VIRGINIA ANDREWS

Flowers in the Attic

HarperCollins*Publishers*

HarperCollins*Publishers*
77–85 Fulham Palace Road,
Hammersmith, London W6 8JB

www.harpercollins.co.uk

This paperback edition 2005
1
First published in Great Britain by
Piatkus 1980

ISBN 978 0 00 787374 6

Set in Ehrhardt by Palimpsest Book Production Limited,
Polmont, Stirlingshire

Printed and bound in Great Britain by
Clays Limited, St Ives plc

'Ballerina' lyrics by Bob Russel, music by Carl Sigman. Publishers,
TRO – The Cromwell Music, Inc. & Harrison Music. (ASCAP).
Reprinted by permission

FLOWERS IN THE ATTIC

Virginia Andrews, who lived in Norfolk, Virginia, studied art at college and during the sixties worked as a fashion illustrator, commercial artist, and later a portrait painter.

Flowers in the Attic was based on a true story and became an immediate bestseller on publication in 1979, receiving tremendous acclaim on both sides of the Atlantic and being adapted for the big screen. It was followed by more books about the Dollanganger family, *Petals on the Wind*, *If There be Thorns*, *Seeds of Yesterday*, and a prequel to *Flowers in the Attic*, *Garden of Shadows*. In addition to these novels, she is also the author of *My Sweet Audrina* and the Casteel family saga: *Heaven*, *Dark Angel*, *Fallen Hearts*, *Gates of Paradise* and *Web of Dreams*, all set in Virginia Andrews' home country, West Virginia, and in Boston.

Virginia Andrews died in 1986, and left a considerable amount of unpublished material.

For automatic updates on your favourite authors visit HarperCollins.co.uk and register for AuthorTracker.

This book is dedicated to my mother.

PART ONE

Shall the clay say to him that fashioneth it,
What makest thou?

Isaiah 45:9

PROLOGUE

It is so appropriate to colour hope yellow, like that sun we seldom saw. And as I begin to copy from the old memorandum journals that I kept for so long, a title comes as if inspired. *Open the Window and Stand in the Sunshine*. Yet, I hesitate to name our story that. For I think of us more as flowers in the attic. Paper flowers. Born so brightly coloured, and fading duller through all those long, grim, dreary, nightmarish days when we were held prisoners of hope, and kept captives by greed. But, we were never to colour even one of our paper blossoms yellow.

Charles Dickens would often start his novels with the birth of the protagonist and, being a favourite author of both mine and Chris's, I would duplicate his style – if I could. But he was a genius born to write without difficulty while I find every word I put down, I put down with tears, with bitter blood, with sour gall, well mixed and blended with shame and guilt. I thought I would never feel ashamed or guilty, that these were burdens for others to bear. Years have passed and I am older and wiser now, accepting, too. The tempest of rage that once stormed within me has simmered down so I can write, I hope, with truth and with less hatred and prejudice than would have been the case a few years ago.

So, like Charles Dickens, in this work of 'fiction' I will hide myself away behind a false name, and live in fake places, and I will pray to God that those who should will hurt when they read what I have to say. Certainly God in his infinite mercy will see that some understanding publisher will put my words in a book, and help grind the knife that I hope to wield.

3

GOODBYE, DADDY

Truly, when I was very young, way back in the 'fifties, I believed all of life would be like one long and perfect summer day. After all, it did start out that way. There's not much I can say about our earliest childhood except that it was very good, and for that, I should be everlastingly grateful. We weren't rich, we weren't poor. If we lacked some necessity, I couldn't name it; if we had luxuries, I couldn't name those, either, without comparing what we had to what others had, and nobody had more or less in our middle-class neighbourhood. In other words, short and simple, we were just ordinary, run-of-the-mill children.

Our daddy was a PR man for a large computer manufacturing firm located in Gladstone, Pennsylvania: population, 12,602. He was a huge success, our father, for often his boss dined with us, and bragged about the job Daddy seemed to perform so well. 'It's that all-American, wholesome, devastatingly good-looking face and charming manner that does them in. Great God in heaven, Chris, what sensible person could resist a fella like you?'

Heartily, I agreed with that. Our father was perfect. He stood six feet two, weighed 180 pounds, and his hair was thick and flaxen blond, and waved just enough to be perfect; his eyes were cerulean blue and they sparkled with laughter, with his great zest for living and having fun. His nose was straight and neither too long nor too narrow, nor too thick. He played tennis and golf like a pro and swam so much he kept a suntan all through the year. He was always dashing off on airplanes to California, to Florida, to Arizona, or to Hawaii, or even abroad on business, while we were left at home in the care of our mother.

When he came through the front door late on Friday afternoons – every Friday afternoon (he said he couldn't bear to be separated from us for longer than five days) – even if it were raining or snowing, the sun shone when he beamed his broad, happy smile on us.

His booming greeting rang out as soon as he put down his suit-case and briefcase. 'Come greet me with kisses if you love me!'

Somewhere near the front door, my brother and I would be hiding, and after he'd called out his greeting, we'd dash out from behind a chair or the sofa to crash into his wide open arms, which seized us up at once and held us close, and he warmed our lips with his kisses. Fridays – they were the best days of all, for they brought Daddy home to us again. In his suit pockets he carried small gifts for us; in his suitcases he stored the larger ones to dole out after he greeted our mother, who would hang back and wait patiently until he had done with us.

And after we had our little gifts from his pockets, Christopher and I would back off to watch Momma drift slowly forward, her lips curved in a welcoming smile that lit up our father's eyes, and he'd take her in his arms, and stare down into her face as if he hadn't seen her for at least a year.

On Fridays, Momma spent half the day in the beauty parlour having her hair shampooed and set and her fingernails polished, and then she'd come home to take a long bath in perfumed-oiled water. I'd perch in her dressing-room, and wait to watch her emerge in a filmy negligée. She'd sit at her dressing-table to metic-ulously apply make-up. And I, so eager to learn, drank in every-thing she did to turn herself from just a pretty woman into a creature so ravishingly beautiful she didn't look real. The most amazing part of this was our father thought she *didn't* wear make-up! He believed she was naturally a striking beauty.

Love was a word lavished about in our home. 'Do you love me? – For I most certainly love you; did you miss me? – Are you glad I'm home? – Did you think about me when I was gone? Every night? Did you toss and turn and wish I were beside you, holding you close? For if you didn't, Corrine, I might want to die.'

Momma knew exactly how to answer questions like these – with her eyes, with soft whispers and with kisses.

We had a funny surname, the very devil to learn to spell. Dollanganger. Just because we were all blond, flaxen-haired, with fair complexions (except Daddy, with his perpetual tan), Jim Johnston, Daddy's best friend, pinned on us a nickname, 'the Dresden dolls'. He said we looked like those fancy porcelain people

5

who grace whatnot shelves and fireplace mantels. Soon everyone in our neighbourhood was calling us the Dresden dolls; certainly it was easier to say than Dollanganger.

When the twins were four, and Christopher was fourteen, and I had just turned twelve, there came a very special Friday. It was Daddy's thirty-sixth birthday party and we were having a surprise party for him. Momma looked like a fairy-tale princess with her freshly washed and set hair. Her nails gleamed with pearly polish, her long formal gown was of softest aqua colour, and her knotted string of pearls swayed as she glided from here to there, setting the table in the dining-room so it would look perfect for Daddy's birthday party. His many gifts were piled high on the buffet. It was going to be a small, intimate party, just for our family and our closest friends.

'Cathy,' said Momma, throwing me a quick look, 'would you mind bathing the twins again for me? I gave them both baths before their naps, but as soon as they were up, they took off for the sandbox, and now they need another bath.'

I didn't mind. She looked far too fancy to give two dirty four-year-olds splashy baths that would ruin her hair, her nails, and her lovely dress.

'And when you finish with them, both you and Christopher jump in the tub and bathe, too, and put on that pretty new pink dress, Cathy, and curl your hair. And, Christopher, no blue jeans, please. I want you to put on a dress shirt and a tie, and wear that light blue sports jacket with your cream-coloured trousers.'

'Ah, heck, Momma, I hate dressing up,' he complained, scuffing his sneakers and scowling.

'Do as I say, Christopher, for your father. You know he does a lot for you; the least you can do is make him proud of his family.'

He grouched off, leaving me to run out to the back garden and fetch the twins, who immediately began to wail. 'One bath a day is enough!' screamed Carrie. 'We're already clean! Stop! We don't like soap! We don't like hair washings! Don't you do that to us again, Cathy, or we'll tell Momma!'

'Hah!' I said. 'Who do you think sent me out here to clean up two filthy little monsters? Good golly, how can the two of you get so dirty so quickly?'

As soon as their naked skins hit the warm water, and the little yellow rubber ducks and rubber boats began to float, and they could splash all over me, they were content enough to be bathed, shampooed, and dressed in their very best clothes. For, after all, they were going to a party – and, after all, this was Friday, and Daddy was coming home.

First I dressed Cory in a pretty little white suit with short pants. Strangely enough, he was more apt to keep himself clean than his twin. Try as I would, I couldn't tame down that stubborn cowlick of his. It curled over to the right, like a cute pig's tail, and – would you believe it? – Carrie wanted her hair to do the same thing!

When I had them both dressed, and looking like dolls come alive, I turned the twins over to Christopher with stern warnings to keep an ever observant eye on them. Now it was my turn to dress up.

The twins wailed and complained while I hurriedly took a bath, washed my hair, and rolled it up on fat curlers. I peeked around the bathroom door to see Christopher trying his best to entertain them by reading to them from *Mother Goose*.

'Hey,' said Christopher when I came out wearing my pink dress with the fluted ruffles, 'you don't look half-bad.'

'Half-bad? Is that the best you can manage?'

'Best I can for a sister.' He glanced at his watch, slammed the picture book closed, seized the twins by their dimpled hands and cried out, 'Daddy will be here any minute – hurry, Cathy!'

Five o'clock came and went, and though we waited and waited, we didn't see our father's green Cadillac turn into our curving drive. The invited guests sat around and tried to keep up a cheerful conversation, as Momma got up and began to pace around nervously. Usually Daddy flung open the door at four, and sometimes even sooner.

Seven o'clock, and still we were waiting.

The wonderful meal Momma had spent so much time preparing was drying out from being too long in the warming oven. Seven was the time we usually put the twins to bed, and they were growing hungry, sleepy and cross, demanding every second, 'When is Daddy coming?'

7

Their white clothes didn't look so virgin now. Carrie's smoothly waved hair began to curl up and look windblown. Cory's nose began to run, and repeatedly he wiped it on the back of his hand until I hurried over with a Kleenex to clean off his upper lip.

'Well, Corinne,' joked Jim Johnston, 'I guess Chris has found himself another super-broad.'

His wife threw him an angry look for saying something so tasteless.

My stomach was growling, and I was beginning to feel as worried as Momma looked. She kept pacing back and forth, going to the wide picture window and staring out.

'Oh!' I cried, having caught sight of a car turning into our tree-lined driveway, 'maybe that's Daddy coming now!'

But the car that drew to a stop before our front door was white, not green. And on the top was one of those spinning red lights. An emblem on the side of that white car read STATE POLICE.

Momma smothered a cry when two policemen dressed in blue uniforms approached our front door and rang our doorbell.

Momma seemed frozen. Her hand hovered near her throat; her heart came up and darkened her eyes. Something wild and frightening burgeoned in my heart just from watching her reactions.

It was Jim Johnston who answered the door, and allowed the two state troopers to enter, glancing about uneasily, seeing, I'm sure, that this was an assembly gathered together for a birthday party. All they had to do was glance into the dining-room and see the festive table, the balloons suspended from the chandelier, and the gifts on the buffet.

'Mrs Christopher Garland Dollanganger?' inquired the older of the two officers as he looked from woman to woman.

Our mother nodded slightly, stiffly. I drew nearer, as did Christopher. The twins were on the floor, playing with tiny cars, and they showed little interest in the unexpected arrival of police officers.

The kindly-looking uniformed man with the deep red face stepped closer to Momma. 'Mrs Dollanganger,' he began in a flat voice that sent immediate panic into my heart, 'we're terribly sorry, but there's been an accident on Greenfield Highway.'

'Oh . . .' breathed Momma, reaching to draw both Christopher

8

and me against her sides. I could feel her quivering all over, just as I was. My eyes were magnetized by those brass buttons; I couldn't see anything else.

'Your husband was involved, Mrs Dollanganger.'

A long sigh escaped from Momma's choked throat. She swayed and would have fallen if Chris and I hadn't been there to support her.

'We've already questioned motorists who witnessed the accident, and it wasn't your husband's fault, Mrs Dollanganger,' that voice continued on, without emotion. 'According to the accounts, which we've recorded, there was a motorist driving a blue Ford weaving in and out of the left hand lane, apparently drunk, and he crashed head-on into your husband's car. But it seems your husband must have seen the accident coming, for he swerved to avoid a head-on collision, but a piece of machinery had fallen from another car, or truck, and this kept him from completing his correct defensive driving manoeuvre, which would have saved his life. But as it was, your husband's much heavier car turned over several times, and still he might have survived, but an oncoming truck, unable to stop, crashed into his car, and again the Cadillac spun over . . . and then . . . it caught on fire.'

Never had a room full of people stilled so quickly. Even the young twins looked up from their innocent play, and stared at the two troopers.

'My husband?' whispered Momma, her voice so weak it was hardly audible. 'He isn't . . . he isn't . . . dead . . . ?'

'Ma'am,' said the red-faced officer very solemnly, 'it pains me dreadfully to bring you bad news on what seems a special occasion.' He faltered and glanced around with embarrassment. 'I'm terribly sorry, ma'am . . . everybody did what they could to get him out . . . but, well, ma'am . . . he was, well, killed instantly, from what the doc says.'

Someone sitting on the sofa screamed.

Momma didn't scream. Her eyes went bleak, dark, haunted. Despair washed the radiant colour from her beautiful face; it resembled a death mask. I stared up at her, trying to tell her with my eyes that none of this could be true. Not Daddy! Not my daddy! He couldn't be dead . . . he couldn't be! Death was for old people, sick people . . . not for somebody as loved and needed, and young.

Yet there was my mother with her grey face, her stark eyes, her hands wringing out the invisible wet cloths, and each second I watched, her eyes sank deeper into her skull.

I began to cry.

'Ma'am, we've got a few things of his that were thrown out on the first impact. We saved what we could.'

'Go away!' I screamed at the officer. 'Get out of here! It's not my daddy! I know it's not! He's stopped by a store to buy ice-cream. He'll be coming in the door any minute! Get out of here!' I ran forward and beat on the officer's chest. He tried to hold me off, and Christopher came up and pulled me away.

'Please,' said the trooper, 'won't someone please help this child?'

My mother's arms encircled my shoulders and drew me close to her side. People were murmuring in shocked voices, and whispering, and the food in the warming oven was beginning to smell burned.

I waited for someone to come up and take my hand and say that God didn't ever take the life of a man like my father, yet no one came near me. Only Christopher came to put his arm about my waist, so we three were in a huddle – Momma, Christopher, and me.

It was Christopher who finally found a voice to speak and such a strange, husky voice: 'Are you positive it was our father? If the green Cadillac caught on fire, then the man inside must have been badly burned, so it could have been someone else, not Daddy.'

Deep, rasping sobs tore from Momma's throat, though not a tear fell from her eyes. She believed! She believed those two men were speaking the truth!

The guests who had come so prettily dressed to attend a birthday party swarmed about us now and said those consoling things people say when there just aren't any right words.

'We're so sorry, Corinne, really shocked . . . it's terrible . . .'

'What an awful thing to happen to Chris.'

'Our days are numbered . . . that's the way it is, from the day we're born, our days are numbered.'

It went on and on, and slowly, like water into concrete, it sank in. Daddy was really dead. We were never going to see him alive again. We'd only see him in a coffin, laid out in a box that would end up in the ground, with a marble headstone that bore his name and his day of birth and his day of death. Numbered the same, but for the year.

I looked around, to see what was happening to the twins, who shouldn't have been feeling what I was. Someone kind had taken them into the kitchen and was preparing them a light meal before they were tucked into bed. My eyes met Christopher's. He seemed as caught in this nightmare as I was, his young face pale and shocked; a hollow look of grief shadowed his eyes and made them dark.

One of the state troopers had gone out to his car, and now he came back with a bundle of things which he carefully spread out on the coffee table. I stood frozen, watching the display of all the things Daddy kept in his pockets: a lizard-skinned wallet Momma had given him as a Christmas gift; his leather notepad and date book; his wristwatch; his wedding band. Everything was blackened and charred by smoke and fire.

Last came the soft pastel animals meant for Cory and Carrie, all found, so the red-faced trooper said, scattered on the highway. A plushy blue elephant with pink velvet ears, and a purple pony with a red saddle and golden reins – oh, that just had to be for Carrie. Then the saddest articles of all – Daddy's clothes, which had burst the confines of his suitcases when the trunk lock sprang.

I knew those suits, those shirts, ties, socks. There was the same tie I had given him on his last birthday.

'Someone will have to identify the body,' said the trooper.

Now I knew positively. It was real, our father would never come home without presents for all of us – even on his own birthday.

I ran from that room! Ran from all the things spread out that tore my heart and made me ache worse than any pain I had yet experienced. I ran out of the house and into the back garden, and there I beat my fists upon an old maple tree. I beat my fists until they ached and blood began to come from the many small cuts; then I flung myself down on the grass and cried – cried ten oceans of tears, for Daddy who should be alive. I cried for us, who would have to go on living without him. And the twins, they hadn't even had the chance to know how wonderful he was – or had been. And when my tears were over, and my eyes swollen and red, and hurt from the rubbing, I heard soft footsteps coming to me – my mother.

She sat down on the grass beside me and took my hand in hers. A quarter-horned moon was out, and millions of stars, and the breezes were sweet with the newborn fragrances of spring. 'Cathy,' she said eventually when the silence between us stretched so long it might never come to an end, 'your father is up in heaven looking down on you, and you know he would want you to be brave.'

'He's not dead, Momma!' I denied vehemently.

'You've been out in this yard a long time; perhaps you don't realize it's ten o'clock. Someone had to identify your father's body, and though Jim Johnston offered to do this, and spare me the pain, I had to see for myself. For, you see, I found it hard to believe too. Your father *is* dead, Cathy. Christopher is on his bed crying, and the twins are asleep; they don't fully realize what "dead" means.'

She put her arms around me, and cradled my head down on her shoulder.

'Come,' she said, standing and pulling me up with her, keeping her arm about my waist, 'You've been out here much too long. I thought you were in the house with the others, and the others thought you were in your room, or with me. It's not good to be alone when you feel bereft. It's better to be with people and share your grief, and not keep it locked up inside.'

She said this dry-eyed, with not a tear, but somewhere deep inside her she was crying, screaming. I could tell by her tone, by the very bleakness that had sunk deeper into her eyes.

With our father's death, a nightmare began to shadow our days. I gazed reproachfully at Momma and thought she should have prepared us in advance for something like this, for we'd never been allowed to own pets that suddenly pass away and teach us a little about losing through death. Someone, some adult, should have warned us that the young, the handsome, and the needed can die, too.

How do you say things like this to a mother who looked like fate was pulling her through a knothole and stretching her out thin and flat? Could you speak honestly to someone who didn't want to talk, or eat, or brush her hair, or put on the pretty clothes that filled her closet? Nor did she want to attend to our needs. It was a good thing the kindly neighbourhood women came in and took us over, bringing with them food prepared in their own kitchens. Our house filled to overflowing with flowers, with home-made casseroles, hams, hot rolls, cakes, and pies.

They came in droves, all the people who loved, admired, and respected our father, and I was surprised he was so well known. Yet I hated it every time someone asked how he died, and what a pity someone so young should die, when so many who were useless and unfit, lived on and on, and were a burden to society.

From all that I heard, and overheard, fate was a grim reaper, never kind, with little respect for who was loved and needed.

Spring days passed on towards summer. And grief, no matter how you try to cater to its wail, has a way of fading away, and the person so real, so beloved, becomes a dim, slightly out-of-focus shadow.

One day Momma sat so sad-faced that she seemed to have forgotten how to smile. 'Momma,' I said brightly, in an effort to cheer her, 'I'm going to pretend Daddy is still alive, and away on another of his business trips, and soon he'll come, and stride in the door, and he'll call out, just as he used to, "Come and greet me with kisses if you love me." And – don't you see? – we'll feel better, all of us, like he *is* alive somewhere, living where we can't see him, but where we can expect him at any moment.'

'No, Cathy,' Momma flared, 'you must accept the truth. You are not to find solace in pretending. Do you hear that! Your father is dead, and his soul has gone on to heaven, and you should under-stand at your age that no one ever has come back from heaven. As for us, we'll make do the best we can without him – and that doesn't mean escaping reality by not facing up to it.'

I watched her rise from her chair and begin to take things from the refrigerator to start breakfast.

'Momma . . .' I began again, feeling my way along cautiously lest she turn hard and angry again. 'Will we be able to go on, without him?'

'I will do the best I can to see that we survive,' she said dully, flatly.

'Will you have to go to work now, like Mrs Johnston?'

'Maybe, maybe not. Life holds all sorts of surprises, Cathy, and some of them are unpleasant, as you are finding out. But remember always you were blessed to have for almost twelve years a father who thought you were something very special.'

'Because I look like you,' I said, still feeling some of that envy I always had, because I came in second after her.

She threw me a glance as she rambled through the contents of the jam-packed fridge. 'I'm going to tell you something now, Cathy, that I've never told you before. You look very much as I did at your age, but you are not like me in your personality. You are much more aggressive, and much more determined. Your father used to say that you were like his mother, and he loved his mother.'

'Doesn't everybody love their mother?'

'No,' she said with a queer expression, 'there are some mothers you just can't love, for they don't want you to love them.'

She took bacon and eggs from the refrigerator, then turned to take me in her arms. 'Dear Cathy, you and your father had a very special close relationship, and I guess you must miss him more because of that, more than Christopher does, or the twins.'

I sobbed against her shoulder. 'I hate God for taking him! He should have lived to be an old man! He won't be there when I dance and when Christopher is a doctor. Nothing seems to matter now that he's gone.'

'Sometimes,' she began in a tight voice, 'death is not as terrible as you think. Your father will never grow old, or infirm. He'll always stay young; you'll remember him that way – young, handsome, strong. Don't cry any more, Cathy, for as your father used to say, there is a reason for everything and a solution for every problem, and I'm trying, trying hard to do what I think best.'

We were four children stumbling around in the broken pieces of our grief and loss. We would play in the back garden, trying to find solace in the sunshine, quite unaware that our lives were soon to change so drastically, so dramatically, that the words 'back-yard' and 'garden' were to become for us synonyms for heaven – and just as remote.

It was an afternoon shortly after Daddy's funeral, and Christopher and I were with the twins in the backyard. They sat in the sandbox with small shovels and sand pails. Over and over again they transferred sand from one pail to another, gibbering back and forth in the strange language only they could understand. Cory and Carrie were fraternal rather than identical twins, yet they were like one unit, very much satisfied with each other. They built a wall about themselves so they were the castle-keeps, and full guardians of their larder of secrets. They had each other and that was enough.

The time for dinner came and went. We were afraid that now even meals might be cancelled, so even without our mother's voice to call us in, we caught hold of the dimpled, fat hands of the twins and dragged them along towards the house. We found our mother seated behind Daddy's big desk; she was writing what appeared to be a very difficult letter, if the evidence of many discarded beginnings meant anything. She frowned as she wrote in long-hand, pausing every so often to lift her head and stare off into space.

'Momma,' I said, 'it's almost six o'clock. The twins are growing hungry.'

'In a minute, in a minute,' she said in an off-hand way. 'I'm writing to your grandparents who live in Virginia. The neighbours have brought us food enough for a week – you could put one of the casseroles in the oven, Cathy.'

It was the first meal I almost prepared myself. I had the table set, and the casserole heating, and the milk poured, when Momma came in to help.

It seemed to me that every day after our father had gone, our mother had letters to write, and places to go, leaving us in the care of the neighbour next door. At night Momma would sit at Daddy's desk, a green ledger book opened in front of her, checking over stacks of bills. Nothing felt good any more, nothing. Often now my brother and I bathed the twins, put on their pyjamas, and tucked them into bed. Then Christopher would hurry off to his room to study, while I would hurry back to my mother to seek a way to bring happiness to her eyes again.

A few weeks later a letter came in response to the many our mother had written home to her parents. Immediately Momma began to cry – even before she had opened the thick, creamy envelope, she cried. Clumsily, she used a letter opener, and with trembling hands she held three sheets, reading over the letter three times. All the while she read, tears trickled slowly down her cheeks, smearing her make-up with long, pale, shiny streaks.

She had called us in from the backyard as soon as she had collected the mail from the box near the front door, and now we four were seated on the living-room sofa. As I watched I saw her soft fair Dresden face turn into something cold, hard, resolute. A cold chill shivered down my spine. Maybe it was because she stared at us for so long – too long. Then she looked down at the sheets held in her trembling hands, then to the windows, as if there she could find some answer to the question of the letter.

Momma was acting so strangely. It made us all uneasy and unusually quiet, for we were already intimidated enough in a fatherless home without a creamy letter of three sheets to glue our mother's tongue and harden her eyes. Why did she look at us so oddly?

Finally, she cleared her throat and began to speak, but in a cold voice, totally unlike her customary soft, warm cadence. 'Your grandmother has at last replied to my letters,' she said in that icy voice. 'All those letters I wrote to her . . . well . . . she has agreed. She is willing to let us come and live with her.'

Good news! Just what we had been waiting to hear – and we should have been happy. But Momma fell into that moody silence again, and she just sat there staring at us. What was the matter with her? Didn't she know we were hers, and not some stranger's four perched in a row like birds on a clothesline?

'Christopher, Cathy, at fourteen and twelve, you two should be old enough to understand, and old enough to co-operate, and help your mother out of a desperate situation.' She paused, fluttered one hand up to nervously finger the beads at her throat and sighed heavily. She seemed on the verge of tears. And I felt sorry, so sorry for poor Momma, without a husband.

'Momma,' I said, 'is everything all right?'

'Of course, darling, of course.' She tried to smile. 'Your father, God rest his soul, expected to live to a ripe old age and acquire in the meantime a sizeable fortune. He came from people who know how to make money, so I don't have any doubts he would have done just what he planned, if given the time. But thirty-six is so young to die. People have a way of believing nothing terrible will ever happen to them, only to others. We don't anticipate accidents, nor do we expect to die young. Why, your father and I thought we would grow old together, and we hoped to see our grandchildren before we both died on the same day. Then neither of us would be left alone to grieve for the one who went first.'

Again she sighed. 'I have to confess we lived way beyond our present means, and we charged against the future. We spent money before we had it. Don't blame him; it was my fault. He knew all about poverty. I knew nothing about it. You know how he used to scold me. Why, when we bought this house, he said we needed only three bedrooms, but I wanted four. Even four didn't seem enough. Look around, there's a thirty year mortgage on this house. Nothing here is really ours: not this furniture, not the cars, not the appliances in the kitchen or laundry-room – not one single thing is fully paid for.'

Did we look frightened? Scared? She paused as her face flushed deeply red, and her eyes moved around the lovely room that set off her beauty so well. Her delicate brows screwed into an anxious frown. 'Though your father would chastise me a little, still he wanted them, too. He indulged me, because he loved me, and I believe I convinced him finally that luxuries were absolute necessities, and he gave in, for we had a way, the two of us, of indulging our desires too much. It was just another of the things we had in common.'

Her expression collapsed into one of forlorn reminiscence before she continued on in her stranger's voice. 'Now all our beautiful things will be taken away. The legal term is repossession. That's what they do when you don't have enough money to finish paying for what you've bought. Take that sofa, for example. Three years ago it cost eight hundred dollars. And we've paid all but one hundred, but still they're going to take it. We'll lose all that we've paid on everything, and that's still legal. Not only will we lose this furniture and the house, but also the cars – in fact, everything but our clothes and your toys. They're going to allow me to keep my wedding band, and I've hidden away my engagement diamond – so please don't mention I ever had an engagement ring to anyone who might come to check.'

Who 'they' were, not one of us asked. It didn't occur to me to ask. Not then. And later it just didn't seem to matter.

Christopher's eyes met mine. I floundered in the desire to understand, and struggled not to drown in the understanding. Already I was sinking, drowning in the adult world of death and debts. My brother reached out and took my hand, then squeezed my fingers in a gesture of unusual brotherly reassurance.

Was I a windowpane, so easy to read, that even he, my arch-tormentor, would seek to comfort me? I tried to smile, to prove to him how adult I was, and in this way gloss over that trembling and weak thing I was cringing into because 'they' were going to take everything. I didn't want any other little girl living in my pretty peppermint pink room, sleeping in my bed, playing with the things I cherished – my miniature dolls in their shadowbox frames, and my sterling-silver music box with the pink ballerina – would they take those, too?

Momma watched the exchange between my brother and me very closely. She spoke again with a bit of her former sweet self showing. 'Don't look so heartbroken. It's not really as bad as I've made it seem. You must forgive me if I was thoughtless and forgot how young you still are. I've told you the bad news first, and saved the best for the last. Now hold your breath! You are not going to believe what I have to tell you – for my parents are rich! Not middle-class rich, or upper-class rich, but very, very rich! Filthy, unbelievably, sinfully rich! They live in a fine big house in Virginia – such a house as you've never seen before. I know, I was born there, and grew up there, and when you see that house, this one will seem like a shack in comparison. And didn't I say we are going to live with them – my mother, and my father?'

She offered this straw of cheer with a weak and nervously fluttering smile that did not succeed in releasing me from doubts which her demeanour and her information had pitched me into. I didn't like the way her eyes skipped guiltily away when I tried to catch them. I thought she was hiding something.

But she was my mother.

And Daddy was gone.

I picked up Carrie and sat her on my lap, pressing her small, warm body close against mine. I smoothed back the damp golden curls that fell over her rounded forehead. Her eyelids drooped, and her full rosebud lips pouted. I glanced at Cory, crouching against Christopher. 'The twins are tired, Momma. They need their dinner.'

'Time enough for dinner later,' she snapped impatiently. 'We have plans to make, and clothes to pack, for tonight we have to catch a train. The twins can eat while we pack. Everything you four wear must be crowded into only two suitcases. I want you to take only your favourite clothes and the small toys you cannot bear to leave. Only one game. I'll buy you many games after you are there. Cathy, you select what clothes and toys you think the twins like best – but only a few. We can't take along more than four suitcases, and I need two for my own things.'

Oh, golly-lolly! This was real! We had to leave, abandon everything! I had to crowd everything into two suitcases my brothers and sister would share as well. My Raggedy Ann doll alone would half fill *one* suitcase! Yet how could I leave her, my most beloved doll, the one Daddy gave me when I was only three? I sobbed.

So, we sat with our shocked faces staring at Momma. We made her terribly uneasy, for she jumped up and began to pace the room.

'As I said before, my parents are extremely wealthy.' She shot Christopher and me an appraising glance, then quickly turned to hide her face.

'Momma,' said Christopher, 'is something wrong?'

I marvelled that he could ask such a thing, when it was only too obvious, *everything* was wrong.

She paced, her long shapely legs appearing through the front opening of her filmy black negligée. Even in her grief, wearing black, she was beautiful – shadowed, troubled eyes and all. She was so lovely, and I loved her, – oh, how I loved her then!

How we all loved her then.

Directly in front of the sofa, our mother spun around and the black chiffon of her negligée flared like a dancer's skirt, revealing her beautiful legs from feet to hips.

'Darlings,' she began, 'what could possibly be wrong about living in such a fine home as my parents own? I was born there; I grew up there, except for those years when I was sent away to school. It's a huge, beautiful house, and they keep adding new rooms to it, though Lord knows they have enough rooms already.'

She smiled, but something about her smile seemed false. 'There is, however, one small thing I have to tell you before you meet my father – your grandfather.' Here again she faltered, and again smiled that queer, shadowy smile. 'Years ago, when I was eighteen, I did something serious, of which your grandfather disapproved, and my mother wasn't approving, either, but she wouldn't leave me anything, anyway, so she doesn't count. But, because of what I did, my father had me written out of his will, and so now I am disinherited. Your father used to gallantly call this "fallen from grace". Your father always made the best of everything, and he said it didn't matter.'

Fallen from grace? Whatever did that mean? I couldn't imagine my mother doing anything so bad that her own father would turn against her and take away what she should have.

'Yes, Momma, I know exactly what you mean,' Christopher piped up. 'You did something of which your father disapproved, and so, even though you were included in his will, he had his lawyer write you out instead of thinking twice, and now you won't inherit any of his worldly goods when he passes on to the great beyond.' He grinned, pleased with himself for knowing more than me. He always had the answers to everything. He had his nose in a book whenever he was in the house. Outside, under the sky, he was just as wild, just as mean as any other kid on the block. But indoors, away from the television, my older brother was a bookworm!

Naturally, he was right.

'Yes, Christopher. None of your grandfather's wealth will come to me when he dies, or through me, to you. That's why I had to keep writing so many letters home when my mother didn't respond.' Again she smiled, this time with bitter irony. 'But, since I am the sole heir left, I am hopeful of winning back his approval. You see, once I had two older brothers, but both have died in accidents, and now I am the only one left to inherit.' Her restless pacing stopped. Her hand rose to cover her mouth; she shook her head, then said in a new parrot-like voice, 'I guess I'd better tell you something else. Your real surname is not Dollanganger; it is Foxworth. And Foxworth is a very important name in Virginia.'

'Momma!' I exclaimed in shock. 'Is it legal to change your name, and put that fake name on our birth certificates?'

Her voice became impatient. 'For heaven's sake, Cathy, names can be changed legally. And the name Dollanganger does belong to us, more or less. Your father borrowed that name from way back in his ancestry. He thought it an amusing name, a joke, and it served its purpose well enough.'

'What purpose?' I asked. 'Why would Daddy legally change his name from something like Foxworth, so easy to spell, to something long and difficult like Dollanganger?'

'Cathy, I'm tired,' said Momma, falling into the nearest chair. There's so much for me to do, so many legal details. Soon enough you'll know everything; I'll explain. I swear to be totally honest; but please, now, let me catch my breath.'

Oh, what a day this was. First we hear the mysterious 'they' were coming to take away all our things, even our house. And then we learn even our own last name wasn't really ours.

The twins, curled up on our laps, were already half-asleep, and they were too young to understand, anyway. Even I, now twelve years old, and almost a woman, could not comprehend why Momma didn't really look happy to be going home again to parents she hadn't seen in fifteen years. Secret grandparents we'd thought were dead until after our father's funeral. Only this day had we heard of two uncles who'd died in accidents. It dawned on me strongly then, that our parents had lived full lives even before they had children, that we were not so important after all.

'Momma,' Christopher began slowly, 'your fine, grand home in Virginia sounds nice, but we like it here. Our friends are here, everybody knows us, likes us, and I know I don't want to move. Can't you see Daddy's attorney and ask him to help find a way so we can stay on, and keep our house and our furnishings?'

'Yes, Momma, please, let us stay here,' I added.

Quickly Momma was out of her chair and striding across the room. She dropped down on her knees before us, her eyes on the level with ours. 'Now listen to me,' she ordered, catching my brother's hand and mine and pressing them both against her breasts. 'I have thought, and I have thought of how we can manage to stay on here, but there is no way – no way at all, because we have no money to meet the monthly bills, and I don't have the skills to earn an adequate salary to support four children and myself as well. Look at me,' she said, throwing wide her arms, appearing vulnerable, beautiful, helpless. 'Do you know what I am? I am a pretty, useless ornament who always believed she'd have a man to take care of her. I don't know how to do anything. I can't even type. I'm not very good with arithmetic. I *can* embroider beautiful needlepoint and crewelwork stitches, but that kind of thing doesn't earn any money. You can't live without money. It's not love that makes the world go 'round – it's money. And my father has more money than he knows what to do with. He has only one living heir – me! Once he cared more for me than he did for either of his sons, so it shouldn't be difficult to win back his affection. Then he will have his attorney draw me into a new will, and I will inherit everything! He is sixty-six years old, and he is dying of heart disease. From what my mother wrote on a separate sheet of paper which my father didn't read, your grandfather cannot possibly live more than two or three months longer at the most. That will give me plenty of time to charm him into loving me like he used to – and when he dies, his entire fortune will be mine! Mine! *Ours!* We will be free for ever of all financial worries. Free to go anywhere we want. Free to do anything we want. Free to travel, to buy what our hearts desire – anything our hearts desire! I'm not speaking of only a million or two, but many, many millions – maybe even billions! People with that kind of money don't even know their own net value, for it's invested here and there, and they own this and that, including banks, airlines, hotels, department stores, shipping lines. Oh, you just don't realize the kind of empire your grand-father controls, even now, while he's on his last legs. He has a genius for making money. Everything he touches turns to gold.'

Her blue eyes gleamed. The sun shone through the front windows, casting diamond strands of light on her hair. Already she seemed rich beyond value. Momma, Momma, how had all of this come about only after our father died?

'Christopher, Cathy, are you listening, using your imaginations? Do you realize what a tremendous amount of money can do? The world, and everything in it is yours! You have power, influence, respect. Trust me. Soon enough I will win back my father's heart. He'll take one look at me, and realize instantly how all those fifteen years we've been separated have been such a waste. He's old, sick, he always stays on the first floor, in a small room beyond the library, and he has nurses to take care of him night and day, and servants to wait on him hand and foot. But only your own flesh and blood means anything, and I'm all he has left, only me. Even the nurses don't find it necessary to climb the stairs, for they have their own bath. *One* night, I will prepare him to meet his four grandchildren, and then I will bring you down the stairs, and into his room, and he will be charmed, enchanted by what he sees: four beautiful children who are perfect in every way – he is bound to love you, each and every one of you. Believe me, it will work out, just the way I say. I promise that whatever my father requires of me, I will do. On my life, on all I hold sacred and dear – and that is the children my love for your father made – you can believe I will soon be the heiress to a fortune beyond belief, and through me, every dream you've ever had will come true.'

My mouth gaped open. I was overwhelmed by her passion. I glanced at Christopher to see him staring at Momma with incredulity. Both the twins were on the soft fringes of sleep. They had heard none of this.

We were going to live in a house as big and rich as a palace.

In that palace so grand, where servants waited on you hand and foot, we would be introduced to King Midas, who would soon die, and then *we* would have all the money, to put the world at our feet. We were stepping into riches beyond belief! I would be just like a princess!

Yet, why didn't I feel really happy?

'Cathy,' said Christopher, beaming on me a broad, happy smile, 'you can still be a ballerina. I don't think money can buy talent, nor can it make a good doctor out of a playboy. But, until the time comes when we have to be dedicated and serious, my, aren't we gonna have a ball?'

I couldn't take the sterling-silver music box with the pink ballerina inside. The music box was expensive and had been listed as something of value for 'them' to claim.

I couldn't take down the shadowboxes from the walls, or hide away the miniature dolls. There was hardly anything I could take that Daddy had given me except the small ring on my finger, with a semi-precious gem stone shaped like a heart.

And, just like Christopher said, after we were rich, our lives would be one big ball, one long, long party. That's the way rich people lived – happily ever after as they counted their money and made their fun plans.

Fun, games, parties, riches beyond belief, a house as big as a palace, with servants who lived over a huge garage that stored away at least nine or ten expensive automobiles. Who would ever have guessed my mother came from a family like that? Why had Daddy argued with her so many times about spending money lavishly, when she could have written letters home before, and done a bit of humiliating begging?

Slowly I walked down the hall to my room, to stand before the silver music box where the pink ballerina stood in arabesque position when the lid was opened, and she could see herself in the reflecting mirror. And I heard the tinkling music play, 'Whirl, ballerina, whirl . . .'

I could steal it, if I had a place to hide it.

Goodbye, pink-and-white room with the peppermint walls. Goodbye, little white bed with the dotted Swiss canopy that had seen me sick with measles, mumps, chicken-pox.

Goodbye again to you, Daddy, for when I'm gone, I can't picture you sitting on the side of my bed, and holding my hand, and I won't see you coming from the bathroom with a glass of water. *I really don't want to go too much, Daddy. I'd rather stay and keep your memory close and near.*

'Cathy' – Momma was at the door – 'don't just stand there and cry. A room is just a room. You'll live in many rooms before you die, so hurry up, pack your things and the twins' things, while I do my own packing.'

Before I died, I was going to live in a thousand rooms or more, a little voice whispered this in my ear . . . and I believed.

THE ROAD TO RICHES

While Momma packed, Christopher and I threw our clothes into two suitcases, along with a few toys and one game. In the early twilight of evening, a taxi drove us to the train station. We had slipped away furtively, without saying goodbye to even one friend, and this hurt. I didn't know why it had to be that way, but Momma insisted. Our bicycles were left in the garage along with everything else too large to take.

The train lumbered through a dark and starry night, heading towards a distant mountain estate in Virginia. We passed many a sleepy town and village, and scattered farmhouses where golden rectangles of light were the only evidence to show they were there at all. My brother and I didn't want to fall asleep and miss out on anything, and oh, did we have a lot to talk about! Mostly we speculated on that grand, rich house where we would live in splendour, and eat from golden plates, and be served by a butler wearing livery. And I supposed I'd have my own maid to lay out my clothes, draw my bath, brush my hair, and jump when I commanded. But I wouldn't be too stern with her. I would be sweet, understanding, the kind of mistress every servant desired – unless she broke something I really cherished! Then there'd be hell to pay – I'd throw a temper tantrum, and hurl a few things I didn't like, anyway.

Looking backward to that night ride on the train, I realize that was the very night I began to grow up, and philosophize. With everything you gained, you had to lose something – so I might as well get used to it, and make the best of it.

While my brother and I speculated on how we would spend the money when it came to us, the portly, balding conductor entered our small compartment and gazed admiringly at our mother from head to toes before he softly spoke: 'Mrs Patterson, in fifteen minutes we'll reach your depot.'

Now why was he calling her 'Mrs Patterson'? I wondered. I

shot a questioning look at Christopher, who also seemed perplexed by this.

Jolted awake, appearing startled and disoriented, Momma's eyes flew wide open. Her gaze jumped from the conductor, who hovered so close above her, over to Christopher and me, and then she looked down in despair at the sleeping twins. Next came ready tears and she was reaching in her purse and pulled out tissues, dabbing at her eyes daintily. Then came a sigh so heavy, so full of woe, my heart began to beat in a nervous tempo. 'Yes, thank you,' she said to the conductor, who was still watching her with great approval and admiration. 'Don't fear, we'll be ready to leave.'

'Ma'am,' he said, most concerned when he glanced at his pocket watch, 'it's three o'clock in the morning. Will someone be there to meet you?' He flicked his worried gaze to Christopher and me, then to the sleeping twins.

'It's all right,' assured our mother.

'Ma'am, it's very dark out there.'

'I could find my way home asleep.'

The grandfatherly conductor wasn't satisfied with this. 'Lady,' he said, 'it's an hour's ride to Charlottesville. We are letting you and your children off in the middle of nowhere. There's not a house in sight.'

To forbid any further questioning, Momma answered in her most arrogant manner, 'Someone *is* meeting us.' Funny how she could put on that kind of haughty manner like a hat, and just as easily discard it.

We arrived at the depot in the middle of nowhere, and we were let off. No one was there to meet us.

It was totally dark when we stepped from the train, and as the conductor had warned, there was not a house in sight. Alone in the night, far from any sign of civilization, we stood and waved goodbye to the conductor on the train steps, holding on by one hand, waving with the other. His expression revealed that he wasn't too happy about leaving 'Mrs Patterson' and her brood of four sleepy children waiting for someone coming in a car. I looked around and saw nothing but a rusty, tin roof supported by four wooden posts, and a rickety green bench. This was our train depot. We didn't sit on that bench, just stood and watched until the train disappeared in the darkness, hearing one single, mournful whistle calling back, as if wishing us good luck and Godspeed.

We were surrounded by fields and meadows. From the deep woods in back of the 'depot', something made a weird noise. I jumped and spun about to see what it was, making Christopher laugh. 'That was only an owl! Did you think it was a ghost?'

'Now there is to be none of that!' said Momma sharply. 'And you don't have to whisper. No one is about. This is farm country, dairy cows mostly. Look around. See the fields of wheat and oats, some barley, too. The nearby farmers supply all the fresh produce for the wealthy people who live on the hill.'

There were hills aplenty, looking like lumpy patchwork quilts, with trees parading up and down to separate them into distinct sections. Sentinels of the night, I called them, but Momma told us the many trees in straight rows acted as windbreaks, and held back the heavy drifts of snow. Just the right words to make Christopher very excited. He loved all kinds of winter sports, and he hadn't thought a southern state like Virginia would have heavy snow.

'Oh, yes, it snows here,' said Momma. 'You bet it snows. We are in the foothills of the Blue Ridge Mountains, and it gets very, very cold here, just as cold as it did in Gladstone. But the summers will be warmer during the day. The nights are always cool enough for at least one blanket. Now if the sun were out, you'd be feasting your eyes on very beautiful countryside, as pretty as there is anywhere in the world. We have to hurry, though. It's a long, long walk to my home, and we have to reach there before dawn, when the servants get up.'

How strange. 'Why?' I asked. 'And why did that conductor call you Mrs Patterson?'

'Cathy, I don't have time to explain to you now. We've got to walk fast.' She bent to pick up the two heaviest suitcases, and said in a firm voice that we were to follow where she led. Christopher and I were forced to carry the twins, who were too sleepy to walk, or make even an attempt.

'Momma!' I cried out, when we had moved on a few steps, 'the conductor forgot to give us *your* two suitcases!'

'It's all right, Cathy,' she said breathlessly, as if the two suitcases she was carrying were enough to tax her strength. 'I asked the conductor to take my two bags on to Charlottesville and put them in a locker for me to pick up tomorrow morning.'

'Why would you do that?' asked Christopher in a tight voice.

'Well, for one thing, I certainly couldn't handle *four* suitcases, could I? And, for another thing, I want the chance to talk to my father first before he learns about my children. And it just wouldn't seem right if I arrived home in the middle of the night after being gone for fifteen years, now would it?'

It sounded reasonable, I guess, for we did have all we could handle since the twins refused to walk. We set off, tagging along behind our mother, over uneven ground, following faint paths between rocks and trees and shrubbery that clawed at our clothes. We trekked a long, long, long way. Christopher and I became tired, irritable, as the twins grew heavier and heavier, and our arms began to ache. It was an adventure already beginning to pall. We complained, we nagged, we dragged our feet, wanting to sit down and rest. We wanted to be back in Gladstone, in our own beds, with our own things – better than here – better than that big old house with servants and grandparents we didn't even know.

'Wake up the twins!' snapped Momma, grown impatient with our complaining. 'Stand them on their feet, and force them to walk, whether or not they want to.' Then she mumbled something faint into the fur collar of her jacket that just barely reached my keen ears: 'Lord knows, they'd better walk outside while they can.'

A ripple of apprehension shot down my spine. I glanced at my older brother to see if he'd heard, just as he turned his head to look at me. He smiled. I smiled in return.

Tomorrow, when Momma arrived at a proper time, in a taxi, she would go to the sick grandfather and she'd smile, and she'd speak, and he'd be charmed, won over. Just one look at her lovely face, and just one word from her soft beautiful voice, and he'd hold out his arms, and forgive her for whatever she'd done to make her 'fall from grace'.

From what she'd already told us, her father was a cantankerous *old* man, for sixty-six did seem like incredibly old age to me. And a man on the verge of death couldn't afford to hold grudges against his sole remaining child, a daughter he'd once loved very much. He'd have to forgive her, so he could go peacefully, blissfully into his grave, and know he'd done the right thing. Then, once she had him under her spell, she'd bring us down from the bedroom, and we'd be looking our best, and acting our sweetest selves, and he'd soon see we weren't ugly, or really bad, and nobody, absolutely nobody with a heart could resist loving the twins. Why, people in shopping centres stopped to pat the twins, and compliment our mother on having such beautiful babies. And just wait until Grandfather learned how smart Christopher was! A straight-A student! And what was even more remarkable, he didn't have to study and study the way I did. Everything came so easily for him. His eyes could scan a page just once or twice, and all the information would be written indelibly on his brain, never to be forgotten. Oh, how I did envy him that gift.

I had a gift too; not the bright and shining coin that was Christopher's. It was my way to turn over all that glittered and look for the tarnish. We had gleaned but a bit of information about that unknown grandfather, but putting the pieces together, I already had the idea he was not the kind to easily forgive – not when he could deny a once-beloved daughter for fifteen years. Yet, could he be so hard he could resist all Momma's wheedling charms, which were considerable? I doubted it. I had seen and heard her wheedle with our father about money matters, and always Daddy was the one to give in and be won over to her way. Just a kiss, a hug, a soft stroking caress and Daddy would brighten up and smile, and agree, yes, somehow or other they could manage to pay for everything expensive she bought.

'Cathy,' said Christopher, 'take that worried look off your face. If God didn't plan for people to grow old and sick, and to eventually die, he wouldn't keep on letting people have babies.'

I felt Christopher staring at me, as if reading my thoughts, and I flushed. He grinned cheerfully. He was the perpetual cock-eyed optimist, never gloomy, doubtful, or moody, as I often was.

We followed Momma's advice and woke up the twins. We stood them on their feet and told them they would have to make an effort to walk, tired or not. We pulled them along while they whined and complained with sniffling sobs of rebellion. 'Don't wanna go where we're going,' sobbed a teary Carrie.

Cory only wailed.

'Don't like walkin' in woods when it's dark!' screamed Carrie, trying to pull her tiny hand free from mine. 'I'm going home! Let me go, Cathy, let me go!'

Cory howled louder.

I wanted to pick Carrie up again, and carry her on, but my arms were just too aching to make another effort. Then Christopher released Cory's hand and ran ahead to assist Momma with her two heavy suitcases, so I had two unwilling, resisting twins to lug along in the darkness.

The air was cool and sharply pungent. Though Momma called this hill country, those shadowy, high forms in the distance looked like mountains to me. I stared up at the sky. It seemed to me like an inverted deep bowl of navy-blue velvet, sparkled all over with crystallized snowflakes instead of stars – or were they tears of ice that I was going to cry in the future? Why did they seem to be looking down at me with pity, making me feel ant-sized, over-whelmed, completely insignificant? It was too big, that close sky, too beautiful, and it filled me with a strange sense of foreboding. Still I knew that under other circumstances, I could love a countryside like this.

We came at last upon a cluster of large and very fine homes, nestled on a steep hillside. Stealthily, we approached the largest and, by far, the grandest of all the sleeping mountain homes. Momma said in a hushed voice that her ancestral home was named Foxworth Hall, and was more than two hundred years old!

'Is there a lake nearby for ice-skating, and swimming?' asked Christopher. He gave serious attention to the hillside. 'It's not good ski country – too many trees and rocks.'

'Yes,' said Momma, 'there's a small lake about a quarter of a mile away.' And she pointed in the direction where a lake could be found.

We circled that enormous house, almost on tiptoes. Once at the back door, an old lady let us in. She must have been waiting, and seen us coming, for she opened that door so readily we didn't even have to knock. Just like thieves in the night, we stole silently inside. Not a word did she speak to welcome us. Could this be one of the servants? I wondered.

Immediately we were inside the dark house, and she hustled us up a steep and narrow back staircase, not allowing us one second to pause and take a look around the grand rooms we only glimpsed in our swift and mute passage. She led us down many halls, past many closed doors, and finally we came to an end room, where she swung open a door and gestured us inside. It was a relief to have our long night journey over, and be in a large bedroom where a single lamp was lit. Heavy, tapestried draperies covered two tall windows. The old woman in her grey dress turned to look us over as she closed the heavy door to the hall and leaned against it.

She spoke, and I was jolted. 'Just as you said, Corrine. Your children are beautiful.'

There she was, paying us a compliment that should warm our hearts – but it chilled mine. Her voice was cold and uncaring, as if we were without ears to hear, and without minds to comprehend her displeasure, despite her flattery. And I was right to judge her so. Her next words proved that.

'But are you sure they are intelligent? Do they have some invisible afflictions not apparent to the eyes?'

'None!' cried our mother, taking offence, as did I. 'My children are perfect, as you can plainly see, physically and mentally!' She glared at that old woman in grey before she squatted down on her heels and began to undress Carrie, who was nodding on her feet. I knelt before Cory and unbuttoned his small blue jacket, as Christopher lifted one of the suitcases up on one of the big beds. He opened it and took out two pairs of small yellow pyjamas with feet.

Furtively, as I helped Cory off with his clothes and into his yellow pyjamas, I studied that tall, big woman, who was, I presumed, our grandmother. As I looked her over, seeking wrinkles and heavy jowls, I found out she was not as old as I had at first presumed. Her hair was a strong, steel-blue colour, drawn back from her face in a severe style which made her eyes appear somewhat long and cat-like. Why, you could even see how each strand of hair pulled her skin up in little resentful hills – and even as I watched, I saw one hair spring free from its moorings!

Her nose was an eagle's beak, her shoulders were wide, and her mouth was like a thin, crooked knife slash. Her dress, a grey taffeta, had a diamond brooch at the throat of a high, severe neckline. Nothing about her appeared soft or yielding; even her bosom looked like twin hills of concrete. There would be no funning with her, as we had played with our mother and father.

I didn't like her. I wanted to go home. My lips quivered. I wanted Daddy alive again. How could such a woman as this make someone as lovely and sweet as our mother? From whom had our mother inherited her beauty, her gaiety? I shivered, and tried to forbid those tears that welled in my eyes. Momma had prepared us in advance for an unloving, uncaring, unrelenting grandfather – but the grandmother who had arranged for our coming – she came as a harsh, astonishing surprise. I blinked back my tears, fearful Christopher would see them and mock me later. But to reassure me, there was our mother smiling warmly as she lifted a pyjamaed Cory into one of the big beds, and then she put Carrie in beside him. Oh, how they did look sweet, lying there, like big, rosy-cheeked dolls. Momma leaned over the twins and pressed kisses on their flushed cheeks, and her hand tenderly brushed back the curls on their foreheads, and then she tucked the covers high under their chins. 'Good night, my darlings,' she whispered in the loving voice we knew so well.

The twins didn't hear. Already they were deeply asleep.

However, standing firmly as a rooted tree, the grandmother was obviously displeased as she gazed upon the twins in one bed, then over to where Christopher and I were huddled close together. We were tired, and half-supporting each other. Strong disapproval glinted in her grey-stone eyes. She wore a fixed, piercing scowl that Momma seemed to understand, although I did not. Momma's face flushed as the grandmother said, 'Your two older children cannot sleep in one bed!'

'They're only children,' Momma flared back with unusual fire. 'Mother, you haven't changed one bit, have you? You still have a nasty, suspicious mind! Christopher and Cathy are innocent!'

'Innocent?' she snapped back, her mean look so sharp it could cut and draw blood. 'That is exactly what your father and I always presumed about you and your half-uncle!'

I looked from one to the other, my eyes wide. I glanced at my brother. Years seemed to melt from him, and he stood there vulnerable, helpless, as a child of six or seven, no more comprehending than I.

A tempest of hot anger made our mother's ruddy colour depart. 'If you think like that, then give them separate rooms, and separate beds! Lord knows this house has enough of them!'

'That is impossible,' the grandmother said in her fire ice voice. 'This is the only bedroom with its own adjoining bath, and where my husband won't hear them walking overhead, or flushing the toilet. If they are separated, and scattered about all over upstairs, he will hear their voices, or their noise, or the servants will. Now, I have given this arrangement a great deal of thought. This is the only safe room.'

Safe room? We were going to sleep, all of us, in only one room? In a grand, rich house with twenty, thirty, forty rooms, we were going to stay in one room? Even so, now that I gave it more thought, I didn't want to be in a room alone in this mammoth house.

'Put the two girls in one bed, and the two boys in the other,' the grandmother ordered.

Momma lifted Cory and put him in the remaining double bed, thus, casually establishing the way it was to be from then on. The boys in the bed nearest the bathroom door, and Carrie and I in the bed nearest the windows.

The old woman turned her hard gaze on me, then on Christopher. 'Now hear this,' she began like a drill sergeant, 'it will be up to you two older children to keep the younger ones quiet, and you two will be responsible if they break even one of the rules I lay down. Keep this always in your mind: if your grandfather learns too soon you are up here, then he will throw all of you out without one red penny – *after* he has severely punished you for being alive! And you will keep this room clean, neat, tidy, and the bathroom, too, just as if no one lived here. And you will be quiet; you will not yell, or cry, or run about to pound on the ceilings below. When your mother and I leave this room tonight, I will close and lock the door behind me. For I will not have you roaming from room to room, and into the other sections of this house. Until the day your grandfather dies, you are here, but you don't really exist.'

33

Oh, God! My eyes flashed to Momma. This couldn't be true! She was lying, wasn't she? Saying mean things just to scare us. I drew closer to Christopher, pressing against his side, gone cold and shaky. The grandmother scowled, and quickly I stepped away. I tried to look at Momma, but she had turned her back, and her head was lowered, but her shoulders sagged and quivered as if she were crying.

Panic filled me, and I would have screamed out something if Momma hadn't turned then and sat down on a bed, and stretched out her arms to Christopher and me. We ran to her, grateful for her arms that drew us close, and her hands that stroked our hair and backs, and smoothed down our wind-rumpled hair. 'It's all right,' she whispered. 'Trust me. One night only will you be in here, and my father will welcome you into his home, to use it as you would your own – all of it, every room, and the gardens, too.'

Then she glared up at her mother so tall, so stern, so forbidding. 'Mother, have some pity and compassion for my children. They are of your flesh and blood too, keep that in *your* mind. They are very good children, but they are also normal children, and they need room to play and run and make noise. Do you expect them to speak in whispers? You don't have to lock the door to this room; you can lock the door at the end of the hall. Now why can't they have all the rooms of this north wing to use as their very own? I know you never cared for this older section very much.'

The grandmother shook her head vigorously. 'Corrine, I make the decisions here – not you! Do you think I can just close and lock the door to this wing and the servants won't wonder why? Everything must stay just as it was. They understand why I keep this particular room locked, for the stairway to the attic is in here, and I don't like for them to snoop around where they don't belong. Very early in the morning, I will bring the children food and milk – before the cook and the maids enter the kitchen. This north wing is never entered except on the last Friday of each month, when it is thoroughly cleaned. On those days, the children will hide in the attic until the maids finish. And before the maids enter, I myself will check everything over to see they leave behind no evidence of their occupancy.'

Momma voiced more objections. 'That is impossible! They are

34

bound to give themselves away, leave a clue. Mother, lock the door at the end of the hall!'

The grandmother gnashed her teeth. 'Corrine, give me time; with time I can figure out some reason why the servants cannot enter this wing at all, even to clean. But I have to tread carefully, and not raise their suspicions. They don't like me; they would run to your father with tales, hoping he would reward them. Can't you see? The closure of this wing cannot coincide with your return, Corrine.'

Our mother nodded, giving in. She and the grandmother plotted on and on, while Christopher and I grew sleepier and sleepier. It seemed an endless day. I wanted so much to crawl into the bed beside Carrie, and nestle down so I could fall into sweet oblivion, where problems didn't live.

Eventually, just when I thought she never would Momma took notice of how tired Christopher and I were, and we were allowed to undress in the bathroom, and then to climb into bed – at long last.

Momma came to me, looking tired and concerned, with dark shadows in her eyes, and she pressed her warm lips on my forehead. I saw tears glistening in the corners of her eyes, and her mascara pooled the tears into black streaks. Why was she crying again?

'Go to sleep,' she said hoarsely. 'Don't worry. Pay no attention to what you just heard. As soon as my father forgives me, and forgets what I did to displease him, he'll open up his arms and welcome his grandchildren – the only grandchildren he's likely to live long enough to see.'

'Momma' – I frowned, full of anguish, 'why do you keep crying so much?'

With jerky movements she brushed away her tears and tried to smile. 'Cathy, I'm afraid it may take more than just one day to win back my father's affection and approval. It may take two days, or more.'

'More?'

'Maybe, maybe even a week, but not longer, possibly much less time. I just don't know exactly . . . but it won't be long. You can count on that.' Her soft hand smoothed back my hair. 'Dear sweet

Cathy, your father loved you so very much, and so do I.' She drifted over to Christopher, to kiss his forehead and stroke his hair, but what she whispered to him, I couldn't hear.

At the door she turned to say, 'Have a good night's rest, and I'll see you tomorrow as soon as I can. You know my plans. I have to walk back to the train depot, and catch another train to Charlottesville where my two suitcases will be waiting, and tomorrow morning, early, I'll taxi back here, and I'll sneak up to visit with you when I can.'

The grandmother ruthlessly shoved our mother through the open doorway, but Momma twisted around to peer back at us over her shoulder, her bleak eyes silently pleading with us even before her voice sounded again: 'Please be good. Behave yourselves. Don't make any noise. Obey your grandmother and her rules, and never give her any reason to punish you. Please, please do this; and make the twins obey, and keep them from crying and missing me too much. Make this seem a game, lots of fun. Do what you can to entertain them until I'm back with toys and games for you all to play. I'll be back tomorrow, and every second I'm gone, I'll be thinking of you, and praying for you, and loving you.'

We promised we'd be as good as gold, and quiet as mice, and like angels we'd obey and keep to whatever rules were laid down. We'd do the best we could for the twins and I'd do anything, say anything, to take the anxiety from her eyes.

'Good night, Momma,' said both Christopher and I as she stood falteringly in the hall with the grandmother's large cruel hands on her shoulders. 'Don't worry about us. We'll all be fine. We know what to do for the twins, and how to entertain ourselves. We're not little children any more.' All of this came from my brother.

'You'll see me early tomorrow morning,' the grandmother said before she pushed Momma into the hall, then closed and locked the door.

Scary to be locked in, children alone. What if a fire started? Fire. Always I was to think of fire and how to escape. If we were going to be here locked in, no one would hear us if we cried out for help. Who *could* hear us in this remote, forbidden room on the second floor, where no one came but once a month, on the last Friday?

Thank God this was just a temporary arrangement – one night.

And then, tomorrow Momma would win over the dying grand-father.

And we were alone. Locked in. All the lights were turned off. Around us, below us, this huge house seemed a monster, holding us in its sharp-toothed mouth. If we moved, whispered, breathed heavily, we'd be swallowed and digested.

It was sleep I wanted as I lay there, not the long, long silence that stretched interminably. For the first time in my life I didn't fall into dreams the moment my head touched the pillow. Christopher broke the silence, and we began, in whispers, to discuss our situation.

'It won't be so bad,' he said softly, his eyes liquid and gleaming in the dimness. 'That grandmother – she can't possibly be as mean as she seems.'

'You mean to tell me you didn't think she was a sweet old lady?'

He sort of chuckled. 'Yeah, you bet, sweet – sweet as a boa constrictor.'

'She's awful big. How tall do you think she is?'

'Gosh, that's hard to guess. Maybe six feet, and two hundred pounds.'

'Seven feet! Five hundred pounds!'

'Cathy, one thing you've got to learn – stop exaggerating! Stop making so much out of small things. Now, take a real look at our situation, and realize this is only a room in a big house, nothing at all frightening. We have one night to spend here before Momma comes back.'

'Christopher, did you hear what the grandmother said about a half-uncle? Did you understand what she meant?'

'No, but I suppose Momma will explain everything. Now go to sleep, and say a prayer. Isn't that about all we can do?'

I got right out of the bed, fell down on my knees, and folded my hands beneath my chin. I closed my eyes tightly and prayed, prayed for God to help Momma be her most charming, disarming, and winning self. 'And God, please don't let the grandfather be as hateful and mean as his wife.'

Then, fatigued and drowning in many emotions, I hopped back into bed, hugged Carrie close against my chest, and fell, as I wanted, into dreams.

THE GRANDMOTHER'S HOUSE

The day dawned dim behind the heavy, drawn draperies that we had been forbidden to open. Christopher sat up first, yawning, stretching, grinning over at me. 'Hi, touslehead,' he greeted. His hair was as tousled as mine, much more so. I don't know why God chose to give him and Cory such curly hair, when he gave Carrie and me only waves. And all boy that he was, he tried with mighty effort to brush out those curls, as I sat and hoped they would jump from his head over to mine.

I sat up and looked around this room that was, perhaps, sixteen-by-sixteen. Large, but with two double beds, a massive highboy, a large dresser, two over-stuffed chairs, a dressing-table between the two front windows, with its own small chair, plus a mahogany table with four chairs, it seemed a small room. Cluttered. Between the two big beds was another table with a lamp. Altogether there were four lamps in the room. Beneath all the ponderous dark furniture was a faded Oriental red rug with gold fringe. At one time it must have been a beautiful thing, but now it was old and worn. The walls were papered in cream with white flocking. The bedspreads were gold-coloured and made of some heavy fabric like quilted satin. There were three paintings on the walls. Golly-lolly, they did steal your breath away! Grotesque demons chased naked people in underground caverns coloured mostly red. Unearthly monsters devoured other pitiful souls. Even as their legs still kicked, they dangled from slobbering mouths filled with long, shiny, sharp teeth.

'You are now gazing on hell, as some might see it,' my know-it-all brother informed me. 'Ten to one, our angel grandmother hung those reproductions herself just to let us know what we're in for if we dare to disobey. Looks like Goya's work to me,' he said.

My brother did know everything. Next to being a doctor, he wanted to be an artist. He was exceptionally good at drawing, using watercolours, oil paints, and so on. He was good at most everything except picking up after himself, and waiting on himself.

Just as I made a move to get up and go into the bath, Christopher jumped from his bed and beat me to it. Why did Carrie and I have to be so far from the bath? Impatiently I sat on the edge of the bed, swinging my legs, and waited for him to come out.

With many little restless movements, Carrie and Cory fluttered awake simultaneously. They sat up and yawned, as if mirrored reflections, rubbed at their eyes, and looked sleepily around. Then Carrie pronounced in definite tones, 'I don't like it here!'

That was not at all surprising. Carrie was born opinionated. Even before she could talk, and she talked at nine months, she knew what she liked and what she hated. There was never a middle road for Carrie – it was down low, or up sky-high. She had the cutest little voice when she was pleased, sounding very much like a sweet little bird chirping happily in the mornings. Trouble was, she chirped all day long, unless she was asleep. Carrie talked to dolls, teacups, Teddy bears and other stuffed animals. Anything that sat and didn't answer back was worthy of her conversation. After a while, I got so I didn't even hear her incessant chatter; I just turned it off and let her rattle on and on.

Cory was entirely different. While Carrie chattered on and on, he'd sit and listen attentively. I recall Mrs Simpson saying Cory was 'a still water that ran deep'. I still don't know what she meant by that, except quiet people did exude some illusion of mystery that kept you wondering just what they really were beneath the surface.

'Cathy,' twittered my baby-faced small sister, 'did you hear me say I don't like it here?'

Hearing this, Cory scrambled from his bed and ran to jump into ours, and there he reached for his twin and held her tight, his eyes wide and scared. In his solemn way, he asked, 'How did we get here?'

'Last night, on a train. Don't you remember?'

'No, I don't remember.'

'And we walked through the woods in the moonlight. It was very pretty.'

'Where is the sun? Is it still night?'

Behind the draperies the sun hid. But if I dared to tell Cory that, then he was for sure going to want to open those draperies and look outside. And once he saw outside, he was going to want to go outside. I didn't know what to say.

Someone in the hall fumbled with the door lock, saving me from giving any answer at all. Our grandmother carried into the room a large tray laden with food, covered with a large white towel. In a very brisk, businesslike way she explained that she couldn't be running up and down the stairs all day carrying heavy trays. Once a day only. If she came too often, the servants might notice.

'I think from now on I'll use a picnic basket,' she said as she set the tray down on the little table. She turned to look at me, as if I were in charge of the meals. 'You are to make this food last throughout the day. Divide it into three meals. The bacon, eggs, toast and cereal are for breakfast. The sandwiches and the hot soup in the small Thermos are for your lunch. The fried chicken, potato salad and string beans are for your dinner. You can eat the fruit for dessert. And if at the end of the day, you are silent and good, I may bring you ice-cream and cookies, or cake. No candy, ever. We can't have you getting tooth cavities. There won't be any trips to a dentist until your grandfather dies.'

Christopher had come from the bathroom, fully dressed, and he, too, stood and stared at the grandmother who could so easily talk of the death of her husband, showing no distress. It was as if she were speaking of some goldfish in China that would soon die in a fishbowl. 'And clean your teeth after every meal,' she went on, 'and keep your hair brushed neatly, and your bodies clean and fully clothed. I do despise children with dirty faces and hands and runny noses.'

Even as she said this, Cory's nose was running. Surreptitiously, I used a tissue to wipe it for him. Poor Cory, he had hay fever most of the time, and she hated children with runny noses.

'And be modest in the bathroom,' she said, looking particularly hard at me and then Christopher who was now lounging insolently against the door-frame of the bath. 'Girls and boys are never to use the bathroom together.'

I felt a hot blush stain my cheeks? What kind of kids did she think we were?

Next we heard something for the first time, which we were to hear over and over again like a needle stuck in a scratched record: 'And remember, children, God sees everything! God will see what evil you do behind my back! And God will be the one to punish when I don't!'

From her dress pocket, she pulled a sheet of paper. 'Now, on this paper, I have listed the rules you are to follow while you are in my home.' She laid the list down on the table and told us we should read and memorize them. Then she spun around to leave . . . but no, she headed towards the closet that we hadn't yet investigated. 'Children, beyond this door, and in the far end of the closet, is a small door concealing the steps to the attic. Up in the attic there is ample space for you to run and play and make a reasonable amount of noise. But you are never to go up there until after ten o'clock. Before ten, the maids will be on the second floor doing their morning chores, and they could hear you running about. Therefore, always be conscious you can be heard below if you are too noisy. After ten, the servants are forbidden to use the second floor. One of them has started stealing. Until that thief is caught red-handed, I'm always present when they straighten up the bedrooms. In this house, we make our own rules, and execute the deserved punishment. As I said last night, on the last Friday of each month, you will go into the attic very early, and sit quietly without talking, or scuffling your feet – do you understand me?' She stared at each of us in turn, impounding her words with mean, hard eyes. Christopher and I nodded. The twins only gazed at her in a strange kind of fascination, close to awe. Further explanations informed us that she would check our room and bath to see we left no hint of ourselves on that Friday.

Everything said, she left. Once more she locked us in.

Now we could breathe.

Grimly, with determination, I set out to make a game of this. 'Christopher Doll, I appoint you the father.'

He laughed, then said with sarcasm, 'What else? As the man, and the head of this family, let it be known hitherto that I am to be waited on hand and foot – the same as a king. Wife, as my inferior, and my slave, set the table, dish out the food, make ready for your lord and master.'

'Repeat again what you said, *brother*.'

'From now on, I am not your brother, but your lord and master; you are to do my bidding, whatever I say.'

'And if I don't do as you say – what will you do next, lord and master?'

'I don't like the tone of your voice. Speak respectfully when you speak to me.'

'La-dee-da, and ho-ho-ho! The day I speak respectfully to you, Christopher, will be the day you *earn* my respect – and that will be the day you stand twelve feet high, and the moon is at noon, and a blizzard blows in a unicorn ridden by a gallant knight wearing pure white shining armour, with a green dragon's head perched on the point of his lance!' And so said, and so satisfied with his disgruntled expression, I caught hold of Carrie's small hand and led her haughtily into the bathroom where we could take our time to wash, dress and brush, and ignore poor Cory, who kept calling out that he had to go.

'Please, Cathy. Let me come in! I won't look!'

Eventually a bathroom grows boring, and we came out, and, believe it or not, Christopher had Cory fully dressed! And what was even more shocking – now Cory didn't need to use the bathroom!

'Why?' I asked. 'Now don't you dare tell me you got back into bed and did it there!'

Silently, Cory pointed to a large blue vase without flowers.

Christopher lounged against the highboy, his arms folded across his chest, pleased with himself. 'That should teach you to ignore a male in need. We men are not like you sit-down females. Any little thing will do in an emergency.'

Before I would allow anyone to begin breakfast, I had to empty the blue vase, and rinse it out well. Really, it wouldn't be such a bad idea to keep the vase near Cory's side of the bed, just in case.

Near the windows we sat down to the little table meant for card-playing. The twins sat on doubled-over pillows so they could see what they were eating. All four lamps were turned on. Still it was depressing, having to eat breakfast in what looked like twilight.

'Cheer up, sober face,' said my unpredictable older brother. 'I was only kidding. You don't have to be my slave. I just love the gems you spurt forth when provoked. I admit, in verbosity you females are blessed, just as we males are gifted with the perfect instrument for picnic bathrooming.' And to prove he wasn't going to be an overbearing brute, he helped me pour the milk, finding out, as I had, that hefting a gallon-sized Thermos and pouring without spilling was no mean feat.

Carrie gave those fried eggs and bacon just one glance and she was wailing. '*We-ee* don't like bacon and eggs! *Cold* CEREAL is what we-ee like! We-ee don't want no hot, lumpy, bumpy food that's greasy. *Cold* CEREAL IS WHAT WE LIKE!' she shrieked. '*Cold* CEREAL WITH RAISINS!'

'Now you listen to me,' said their new, smaller-edition father, 'you will eat what is put before you, and you will make no complaints, and you will not yell, or cry, or scream! Hear that? And it is not hot food, it is cold food. You can scrape off the grease. It is solid, anyway.'

In a wink Christopher gobbled down his cold, greasy food, plus his cold toast without butter. Those twins, for some odd reason I'll never understand, ate their breakfast without another word of complaint. I had the uneasy queasy feeling our luck with the twins just couldn't hold out. They might be impressed now by a forceful older brother, but watch out later!

The meal finished, I neatly stacked the dishes back on the tray. And only then did I remember we'd forgotten to say grace. Hastily we gathered together at the table and sat down to bow our heads, and clasp our palms together.

'Lord, forgive us for eating without asking your permission. Please don't let the grandmother know. We vow to do it right next time. Amen.' Finished, I handed Christopher the list of do's and don'ts that were carefully typed in capital letters as if we were so stupid we couldn't understand longhand.

And just so the twins, who'd been too sleepy last night to understand our situation, fully realized what they were in for, my brother began at the top of the list of rules not to be broken – or else!

First he pursed his mouth up in a good imitation of the grand-

43

mother's hateful lips, and you'd never believe such a finely shaped mouth as his could be made to look so grim, but somehow he managed to mimic her austerity.

'One:' – he read in a cold, flat voice – 'you are *always* to be fully dressed.' And, boy, did he make *'always'* sound impossible.

'Two: you will never take the Lord's name in vain, and will *always* say grace before each meal. And if I am not in the room to see that you do this, you may be sure that He above will be listening, and watching.

'Three: you are *never* to open the draperies, not even to peek out.

'Four: you will *never* speak to me unless I speak to you first.

'Five: you will keep this room neat and orderly, *always* with the beds made.

'Six: you are *never* to be idle. You will devote five hours each day to studying, and use the remainder of your time to develop your abilities in some meaningful way. *If* you have any skills, abilities or talents, you will seek to improve upon them, and if you have no abilities or talents, or skills, you will read the Bible; and if you cannot, then you will sit and stare at the Bible, and try to absorb through the purity of your thoughts the meaning of the Lord and his ways.

'Seven: you will clean your teeth after breakfast each day, and before retiring each night.

'Eight: if I ever catch boys and girls using the bathroom at the same time, I will quite relentlessly, and without mercy, peel the skins from your backs.'

My heart seemed to flip over. Good-golly day, what kind of grandmother did we have?

'Nine: you will, all four, be modest and discreet at *all* times – in deportment, in speech, and in thought.

'Ten: you *will not* handle or play with the private parts of your bodies; nor will you look at them in the mirrors; nor will you think about them, even when you are cleansing those parts of your bodies.'

Unabashed, with a funny little gleam in his eyes, Christopher read on, mimicking the grandmother with some skill.

'Eleven: you *will not* allow wicked, sinful, or lusting thoughts

44

to dwell in your minds. You will keep your thoughts clean, pure, and away from wicked subjects that will corrupt you morally.

'Twelve: you will refrain from looking at members of the opposite sex unless it is absolutely necessary.

'Thirteen: those of you who can read, and I hope at least two of you can, will each, alternately, take turns reading aloud from the Bible at least one page per day, so the two younger children will benefit from the Lord's teachings.

'Fourteen: you will each bathe daily, and clean the ring from the tub, and keep the bathroom as spotless as it was when you found it.

'Fifteen: you will each learn, including the twins, at least one quote from the Bible per day. And if I so request, you will repeat to me such quotes as I demand, as I keep track of what passages you have read.

'Sixteen: you will eat all of the food I bring to you, and not waste one single bit, or throw it away, or hide it away. It is sinful to waste good food when so many in this world are starving.

'Seventeen: you will not stride about in the bedroom wearing only your nightclothes, even if you are only going from bed to bath, or bath to bed. You will, at *all* times, wear a robe of some kind over your nightclothes, and over your undergarments if at some time you feel the need to suddenly leave the bathroom without fully dressing yourself, so that another child may enter in an emergency. I demand that everyone who lives under this roof be modest and discreet – in all things, and in all ways.

'Eighteen: you will stand at attention when I enter your room, with your arms straight down at your sides; you will not clench your hands into fists to show silent defiance; nor will you allow your eyes to meet with mine; nor will you seek to show signs of affection towards me, nor hope to gain my friendship, nor my pity, nor my love, nor my compassion. All of that is impossible. Neither your grandfather nor myself can allow ourselves to feel anything for what is not wholesome.'

Ohhh! Those were words to really sting! Even Christopher paused, and a flicker of despair fleeted over his face, quickly put away by a grin as his eyes met with mine. He reached out and

45

tickled Carrie to make her giggle, and then he tweaked Cory's nose, so he, too, giggled.

'Christopher,' I cried, alarm in my voice. 'From the way she put it, our mother can never hope to win over her father again! Much less will he want his eyes to rest upon us! Why? What have we done? We weren't here the day our mother fell from grace by doing something so terrible her father disinherited her! We weren't even born then! Why do they hate us?'

'Keep your cool,' said Chris, his eyes scanning down the long list. 'Don't take any of this seriously. She's a nut, a loony-bird. Nobody as smart as our grandfather can have the idiot ideas his wife does – or else how could he make millions of dollars?'

'Maybe he didn't make the money, but inherited it.'

'Yes, Momma told us he inherited some, but he has increased that a hundred times over, so he must have a *little* brains in his head. But he somehow picked the Queen Bee nut from the barmy tree for his wife.' He grinned and then went on with the rule reading.

'Nineteen: when I come into this room to bring you food and milk, you will not look at me, or speak to me, or think of me with disrespect, or of your grandfather with disrespect, for God is above and is able to read your minds. My husband is a very determined man, and seldom has any one bested him in any way. He has an army of doctors and nurses and technicians to tend to his every need, and machines to function for his organs in case they fail, so don't think something as weakly motivated as his heart can fail a man made of steel.'

Wow! A man of steel to make the opposite book-end to his wife. His eyes must be grey, too. Flint, hard, steel-grey eyes – for, as our very own mother and father had proved, likes do attract.

'Twenty:' – read Christopher – 'you will not jump, yell, shout, or speak in loud voices so the servants below can hear you. And you will wear sneakers and never hard-soled shoes.

'Twenty-One: you will not waste toilet tissue, or the soap, and you will clean up the mess if you clog up the toilet bowl so it overflows. And if you put it out of order, then it will stay that way until the day you leave, and you will use the chamberpots that you will find in the attic, and your mother can empty them for you.

'Twenty-Two: the boys will wash their own clothes in the bathtub, as will the girls. Your mother will take care of the bed linen and the towels you use. The quilted mattress covers will be changed once a week, and if a child soils the covers, then I will order your mother to bring you rubber sheets to use, and thrash severely the child who cannot be toilet trained.'

I sighed and put my arm about Cory who whimpered and clung to me on hearing this. 'Ssssh! Don't be afraid. She'll never know what you do. We'll protect you. We'll find a way to cover up your mistakes, if you make any.'

Chris read: 'Conclusion, and this is not a do or a don't, just a warning. She's written: "You may rightly assume that I will add to this list from time to time as I see the need arise, for I am a very observant woman who misses nothing. Do not think you can deceive me, mock me, or play jokes at my expense, for if you do, your punishment will be so severe that your skins, and your egos, will bear lifetime scars, and your pride will go down in permanent defeat. And let it be known from now on, that never in my presence will you mention your father's name, or refer to him in the slightest way, and I, myself, will refrain from looking at the child who resembles him most."'

It was over. I flashed Christopher a questioning look. Was he inferring, as I was, what that last paragraph implied – that for some reason our father was the cause of our mother being disinherited, and now hated by her parents?

And did he infer, too, that we were going to be locked up here for a long, long time?

Oh God, oh God, oh God! I couldn't stand even a week!

We weren't devils, but most certainly we weren't angels, either! And we needed each other, to touch, to look at.

'Cathy,' said my brother calmly, a wry smile cocking his lips while the twins looked from one to the other of us, ready to mimic our panic, our joy, or our screams, 'are we so ugly and without charm that an old woman who very obviously hates our mother, and also our father, for some reason I don't know, can for ever resist us? She's a fake, a fraud. She doesn't mean any of this.' He gestured towards the list, which he folded and flung away towards the dresser. It made a poor airplane.

47

'Are we to believe an old woman like that, who must be demented, and should be locked up – or should we believe the woman who loves us, the woman we know and trust? Our mother will take care of us. She knows what she's doing, on that you can depend.'

Yes, of course, he was right. Momma was the one to believe in and trust, not that stern old crazy woman with her idiot ideas, and her gunshot eyes, and her crooked, knife-slashed mouth.

In no time at all the grandfather downstairs would succumb to our mother's beauty and charm, and down the stairs we'd trip, dressed in our best, wearing happy smiles. And he'd see us, and know we weren't ugly, or stupid, but normal enough to like a little, if not a lot. And perhaps, who knows, maybe some day he might even find a *little* love to give to his grandchildren.

THE ATTIC

The morning hour of ten came and went.

What remained of our daily ration of food, we stored in the coolest spot we could find in the room, under the highboy. The servants who made the beds, and tidied up in the upstairs rooms of other wings, must surely have departed for lower sections, and they would not see this floor again for another twenty-four hours.

We were, of course, already tired of that room, and very eager to explore the outer confines of our limited domain. Christopher and I each caught hold of a twin's hand, and we headed silently towards the closet that held our two suitcases with all the clothes still inside. We'd wait to unpack. When we had more roomy, pleasant quarters, the servants could unpack for us, as they did in movies, and we could take off outdoors. Indeed, we wouldn't be in this room when the servants came in on the last Friday of the month to clean. We'd be set free by then.

With my older brother in the lead, holding on to the small hand of my younger brother so he wouldn't trip or fall, and with me close at Cory's heels, as Carrie clung to my hand, we headed up the dark, narrow, steep steps. The walls of that passageway were so narrow your shoulders almost brushed them.

And there it was!

Attics we'd seen before, who hasn't? But never such an attic as this one!

We stood as if rooted, and gazed around with incredulity. Huge, dim, dirty, dusty, this attic stretched for miles! The farthest walls were so distant they seemed hazy, out of focus. The air was not clear, but murky; it had an odour, an unpleasant odour of decay, of old rotting things, of dead things left unburied, and because it was cloudy with dust, everything seemed to move, to shimmer, especially in the darker, gloomier corners.

Four sets of deep dormer windows stretched across the front, four sets across the back. The sides, what we could see of them, were without windows – but there were wings where we couldn't see unless we dared to move forward and brave the stifling heat of the place.

Step by step we moved as one away from the stairwell.

The floor was of wide wooden planks, soft and rotting. As we inched along cautiously, feeling fearful, small creatures on the floor went scuttling off in all directions. There was enough furniture stored in the attic to furnish several houses. Dark, massive furniture, and chamberpots, and pitchers set in larger bowls, perhaps twenty or thirty sets of them. And there was a round wooden thing that looked like a tub banded with iron. Imagine keeping a bathtub like that!

Everything that seemed of value was draped over by sheets where dust had accumulated to turn the white cloth dingy grey. And what was covered by sheets for protection shivered my spine, for I saw these things as weird, eerie, furniture ghosts, whispering, whispering. And I didn't want to hear what they had to say.

Dozens of old leather-bound trunks with heavy brass locks and corners lined one entire wall, each trunk stuck all over with travel labels. Why, they must have been around the world several or more times. Big trunks, fit for coffins.

Giant armoires stood in a silent row against the farthest wall, and when we checked, we found each one full of ancient clothes. We saw both Union and Confederate uniforms, giving Christopher and me much to speculate upon as the twins cringed close against us and looked around with big, scared eyes.

'Do you think our ancestors were so undecided during the Civil War they didn't know which side they were on, Christopher?'

'The War Between the States sounds better,' he answered.

'Spies, you think?'

'How would I know?'

Secrets, secrets, everywhere! Brother against brother I saw it – oh, what fun to find out! If only we could find diaries!

'Look here,' said Christopher, pulling out a man's suit of pale cream-coloured wool, with brown velvet lapels, and piped smartly with darker brown satin. He waved the suit. Disgusting winged creatures took off in all directions, despite the stench of mothballs.

I yelped, as did Carrie.

'Don't be such babies,' he said, not in the least disturbed by those things. 'What you saw were moths, harmless moths. It's the larvae that do the chewing and make the holes.'

I didn't care! Bugs were bugs – infants or adults. I don't know why that darned suit interested him so much anyway. Why did we have to examine the fly to see if men in those days used buttons or zippers? 'Gosh,' he said, finally disturbed, 'what a pain to unfasten buttons every time.'

That was his opinion.

In my opinion, olden-day people really knew how to dress! How I would love to flounce around in a frilly chemise over pantaloons, with dozens of fancy petticoats over the wire hoops, all bedecked in ruffles, lace, embroidery, with flowing ribbons of velvet or satin, and my shoes would be of satin and over all this bedazzling finery would be a lacy parasol to shade my golden curls, and keep the sun from my fair, unwrinkled complexion. And I'd carry a fan to elegantly cool myself, and my eyelids would flutter and bewitch. Oh, what a beauty I'd be!

Subdued by the immense attic until now, Carrie let out a howl that took me swiftly from sweet speculations and right back to the here and now, which was where I didn't want to be.

'It's hot up here, Cathy!'

'Yes, it is.'

'I hate it up here, Cathy!'

I glanced at Cory, his small face awed as he looked around and clung to my side, and catching his hand, and Carrie's, I left behind the fascination of the old clothes, and all of us wandered off to pry into everything this attic had to offer. And that was considerable. Thousands of old books in stacks, dark ledgers, office desks, two upright pianos, radios, phonographs, cartons filled with the unwanted accoutrements of generations long gone. Dress forms, all sizes and shapes, bird-cages and stands to hold them, rakes, shovels, framed photographs and peculiar pale and sickly-looking people who were, I presumed, dead relatives of ours. Some had light hair, some dark; all had eyes sharp, cruel, hard, bitter, sad, wistful, yearning, hopeless, empty, but never, I swear, never did I see any happy eyes. Some smiled. Most didn't. I was drawn in particular to a pretty girl of perhaps eighteen; she wore a faint, enigmatic smile which reminded me of Mona Lisa, only she was more beautiful. Her bosom swelled out beneath a ruffled bodice most impressively, making Christopher point to one of the dress forms and declare emphatically, 'Hers!'

I looked. 'Now,' he continued with admiring eyes, 'that is what you call an hourglass figure. See the wasp waist, the ballooning hips, the swelling bosom? Inherit a shape like that, Cathy, and you will make a fortune.'

'Really,' I said in disgust, 'you don't know very much. That is not a woman's natural form. She's wearing a corset, cinched in at the waist so much her flesh is squeezed out at the top and the bottom. And that is exactly why women used to faint so much and then call for smelling salts.'

'How can one faint and still manage to call for smelling salts?' he asked sarcastically. 'Besides, you can't squeeze out at the top what isn't there.' He took another look at the shapely young woman. 'You know, she kind of looks like Momma – If she wore her hair differently and her clothes were modern – she'd be Momma.'

Hah! Our mother would have more sense than to wear a laced-up cage and suffer. 'But this girl is only pretty,' Christopher concluded. 'Our mother is beautiful.'

The silence of that huge space was so deep you could hear your heartbeat. Yet it would be fun to explore every trunk; to examine the contents of every box; to try on all those rotting, smelly, fancy clothes, and pretend, pretend, pretend. But it was so hot! So stifling! So stuffy! Already my lungs seemed clogged with dirt and dust and stale air. Not only that, spider webs laced the corners and draped down from the rafters, and crawling or slithering things rambling about on the floor or up the walls. Though I didn't see any, I thought of rats and mice. We'd seen a movie once on TV where a man went crazy and hanged himself from an attic rafter. And in another movie, a man shoved his wife in an old trunk with brass corners and locks, just like these, and then he slammed down the lid and left her there to die. I took another look at those trunks, wondering what secrets they held that the servants shouldn't know.

Disconcerting, the curious way my brother was watching me and my reactions. I whirled to hide what I was feeling – but he saw. He stepped closer and caught my hand, and said so much like Daddy, 'Cathy, it is going to be all right. There must be very simple explanations for everything that seems to us very complex and mysterious.'

Slowly I turned to him, surprised he'd come to comfort and not to tease. 'Why do you suppose the grandmother hates us, too? Why should the grandfather hate us? What have *we* done?'

He shrugged, as baffled as I was, and with his hand still holding mine, we both pivoted to look the attic over again. Even our untrained eyes could tell where new sections had been added to the older house. Thick, square, upright beams divided the attic into distinct sections. I thought if we wandered here, and wandered there, we would come upon a place for comfortable, fresh breathing.

The twins began to cough and sneeze. They fixed resentful blue eyes on us for keeping them where they didn't want to be.

'Now look,' said Christopher when the twins started to really complain, 'we can open up the windows an inch or so, enough to let in a little fresh air, and no one will notice such a little opening from the ground.' Then he released my hand and ran on ahead, leaping over boxes, trunks, furniture, showing off, while I stood frozen, holding to the hands of both my little ones, who were terrified of where they were.

'Come see what I've found!' called Christopher, who was out of sight. Excitement was in his voice. 'You just wait and see my discovery!'

We ran, eager to see something exciting, wonderful, fun – and all he had to show us was a room – a real room with plaster walls. It had never been painted, but it did have a regular ceiling, not just beams. This seemed to be a schoolroom with five desks, facing a larger desk up front. Blackboards lined the walls over low bookcases filled with faded and dusty old volumes that my perpetual seeker of all knowledge had to immediately inspect by crawling around and reading the book titles aloud. Books were enough to send him off on a high tangent, knowing he had a way to escape to other worlds.

I was drawn to the small desks, where names and dates were etched, such as Jonathan, age 11, 1864! And Adelaide, age 9, 1879! Oh, how very old this house was! They were dust in their graves by now, but they had left their names behind to let us know that once, they, too, had been sent up here. But why would parents send their children into an attic to study? They had been wanted children, surely – unlike us, whom the grandparents despised. Maybe for *them* the windows had been opened wide. And for them, servants had carried up coal or wood to burn in the two stoves we saw in the corners.

An old rocking-horse with a missing amber eye wobbled unsteadily, and his matted yellow tail was a woebegone thing. But this white-and-black-spotted pony was enough to bring a delighted cry from Cory. Instantly he clambered up on the peeling red saddle, crying out, 'Getty-up, horsy!' And the pony, not ridden for ever so long, galloped along, squealing, rattling, protesting with every rusty joint.

'I want to ride, too!' bellowed Carrie. 'Where is my horsy?'

Quickly I ran to lift Carrie up behind Cory, so she could cling to his waist, and laugh, and kick her heels to make the dilapidated horse go faster and faster. I marvelled that the poor thing stayed hinged together.

Now I had the chance to look over the old books that had charmed Christopher. Heedlessly, I reached in and took out a book, not caring what the title read. I flipped through the pages and sent legions of flat bugs with centipede legs madly scampering everywhere! I dropped that book, – then stared down at the loose pages that had scattered. I hated bugs, spiders most of all, worms next. And what swarmed from those pages seemed a combination of both.

Such a girlish performance was enough to send Christopher into hysterics, and when he calmed down he called my squeamishness overdone. The twins reined in their bucking bronco and stared at me in astonishment. Quickly I had to reach for my poise. Even pretend mothers didn't squeal at the sight of a few bugs.

'Cathy, you're twelve, and it's time you grew up. Nobody screams to see a few bookworms. Bugs are a part of life. We humans are the masters, the supreme rulers over all. This isn't such a bad room at all. Lots of space, full of big windows, plenty of books, and even a few toys for the twins.'

Yeah. There was a rusty red wagon with a broken handle, and a missing wheel – great. A broken green scooter, too. Terrific. Yet there stood Christopher looking around and expressing his pleasure in finding a room where people hid away their children so they couldn't see them, or hear them, or maybe not even think about them, and he saw it as a room with possibilities.

Sure, somebody could clean all the dark secret places where creeping horrors lived, and they could spray all over with insect repellent so nothing sinister was left that was small enough to step on. But how to step on the grandmother, the grandfather? How to turn an attic room into a paradise where flowers bloomed, and not just another prison like the one below?

I ran to the dormer windows and climbed upon a box to reach the high window ledge. Desperate to see the ground, to see how far we were above it, and if we jumped how many bones we'd break. Desperate to see the trees, the grass, where the flowers grew, where sunlight was, where birds flew, where real life lived. But all I saw was a slate black roof expanding wide beneath the windows, blocking out the view of the ground. Beyond the roofs were tree-tops; beyond the tree-tops, enclosing mountains hovered over by blue mists.

Christopher climbed up beside me and looked, too. His shoulder brushing mine quivered, as did his voice when he said softly, 'We can still see the sky, the sun, and at night we'll see the moon and stars, and birds and planes will fly over. We can watch them for amusement until the day we don't come up here again.'

He paused, seeming to think back to the night we came – was it only last night? 'I'll bet if we leave a window open wide, an owl might fly in. I've always wanted an owl for a pet.'

'For heaven's sake, why in the world would you want one of those things?'

'Owls can turn their heads all the way around. Can you do that?'

'I don't want to do that.'

'But if you wanted to, you still couldn't.'

'Well, neither can you!' I flared, wanting to make him face up to reality, like he insisted I do. No bird as wise as an owl would want to live locked up with us for even an hour.

'I want a kitty,' spoke up Carrie, holding her arms up so she could be lifted to where she could see, too.

'I want a puppy,' said Cory before he glanced out of the window. Then he quickly forgot about pets, for he began to chant, 'Outside, outside, Cory wants outside. Cory wants to play in the garden. Cory wants to swing!'

Quickly Carrie followed suit. She too wanted outside, the garden, and the swings. And with her bullmoose voice, she was far more persistent with her wants than Cory.

Now they were both near driving Christopher and me up the wall with their demands to go outside, outside, outside!

'Why can't we go outside?' screamed Carrie, doubling up her fists and beating them against my chest. 'We-ee don't like it here! Where is Momma? Where is the sunshine? Where did the flowers go? Why is it so hot?'

'Look,' said Christopher, catching her small battering fists and saving me from a bruising, 'think of this place as outside. There's no reason you can't swing up here, like in a garden. Cathy, let's search around and see if we can't find some rope.'

We did search. And we did find rope in an old trunk that held all sorts of junk. It was very apparent the Foxworths didn't throw anything away – they stored their trash in the attic. Maybe they were afraid of one day being poor, and suddenly needing what was put away so miserly.

With great diligence my older brother worked to make swings for both Cory and Carrie, for when you have twins, you must never, ever give them only one of a kind – of anything. For seats he used boards ripped from a lid of a trunk. He found sandpaper and smoothed away the splinters. While he did this, I hunted around until I found an old ladder with a few missing rungs that didn't hinder Christopher in the least from quickly reaching the rafters high above. I watched him climbing nimbly around up there, crawling out on a wide beam – and every move he made endangered his life! He stood up to show off his balancing skill. He swayed suddenly off balance! Quickly he adjusted himself by putting out his arms, but my heart had jumped up, terrified to see him taking such chances, risking his life, just to show off! There was no adult to call him down. If I tried to order him down, he'd laugh, and do even more foolish things. So I kept my mouth shut and closed my eyes, and I tried to shut out the visions I had of him falling, splattering down, breaking his arms, legs or, even worse, his back or neck! And he didn't have to put on any act. I knew he was brave. He had the knots securely tied, so why couldn't he come down and give my heart a chance to beat normally again?

It had taken Christopher hours to make those swings, and then he risked his life to hang them. And when he was down, and the twins were seated on the swings, fanning back and forth and stirring up the dusty air, they were satisfied for, perhaps, three minutes.

Then it began. Carrie started off. 'Take us out of here! Don't like these swings! Don't like in here! This is a baa-ad place!'

No sooner did her wails cease than Cory's began. 'Outside, outside, we want outside! Take us outside! Outside!' And Carrie added her chants to his. Patience – I had to have patience, deep self-control, act adult, not scream just because I wanted outside just as much as they did.

'Now stop that racket!' snapped Christopher to the twins. 'We're playing a game, and all games have rules. The main rule of this game is to stay inside and be as quiet as possible. Screaming and yelling is forbidden.' His tone turned softer as he gazed down at their tear-streaked, grimy faces. 'Pretend this is the garden under a bright blue sky, and tree leaves are overhead, and the sun is shining bright. And when we go downstairs, that room will be our home with many rooms.'

He gave us all a whimsical, disarming smile. 'When we're rich as Rockefellers, we'll never need to see this attic again, or that bedroom below. We'll live like princesses and princes.'

'Do you think the Foxworths have as much money as the Rockefellers?' I asked disbelievingly. Golly-day, wow! We'd be able to have everything! Yet, yet, I was terribly troubled . . . that grandmother, something about her, the way she treated us, as if we didn't have a right to be alive. Such horrible words she'd said: 'You are here, but you don't really exist.'

We rambled about the attic, half-heartedly exploring this and that, until someone's stomach rumbled. I glanced at my wristwatch. Two. My older brother stared at me, as I glanced at the twins. It must have been one of their stomachs, for they ate so little, but, nevertheless, their digestive systems were automatically set on seven for breakfast, twelve for lunch, and five for dinner, and seven for bedtime, and a snack before.

'Lunchtime,' I announced cheerfully.

Down the stairs we tripped single file, back into that hateful dim room. If only we could open the draperies wide to let in some light and cheer. If only . . .

My thoughts could have been spoken aloud, for Christopher was perceptive enough to say that even if the draperies were opened wide, this room faced north and the sunlight would never enter.

And my, just look at the chimney sweeps in the mirrors! Just like those from *Mary Poppins*, a spoken comparison to put smiles on the dirty faces of the twins. They dearly loved being compared with those charming people who lived in their kind of picture books.

Since we'd been taught from our earlier years never to sit down to eat when we were less than spotlessly clean, and since God had His keenest eye riveted on us, we would obey all the rules and please Him. Now, it didn't really offend God's eyes if we put Cory and Carrie in the same bathtub, when they'd come from the same womb, did it? Christopher took over Cory, as I shampooed Carrie, then bathed her, dressed her, and brushed her silky hair until it shone, and then I curled her hair around my fingers till it spiralled down in pretty coils. Next I tied on a green satin ribbon.

And it wouldn't really hurt anyone if Christopher talked to me while I bathed. We weren't adults – yet. It wasn't the same thing as 'using' the bathroom together. Momma and Daddy had seen nothing wrong about bare skin, but as I washed my face, the memory of the grandmother's stern, uncompromising expression flashed before my eyes. She would think it was wrong.

'We can't do this again,' I said to Christopher. 'That grandmother – she might catch us, and then she would think it evil.'

He nodded as if it didn't really matter. He must have seen something on my face that made him move forward to the tub so he could put his arms about me. How did he know I needed a shoulder to cry on? Which was exactly what I did.

'Cathy,' he soothed while my head was tucked down on his shoulder and my sobs came, 'keep thinking about the future, and all that will be ours when we're rich. I've always wanted to be filthy rich so I can be a playboy for a while, only a little while, for Daddy said everybody should contribute something useful and meaningful to mankind, and I'd like to do that. But until I'm in college, and med. school I could sneak in a little fooling around until I settle down seriously.'

'Oh, I see you mean to do everything a poor guy can't afford to do. Well, if that's what you want, go to it. But what I want is a horse. All my life I've wanted a pony, and we've never lived in a place that would allow a pony, and now I'm too big for a pony. So it will have to be a horse. And, of course, all the while I'll be working my way to fame and fortune as the world's leading prima ballerina. And you know how dancers have to eat and eat or else they'd be just skin and bones, so I'm going to eat a whole gallon of ice-cream each day, and one day I'm going to eat nothing but cheese – every kind of cheese there is, put on cheese crackers, and top it off with ice-cream. And I'll work off the fat by dancing.'

He was stroking my wet back, and when I turned to see his profile, he looked dreamy, wistful.

'You see, Cathy, it's not going to be so bad, this short time while we're shut up here. We won't have time to feel depressed, for we'll be too busy thinking of ways to spend all of our money. Let's ask Momma to bring us a chess game. I've always wanted to learn to play chess. And we can read; reading is almost as good as doing. Momma won't let us get bored; she'll bring us new games and things to do. This week will pass in a flash.' He smiled at me brilliantly. 'And please stop calling me Christopher! I can't be confused with Daddy any more, so from now on, I am only Chris, okay?'

'Okay, Chris,' I said. 'But the grandmother – what do you think she'd do if she caught us in the bathroom together?'

'Give us hell – and God knows what else.'

Still, when I was out of the tub, drying off, I started to tell him not to look. However, he wasn't looking. Already we knew each other's bodies well, having been looking at them naked since I could remember. And in my opinion, mine was the best. Neater.

All of us wearing clean clothes, and smelling good, we sat down to eat our ham sandwiches, and lukewarm vegetable soup from the small Thermos, and more milk to drink. Lunch without cookies was an abysmal thing.

Furtively, Chris kept glancing at his watch. It might be a long, long time before our mother showed up. The twins prowled around restlessly after lunch was over. They were cranky, and they expressed their displeasure with everything by kicking at it, and from time to time as they prowled the room, they shot both me and Chris scowling looks. Chris headed for the closet, and the attic, to the schoolroom for books to read, and I started to follow.

'No!' screamed Carrie. 'Don't go up in the attic! Don't like it up there! Don't like it down here! Don't like nothin'! Don't want you being my momma, Cathy! Where is my real momma? Where'd she go? You tell her to come back and let us go out to the sandbox!' She took off for the door to the hall and turned the knob, then screamed like an animal in terror when the door wouldn't open. Wildly she beat her small fists against the hard oak and all the while she screamed for Momma to come and take her out of this dark room!

I ran to catch her up in my arms while she kicked and kept right on yelling. It was like holding a wildcat. Chris seized Cory, who ran to protect his twin. All we could do was put them down on one of the big beds, haul out their story books, and suggest naps. Teary and resentful, both twins glared up at us.

'Is it night already?' whimpered Carrie, gone hoarse from so many fruitless screams for freedom, and a mother who wouldn't come. 'I want my momma so bad. Why don't she come?'

'*Peter Rabbit*,' I said, picking up Cory's favourite story book with colourful illustrations on every page, and this alone made *Peter Rabbit* a very good book. Bad books had no pictures. Carrie had a fondness for *The Three Little Pigs*, but Chris would have to read like Daddy used to, and huff and puff, and make his voice deep like the wolf's. And I wasn't sure he would.

'Please let Chris go up in the attic and find himself a book to read, and while he does that, I'll read to you from *Peter Rabbit*. And let's see if Peter will steal into the farmer's garden tonight and eat his fill of carrots and cabbages. And if you fall asleep while I'm still reading, the story will end in your dreams.'

Maybe five minutes passed before both the twins were asleep. Cory clutched his story book against his small chest to make the transportation of *Peter Rabbit* into his dreams as easy as possible. A soft, warm feeling swept over me, making my heart ache for little ones who really needed a grown-up mother, not one only twelve. I didn't feel much different than I had at ten. If womanhood was just around the corner, it hadn't reared its head to make me feel mature and capable. Thank God we weren't going to be shut up here long, for what would I do if they got sick? What would happen if there was an accident, a fall, a broken bone? If I banged hard on the locked door, would the despicable grandmother come running in response? There was no telephone in this room. If I cried out for help, who would hear me from this remote, forbidden wing?

While I stewed and fretted, Chris was up in the attic school-room, collecting an assortment of dusty, buggy books to bring down to the bedroom for us to read. We had brought along a checker-board, and that's what I wanted to do – not stick my nose in an old book.

'Here,' he said, thrusting an old book into my hands. He said he'd shaken it free of all bugs that might send me off into hysteria again. 'Let's save the checkers until later when the twins are awake. You know how you cut up when you lose.'

He settled down in a comfortable chair, flinging his leg across the fat, rounded chair arm, and opened up *Tom Sawyer*. I flung myself down on the only empty bed and began to read about King Arthur and the Knights of the Round Table. And, believe it or not, that day a door opened I hadn't known existed before: a beautiful world when knighthood was in flower, and there was romantic love, and fair ladies were put on pedestals and worshipped from afar. A love affair with the medieval age began that day for me, one I was never to lose, for, after all, weren't most ballets based on fairy tales? And weren't all fairy tales written from folklore of medieval times?

I was the kind of child who'd always looked for fairies dancing on the grass. I wanted to believe in witches, wizards, ogres, giants, and enchanted spells. I didn't want all of the magic taken out of the world by scientific explanation. I didn't know at that time that I had come to live in what was virtually a strong and dark castle, ruled over by a witch and an ogre. I didn't guess that some modern-day wizards could weave money to create a spell . . .

As daylight drew away behind the heavy drawn draperies, we sat down at our small table to eat our meal of fried chicken (cold) and potato salad (warm) and string beans (cold and greasy). At least Chris and I ate most of our meal, cold and unappetizing or not. But the twins just picked at their food, complaining all the time that it didn't taste good. I felt that if Carrrie had said less, then Cory would have eaten more.

'Oranges are not funny looking,' said Chris, handing me an orange to peel, 'or supposed to be hot. Actually, oranges are liquid sunshine.' Boy, he did say the right thing that time. Now the twins had something they could eat with pleasure – liquid sunshine.

Now it was night, and really not much different than the day had been. We turned on all four lamps, and one tiny little rose nightlamp our mother had brought along to comfort the twins who didn't like the dark.

After their naps, we had dressed the twins again in their clean clothes, and brushed their hair, and washed their faces, so they looked sweet and appealing as they settled down on the floor to put large pieces of puzzles together. Those puzzles were old ones and they knew exactly which piece fitted into the other, and it was not so much of a problem, but a race to see who could fit in the most pieces first. Soon the race to put puzzles together bored the twins, so we all piled on one of the beds and Chris and I told stories we made up. That too grew boring for the twins, though my brother and I could have gone on longer, competing to see who had the most imagination. Next we hauled the small cars and trucks from the suitcases so the twins could crawl around and push cars from New York to San Francisco, by route of wriggling under the beds and between the table legs – and soon they were dirty again. When we tired of that, Chris suggested we play checkers, and the twins could transport orange peels in their trucks and dump them down in Florida, which was the trash can in the corner.

'You can have the red pieces,' announced Chris patronizingly. 'I don't believe as you do, that black is a losing colour.'

I scowled, sulked away. It seemed an eternity had passed between dawn and dusk, enough to change me so I'd never be the same again. 'I don't want to play checkers!' I said nastily.

So I fell on a bed and gave up the struggle to keep my thoughts from roaming up and down endless alleys of dark suspicious fears, and tormenting nagging doubts, wondering always if Momma had told us all of the truth. And while we all four waited, and waited, and waited for Momma to show up, there wasn't a calamity my thoughts didn't touch upon. Mostly fire. Ghosts, monsters, and other spectres lived in the attic. But in this locked room fire was the uppermost threat.

And time passed so slowly. Chris in his chair, with his book, kept sneaking glances at his watch. The twins crawled to Florida, dumped their orange peels, and now they didn't know where to go. There were no oceans to cross, for they had no boats. Why hadn't we brought a boat?

I whipped a glance at the paintings depicting hell and all its torments, and marvelled at how clever and cruel the grandmother was. Why did she have to think of everything? It just wasn't fair for God to keep an ever watchful eye on four children, when outside in the world so many others were doing worse. In God's place, from His all-seeing perspective, I wouldn't waste my time looking at four fatherless children locked up in a bedroom. I'd be staring at something far more entertaining. Besides, Daddy was up there – he'd make God take good care of us, and overlook a few mistakes.

Disregarding my sulky ways and objections, Chris put down his book and carried over the gaming box, which held equipment enough to play forty different games.

'What's the matter with you?' he asked, as he began to place the red and black rounds on the board. 'Why are you sitting so quiet, so scared looking? Afraid I'll win again?'

Games, I wasn't thinking of games. I told him my thoughts of fire, and my idea of ripping up sheets and knotting them together to form a ladder to reach the ground, just like they did in many an old movie. Then if a fire started, maybe tonight, we'd have a way to reach the ground after we broke a window, and each of us could tie a twin to our back.

I'd never seen his blue eyes show so much respect as they lit up with admiration. 'Wow, what a fantastic idea, Cathy! Terrific! Exactly what we'll do if a fire starts – which it won't. And boy, it sure is good to know you're not going to be a cry-baby after all. When you think ahead and plan for unexpected contingencies it shows you're growing up, and I like that.'

Golly-day, in twelve years of hard striving, I had at last won his respect and approval, and reached a goal I thought impossible. It was sweet knowing we could get along when shut up so close. Our exchanged smiles promised that together we were going to manage to survive until the end of the week. Our new-found camaraderie constructed some security, a bit of happiness to grab hold of, like hands clasping.

Then, what we'd found was shattered. Into our room came our mother, walking so funny, wearing the strangest expression. We'd waited so long for her return, and somehow it didn't give us the anticipated joy to be with her again. Maybe it was only the grandmother who followed so close at her heels, with her flint hard, mean grey eyes that quickly quelled our enthusiasm.

My hand rose to my mouth. Something dreadful had happened. I knew it! I just knew it!

Chris and I were sitting on a bed, playing a checker game and from time to time looking at each other while we rumpled the bedspread.

One rule broken . . . no, two . . . looking was forbidden as well as rumpling.

And the twins had puzzle pieces here and there, and their cars and marbles were scattered about, so the room wasn't exactly tidy.

Three rules broken.

And boys and girls had been in the bathroom together.

And maybe we'd even broken another rule, for we were always to feel, no matter what we did, that God and the grandmother had some secret communication between them.

THE WRATH OF GOD

Momma came into our room this first night, tight-limbed and stiff-jointed, as if every movement she made hurt. Her lovely face was pale and bloated; her swollen eyes red-rimmed. At the age of thirty-three, someone had humiliated her so much she couldn't squarely meet a pair of our eyes. Looking defeated, forlorn, humbled, she stood in the centre of the room like a child brutally chastised. Thoughtlessly, the twins ran to greet her. They threw enthusiastic arms about her legs, laughing and crying out in happy voices, 'Momma, Momma! Where have you been?'

Chris and I ambled over to tentatively hug her. One might have thought she had been gone a decade of Sundays, and not just one Wednesday, but she represented our hope, our reality, our line to the world outside.

Did we kiss her too much? Did our eager, hungry, clinging embraces make her wince from pain, or from the obligations? While fat and slow tears slid silently down her pale cheeks, I thought she cried only for the pity she felt for us. When we sat, all wanting to be as close to her as possible, it was on one of the big beds. She lifted both twins to her lap so Chris and I could cuddle close on either side. She looked us over, and complimented our glowing cleanliness, and smiled because I had tied a green ribbon in Carrie's hair to match the green stripes on her dress. She spoke, her voice hoarse, as if she had a cold, or that fabled frog had lodged in her throat. 'Now, tell me honestly, how did it go for you today?'

Resentfully, Cory's plump face pouted, mutely saying his day had not gone well at all. Carrie put her unspoken umbrage into words. 'Cathy and Chris are mean!' she screamed, and it was no sweet bird twitter. 'They made us stay inside all day! We don't like inside! We don't like that big dirty place they told us was nice! Momma, it's not nice!'

Troubled and pained looking, Momma tried to soothe Carrie,

telling the twins that circumstances had changed, and now they had to mind their older brother and sister, and think of them as parents to obey.

'No! No!' shrilled an even more irate bundle of red-faced fury. 'We hate it here! We want the garden; it's dark here. We don't want Chris and Cathy, Momma, we want you! Take us home! Take us out of here!'

Carrie hit at Momma, at me, at Chris, yelling how much she wanted her home, as Momma sat there not defending herself, apparently unhearing, and not knowing how to handle a situation in which a five-year-old ruled. The more unhearing Momma became, the louder Carrie screamed. I covered my ears.

'Corrine!' commanded the grandmother. 'You stop that child from screaming this very second!' I knew, just looking at her stone cold face, that she would know exactly how to shut Carrie up, and at once. However, sitting on Momma's other knee was a little boy whose eyes grew wide as he stared up at the tall grandmother – someone who threatened his twin sister, who had jumped down from Momma's lap and was now standing in front of the grandmother. Planting her small feet wide apart, Carrie threw back her head, opened up her rosebud mouth and she really let go! Like an opera star who'd saved her best for the grand aria finale, her former cries seemed like weak mewings from a small kitten. Now we had a tigress – enraged!

Oh, boy, was I impressed, awed, terrified of what would happen next.

The grandmother seized hold of Carrie by the hair, lifting her up enough to make Cory jump from Momma's lap. Quick as a cat he pounced on the grandmother! Faster than I could wink, he ran to bite her leg! I cringed inside, knowing now we were all in for it. She gazed down at him, then shook him off as one does a small, annoying lap-dog. But the bite did make her release Carrie's hair. Down she dropped to the floor, to quickly scamper to her feet, and take a quick swipe, just missing the grandmother's leg with her foot.

Not to be outdone by his twin sister, Cory raised his small white shoe, took careful aim, then kicked the grandmother's leg as hard as he could manage.

In the meanwhile, Carrie had scuttled over to the corner where she crouched down and wailed like an Irish banshee set on fire!

Oh, indeed, it was a scene worthy of remembering, and recording.

So far Cory hadn't said a word, or uttered one cry, as was his silent and resolute way. But no one was going to hurt or threaten his twin sister – even if that 'no one' stood close to six feet, and weighed in at close to 200 pounds! And Cory was very small for his age.

If Cory didn't like what was happening to Carrie, or the potential threat to himself, the grandmother didn't like what was happening to her either! She glared down at his small, defiant, angry face, which was tilted up to hers. She waited for him to cower, to take the scowl from his face, and the defiance from his blue eyes, but he stood determinedly before her, daring, challenging her to do her worst. Her thin and colourless lips tightened into a fine, crooked pencil line.

Up came her hand – a huge, heavy hand, flashing with diamond rings. Cory didn't flinch, his only reaction to this very obvious threat was a deeper, more fierce scowl as his small hands knotted into fists raised in professional boxer technique.

Good-golly day! Did he think he could fight her – and win?

I heard Momma call Cory's name, her voice so choked it was only a whisper.

Decided on her course of action now, the grandmother delivered against his round, defiant baby face a stinging slap so hard it sent him reeling! He stumbled backwards, then fell to the floor, but was up in a flash, spinning around to consider a fresh assault against that huge mountain of hateful flesh. His indecision then was a pitiful thing. He faltered, reconsidered, and common sense won out over anger. He scampered over to where Carrie crouched, half-crawling, half-running, and then flinging his arms about her, they knelt, holding one to the other, cheek pressed to cheek, and he added his siren howls to hers!

Beside me, Chris mumbled something that sounded like a prayer.

'Corrine, they are your children – shut them up! This instant!'

However, the buttercup twins, once started, were practically

67

impossible to quiet. Reasoning never reached their ears. They heard only their own terror, and like mechanical toys, they had to run down from pure exhaustion.

When Daddy was alive and knew how to handle situations like this, he would pick them up as sacks of corn, one under each arm, and off he'd carry them to their room and order them sternly to shut up, or else they'd stay alone until they could, without TV, toys, without anything. Without an audience to witness their defiance, or hear their impressive wails, their screams seldom lasted more than a few minutes after the door closed on them. Then they would sulk out, quiet, meek and they would snuggle down on Daddy's lap and say in small voices, 'We're sorry.'

But Daddy was dead. There wasn't a distant bedroom where they could wind down. This one room was our mansion, and in here the twins held their captive audience painfully enthralled. They screamed until their faces went from red to magenta, and then on to purple. Their blue eyes went glassy and unfocused from their combined efforts. Oh, it was a grand show all right – and a foolhardy one!

Apparently, until now our grandmother had been held mesmerized by such a display. Then, whatever had held her motionless released its spell. She came alive. Purposefully, she strode over to the corner where the twins huddled. Down she reached to seize up ruthlessly, by their scruffs, two yelling children. Holding them stiff-armed away from her, as they kicked, hollered, and flailed their arms, trying ineffectively to inflict some injury on their tormentor, the twins were hauled up before our mother. Then down on the floor they were dropped like so much unwanted trash. In a loud, firm voice that punctuated through their yelling, she stated flatly, 'I will whip you both until the blood runs from your skin if you don't stop that yelling this very instant!'

That inhuman quality, plus the cold force of this appalling threat, convinced the twins, as it did me, that she meant exactly what she said. In astonished and horrified belief, the twins stared up at her – and with open mouths they choked off their cries. They knew what blood was, and pain came with it. It hurt to see them handled so brutally, as if she didn't care if frail bones broke, or tender flesh was bruised. She towered above them, above all of us. Then, she pivoted about and fired at our mother: 'Corrine, I will not have a scene so disgusting as this happen again! Obviously your children have been spoiled and indulged, and are in desperate need of lessons in discipline and obedience. No child who lives in this house will disobey, or scream, or show defiance. Hear that! They will speak when spoken to. They will jump to obey my voice. Now take off your blouse, daughter, and show those who disobey just how punishment is dealt out in this house!'

During this our mother had risen. She seemed to shrink smaller into her high-heeled shoes as she turned waxen white. 'No!' she breathed, 'that is not necessary now. See, the twins have stopped crying . . . they are obeying now.'

The old woman's face grew very grim. 'Corrine, are you heedless enough to disobey? When I tell you to do something, you will do it without question! And immediately! Look at what you have raised. Weak, spoiled, unruly children, all four! They think they can scream and get what they want. Screams will not avail them here. They might as well know there is no mercy for those who disobey and break my rules. You should know that, Corrine. Did I ever show you mercy? Even before you betrayed us, did I ever let your pretty face and beguiling ways stay my ready hand? Oh, I remember when your father loved you well, and he would turn against me in defence of you. But those days are over. You proved to him you are just what I always said you were – a deceitful, lying bit of trash!'

She turned those hard, flintstone eyes on Chris and me. 'Yes, you and your half-uncle did make exceedingly beautiful children, I readily admit that, though they should never have been born. But they also appear soft, useless nothings!' Her mean eyes raked over our mother scornfully, as if we had caught all these demeaning faults from her. But she had not yet finished.

'Corrine, definitely your children need an object lesson. When they observe what has happened to their mother, then they will have no doubt as to what can happen to them.'

I saw my mother straighten and stiffen her spine, facing up bravely to the large, raw-boned woman who topped her by at least four inches, and was many, many pounds heavier.

'If you are cruel to my children,' began Momma in a voice that quavered, 'I will take them out of this house tonight, and you will never see them, or me, again!' This she stated defiantly, lifting her beautiful face and staring with some determined fierceness at that hulking woman who was *her* mother!

A small smile, tight and cold, met Momma's challenge. No, it was not a smile, it was a sneer. 'Take them away tonight – now! Take yourself away, Corrine! If I never see your children again, or hear from you again, do you think I care?'

Our mother's Dresden blues clashed with those steely tones while we children watched. Inside I was screaming with joy. Momma was going to take us out of here. We were leaving! *Goodbye, room! Goodbye, attic! Goodbye, all those millions I don't want anyway!*

But, as I watched, as I waited for Momma to spin on her heel and head for the closet, for our suitcases, I saw instead something that was noble and fine in our mother crumble. Her eyes lowered in defeat and slowly her head bowed to hide her expression.

Shaken and trembling myself, I watched the grandmother's sneer become a large, cruel smile of victory. Momma! Momma! Momma! My soul was screaming. Don't let her do this to you!

'Now, Corrine, *take off that blouse.*'

Slowly, reluctantly, her face as white as death, Momma pivoted around, presenting her back just as a violent shudder shivered down her spine. Stiffly her arms lifted. With great difficulty each button of her white blouse was unfastened. Carefully, she eased down the blouse to expose her back.

Under the blouse she didn't wear a slip, or a bra, and it was easy enough to see why. I heard Chris pull in his breath. And Carrie and Cory must have looked, for their whimpers reached my ears. Now I knew why Momma, usually so graceful, had walked stiffly into our room, with eyes red from weeping.

Her back was striped with long, angry red welts from her neck on down to the waistband of her blue skirt. Some of the puffier welts were crusted over with dried blood. There was barely an inch of uncut, unmarred skin between the hideous whip marks.

Unfeeling, uncaring, disregarding our sensitivities, or those of our mother, new instructions issued from our grandmother: 'Take a good long look, children. Know that those whip marks go *all* the way down to your mother's feet. Thirty-three lashes, one for each year of her life. And fifteen extra lashes for each year she lived in sin with your father. Your grandfather ordered this punishment, but I was the one who applied the whip. Your mother's crimes are against God, and the moral principles society lives by. Hers was an unholy marriage, a sacrilege! A marriage that was an abomination in the eyes of the Lord. And, as if that wasn't enough, they had to have children – four of them! Children spawned from the Devil! Evil from the moment of conception!'

My eyes bulged at the sight of those pitiful welts on the creamy tender flesh that our father had handled with so much love and gentleness. I floundered in a maelstrom of uncertainty, aching inside, not knowing who or what I was, if I had the right to be living on an earth the Lord reserved for those born with his blessings and permission. We had lost our father, our home, our friends and our possessions. That night I no longer believed that God was the perfect judge. So, in a way, I lost God too.

I wanted a whip in my hands to strike back at that old woman who had ruthlessly ripped so much from us. I stared at the ladder of bloody welts on Momma's back, and never had I felt such hate before, or such anger. I hated not only for what she had done to our mother, but for the ugly words that gushed forth from that mean mouth.

She looked at me then, that detestable old woman, as if sensing all that I felt. I glared back defiantly, hoping that she *could* see how I denied her blood relationship from that moment on – not only her, but that old man downstairs as well. Never again would I pity him.

Perhaps my eyes were only glass to reveal all the spinning wheels of revenge I harboured, and vowed to let loose one day. Maybe she did see something vengeful on those white worms of brains, for she directed her next words solely at me, though she used the noun 'children'.

'So you see, children, this house can be hard and relentless in dealing with those who disobey and break our rules. We will dole out food, drink, and shelter, but never kindness, sympathy or love. It's impossible to feel anything but revulsion for what is not wholesome. Keep to my rules, and you won't feel the bite of my whip, nor will you be deprived of necessities. Dare to disobey me, and you will soon learn all I can do to you, and all I can keep from you.' She stared in turn at each of us.

Yes, she wanted to make us undone that night, when we were young, innocent, trusting, having known only the sweetest part of living. She wanted to wither our souls and shrivel us small and dry, perhaps never to feel pride again.

But she didn't know us.

Nobody was ever going to make me hate my father or my mother! Nobody was going to have the power of life and death over me – not while I was alive and could still fight back!

I shot Chris a quick glance. He was staring at her, too. His eyes swept up and down her height, considering what damage he could inflict if he attacked. But he was only fourteen. He would have to grow into a man before he could overcome the likes of her. Still, his hands clenched into fists, which he forced to keep tight at his sides. The restraint pressed his lips into a line as thin and hard as the lips of the grandmother. Only his eyes were cold, hard as blue ice.

Of us all, he loved our mother best. He had her high on a pedestal of perfection, considering her the dearest, sweetest, most understanding woman alive. He'd already told me when he grew up, he'd marry a woman who was like our mother. Yet he could only glare fiercely. He was too young to do anything.

Our grandmother bestowed on us one last, long, contemptuous look. Then she shoved the door key into Momma's hand and left the room.

One question loomed sky-high, above all others.

Why? *Why* had we been brought to *this* house?

This was no safe harbour, no refuge, no sanctuary. Certainly Momma must have known how it would be, and yet, she'd led us here in the dead of night. Why?

MOMMA'S STORY

After the grandmother's departure, we did not know what to do, or what to say, or how to feel, except unhappy and miserable. My heart was fluttering madly as I watched Momma slip up her blouse, button it, and tuck it into the waistband of her skirt before she turned to give us all a tremulous smile that sought to reassure. Pitiful that I could find a straw to grasp in such a smile as that one. Chris lowered his eyes to the floor; his restless torment was expressed by his shoe diligently following the intricate scrollwork of the Oriental rug.

'Now look,' said Momma with forced cheerfulness, 'it was just a willow switching, and it didn't hurt too much. My pride suffered more than my flesh. It's humiliating to be whipped like a slave, or an animal, and by your own parents. But don't worry that such a whipping will occur again, for it never will. Only this one time. I would suffer a hundred times over what whip weals I bear to live again those fifteen years of happiness I had with your father, and with you. Though it cringes my soul, she made me show what they did . . .' She sat on a bed and held out her arms so we could cluster close about and be comforted, though I was careful not to embrace her again and cause more pain. She lifted the twins to her lap and patted the bed to indicate we should crowd up against her. Then she began to talk. What she said was obviously hard to say, and equally difficult for us to hear.

'I want you to listen very carefully, and remember all your lives every word I say tonight.' She paused, hesitating as she scanned the room and stared at the cream-flocked walls as if they were transparent, and through them she could see into all the rooms of this gigantic house. 'This is a strange house, and the people who reside here are even stranger – not the servants, but my parents. I should have warned you that your grandparents are fanatically religious. To believe in God is a good thing, a right thing. But when you reinforce your belief with words you take from the Old Testament that you seek out, and interpret in the ways that suit your needs best, that is hypocrisy, and that is exactly what my parents do.

'My father is dying, yes, but every Sunday he is carried into church either in his wheelchair, if he is feeling that well, or lying on a stretcher if he is feeling worse, and he gives his tithe – a tenth share of his yearly income, which is considerable. So naturally, he is very welcomed. He paid to have the church built, he bought all the stained-glass windows, he controls the minister and his sermons, for he is paving his way to heaven with gold, and if St Peter can be bribed, my father will surely gain entrance. In that church he is treated like a god himself, or a living saint. And then he comes home, feeling completely justified in doing anything he wants, because he has done his duty, and paid his way, and therefore he is safe from hell.

'When I was growing up, with my two older brothers, we were literally forced to go to church. Even if we were sick enough to stay in bed, we still had to go. Religion was rammed down our throats. Be good, be good, be good – that's all we ever heard. Every day, normal pleasures that were right for other people were made sinful for us. My brothers and I were not allowed to go swimming, for that meant wearing bathing-suits and exposing most of our bodies. We were forbidden card games, or any sort of game that implied gambling. We weren't allowed to go to dances, for that meant your body might be pressed close to that of the other sex. We were ordered to control our thoughts, to keep them off lusting, sinful subjects for they said the thought was as evil as the deed. Oh, I could go on and on about all we were forbidden to do – it seemed everything that was fun and exciting was sinful to them. And there is something in the young that rebels when life is made too strict, making us want to do most of all the very things denied to us. Our parents, in seeking to make their three children into living angels or saints, only succeeded in making us worse than we would have been otherwise.'

My eyes widened. I sat spellbound, all of us did, even the twins.

'Then one day,' Momma went on, 'into all this, a beautiful young man came to live. His father had been my grandfather, a

74

man who died when this young man was only three. His mother was named Alicia, and she was only sixteen when she married my grandfather who was fifty-five years old. So, when she gave birth to a boy, she should have lived to see him a man. Unfortunately, Alicia died very young. My grandfather's name was Garland Christopher Foxworth, and when he died, half of his estate should have gone to his youngest son, who was three. But Malcolm, my father, gained control of his father's estate by having himself appointed administrator, for, of course, a three-year-old boy had no voice in the matter, nor was Alicia given a vote. Once my father had everything under his thumb, he kicked out Alicia and her young son. They fled back to Richmond, to Alicia's parents, and there she lived until she married a second time. She had a few years of happiness with a young man she'd loved since her childhood, and then he, too, died. Twice married, twice widowed, left with a young son, and now her parents were dead as well. And then one day she found a lump in her breast, and a few years later she died of cancer. That was when her son, Garland Christopher Foxworth the Fourth, came to live here. We never called him anything but Chris.' She hesitated, tightened her arms about Chris and me. 'Do you know who I'm talking about? Have you guessed who this young man was?'

I shivered. The mysterious half-uncle. And I whispered, 'Daddy . . . you're talking about Daddy.'

'Yes,' she said, then sighed heavily.

I leaned forward to glance at my older brother. He sat so still, with the queerest expression on his face, and his eyes were glassy.

Momma continued: 'Your father was my half-uncle, but he was only three years older than I, I remember the first time I saw him. I knew he was coming, this young half-uncle I'd never seen or heard much about, and I wanted to make a good impression, so all day I prepared myself, curling my hair, bathing and I put on what I thought were my prettiest and most becoming clothes. I was fourteen years old – and that is an age when a girl just begins to feel her power over men. And I knew I was what most boys and men considered beautiful, and I guess, in a way, I was ripe for falling in love.

'Your father was seventeen. It was late spring, and he was

standing in the middle of the hall with two suitcases near his shabby shoes – his clothes were very worn looking, and he'd outgrown them. My mother and father were with him, but he was turning around, staring at everything, dazzled by the display of wealth. I myself had never paid much attention to what was around me. It was there, I accepted it as part of my heritage, and until I was married, and began to live a life without wealth, I hardly realized that I'd been raised in an exceptional home.

'You see, my father is a "collector". He buys everything that is considered a unique work of art – not because he appreciates art, but he likes to own things. He would like to own *everything*, if possible, especially beautiful things. I used to think I was part of his collection of *objets d'art* . . . and he meant to keep me for himself, not to enjoy, but to keep others from enjoying what was his.'

My mother continued, her face flushed, her eyes staring off into space, apparently looking backwards to that exceptional day when a young half-uncle came into her life to make such a difference.

'Your father came to us so innocent, so trusting, so sweet, and vulnerable, having known only honest affection, and genuine love, and a great deal of poverty. He came from a four-room cottage into this huge, grand house that widened his eyes and dazzled his hopes, and he thought he had stumbled on to good luck, into heaven on earth. He was looking at my mother and father with all of that gratefulness plain in his eyes. Hah! The pity of him coming here and being grateful still hurts. For half of what he was looking at, by all rights, should have been his. My parents did all they could to make him feel like a poor relation.

'I saw him there, standing in the sunlight, beaming down through the windows, and paused halfway down the staircase. His golden hair was haloed by an aura of silver light. He was so beautiful, not just handsome, but beautiful – there's a difference, you know. Real beauty radiates from the inside out, and he had that.

'I made some slight noise that made him lift his head, and his blue eyes lit up – and oh, I can remember how they lit up – and then when we were introduced, the light went out. I was his half-niece, and forbidden, and he was disappointed, just as I was. For on that very day, with me on the staircase and him down there on the floor, a spark was lit between us, a little red glow that was to grow larger and larger until we could deny it no longer.

'I won't embarrass you with the telling of our romance,' she said uneasily when I shifted, and Chris moved to hide his face. 'Let it suffice to say that it was love at first sight with us, for it happens that way sometimes. Perhaps he was ready to fall in love, as was I, or perhaps it was because we were both needing someone to give us warmth and affection. My older brothers were both dead by this time, killed by accidents; I had only a few friends, for no one was "good enough" for the daughter of Malcolm Foxworth. I was his prize, his joy; if ever a man took me from him, it would be for a dear, dear price. So, your father and I would meet furtively in the gardens and just sit and talk for hours and hours, and sometimes he'd push me in a swing, or I'd push him, and sometimes we'd stand on the swing and work it with our legs, and just look at each other as we flew higher and higher. He told me all his secrets and I told him all of mine. And soon enough it had to come out, we had to confess that we were deeply in love, and right or wrong, we had to marry. And we had to escape this house, and the rule of my parents, before they had a chance to make us into duplicates of themselves – for that was their purpose, you know, to take your father and change him, make him pay for the evil his mother had done in marrying a man so much older. They gave him everything, I will admit that. They treated him as their own son, for he was to replace the two sons they had lost. They sent him to Yale, and he was brilliant. You get your intelligence from him, Christopher. He graduated in three years – but he could never use the master's degree he earned, for it had his rightful name on it, and we had to hide who we were from the world. It was hard for us in the first years of our marriage because he had to deny his college education.'

She paused. She glanced reflectively at Chris, then at me. She hugged the twins and kissed the top of their fair heads, and a troubled frown came to worry her face and pucker her brow. 'Cathy, Christopher, you are the ones I am expecting to understand. The twins are too young. You *are* trying to understand how it was with us?'

Yes, yes, both Chris and I nodded.

She was talking my language, the language of music and ballet, romance, and love, beautiful faces in lovely places. Fairy tales can come true!

Love at first sight. Oh, that was going to happen to me, I just knew it would and he'd be as beautiful as Daddy had been, radiating beauty, touching my heart. You had to have love or you withered away and died.

'Listen attentively, now,' she said in a low voice, and this gave her words greater impact. 'I am here to do what I can to make my father like me again, and forgive me for marrying his half-brother. You see, as soon as I reached my eighteenth birthday, your father and I eloped, and two weeks later we came back and told my parents. My father nearly threw a fit. He raged, he stormed, he ordered us both out of his house, and told us never to come back, never! And that is why I was disinherited, and your father too – for I think my father did plan to leave him a little, not much, but some. The main portion was to be mine, for my mother has money in her own right. Why, to hear tell it, the money she inherited from her parents is the main reason why my father married her, though in her youth she was what is called a *handsome* woman, not a great beauty, but she had a regal, powerful kind of noble good looks.'

No, I thought bitterly to myself . . . that old woman was born ugly!

'I am here to do what I can to make my father like me again, and forgive me for marrying my half-uncle. And in order to do this, I am going to have to play the role of the dutiful, humbled, thoroughly chastised daughter. And sometimes, when you begin to play a role you assume that character, so I want to say now, while I am still fully myself, all you have to hear. That's why I'm telling you all of this, and being as honest as I can. I confess, I am not strong-willed, nor am I a self-starter. I was strong only when I had your father to back me up, and now I don't have him. And downstairs, on the first floor, in a small room beyond a giant library, is a man the likes of whom you have never encountered. You have met my mother, and know a little of what she is like, but you have not met my father. And I don't want you to meet

78

him until he forgives me and accepts the fact that I have four children fathered by his much younger half-brother. This is going to be very difficult for him to take. But I don't think it is going to be *too* difficult for him to forgive me, since your father *is* dead, and it is difficult to hold grudges against the dead and buried.'

I don't know why I felt so scared.

'In order to have my father write me into his will again, I am going to be forced to do anything he wants.'

'What could he want from you but obedience and a show of respect?' asked Chris in the most sombre, adult way, as if he understood what this was all about.

Momma gave him the longest look, full of sweet compassion as her hand lifted to caress his boyish cheek. He was a younger smaller edition of the husband she'd so recently buried. No wonder tears came into her eyes.

'I don't know what he'll want, darling, but whatever I have to do, I will do. Somehow he must include me in his will. But let's forget all of that now. I saw your faces when I was talking. I don't want you to feel what my mother said is true. What your father and I did was *not* immoral. We were properly married in church, just as any other young couple in love. There was nothing 'unholy' about it. And you are not the Devil's spawn, or evil – your father would call that hogwash. My mother would have you think your-selves unworthy as another way to punish me, and you. People make the rules of society, not God. In some parts of the world closer relatives marry and produce children, and it is considered perfectly all right, though I'm not going to try and justify what we did, for we do have to abide by the laws of our own society. That society believes closely related men and women should not marry, for if they do, they can produce children who are mentally or physically less than perfect. But who is perfect?'

Then she was laughing, half-crying, and hugging us all close. 'Your grandfather predicted our children would be born with horns, humped backs, forked tails, hooves for feet – he was like a crazy man, trying to curse us, and make our children deformed, because he wanted us cursed! Did any of his dire predictions come true?' she cried, seemingly half-wild herself. 'No!' She answered her own question. 'Your father and I did worry some when I was pregnant the first time. He paced the hospital corridors all night, until nearly dawn, when a nurse came up and told him he had a son, perfect in every way. Then he had to run to the nursery to see for himself. You should have been there to see the joy on his face when he entered my room, bearing in his arms two dozen red roses, and tears were in his eyes when he kissed me. He was so proud of you, Christopher, so proud. He gave away six boxes of cigars, and went right out and bought you a plastic baseball bat, and a catcher's mitt, and a football, too. When you were teething, you'd chew on the bat, and beat on the crib and the wall to let us know you wanted out.

'Next came Cathy, and you, darling, were just as beautiful, and just as perfect as your brother. And you know how your father loved you, his beautiful dancing Cathy, who would make the world sit up and take notice when she came on stage. Recall your first ballet performance, when you were four? You wore your first pink tutu, and made a few mistakes, and everybody in the audience laughed, and you clapped your hands like you were proud, even so. And your father sent you a dozen roses – remember? He never saw any mistakes you made. In his eyes you were perfect. And seven years after you came to bless us, our twins were born. Now we had two boys, and two girls, and had tempted fate four times – and had won! Four perfect children. So if God had wanted to punish us, he had four chances to give us deformed or mentally retarded children. Instead, he gave us the very best. So never let your grandmother or anyone else convince you that you are less than competent, less than worthy, or less than wholly pleasing in God's eyes. If there was a sin committed, it was the sin of your parents, not yours. You are the same four children all our friends in Gladstone envied and called the Dresden dolls. Keep remembering what you had in Gladstone – hold on to that. Keep believing in yourselves, and in me, and in your father. Even if he is dead, keep on loving and respecting him. He deserves that. He tried so hard to be a good parent. I don't think there are many men who care as much as he did.' She smiled brightly through glistening tears. 'Now, tell me who you are.'

'The Dresden dolls!' Chris and I cried out.

'Now, will you ever believe what your grandmother says about being the Devil's spawn?'

No; *Never, never!*

Yet, yet, half of what I'd heard from both women I would have to ponder over later, and ponder deeply too. I wanted to believe God was pleased with us, and in who and what we were. I had to believe, needed to believe. Nod, I told myself, say yes, just as Chris did. Don't be like the twins who only stared at Momma, not comprehending anything. Don't be so suspicious – don't!

Chris chimed up in the firmest of convincing voices, 'Yes, Momma, I do believe what you say, for if God had disapproved of your marriage to our father, then he *would* have punished you and Daddy through your children. I believe God is not narrow-minded and bigoted – not as our grandparents are. How can that old woman speak so ugly, when she does have eyes, and she can see we are not ugly, and not deformed, and certainly we are not retarded?'

Relief, like a river dammed and released, caused tears to stream down Momma's beautiful face. She drew Chris close against her breast, kissing the top of his head. Then she cupped his face between her palms, stared deep into his eyes, ignoring the rest of us. 'Thank you, my son, for understanding,' she said in a husky whisper. 'Thank you again for not condemning your parents for what they did.'

'I love you, Mama. No matter what you did, or do, I'll always understand.'

'Yes,' she murmured, 'you will, I know *You* will.' Uneasily she glanced at me who stood back, taking all of this in, weighing it, and her. 'Love doesn't always come when you want it to. Sometimes it just happens, despite your will.' She bowed her head, reaching for my brother's hands, and clinging to them. 'My father adored me when I was young. He wanted to keep me always for himself. He never wanted me to marry anyone. I recall when I was only twelve, he said he'd leave me his entire estate if I stayed with him until he died of old age.'

Suddenly, she jerked up her head and looked at me. Did she see something doubting, something questioning? Her eyes shad-owed, grew deep, dark. 'Join hands,' she ordered forcefully, bracing her shoulders, releasing one of Chris's hands. 'I want you to repeat after me: We are perfect children. Mentally, physically, emotionally, we are wholesome, and godly in every way possible. We have as much right to live, love, and enjoy life as any other children on this earth.'

She smiled at me, and reached for my hand to hold in her free one, and asked that Carrie and Cory join the family chain. 'Up here, you are going to need small rituals to get you through the days, little stepping-stones. Let me lay down a few for you to use when I'm gone. Cathy, when I look at you, I see myself at your age. Love me, Cathy, trust me, please.'

Haltingly, we did as she directed, and repeated the litany that was ours to say whenever we felt in doubt. And when we had finished, she smiled at us with approval and reassurance.

'There!' she said with a happier look. 'Now don't think I have lived through this day without the four of you constantly on my mind. I have thought and I have thought of our future, and I've decided we cannot continue to live here, where all of us are ruled over by my mother and father. My mother is a cruel, heartless woman who just happened to give birth to me, but who's never given me an ounce of love – she gave all of that to her sons. It was my foolish belief, when her letter came, that she would treat you differently from the way she treated me. I thought by now she would have mellowed with age, and once she saw you, and knew you, she would be like all grandmothers and welcome you with open arms, and be charmed and delighted to have children to love again. I so hoped once she got a look at your faces . . .' She choked up, near tears again, as if no one with good sense could help but love her children. 'I can understand her dislike for Christopher' – and here she hugged him tightly, and kissed his cheek – 'for he looks so much like his father. And I know she can look at you, Cathy, and see me, and she never liked me – I don't know why, except, perhaps, my father liked me too much, and that made her jealous. But never did it cross my mind that she could be cruel to any of you, or my little twins. I made myself believe people change with age, and they realize their mistakes, but now I know how wrong I was.' She wiped away her tears.

'So, that is why tomorrow morning, early, I am driving away from here, and in the nearest big city, I will enrol in a business school that will teach me how to be a secretary. I'll learn to type, take shorthand, do book-keeping and how to file – and everything a good secretary has to know, I'll learn. When I know how to do all of these things, I'll be able to find a good job that will pay an adequate salary. And then I'll have enough money to take you all out of this room. We'll find an apartment somewhere nearby, so I can still visit my father. Soon, we'll all be living under the same roof, our roof, and we'll be a real family again.'

'Oh, Momma!' Chris cried happily, 'I knew you would find a way! I knew you wouldn't keep us locked up in this room.' He leaned forward to give me a look of smug satisfaction, as if he'd known all along *his* beloved mother would solve all problems, no matter how complicated.

'Trust me,' said Momma, smiling and confident now. Again she had kisses for Chris.

I wished somehow I could be like my brother Chris, and take everything she said as a sacred vow. But my treacherous thoughts were dwelling overlong on her words of not being strong-willed or a self-starter, without Daddy nearby to give her support. Dejectedly, I put in my question. 'Just how long does it take to learn how to be a good secretary?'

Quickly – I thought too quickly – she answered. 'Only a little while, Cathy. Perhaps a month. But if it takes a bit longer, you have to be patient and realize I'm not too smart about things like that. It's not really my fault,' she went on hastily, as if she could see I was blaming her for being inadequate.

'When you're born rich, and you're educated in boarding schools only for the daughters of the extremely rich and powerful, and then you're sent to a girls' finishing school, you are taught polite rules of social etiquette, academic subjects, but most of all, you're made ready for the whirl of romance, debutante parties, and how to entertain and be the perfect hostess. I wasn't taught anything practical. I didn't think I'd ever need any business skills. I thought I'd always have a husband to take care of me, and if not a husband, then my father would – and besides, all the time I was in love with your father. I knew the day I turned eighteen we'd be married.'

She was at that very minute teaching me well. Never would I become so dependent on a man I couldn't make my way in the world, no matter what cruel blow life delivered! But most of all I felt mean, mad, ashamed, guilty – feeling she was to blame for everything, and how could she have known what lay ahead?

'I'm going now,' she said as she stood to leave. The twins burst into tears.

'Momma, don't go! Don't leave us!' They both wrapped their small arms around her legs.

'I'll be back early tomorrow morning, before I leave for that school. Really, Cathy,' she said, looking straight at me, 'I promise to do the best I can. I want you out of this place just as much as you want to be out.'

At the door she said it was a good thing we'd seen her back, for now we knew how heartless her mother could be. 'For God's sake, keep to her rules. Be modest in the bathroom. Realize she can be inhuman not only to me, but to those who are mine.' She held out her arms to all of us, and we ran into them, forgetting her whip-lashed back. 'I love all of you so much,' she sobbed. 'Hold on to that. I'll apply myself as never before, I swear. I feel as much a prisoner as you do, just as trapped by circumstances as you are, in a way. Go to bed tonight with happy thoughts, know that no matter how bad it may seem, seldom is anything *that* bad. I am likable, you know that, and my father did love me extremely well once. So that will make it easy for him to love me again, won't it?'

Yes, yes, it would. To love anything once extremely well made you vulnerable to another loving attack. I knew; I'd already been in love six times.

'And while you're in your beds, and in the dimness of this room, remember that tomorrow after I enrol in that school, I'll go shopping for new toys and games to keep your hours up here busy and happy. And it's not going to be a long time until I have my father loving me again, and forgiving me for everything.'

'Momma,' I said, 'do you have enough money to buy us things?'

'Yes, yes,' she said hurriedly. 'I have enough, and my mother and father are proud people. They would not have me seen by their friends and neighbours looking shabby, or ill-groomed. They will provide for me and they'll provide for you, as well. You'll see. And every spare minute I have, and every spare dollar I don't use, I'll put away, and I'll plan for the day when we can all be free to live in our own home, as we used to, and be a family again.'

Those were her parting words before she blew us kisses, and then she closed and locked the door.

Our second night behind a locked door.

Now we knew so much more . . . maybe too much.

After Momma had left, both Chris and I settled into bed. He grinned over at me as he curled his body against Cory's back, and already his eyes were sleepy, too. He closed his eyes and murmured, 'Good night, Cathy. Don't let the bedbugs bite.'

As Christopher had done, I curled around Carrie's small warm body, and she was cupped spoon-like in my arms, and my face lowered into her sweet, soft hair.

I was restless, and soon enough I was supine, staring upwards, and sensing the great silence of this huge house as it settled down, and went to sleep. I heard not a whisper of movement in the huge house; not the faint shrills of a telephone ringing; not a kitchen appliance could be heard switching on and off; not even a dog barked outside; nor did a car pass to throw light that might, hopefully, penetrate through the heavy draperies.

Snide thoughts came and told me we were unwanted, locked up . . . Devil's spawn. Those thoughts wanted to lounge around in my head and make me miserable. I had to find a way to drive them out. Momma, she loved us, she wanted us, she'd try hard to be a good secretary to some lucky man. She would. I knew she would. She would resist the ways the grandparents sought to turn her away from us. She would, she would.

God, I prayed, please help Momma learn quickly!

It was horribly hot and stuffy in that room. Outside, I could hear the wind rustling the leaves, but not enough of it came in to cool us off, only enough to hint that it was cool out there, and would be in here if only we could open the windows wide. Wistfully, I sighed, longing for fresh air. Hadn't Momma told us mountain nights, even in the summertime, were always cool? And this was summertime and it wasn't cool with the windows down.

In the rosy darkness, Chris whispered my name. 'What are you thinking?'

'About the wind. It sounds like a wolf.'

'I knew you'd be thinking something cheery like that. Gosh, if you aren't the one to take the cake for depressing thoughts.'

'I've got another goodie – whispering winds like dead souls trying to tell us something.'

He groaned. 'Now you listen to me, Catherine Doll (the stage name I planned to use one day), I order you *not* to lie there and think your kind of scary thoughts. We will take each hour as it comes, and never pause to think ahead to the next one, and by using this method, it will be much easier than thinking in terms of days and weeks. Think about music, about dancing, singing. Haven't I heard you say you never feel sad when music is dancing in your head?'

'What will you think about?'

'If I were less sleepy, I would pour out ten volumes of thoughts, but as it is, I'm too tired to answer. And you know my goal, anyway. As for now, I'll just think of the games we'll have time to play.' He yawned, stretched, and smiled over at me. 'What did you think of all that talk, about half-uncles marrying half-nieces, and creating children with hooves, tails, and horns?'

'As a seeker of all knowledge, and a future doctor, is it medically, scientifically possible?'

'Nope!' he answered, as if well-educated on the subject. 'If so, the world would abound in freaks resembling devils and to tell you the truth, I would like to see a devil, just once.'

'I see them all the time, in my dreams.'

'Hah!' he scoffed. 'You and your crazy dreams. Weren't the twins something, though? I was really rather proud of them when they faced up to that giant grandmother so defiantly. Gosh, they got spunk. But then I was afraid she'd really do something awful.'

'What she did wasn't awful? She picked Carrie up by her hair. That must have hurt. And she slapped Cory and sent him reeling, and that must have hurt. What more did you want?'

'She could have done worse.'

'I think she's crazy herself.'

'You might be right,' he mumbled sleepily.

'The twins are only babies. Cory was only protecting Carrie – you know how he is about her, and she is about him.' I hesitated.

'Chris, did our mother and father do right by falling in love? Couldn't they have done something to stop it?'

'I don't know. Let's not talk about that; it makes me feel uneasy.'

'Me, too. But I guess that explains why we all have blue eyes and blond hair.'

'Yeah,' he yawned, 'the Dresden dolls; that's us.'

'You're right. I've always wanted to play games all day long. And just think, when our mother does bring us that new deluxe Monopoly game, we will at last have time to finish a game.' For we had never finished a game. 'And Chris, the silver ballerina slippers are to be mine.'

'Right,' he murmured, 'and I'll take the top hat, or the racing car.'

'The top hat, please.'

'Right. Sorry, I forgot. And we can teach the twins to be bankers and count out the money.'

'First we'll have to teach them to count.'

'That will be no trick at all, for Foxworths know all about money.'

'We are *not Foxworths*!'

'Then what are we?'

'Dollangangers! That's who!'

'Okay, have it your way.' And again he said good night.

Once more I knelt by the side of the bed and put my hands in prayer position under my chin. Silently I began: *Now I lay me down to sleep, I pray the Lord my soul to keep* . . . But somehow I just couldn't say those words about taking my soul if I should die before I wake. Again I had to skip that part, and again I asked blessings for Momma, for Chris, and the twins, and for Daddy, too, wherever he was in heaven.

Then, when I was back in bed again, I had to go and think of the cake or cookies, and the ice-cream the grandmother had half-promised last night – if we were good.

And we had been good.

At least until Carrie started cutting up – and still the grand-mother hadn't come into the room with desserts.

How could she have known that later on we would be so un-deserving?

'What are you thinking now?' asked Chris in a sleepy monotone. I thought he was already asleep, and certainly not watching me.

'Nuthin' much. Just little thoughts of the ice-cream, and cake or cookies the grandmother said she'd bring if we were good.'

'Tomorrow's another day, so don't give up on treats. And maybe tomorrow the twins will forget about outdoors. They don't have very long memories.'

No, they didn't. Already they'd forgotten Daddy, and he'd been killed only last April. How easily Cory and Carrie let go of a father who had loved them very much. And I couldn't let him go; I was never going to let him go, even if I couldn't see him so clearly now . . . I could feel him.

MINUTES LIKE HOURS

All the days dragged by. Monotonously.

What did you do with time when you had it in super-abundance? Where did you put your eyes when you had already seen everything? What direction should your thoughts take, when daydreams could lead you into so much trouble? I could imagine how it would be to run outside, wild and free in the woods, with dry leaves crackling under my feet. I could picture swimming in the nearby lake, or wading in a cool mountain stream. But daydreams were merely cobwebs, easily torn into shreds, and I'd quickly be dropped back into reality. And where was happiness? In the yesterdays? In the tomorrows? Not in this hour, this minute, this second. We had one thing, and one thing only, to give us a spark of joy. Hope.

Chris said it was a deadly crime to waste time. Time was valuable. No one ever had time enough, or lived long enough to learn enough. All about us the world was on the way to the fire, crying, 'Hurry, hurry, hurry!' And look at us: we had time to spare, hours to fill, a million books to read, time to let our imaginations take wing. The creative genius begins in the idle moment, dreaming up the impossible, and later making it come true.

Momma came to see us, as she promised, bearing new games and toys to occupy our time. Chris and I adored Monopoly, Scrabble, Chinese checkers, plain checkers, and when Momma brought us a double deck of bridge cards, and a book on how to play card games, boy, did we become the card sharks!

It was harder with the twins, who weren't old enough to play games with rules. Nothing held their interest for long, not the many tiny cars Momma bought, nor the dump trucks, nor the electric train that Chris hooked together so the tracks ran under our beds, under the dressing-table, over to the dresser, and under the highboy. No matter where we turned something was underfoot. One thing for sure, they did hate the attic – everything about it seemed scary to them.

Every day we got up early. We didn't have an alarm clock, only our wristwatches. But some automatic timing-system in my body took over and wouldn't let me sleep late, even when I wanted to.

As soon as we were out of bed, on alternate days, the boys would use the bathroom first, and then Carrie and I would go in. We had to be fully dressed before the grandmother entered – or else.

Into our grim, dim room the grandmother would stalk, while we stood at attention, waiting for her to put down the picnic basket and depart. Seldom did she speak to us, and when she did, it was only to ask if we had said grace before every meal, said prayers before retiring and had read a page from the Bible yesterday.

'No,' said Chris one morning, 'we don't read a page – we read chapters. If you consider reading the Bible a form of punishment, then forget it. We find it fascinating reading. It's bloodier and lustier than any movie we ever saw, and talks more about sin than any book we ever read.'

'Shut up, boy!' she barked at him. 'I was asking your sister, *not you!*'

Next she was asking me to repeat some quote I'd learned, and in this way we often had our little jokes, at her expense, for when you looked hard and long enough, you found words in the Bible to suit any occasion. I answered on this particular morning, 'Wherefore have you rewarded evil for good? Genesis forty-four: four.'

She scowled and pivoted about and left us. It was another few days before she snapped at Chris, without looking his way, and keeping her back turned, 'Repeat to me a quote from the Book of Job. And do not try to fool me into believing you read the Bible when you do not!'

Chris seemed well prepared and confident. 'Job, twenty-eight: twelve – But where shall wisdom be found? And where is the place of the understanding? Job twenty-eight: twenty-eight – Behold, the fear of the Lord, that is wisdom; and to depart from evil is understanding. Job, thirty-one: thirty-five – My desire is that the Almighty would answer me, and that mine adversity had written a book. Job, thirty-two: nine – Great men are not always wise.' And he would have gone on and on endlessly, but anger coloured the grandmother's face. Never again did she ask Chris to quote from the Bible. She eventually stopped asking me also, for I, too, could always come up with some stinging quote.

Around six o'clock each evening Momma would show up, breathless, always in a great hurry. She came loaded down with gifts, new things for us to do, new books to read, more games to play. Then she'd dash off to bathe and dress in her suite of rooms for a formal dinner downstairs, where a butler and a maid waited on the table, and it seemed, from what she breathlessly explained, that often guests dined with them. 'A great deal of business is done over lunch and dinner tables,' we were informed.

The best times were when she sneaked up fancy little canapés, and tasty hors d'oeuvres, but she never brought us candy to rot our teeth.

Only on Saturdays and Sundays could she spend more than a few moments with us, and sit down at our small table to eat lunch. Once she patted her stomach. 'Look how fat I'm becoming, eating lunch with my father, then saying I want to nap, so I can come up and eat again with my children.'

Meals with Momma were wonderful, because it reminded me of the old days when we were living with Daddy.

One Sunday Momma came in, smelling fresh from outside, bringing a quart of vanilla ice-cream and a chocolate cake from a bakery. The ice-cream had melted almost to soup, but still we ate it. We begged her to stay all night, to sleep between Carrie and me, so we could wake up in the morning and we could see her there. But she took a long look around the cluttered bedroom, and shook her head. 'I'm sorry, I can't, I really can't. You see, the maids would wonder why my bed wasn't used. And three in a bed would be too crowded.'

'Momma,' I asked, 'how much longer? We've been here two weeks – it seems like two years. Hasn't the grandfather forgiven you yet for marrying Daddy? Have you told him about us yet?'

'My father has given me one of his cars to drive,' she said with what I considered evasiveness. 'And I believe he is going to forgive me, or else he wouldn't be letting me use his car, or sleep under his roof, or eat his food. But no, I haven't had the nerve to tell him yet that I have four children hidden away. I have to time this very carefully, and you have to have patience.'

'What would he do if he knew about us?' I asked, ignoring Chris, who kept frowning at me. Already he'd told me if I kept asking so many questions, Momma would stop coming to see us every day. Then what would we do?

'God knows what he'd do,' she whispered fearfully. 'Cathy, promise me you will not try to make the servants hear! He is a cruel, heartless man, and one who wields a great deal of power. Let me time carefully the moment I believe he's *ready* to hear.'

She went away about seven, and soon after we retired. We went to bed early, because we got up early. And the longer you could stay asleep, the shorter were the days. We would drag our twins into the attic as soon as the hour of ten passed. Exploring the giant attic was one of the best ways to occupy our time. There were two pianos up there, uprights. Cory climbed on a round seat that twirled higher or lower, and round and round he spun. He banged on the yellow piano keys, cocked his head and listened attentively. It was out of tune, and the noise he made was so discordant it made your head ache. 'Don't sound right,' he said. 'Why don't it sound right?'

'It needs tuning,' said Chris, who tried to tune it, but when he did, the wires broke. That was the end of trying to make music on two old pianos. There were five Victrolas, each with a small, white dog that cocked its head charmingly, as if enchanted to hear the music – but only one of these machines worked well. We'd wind up this one, put on a warped old record, and listen to the weirdest music we'd ever heard!

There were stacks and stacks of Enrico Caruso records, but, unfortunately, they were not well cared for, just stacked on the floor, not even put in cardboard cartons. We sat in a semicircle to listen to him sing. Christopher and I knew he was the greatest of all male singers, and now was our chance to hear him. His voice was so high-pitched it sounded false, and we wondered what had been so great about him. But for some crazy reason, Cory loved it.

Then, slowly, slowly, the machine would wind down, and would spin Caruso's voice into only a whine, and that's when one of us would race like mad to crank the handle so tight he'd sing fast and funny so he sounded like Donald Duck talking jibberty-junk – and the twins would break up in laughter. Naturally. It was their kind of talk, their secret language.

Cory would spend all of his days in the attic, playing the records. But Carrie was a restless prowler, ever discontented, an incessant seeker of something better to do.

'I don't like this *big bad place*!' she wailed for the zillionth time. 'Take me out of this *baa-aad place*! Take *me out now! This minute! You take me out or I'm gonna kick down the walls! I will! I can! I can, too!*'

She ran to the walls to attack with small feet and flailing little fists that she managed to bruise severely before she gave up.

I felt sorry for her, and for Cory. All of us would have liked to kick down the walls and escape. With Carrie, though, it was more likely the walls would tumble down just from the crescendo trumpet of her powerful voice, like the walls of Jericho tumbling down.

Indeed, it was a relief when Carrie braved the dangers of the attic and found her own way to the stairway, and to the bedroom below, where she could play with her dolls, and her teacups, and her tiny stove, and her little ironing-board with the iron that didn't heat up.

For the first time, Cory and Carrie could spend a few hours separated from each other, and Chris said that was a good thing. Up in the attic was the music which charmed Cory, while Carrie would chatter on to her 'things'.

Taking many baths was another way to use up excess time, and shampooing hair made it last longer – oh, we were the cleanest children alive. We napped after lunch, which lasted as long as we could stretch it. Chris and I made a contest of peeling apples so the skin came off in one long, long spiralling cord. We peeled oranges and took off every bit of white string that the twins detested. We had little boxes of cheese crackers that we counted out to divide equally into four portions.

Our most dangerous and amusing game was to mimic the grandmother – ever fearful she'd walk in and catch us draped with some filthy grey sheet from the attic, to represent her grey taffeta

93

uniforms. Chris and I were the best at this. The twins were too afraid of her to even lift their eyes when she was in the room.

'Children!' snapped Chris while he stood by the door, holding an invisible picnic basket. 'Have you been decent, honourable, proper? This room looks a terrible mess! Girl – you over there – smooth out that rumpled pillow before I crush your head in with the mere glare of my eyes!'

'Mercy, Grandmother!' I cried, falling down on my knees and crawling to her with my hands folded under my chin. 'I was dead tired from scrubbing down all the walls in the attic. I had to rest.'

'*Rest!*' snapped the grandmother at the door, her dress about to fall off. 'There is no *rest* for the evil, the corrupt, the unholy and the unworldly – there is only work until you are dead, and hung for ever over hell's eternal roasting fires!' Then he lifted his arms beneath the sheet in some horrible gestures that made the twins shriek from fright, and in a witch's way, the grandmother disappeared, and only Chris was left, grinning at us.

The first weeks were like seconds turned into hours despite all we did to entertain ourselves, and we managed to do quite a lot. It was the doubts and the fears, the hopes and expectations that kept us so in suspense, waiting, waiting – and we were no closer to being let out and taken downstairs.

Now the twins ran to me with their small cuts and bruises, and the splinters garnered from the rotten wood in the attic. I carefully plucked them out with tweezers, Chris would apply the antiseptic, and the adhesive plaster they both loved. An injured small finger was enough reason to demand cuddly-baby things, and lullabies sung as I tucked them into bed, and kissed their faces, and tickled where laughter had to be freed. Their thin little arms wrapped tightly about my neck. I was loved, very loved . . . and needed.

Our twins were more like three-year-olds than children of five. Not in the way they talked, but in the way they rubbed their eyes with small fists, and pouted when they were denied anything, and the way they had of holding their breath until they turned magenta and forced you to give them what they wanted. I was much more susceptible to this kind of ploy than Chris, who reasoned it was impossible for anyone to suffocate themselves in such a way. Still, to see them purple was a terrifying sight.

'Next time they behave like that,' he told me in private, 'I want you to ignore them, even if you have to go into the bathroom and lock the door. And, believe me, they won't die.'

That was exactly what they forced me to do – and they didn't die. That was the last time they pulled that stunt as a way to keep from eating food they didn't like – and they didn't like anything, or hardly anything.

Carrie had the swayback posture of all little girls, protruding in front in a strong arc, and she adored skipping around the room, holding out her skirts so her ruffled panties showed. (Lace ruffled panties were the only kind she would wear.) And if they had little roses made of ribbons, or embroidered somewhere in front, you had to see them at least a dozen times a day, and comment on how charming she looked in her panties.

Of course, Cory wore briefs like Chris, and he was very proud of this. Somewhere, lurking in his memory, were the diapers not too long ago discarded. If he had a temperamental bladder, Carrie was the one who got diarrhoea if she ate one teensy bit of any fruit but citrus. I actually hated the days when peaches and grapes were brought up to us – for dear Carrie adored green grapes without seeds, and peaches, and apples . . . and all three had the same effect. Believe me, when fruit came in the door, I blanched, knowing who would have to wash the ruffled, lacy panties unless I moved fast as lightning, running with Carrie under my arm, and plopping her down in the nick of time. Chris's laughter would ring out when I didn't make it – or Carrie *did* make it. He kept that blue vase handy, for when Cory had to go, he had to let loose immediately, and woe if a girl was in the bathroom with the door locked. More than once he had wet his short pants, and then he'd bury his face in my lap, so ashamed. (Carrie was never ashamed – my fault for being slow.)

'Cathy, when do we get to go outside?' he whispered after one accident.

'As soon as Momma says we can.'

'Why doesn't Momma say we can?'

'There is an old man downstairs who doesn't know we're up here. And we have to wait until he likes Momma again, enough to accept us too.'

'Who is the old man?'

'Our grandfather.'

'Is he like the grandmother?'

'Yeah, I'm afraid he is.'

'Why doesn't he like us?'

'He doesn't like us because . . . because, well, because he hasn't got good sense. I think he's sick in the head, as well as in the heart.'

'Does Momma still like us?'

Now, that was a question to keep me awake at night.

More than weeks had passed when a Sunday came where Momma didn't show up during the day. It hurt not having her with us, when we knew she had the day off from school, and we knew she was somewhere in this very house.

I lay flat on my stomach on the floor where it was cooler, reading *Jude the Obscure*. Chris was up in the attic searching for new reading material, and the twins were crawling around pushing tiny cars and trucks.

The day dragged on into evening before finally the door opened and Momma came gliding into our room, wearing tennis shoes, white shorts and a white top with a sailor collar trimmed in red and blue braid, and an anchor design. Her face was rosy tan from being outdoors. She looked so vibrantly healthy, so unbelievably happy, while we wilted and felt half-sick from the oppressive heat of this room.

Sailing clothes – oh I knew them – that's what she'd been doing. I stared at her resentfully, longing for my skin to be tanned by the sun, with my legs as healthily coloured as hers. Her hair was windblown, and it flattered her well, making her seem almost ten times more beautiful, earthy, sexy. And she was almost old, almost forty.

Very obviously, this afternoon had given her more pleasure than any day since our father died. And it was almost five o'clock. Dinner was served at seven downstairs. That meant she would have very little time to spend with us before she had to leave for her own rooms, where she could bathe, then change into some-thing more suitable for the meal.

I laid aside my book and turned over to sit up. I was hurting, and I wanted to hurt her, too: 'Where have you been?' I demanded in an ugly tone. What right did she have to be enjoying herself when we were locked away, and kept from doing the youthful things that were our right? I would never have a summer when I was twelve again, nor would Chris enjoy this fourteenth summer, or the twins their fifth.

The ugly, accusing tone of my voice paled her radiance. She blanched and her lips quivered, and perhaps she regretted bringing us a big wall calendar so we could know when it was Saturday or Sunday. The calendar was filled with our big red Xs to mark off our imprisoned days, our hot, lonely, suspenseful, hurting days.

She fell into a chair and crossed her lovely legs, picking up a magazine to fan herself. 'I'm sorry to have kept you waiting,' she said, with a loving smile in my direction. 'I wanted to stop by and visit this morning, but my father demanded all of my attention, and I'd made plans for this afternoon, though I did cut them short so I could spend some time with my children before dinner.' Though she didn't look sweaty, she raised a sleeveless arm and fanned her armpit as though this room was more than she could bear. 'I've been sailing, Cathy,' she said. 'My brothers taught me how to sail when I was nine, and then when your father came here to live, I taught him how. We used to spend a lot of time on the lake. Sailing is almost like flying . . . wonderful fun,' she ended lamely, realizing her fun had stolen *our* fun.

'Sailing?' I just about screamed. 'Why weren't you downstairs telling the grandfather about us? How long do you intend to keep us locked up here? For ever?'

Her blue eyes skipped nervously about the room; she appeared on the verge of getting up from the chair we seldom used, for we saved it especially for her – her throne. Maybe she would have gone then and there if Chris hadn't come down from the attic with his arms loaded down with encyclopaedias so old they didn't include television or jet planes.

'Cathy, don't shout at our mother,' he scolded. 'Hi, Mom. Boy, do you look great! I love that sailing outfit you've got on.' He put down his load of books on the dressing-table he used for a desk,

97

then strolled over to put his arms around her. I felt betrayed, not only by Momma, but by my brother. The summer was almost over, and we hadn't done anything, been on a picnic or had a swim, or walked in the woods, even seen a boat or put on a bathing-suit to wade in a backyard pool.

'Momma!' I cried out, jumping to my feet, and ready to do battle for our freedom. 'I think it's time you told your father about us! I'm sick of living in this one room, and playing in the attic! I want our twins out in the fresh air and sunshine, and I want out, too! *I* want to go sailing! If the grandfather has forgiven you for marrying Daddy, then why can't he accept us? Are we so ugly, so terrible, so stupid he'd be ashamed to claim us as his blood kin?'

She shoved Chris away from her, then sank weakly down into the chair she'd just abandoned, leaned forwards, and bowed her face down into her hands. Intuitively, I guessed she was going to reveal some truth she'd previously held back. I called to Cory and Carrie and told them to sit close at my sides so I could put my arm about each. And Chris, though I thought he would stay close by Momma's side, came over to sit on the bed next to Cory. We were again, as we'd been before, small fledgling birds sitting on a clothesline waiting for a strong gust of wind to blow us asunder.

'Cathy, Christopher,' she began, her head still bowed, though her hands were in her lap nervously working, 'I haven't been completely honest with you.'

As if I hadn't guessed that already.

'Will you be staying for dinner with us tonight?' I asked, for some reason wanting to put off the full truth.

'Thank you for asking me. I'd like to stay, but I've made other plans for this evening.'

And this was our day, our time to be with her until dark. And yesterday she'd spent only half an hour with us.

'The letter,' she murmured, and her head lifted and shadows darkened the blue of her eyes into green, 'the letter my mother wrote when we were still in Gladstone. That letter invited us to live here. I didn't tell you that my father wrote a short note on the bottom.'

'Yes, Momma, go on,' I urged. 'Whatever you have to tell us, we can take it.'

Our mother was a poised woman, cool and self-possessed. But there was one thing she could never control, and that was her hands. Always they betrayed her emotions. One wilful, capricious hand rose to flutter near her throat, fingering there, seeking some string of pearls to twist and untwist, and since she wore no jewellery, her fingers just endlessly sought. The fingers on the hand she kept in her lap restlessly rasped together, as if to cleanse themselves.

'Your grandmother, she wrote the letter, signed it, but at the end, my father added his note.' She hesitated, closing her eyes, waited a second or two, and then opened them to glance at us again. 'Your grandfather wrote he was glad your father was dead. He wrote the evil and corrupt always get what they deserve. He wrote the only good thing about my marriage was it hadn't created any Devil's issue.'

Once I would have asked: What was that? Now I knew. Devil's issue was the same as Devil's spawn – something evil, rotten, born to be bad.

I sat on the bed with my arms about the twins, and I looked at Chris, who must be much like Daddy had been at his age, and a vision flashed of my father in his white tennis clothes, standing tall, proud, golden-haired, and bronze-skinned. Evil was dark, crooked, crouched and small – it didn't stand straight and smile at you with clear sky-blue eyes that never lied.

'My mother made the plans for your concealment on a page of the letter my father didn't read,' she concluded lamely, her face flushed.

'Was our father considered evil and corrupt only because he married his half-niece?' asked Chris, in the same controlled, cool voice our mother had used. 'Is that the only thing he ever did wrong?'

'Yes!' she cried, happy that he, her beloved, understood. 'Your father in all his life committed one single, unforgivable sin – and that was to fall in love with me. The law forbids marriage between an uncle and niece, even those who are only half-related. Please don't condemn us. I explained how it was with us. Of us all, your father was the best . . .' She faltered, on the verge of tears, and pleaded with her eyes, and I knew, I knew what was coming next.

'What is evil, and what is corrupt, is in the eyes of the beholder,' she rushed on, eager to make us see it her way. 'Your grandfather could find these faults in an angel. He is the kind of man who expects perfection from everyone in his family, and he is far from perfect. But just try and tell him that, and he would smack you down.' She swallowed nervously then, appearing near sick with what she had to say. 'Christopher, I thought once we were here, and I could tell him about you, how you were the most brilliant boy in your class, and always have been a straight-A student, and I thought when he saw Cathy, and knew of her great talent for dancing – I thought surely those two things alone would win him over without him even seeing the twins, how beautiful they are and how sweet – and who knows what talent they have waiting to be developed? I thought, foolishly, hopefully, that he would easily yield and say he'd made a mistake in believing our marriage was so wrong.'

'Momma,' I said weakly, almost crying myself, 'you make it sound as if you're never going to tell him. He's never going to like us, no matter how pretty the twins are, or how smart Chris is, or how good I can dance. None of it's gonna make any difference to him. He'll still hate us, and think of us as Devil's issue, won't he?'

She got up and came to us, and she fell down on her knees again and tried to wrap us all in her embrace. 'Haven't I told you before he hasn't got long to live? He gasps for breath every time he exerts himself in the least way? And if he doesn't die soon, I'll find a way to tell him about you. I swear I will. Just have patience. Be understanding. What fun you lose now, I'll make up for later on, a thousandfold!'

Her teary eyes were beseeching. 'Please, please, for me, because you love me, and I love you, keep on having patience. It won't be long, it can't be long, and I'll do what I can to make your lives as enjoyable as possible. And think of the riches we'll have one day soon!'

'It's all right, Momma,' said Chris, drawing her into his embrace just as our father would. 'What you ask isn't too much, not when we have so much to gain.'

'Yes,' Momma said eagerly, 'just a short while more to sacrifice, and a little more patience, and all that is sweet and good in life will be yours.'

What was there left for me to say? How could I protest? Already we'd sacrificed over three weeks – what was a few more days, or weeks, or even another month?

At the end of the rainbow waited the pot of gold. But rainbows were made of faint and fragile gossamer – and gold weighed a ton – and since the world began, gold was the reason to do most anything.

TO MAKE A GARDEN GROW

Now we knew the full truth.

We would be in this room until the day our grandfather died. And it came to me in the night, when I was low and dreary, that perhaps she had known from the very beginning that her father was not the kind to forgive anyone anything.

'But,' said my cheerful optimist Christopher, 'any day could see him gone. That is the way of heart disease. A clot could break free and find its way to his heart or lung and snuff him out like a candle.'

Chris and I said cruel and irreverent things between ourselves, but in our hearts we ached, knowing it was wrong, and we were disrespectful as a way to salve the pain of our bleeding self-esteem.

'Now look,' he said, 'since we are going to be up here a while longer, we should set about with more determination to placate the twins, and ourselves, with more entertaining things to do. And when we really apply ourselves, gosh knows, we might just dream up some pretty wild and fantastic things.'

When you have an attic full of junk, and great armoires full of rotting, stinking, but nevertheless very fancy costumes, you are inspired to put on plays, naturally. And since one day I was going to be on stage, I would be the producer, the director, the choreographer, as well as the female star. Chris, of course, would have to play all the male lead roles, and the twins could participate and play minor parts.

But they didn't want to participate! They wanted to be the audience, and sit and watch and applaud.

It wasn't such a bad idea, for what was a play without an audience! It was a great pity they didn't have any money to buy tickets.

'We'll call this dress rehearsal,' said Chris, 'and since you seem to be everything else, and know everything about theatrical productions, you write the script.'

Hah! As if I needed to write the script. This was my chance to play Scarlett O'Hara. We had the hoops to wear under the flouncy ruffled skirts, and the stays to squeeze you tight, and just the clothes for Chris to wear, and fancy parasols with a few holes. The trunks and the armoires offered a great deal to select from, and I had to have the best costume, hauled from one of the armoires, and the underwear and petticoats came from one of the trunks. I'd curled my hair in rags so it hung in long, spiralling curls, and on my head I wore a floppy old Leghorn hat of straw, bedecked with faded silk flowers and banded by green satin ribbon, that was browning about the edges. My ruffled gown worn over wire hoops was of some flimsy stuff that felt like voile. Once, I think, it might have been pink, now it was hard to say just what colour it was.

Rhett Butler wore the fancy costume of cream-coloured trousers, and a brown velvet jacket with pearl buttons, and a satin vest underneath with faint red roses scattered on it. 'Come, Scarlett,' he said to me. 'We've got to escape Atlanta before Sherman reaches here and sets the town on fire.'

Chris had strung ropes on which we draped blankets to act as stage curtains, and our audience of two were stomping their feet impatiently, eager to see Atlanta burn. I followed Rhett on to the 'stage' and was ready to taunt and tease, flirt and bewitch, and put *him* on fire before I rushed off to some pale-haired Ashley Wilkes, when one of my bedraggled ruffles caught beneath my too large, funny-looking old shoes, and down I sprawled in an undignified heap that showed my dirty pantaloons with lace hanging in ragged strings. The audience gave me a standing ovation, thinking this was a pratfall and part of the act. 'Play's over!' I announced, and began to rip off the smelly old clothes.

'Let's eat!' cried Carrie, who'd say anything to take us down from this despised attic.

Cory pouted his lower lip and looked around. 'I wish we had the garden again,' he said so wistfully it hurt. 'I don't like to swing when the flowers don't sway in the wind.' His flaxen hair had grown long enough to touch his shirt collar, and it curled in ringlets, while Carrie's hair hung halfway down her back and rippled like cascading wave. They were wearing blue today, for Monday. We had colours for each day. Yellow was our Sunday colour. Red was for Saturday.

The wish spoken by Cory put thoughts into Chris's head, for he turned in a slow circle, giving the huge attic an appraising survey. 'Admittedly this attic is a grim and dreary place,' he mused, 'but why can't we, as a constructive way to use our creative talents, bring about a metamorphosis and turn this ugly caterpillar into a brilliant soaring butterfly?' He smiled at me, at the twins, in such a charming, convincing way that I was immediately won over. It *would* be fun to attempt to pretty up this dismal place, and give the twins a colourful fake garden where they could swing and enjoy looking at beauty. Of course, we'd never finish decorating all of the attic, it was so tremendous – and any day the grandfather could die, and then we'd leave, never to return again.

We couldn't wait for Momma to come that evening, and when she did, Chris and I enthusiastically told her our plans of decorating the attic, and turning it into a cheerful garden the twins wouldn't be afraid of. The strangest expression flickered momentarily in her eyes.

'Well, now,' she said brightly, 'if you're going to make the attic pretty, first you must make it clean. And I'll do what I can to help.'

Momma sneaked up mops, pails, brooms, scrub-brushes, and boxes of soap powder. She went down on her knees beside us to scrub in the attic corners, and around the edges, and under the large pieces of furniture. I marvelled that our mother knew how to scrub and clean. When we lived in Gladstone, we had a twice weekly maid who came in to do all the hard, dreary things that would redden Momma's hands and break her fingernails. And here she was, on her hands and knees, wearing faded old blue jeans, an old shirt, her hair pinned up in a bun. I really admired her. It was hard, hot, demeaning work – and she never once complained, only laughed and chatted and acted as if this was great fun.

In a week of hard work, we had most of the attic as clean as possible. Then she brought us insect repellent to kill what bugs had hidden from us while we cleaned. We swept up dead spiders and other crawlers by the bucketfuls. We threw them out of a back window, where they rolled to a lower section of the roof.

Later the rain came to wash them down into the gutters. Then the birds found them and had a grisly feast while we four sat on a window ledge and watched. We never saw a rat or a mouse – but we saw droppings. We presumed they were waiting for all the hustle and bustle to calm down before they ventured out of their dark and secret places.

Now that the attic was clean, Momma brought us green plants, plus a spiky amaryllis that was supposed to bloom at Christmastime. I frowned when she said this – for we wouldn't be here then. 'We'll take it with us,' said Momma, reaching out to stroke my cheek. 'We'll take all of our plants when we go, so don't frown and look unhappy. We wouldn't want to leave anything living, and loving of sunshine, in this attic.'

We put our plants in the attic schoolroom for that room had windows facing east. Happy and gay, we all tripped down the narrow stairs, and Momma washed up in our bathroom, then fell exhausted into her special chair. The twins climbed up on her lap as I set the table for lunch. That was a good day, for she stayed until dinnertime, then sighed and said she'd have to go. Her father made such demands on her, wanting to know where she went every Saturday, and why she stayed so long.

'Can you sneak back to see us before bedtime?' Chris asked.

'I'm going to the movies tonight,' she said evenly, 'but before I leave, I'll slip in to see you again. I've got some of those little boxes of raisins that you can snack on between meals. I forgot to bring them with me.'

The twins were crazy about raisins, and I was happy for them. 'Are you going to the movies alone?' I asked.

'No. There's a girl I grew up with – she used to be my best friend, and she's married now. I'm going to the movies with them. She lives only a few houses from here.' She got up and went to the windows, and when Chris had the lights turned out, she parted the draperies and pointed in the direction of the house where her best friend lived. 'Elena has two unmarried brothers, one is studying to be a lawyer. He goes to Harvard Law School, and the other is a tennis pro.'

'Momma!' I cried. 'Are you dating one of those brothers?'

She laughed and let the draperies fall. 'Turn on the lights,

Chris. No, Cathy, I am not dating anyone. To tell you the truth, I'd rather go right to bed, I'm that tired. I really don't care for musicals, anyway. I'd rather stay with my children, but Elena keeps insisting I get out, and when I keep refusing, she keeps asking why. I don't want people to wonder why I stay home every week-end; that's why occasionally I do have to go sailing, or to the movies.'

To make the attic even pretty seemed highly improbable – to make it a beautiful garden soared over the rainbow! It was going to take an enormous amount of hard work and creative ability, but that darned brother of mine was convinced we could do it *in no time at all*. He soon had our mother so sold on the idea that every day she went to secretarial school, she came back to us bearing colouring books from which we could cut out pre-drawn flowers. She brought us watercolour sets, many brushes, boxes of crayons, huge amounts of coloured craft paper, fat pots of white paste, and four pairs of blunt-nosed scissors.

'Teach the twins to colour and cut out flowers,' she instructed, 'and let them participate in all you undertake. I nominate you their kindergarten teachers.'

She came from that city an hour's train ride away, glowing with radiant good health, her skin fresh and rosy from outside air, her clothes so beautiful they took my breath away. She had shoes of every colour, and bit by bit she was accumulating new pieces of jewellery which she called 'junk' jewellery, but somehow those rhinestones looked more like diamonds to me from the way they sparkled. She fell into 'her' chair, exhausted, but happy, and told us of her day. 'Oh, how I wish those typewriters had letters on the keys. I can't seem to remember but one row. I have to look up at the wall chart every time and that slows me down, and I'm not very good at remembering the bottom row, either. But I do know where all the vowels are. You use those keys more than any others, you know. So far my typing speed is twenty words per minute, and that's not too good. Plus I make about four mistakes in those twenty words. And those shorthand squiggles . . .' She sighed, as if they, too, had her baffled. 'Well,

I guess I'll learn eventually; after all, other women do, and if they can, then I can.'

'Do you like your teachers, Momma?' asked Chris.

She giggled girlishly before she answered. 'First, let me tell you about my typing teacher. Her name is Mrs Helena Brady. She's shaped very much like your grandmother – huge. Only her bosom is much larger! Really, hers is the most remarkable bosom I've ever seen! And her bra straps keep slipping off her shoulders, and if it isn't her bra straps, then it's her slip straps, and she's always reaching into the neckline of her dress to haul them back into place, and the men in the class always snicker.'

'Do men take typing classes?' asked I, very surprised.

'Yes, there are a few young men there. Some are journalists, writers, or have some good reason for wanting to know how to type. And Mrs Brady is divorced, and has a keen eye for one of those young men. She flirts with him, while he tries to ignore her. She's about ten years older than he is, at least, and he keeps looking at me. Now don't get any ideas, Cathy. He's much too short for me. I couldn't marry a man who couldn't pick me up and carry me over the threshold. I could pick *him* up – he's only five feet two.'

We all had a good laugh, for Daddy had been a full foot taller, and he had easily picked our mother up. We'd seen him do that many times – especially on those Friday nights when he came home, and they'd look at each other so funny.

'Momma, you're not thinking of getting married again, are you?' Chris asked in the tightest of voices. Swiftly her arms went around him. 'No darling, of course not. I loved your father dearly. It would take a very special man to fill his shoes, and so far I haven't met one who measured up to even his outgrown socks.'

To play kindergarten teachers was great fun, or could have been, if our student body had been the least bit willing. But as soon as we had breakfast finished, our dishes washed and put away, our food stashed in the coldest place, and the hour of ten had come and gone with servants from the second floor, Chris and I each dragged a wailing twin up into the attic schoolroom. There we could sit at the student desks and make a grand mess cutting flower forms from the coloured craft paper, using the crayons to glorify the colours with stripes and polka-dots. Chris and I made the best flowers – what the twins made looked like coloured blobs.

'Modern art,' Chris named the flowers they made.

On the dull and grey slat walls we pasted up our goliath flowers. Chris ascended the old ladder with the missing rungs again so he could dangle down long strings tied to the attic rafters, and to these strings we fastened colourful blossoms that constantly moved in the attic draughts.

Our mother came up to view our efforts, and she gave us all a pleased smile. 'Yes, you're doing marvellously well. You *are* making it pretty up here.' And thoughtfully she moved closer to the daisies, as if considering something else she could bring us. The next day she came with a huge flat box containing coloured glass beads and sequins, so we could add sparkle and glamour to our garden. Oh, we did slave over making those flowers, for whatever occupation we pursued, we pursued it with diligent, fervid zeal. The twins caught some of our enthusiasm, and they stopped howling and fighting and biting when we mentioned the word attic. For after all, the attic was slowly, but surely, turning into a cheerful garden. And the more it changed, the more determined we became to cover over every last wall in that endless attic!

Each day, of course, when Momma was home from that secretarial school, she had to view the day's accomplishments. 'Momma,' gushed Carrie in her breathless bird twitter, 'that's all we do all day, make flowers, and sometimes Cathy, she don't want us to go downstairs and eat lunch!'

'Cathy, you mustn't become so preoccupied with decorating the attic that you forget to eat your meals.'

'But, Momma, we're doing it for them, so they won't be so scared up there.'

She laughed and hugged me. 'My, you are the persistent one, you and your older brother both. You must have inherited that from your father, certainly not from me. I give up so easily.'

'Momma!' I cried, made uneasy. 'Are you still going to school? You are getting better at typing, aren't you?'

'Yes, of course I am.' She smiled again, and then settled back in her chair, holding up her hand and seeming to admire the bracelet she wore. I started to ask why she needed so much jewellery to attend secretarial school, but she spoke instead. 'What you need to make now is animals for your garden.'

'But, Momma, if roses are impossible to make, how can we even *draw* animals?'

She gave me a wry little smile as she traced a cool finger over my nose. 'Oh, Cathy, what a doubting Thomas you are. You question everything, doubt everything, when you should know by now, you can do anything you want to, if you want to badly enough. And I'm going to tell you a secret I've known about for some time – in this world, where everything is complicated, there is also a book to teach you how simple everything can be.'

That I was to find out.

Momma brought us art instruction books by the dozen. The first of these books taught us to reduce all complicated designs into basic spheres, cylinders, cones, rectangles and cubes. A chair was just a cube – I hadn't known that before. A Christmas tree was just an inverted ice-cream cone – I hadn't known that before, either. People were just combinations of all those basic forms: spheres for heads; arms, necks, legs, torso, upper and lower, were only rectangular cubes or cylinders, and triangles made for feet. And believe it or not, using this basic method, with just a few simple additions, we soon had rabbits, squirrels, birds, and other small friendly creatures – all made by our very own hands.

True, they were peculiar looking. I thought their oddities made them all the sweeter. Chris coloured all his animals realistically. I decorated mine with polka-dots, gingham checks, plaids, and put lace-edged pockets on the laying hens. Because our mother had shopped in a sewing notions store, we had lace, cords of all colours, buttons, sequins, felt, pebbles and other decorative materials. The possibilities were endless. When she put that box into my hands, I know my eyes must have shown all the love I felt for her then. For this did prove she thought of us when she was out in the world. She wasn't just thinking of new clothes for herself, and new jewellery and cosmetics. She *was* trying to make our confined lives as pleasant as possible.

One rainy afternoon Cory came running to me with an orange paper snail he'd laboriously worked on the entire morning, and half of the afternoon. He'd eaten but a little of his favourite lunch, peanut-butter-and-jelly sandwiches, he was that anxious to get back to his 'work' and put on the 'things that stick out of the head'.

Proudly, he stood back, small legs spread wide, as he watched each flicker of expression on my face. What he'd made resembled nothing more than a lop-sided beachball with trembling feelers.

'Do you think it's a good snail?' he asked, frowning up and looking worried when I couldn't find words to say.

'Yes,' I said quickly, 'it's a wonderful, beautiful snail.'

'You don't think it looks like an orange?'

'No, of course not – oranges don't have swirls, like this snail does – or crooked feelers.'

Chris stepped closer to view the pitiful creature I held in my hands. 'You don't call those things feelers,' he corrected. 'A snail is a member of the mollusc family, which have soft bodies without any backbones – and those little things are called antennae, which are connected to its brain; it has tubular intestines that end with its mouth, and it moves by a gear-edged foot.'

'Christopher,' I said coolly, 'when Cory and I want to know about a snail's tubular intestines, we'll send you a telegram, and please go sit on a tack and wait for it.'

'Do you want to be ignorant all your life?'

'Yes!' I flared back. 'When it comes to snails, I prefer knowing nothing!'

Cory tagged behind me as we went to watch Carrie pasting pieces of purple paper together. Her working method was slap-dash, unlike Cory's careful plodding. Carrie used her pair of scissors to ruthlessly stab a hole into her purple . . . thing. Behind the hole she pasted a bit of red paper. When she had this . . . thing . . . put together, she named it a worm. It undulated like a giant boa constrictor, flashing a single mean red eye with black spider-leg lashes. 'Its name is Charlie,' she said, handing over her four feet of 'work' to me. (When things came to us without a name of their own, we made their names begin with a C to make them one of us.)

On the attic walls, in our beautiful garden of paper flowers, we pasted up the epileptic snail beside the fierce and menacing worm.

Oh, they did make a pair. Chris sat down and lettered a big sign in red: ALL ANIMALS BEWARE OF EARTH-WORM!!!

I lettered my own sign, feeling Cory's small snail was the one in jeopardy. IS THERE A DOCTOR IN THE HOUSE? (Cory named this snail Cindy Lou.)

Momma viewed this day's accomplishments with laughter, all smiles, because we were having fun. 'Yes, of course there is a doctor in the house,' she said, and leaned to kiss Chris's cheek. 'This son of mine has always known what to do for a sick animal. And Cory, I adore your snail – she looks . . . so . . . so sensitive.'

'Do you like my Charlie?' asked Carrie anxiously. 'I made him good. I used all the purple to make him big. Now we don't have no more purple.'

'It's a beautiful worm, really a gorgeous worm,' said Momma, taking the twins on to her lap and giving them the hugs and kisses she sometimes forgot. 'I especially like the black lashes you put around that red eye – very effective.'

It was a cozy, homey scene, the three of them in her chair, with Chris perched on the arm, his face close to his mother's. Then I had to go and spoil it all, as was my hateful way.

'How many words can you type per minute now, Momma?'

'I'm getting better.'

'How much better?'

'I'm doing the best I can, really, Cathy – I told you the keyboard doesn't have any letters.'

'What about shorthand – how fast can you take dictation?'

'I'm trying. You've got to have patience. You don't learn things like that overnight.'

Patience. I coloured patience grey, hung over with black clouds. I coloured hope yellow, just like that sun we could see for a few short morning hours. Too soon the sun rose high in the sky and disappeared from view, leaving us bereft, and staring at blue.

When you grow up, and have a million adult things to do, you forget how long a day can be for a child. It seemed we lived through four years in the course of seven weeks. Then came another dreaded Friday when we had to get up at dawn and scurry around like mad to rid the bedroom, and the bathroom, of all evidence that we existed. I stripped off the sheets from the bed and rolled them into a ball along with the pillowcases and blankets, and I put the bedspreads directly over the mattress covers – the way the grandmother had ordered me to do. The night before, Chris had taken apart the train tracks. Like crazy we worked to make the room neat, spotless, plus the bathroom, and then the grandmother came in with the picnic basket and ordered us to take it into the attic, and we could eat breakfast there. I had most carefully wiped away all our fingerprints, and the mahogany furniture shone. She scowled heavily when she saw this, and darn if she didn't use dust from a vacuum cleaner bag to make all the furniture tops dull again.

At seven we were in the attic schoolroom, eating our cold cereal with raisins and milk. Down below we could faintly hear the maids moving around in our room. On tippy-toes we moved to the stairwell, and huddled there on the top step listening to what went on below, though we were scared every minute of being discovered.

Hearing the maids move about, laughing and chatting, while the grandmother hovered near the closet door directing them to clean the mirrors, use the lemon wax, air the mattresses – it all gave me the queerest feeling. Why didn't those maids notice something different? Didn't we leave any odour behind to let them know Cory often wet his bed? It was as if we really *didn't* exist, and weren't alive, and the only scents we had were imaginary. We wrapped our arms about each other and held on to each other tightly, tightly.

The maids didn't enter the closet; they didn't open the tall, narrow door. They didn't see us, or hear us, nor did they seem to think it odd the grandmother never left the room for a second while they were in there scrubbing the tub, cleaning the toilet bowl, scrubbing the tile floor.

That Friday did something strange to all of us. I believe we shrivelled in our own estimations of ourselves, for afterwards we couldn't find words to say. We didn't enjoy our games, or our books, and so silently we cut out tulips and daisies and waited for Momma to come and bring hope with her again.

Still, we were young, and hope has strong roots in the young, right down to their toes, and when we entered the attic and saw our growing garden, we could laugh, and pretend. After all, we were making our mark in the world. We were making something beautiful out of what had been drab and ugly.

Now the twins took off like butterflies, fluttering through the mobile flowers. We pushed them high on the swings and created windstorms to shake the flowers madly. We hid behind cardboard trees no taller than Chris, and sat on mushrooms made of papier-mâché, with colourful foam cushions on top, which were, honestly, better than the real thing – unless you had an appetite for eating mushrooms.

'It's pretty!' cried Carrie, spinning around and around, holding to her short pleated skirt so we just had to see the new lace ruffled panties Momma had given her yesterday. All new clothes and shoes had to spend their first night with Carrie and Cory in their beds. (It's terrible to wake up at night with your cheek resting on the sole of a sneaker.) 'I'm going to be a ballerina, too,' she said happily spinning and spinning until she eventually fell, and Cory went rushing to see if she had hurt herself. She screamed to see the blood ooze from a cut on her knee. 'Oh – I don't want to be a ballerina if it hurts!'

I didn't dare let her know it hurt – oh, boy, did it hurt!

Yesterdays ago, I'd ambled through real gardens, real forests – and always I felt their mystical aura – as if something magic and marvellous was waiting just around the bend. To make our attic garden enchanted, too, Chris and I crawled around and drew white-chalk daisies on the floor, joining them in a ring. Inside that fairy ring of white flowers, all that was evil was banished. There we could sit cross-legged on the floor, and by the light of a single candle burning, Chris and I would spin long, involved tales of good fairies who took care of small children, and wicked witches who always went down in defeat.

Then Cory spoke up. As always, he was the one to ask the most difficult questions to answer. 'Where has all the grass gone?'

'God took the grass to heaven.' And thusly, Carrie saved me from answering.

'Why?'

'For Daddy. Daddy likes to mow the lawn.'

Chris's eyes met with mine – and we'd thought they'd forgotten Daddy.

Cory puckered up his faint brows, staring at the little cardboard trees Chris had made. 'Where are all the big trees?'

'Same place,' said Carrie. 'Daddy likes big trees.' This time my eyes took wild flight. How I hated lying to them – telling them this was only a game, an endless game they seemed to endure with more patience than Chris or me. And they never once asked why we had to play such a game.

Never once did the grandmother come up to the attic to ask what we were doing, though very often she opened the bedroom door as silently as possible, hoping we wouldn't notice the noise of the key turning in the lock. She'd peer in the crack, trying to catch us doing something 'unholy' or 'wicked'.

In the attic we were free to do anything we wanted without fear of retaliation, unless God wielded a whip. Not one time did the grandmother leave our room without reminding us that God was up above to see, even when she was not. Because she never went even into the closet to open the door of the attic stairwell, my curiosity was aroused. I reminded myself to ask of Momma as soon as she came in, so I wouldn't forget again. 'Why doesn't the grandmother go into the attic herself and check to see what we do? Why does she just ask, and think we'll tell the truth?'

Tired and dejected looking, Momma wilted in her special chair. Her new green wool suit looked very expensive. She had been to a hairdresser, and the style was changed. She answered my question in an offhand manner, as if her thoughts were dwelling on something more appealing, 'Oh, haven't I told you before? Your grandmother suffers from claustrophobia. That's an emotional affliction that makes it difficult for her to breathe in any small, confined area. You see, when she was a child, her parents used to lock her in a closet for punishment.'

Wow! How difficult to think that large old woman had once been young, and small enough to punish. I could almost feel sorry for the child she'd been, but I knew she was happy to see *us* locked up. Every time she glanced our way, it showed in her eyes – her smug satisfaction to have us so neatly captured. Still, it was a peculiar thing that fate would give her such a fear, and thus give Chris and me reason enough to kiss the dear, sweet, close walls of that narrow passageway. Often Chris and I speculated on how all the massive furniture had been taken up into the attic. Certainly it couldn't have been manoeuvred up through the small closet and then up the stairway, which was barely more than a foot wide. And though we searched diligently to find another larger doorway into the attic, we never found one. Maybe one was hidden behind one of the giant armoires too heavy for us to move. Chris thought the largest furniture could have been hauled up to the roof, then passed through one of the big windows.

Every day the witch-grandmother came into our room, to stab with her flintstone eyes, to snarl with her thin, crooked lips. Every day she asked the same old questions: 'What have you been up to? What do you do in the attic? Did you say grace before today's meals? Did you go down on your knees last night and ask God to forgive your parents for the sin they committed? Are you teaching the youngest two the words of the Lord? Do you use the bathroom together, boys and girls?' Boy, did her eyes flash mean then; 'Are you modest, always? Do you keep the private parts of your bodies from the eyes of others? Do you touch your bodies when it's not necessary for cleanliness?'

God! How dirty she made skin seem. Chris laughed when she was gone. 'I think she must glue on her underwear,' he joked.

'No! She nails it on!' I topped.

'Have you noticed how much she likes the colour grey?'

Noticed? Who wouldn't notice? Always grey. Sometimes the grey had fine pinstripes of red or blue, or a dainty plaid design, very faint, or jacquard – but always the fabric was taffeta with the diamond brooch at the throat of a high and severe neckline, softened a bit by hand-crocheted collars. Momma had already told us a widow-lady in the nearest village custom made these uniforms that looked like armour. 'This lady is a dear friend of my mother's. And she wears grey because it is cheaper to buy material by the bolt than by the yard – and your grandfather owns a mill that makes fine fabrics down in Georgia somewhere.'

Good golly, even the rich had to be stingy.

One September afternoon I raced down the attic stairs in a

terrible hurry to reach the bathroom – and I collided smack into the grandmother! She seized hold of my shoulders, and glared down into my face. 'Watch where you're going, girl!' she snapped. 'Why are you in such a hurry?'

Her fingers felt like steel through the thin fabric of my blue blouse. She had spoken first, so I could answer. 'Chris is painting the most beautiful landscape,' I breathlessly explained, 'and I've got to get right back with fresh water before his large wash dries. It's important to keep the colours clean.'

'Why doesn't he come for his own water? Why do you wait on him?'

'He's painting, and he asked if I'd mind fetching him fresh water, and I wasn't doing anything but watching, and the twins would spill the water.'

'Fool! Never wait on a man! Make him wait on himself. Now, spill out the truth – what are you *really* doing up there?'

'Honest, I'm telling the truth. We're working hard to make the attic pretty so the twins won't be afraid up there, and Chris is a wonderful artist.'

She sneered and asked with contempt, 'How would *you* know?'

'He is gifted artistically, Grandmother – all his teachers said so.'

'Has he asked you to pose for him – without clothes?'

I was shocked. 'No. Of course not!'

'Then why are you trembling?'

'I'm . . . I'm scared of . . . of you,' I stammered. 'Every day you come in and ask what sinful, unholy thing we're doing, and truly, I don't know what it is you think we're doing. If you don't tell us exactly, how can we avoid doing something bad, not knowing it *is* bad?'

She looked me over, down to my bare feet, and smiled sarcastically. 'Ask your older brother – he'll know what I mean. The male of the species is born knowing everything evil.'

Boy, did I blink! Chris wasn't evil, or bad. There were times when he was tormenting, but not unholy. I tried to tell her this, but she didn't want to hear.

Later on in the day she came into our room bearing a clay pot of yellow chrysanthemums. Striding directly to me, she put that pot in my hands. 'Here are real flowers for your fake garden,' she said without warmth. It was such an unwitch-like thing for her to do, it took my breath away. Was she going to change, see us differently? Could she learn to like us? I thanked her effusively for the flowers, perhaps too much, for she spun around and stalked out, as if embarrassed.

Carrie came running to put her small face into the mass of yellow petals. 'Pretty,' she said. 'Cathy, can I have them?' Of course she could have them. With reverence that pot of flowers was placed on the eastern windowsills in the attic to receive the morning sunshine. There was nothing to see but hills and far-off mountains and the trees in between, and above everything hovered a blue mist. The real flowers spent the nights with us, so the twins could wake up in the morning and see something beautiful and alive growing near them.

Whenever I think of being young, I see again those blue-misted mountains and hills, and the trees that paraded stiffly up and down the slopes. And I smell again the dry and dusty air that was ours to breathe daily. I see again the shadows in the attic that blended so well with the shadows in my mind, and I hear again the unspoken, unanswered questions of Why? When? How much longer?

Love . . . I put so much faith in it.

Truth . . . I kept believing it falls always from the lips of the one you love and trust the most.

Faith . . . it's all bound up to love and trust. Where does one end and the other start, and how do you tell when love is the blindest of all?

More than two months had passed, and still the grandfather lived on.

We stood, we sat, we lay on the wide ledges of the attic dormer windows. We wistfully watched as the tree-tops of summer's old dark green turned overnight into the brilliant scarlets, golds, oranges, and browns of autumn. It moved me; I think it moved all of us, even the twins, to see the summer go away, and see the fall begin. And we could only watch, but never participate.

My thoughts took frantic flight, wanting to escape this prison, and seek out the wind so it could fan my hair and sting my skin, and make me feel alive again. I yearned for all those children out there who were running wild and free on the browning grass, and scuffling their feet in the dry, crackling leaves, just as I used to do.

Why was it I never realized when I was able to run wild and free that I was experiencing happiness? Why did I think back then, that happiness was always just ahead in the future, when I would be an adult, able to make my own decisions, go my own way, be my own person? Why had it seemed that being a child was never enough? Why had I thought that happiness reserved itself for those grown to full size?

'You're looking sad,' said Chris, who was crowded close beside me, with Cory on the other side of him, and Carrie on the other side of me. Nowadays Carrie was my little shadow to follow where I led, and mimic what I did, and imitate the way she thought I felt – just as Chris had his small mimicking shadow too, in Cory. If there were ever four siblings closer than we were, they would have had to have been Siamese quadruplets.

'Aren't you going to answer me?' asked Chris. 'Why are you looking so sad? The trees look beautiful, don't they? When it's summer, I like summer best; yet when fall comes, I like fall best, and when winter comes, then that's my favourite season, and then comes spring, and I think spring is best.'

Yes, that was my Christopher Doll. He could make do with the here and now, and always think it best, no matter what the circumstances.

'I was thinking back to old Mrs Bertram and her boring talk of the Boston Tea Party. She made history seem so dull, and the people so unreal. Yet, I'd like to be bored like that again.'

'Yeah,' he agreed, 'I know what you mean. I thought school a bore, too, and history a dull subject, particularly American history – all but the Indians, and the old West. But at least when we were in school, we were doing what other kids our ages did. Now we're just wasting time, doing nothing. Cathy, let's not waste one minute! Let's prepare ourselves for the day we get out. If you don't set your goals firmly in mind, and strive always to reach them, then you never do. I'll convince myself if I can't be a doctor, then I won't want to be anything else, or want anything more that money can buy!'

He said that so intensely. I wanted to be a prima ballerina, though I would settle for something else. Chris scowled as if reading my mind. He turned his summer-blue eyes on me and scolded because I hadn't practised my ballet exercises once since I'd come upstairs to exist. 'Cathy, tomorrow I'm attaching a barre in the portion of the attic we've finished decorating – and five or six hours each day, you are going to practice, just like in ballet class!'

'I am not! Nobody is going to tell me I have to do anything! Besides, you can't do ballet positions unless you are properly dressed for it!'

'What a stupid thing to say!'

'That's because I *am* stupid! *You*, Christopher, have *all* the brains!' With that I burst into tears and fled from the attic, racing past all the paper flora and fauna. Run, run, run for the stairs. Fly, fly, fly down the steep and narrow wooden steps, daring fate to make you fall. Break a leg, a neck, put you in a coffin dead. Make everybody sorry then; make them cry for the dancer I should have been.

I threw myself down on my bed and sobbed into the pillow. There was nothing here but dreams, hopes – nothing real. I'd grow old, ugly, never see lots of people again. That old man downstairs could live to be a hundred and ten! All those doctors would keep him living for ever – and I would miss out on Halloween – no tricking, no treating, no parties, no candy. Oh, I felt sorry for myself, and I vowed somebody was going to pay, pay, pay for all of this, somebody was, somebody was!

Wearing their dirty white sneakers, they came to me, my two brothers, my small sister, and each sought to give me comfort with small gifts of cherished possessions: Carrie's red and purple crayons, Cory's *Peter Rabbit* story book; but Chris, he just sat and looked at me. I never felt so small.

One evening quite late, Momma came in with a large box that she put in my hands to open. There amidst sheets of white tissue were ballet costumes, one a bright pink, the other azure-blue, with leotards and toe shoes to match the tulle tutus. 'From

Christopher,' was written on the enclosed small card. And there were records of ballet music. I started to cry as I flung my arms around my mother, then around my brother. This time they weren't tears of frustration, or despair. Now I had something to work towards.

'I wanted most of all to buy you a white costume,' said Momma, still hugging me. 'They had a beauty in a size too large to fit you, and with it comes a tight cap of white feathers that curl over your ears – for *Swan Lake* – and I ordered it for you, Cathy. Three costumes should be enough to give you inspiration, shouldn't they?'

Oh, yes! When Chris had the barre nailed securely to an attic wall, I practised for hours on end while the music played. There wasn't a large mirror behind the barre, like there had been in the classes I had attended, but there was a huge mirror in my mind, and I saw myself as Pavlova, performing before ten thousand enraptured people, and encore after encore I took, bowing and accepting dozens of bouquets, every one red roses. In time, Momma brought me every one of Tchaikovsky's ballets to play on the record player, which had been hooked up to a dozen extension cords, which went down the stairs and plugged into a socket in our bedroom.

Dancing to beautiful music took me out of myself, and made me forget momentarily that life was passing us by. What did it matter when I was dancing? Better to pirouette and pretend I had a partner to support me when I did the most difficult positions. I'd fall, get up, then dance on again until I was out of breath and ached in every muscle, and my leotards were glued to me with sweat, and my hair was wet. I'd fall down flat on the floor to rest, and pant, then up again at the barre to do pliés. Sometimes I would be the Princess Aurora in *The Sleeping Beauty* and sometimes I'd dance the part of the prince, as well, and leap high into the air and beat my feet together.

Once I looked up from my concluding dying swan spasms, and I saw Chris standing in the attic shadows, watching with the oddest expression on his face. Soon he'd be having a birthday, his fifteenth. How had it come about that already he seemed a man and not a boy? Was it only that vague look in his eyes that said he was moving quickly from childhood?

On full pointe I performed a sequence of those very small, even steps which are supposed to give the impression the dancer is gliding across the stage and creating what is poetically called 'a string of pearls'. In such a way I flitter-glided over to Chris and held out my arms. 'Come, Chris, be my *danseur*; let me teach you the way.'

He smiled, seeming bemused, but he shook his head and said that was impossible. 'Ballet dancing is not for me. But I'd like to learn to waltz – if the music is Strauss.'

He made me laugh. At that time the only waltz music we had (except ballet) was old Strauss records. I hurried over to the record player to take off the *Swan Lake* records, and I put on *The Blue Danube*.

Chris was clumsy. He held me awkwardly, as if embarrassed. He stepped on my pink pointe shoes. But it was touching how hard he tried to get simple steps right, and I couldn't tell him all his talents must reside in his brain, and in the skill of his artistic hands, for certainly none of it drifted down to his legs and feet. And yet, and yet, there was something sweet and endearing about a Strauss waltz, easy to do, and romantic, and so unlike those athletic ballet waltzes that put you in a sweat, and left you panting for breath.

When Momma finally came through the door with that smashing white outfit for dancing *Swan Lake*, a beautifully feathered brief bodice, tight cap, white slippers, and white leotards so sheer the pink of my skin showed through, I gasped!

Oh, it seemed that love, hope, and happiness *could be* brought upstairs in one single giant-sized slippery-satin white box with a violet ribbon and given to me by someone who really cared when another who really cared, put this idea in her head.

> 'Dance, Ballerina, dance, and do your pirouette
> In rhythm with your aching heart,
> Dance, Ballerina, dance, you mustn't once forget
> A dancer has to dance the part,
> Once you said his love must wait its turn,
> You wanted fame instead, I guess that's your concern,
> We live and learn . . . and love is gone, Ballerina,
> gone . . .'

Eventually, Chris could do the waltz and the foxtrot. When I tried to teach him the Charleston, he refused: 'I don't need to learn every kind of dance, like you do. I'm not going to be on stage; all I want to learn is how to get out on the dance floor with a girl in my arms, and not make a jackass of myself.'

I'd always been dancing. There wasn't any kind of dance I couldn't do, and didn't want to do.

'Chris, there's one thing you've got to know: you cannot waltz your whole life through, or do the foxtrot. Every year brings about changes, like in clothes. You've got to keep up with the times, and adapt. Come on, let's jazz it up a bit, so you can limber up your creaky joints that must be going stiff from so much sitting and reading.'

I stopped waltzing and ran to put on another record: 'You ain't nothin' but a hound dog.'

I raised my arms, and began to gyrate my hips.

'Rock 'n' roll, Chris, you've got to learn how. Listen to the beat, let go, and learn to swivel your hips like Elvis. Come on, half-close your eyes, look sleepy, sexy, and pout your lips, for if you don't, no girl is ever going to love you.'

'Then no girl is ever gonna love me.'

That's the way he said it, dead flat, and dead serious. He would never let anyone force him to do anything that didn't fit his image of himself, and in a way I liked him for being what he was, strong, resolute, determined to be his own person, even if his kind of person had long ago gone out of style. My Sir Christopher, the knight gallant.

God-like, we changed the seasons in the attic. We took down the flowers and hung up autumn leaves of brown, russet, scarlet and gold. If we were still here when winter's snowflakes fell, we'd then substitute lacy white designs that we were all four cutting out in preparation, just in case. We made wild ducks and geese from white, grey, and black craft paper, and aimed our mobile birds in wide-arrowed skeins, heading them south. Birds were easy to make: just elongated ovals with spheres for heads, teardrops with wings.

When Chris wasn't sitting with his head stuck in a book, he

was painting watercolour scenes of snow-covered hills with lakes where ice skaters skimmed. He put small houses of yellow and pink deeply buried in snow, and smoke curled from the chimneys, and in the distance rose a misty church steeple. And when he was done, he painted all around this a dark window-frame. When this was hung on the wall, we had a room with a view!

Once Chris had been a tease I could never please. An older brother . . . But, we changed up there, he and I, just as much as we altered our attic world. We lay side by side on an old mattress, stained and smelly, for hours on end, and talked and talked, making plans for the kind of lives we'd live once we were free and rich as Midas. We'd travel around the world. He would meet and fall in love with the most beautiful, sexy woman who was brilliant, understanding, charming, witty and enormous fun to be with; she'd be the perfect housekeeper, the most faithful of devoted wives, the best of mothers, and she'd never nag, or complain, or cry, or doubt his judgment, or be disappointed or discouraged if he made stupid mistakes on the stock market and lost all of their money. She'd understand he'd done his best, and soon he'd make a fortune again with his wits and clever brains.

Boy, did he leave me feeling low. How in the world was I ever going to fill the needs of a man like Chris? Somehow or other, I knew he was setting the standard from which I'd judge all my future suitors.

'Chris, this intelligent, charming, witty, gorgeous woman, can't she have even one little flaw?'

'Why should she have flaws?'

'Take our mother, for instance, you think she is all of those things, except, perhaps, brilliant.'

'Momma's not stupid!' he defended vehemently. 'She's just grown up in the wrong kind of environment! She was put down as a child, and made to feel inferior because she was a girl.'

As for me, after I'd been a prima ballerina for a number of years and was ready to marry and settle down, I didn't know what kind of man I wanted if he didn't measure up to Chris, or my father. I wanted him handsome, I knew that, for I wanted beautiful children. And I wanted him brilliant, or I might not respect him. Before I accepted his diamond engagement ring, I'd sit him down to play games, and if I won time and again, I'd smile, shake my head, and tell him to take his ring back to the store.

And as we made our plans for the future, our pots of philodendron drooped limp; our ivy leaves turned yellow before they died. We bustled about, giving our plants tender loving care, talking to them, pleading with them, asking them to please stop looking sick, and perk up and straighten up their necks. After all, they were getting the healthiest of all sunlight – that eastern morning light.

In a few more weeks Cory and Carrie stopped pleading to go outside. No longer did Carrie beat her small fists against the oak door, and Cory stopped trying to kick it down with his ineffectual small feet, wearing only soft sneakers that didn't keep his small toes from bruising.

They now docilely accepted what before they'd denied – the attic 'garden' was the only 'outside' available to them. And in time, pitiful as it was, they soon forgot there was a world other than the one we were locked up in.

Chris and I had dragged several old mattresses close to the eastern windows, so we could open the windows wide and sunbathe in the beneficial rays that didn't have to pass through dirty window glass first. Children needed sunlight in order to grow. All we had to do was look at our dying plants, and register what the attic air was doing to our greenery.

Unabashedly, we stripped off all our clothes and sunbathed in the short time the sun visited our windows. We saw each other's differences, and thought little about them, and frankly told Momma what we did, so we, too, wouldn't die from lack of sunlight. She glanced from Chris to me and weakly smiled. 'It's all right, but don't let your grandmother know. She wouldn't approve, as you well know.'

I know now that she looked at Chris, and then at me for signs to indicate our innocence, or our awakening sexuality. And what she saw must have given her some assurance we were still only children, though she should have known better.

The twins loved to be naked and play as babies. They laughed and giggled when they used terms such as 'do-do' and 'twiddle-dee', and enjoyed looking at the places where do-do came from, and wondered why Cory's twiddle-dee maker was so different from Carrie's.

'Why, Chris?' asked Carrie, pointing at what he had, and Cory had, and she and I didn't have.

I went right on reading *Wuthering Heights* and tried to ignore such silly talk.

But Chris tried to give an answer that was correct as well as truthful: 'All male creatures have their sexual organs on the outside and females have theirs tucked away inside.'

'*Neatly* inside,' I said.

'Yes, Cathy, I know you approve of your *neat* body and I approve of my *un-neat* body, so let all of us rejoice that we have what we do. Our parents accepted our bare skins just as they did our eyes and hair, and so shall we. And I forgot, male birds have their organs 'neatly' tucked away inside, too, like females.'

Intrigued, I asked, 'How do you know?'

'I just know.'

'You read it in a book?'

'What else – do you think I caught a bird and examined it?'

'I wouldn't put it past you.'

'At least I read to improve my brain, not just to entertain it.'

'You are going to make a very dull man, I'm warning – and if a male bird has tucked away sexual organs, doesn't that make him a her?'

'*No!*'

'But, Christopher, I don't understand: Why are birds different?'

'They have to be streamlined in order to fly.'

It was another of those puzzlements, and he had the answers. I just knew the brain of brains had the answers.

'All right, but why are male birds made the way they are? And leave out the streamlined part.'

He floundered, his face turned deeply red, and he sought a way to say something delicately. 'Male birds can be aroused, and that makes what is in, come out.'

'How are they aroused?'

'Shut up and read your book – and let me read mine!'

* * *

125

Some days were too chilly for sunbathing. Then it grew frigid, so even wearing our heaviest and warmest clothes, we still shivered unless we ran. Too soon the morning sun stole away from the east, leaving us desolate and wishing there were windows on the southern side. But the windows were shuttered over and locked.

'It doesn't matter,' said Momma, 'the morning sun is the healthiest.'

Words that didn't cheer us, since our plants were dying one by one while living in the healthiest sunlight of all.

As November began, the attic began to turn Arctic cold. Our teeth chattered, our noses ran, we sneezed often and complained to Momma that we needed a stove with a chimney, since the two stoves in the schoolroom had been disconnected. Momma spoke of bringing up an electric or gas heater. But she feared an electric stove might start a fire if connected to many extension cords. And a chimney was also needed for a gas heater.

She brought us long heavy underwear, and thick ski jackets with attached hoods, and bright ski pants with wool fleece lining. Wearing these clothes, we went daily into the attic where we could run free and escape the grandmother's ever observant eyes.

In our cluttered bedroom we barely had room to walk without colliding into something to bruise our shins. In the attic we went frantic, screaming as we chased one another: hiding, finding, putting on small plays with frenzied activity. We fought sometimes, argued, cried, then went back to fierce play. We had a passion for hide and seek. Chris and I enjoyed making this game terribly threatening but only mildly so for the twins, who were already terrified enough of the many 'bad things' that lingered in the dark attic shadows. Carrie earnestly said she saw monsters hiding behind the shrouded furniture.

One day, we were up in the attic polar zone, and searching to find Cory. 'I'm going downstairs,' said Carrie, her small face resentful, her lips pouted. No good to try and make her stay and exercise – she was too stubborn. She sashayed off in her little red ski outfit, leaving me and Chris to hunt around to find Cory. Customarily, he was just too easy to find. His way was to choose the last place Chris had hidden. So it was our belief we could go straight to the third massive armoire and there would be Cory, crouched down on the floor, hiding under the old clothes, and grinning up at us. We indulged him, avoiding this particular wardrobe for a specific length of time. Then we decided to 'find' him. And lo, when we looked – he wasn't there!

'Well, I'll be damned!' exclaimed Chris. 'He's finally going to be innovative and find an original place to hide.'

That's what came of reading so many books. Big words stuck to his brains. I swiped at my leaky nose, and then took another look around. If truly innovative, there were a million good hiding places in this multi-winged attic. Why, it might take us hours and hours to find Cory. And I was cold, tired and irritable, sick of playing this game Chris insisted on daily to keep us active.

'Cory!' I yelled. 'Come out from wherever you are! It's time to eat lunch!' Now, that should bring him. Meals were a cosy and homey thing to do, and they broke up our long days into separate portions.

Still, he didn't answer. I flashed angry eyes at Chris. 'Peanut-butter-and-grape-jelly sandwiches,' I added. Cory's favourite meal, which should bring him running. Still, not a sound, not a cry, nothing.

Suddenly I was scared. I couldn't believe Cory had overcome his fear of the immense, shadowy attic, and was at last taking the game seriously – but just suppose he was trying to imitate Chris or me? Oh, God! 'Chris!' I cried. 'We've got to find Cory, and fast!'

He caught my panic, and whirled about to run, crying out Cory's name, ordering him to come out, stop hiding! Both of us ran and hunted, calling Cory repeatedly. Hide-and-seek-time was over – lunchtime now! No answer, and I was nearly freezing, despite all my clothes. Even my hands looked blue.

'Oh, my God,' murmured Chris, pulling up short, 'just suppose he hid in one of the trunks, and the lid came down and accidentally latched?'

Cory would suffocate. He'd die!

Like crazy we ran and looked, throwing open the lids of every old trunk. We tossed out pantaloons, shifts, camisoles, petticoats, stays, suits, all with insane, distressed terror. And while I ran and searched, I prayed over and over again for God not to let Cory die.

'Cathy, I've found him!' shouted Chris. I spun around to see Chris lifting Cory's small, inert form from a trunk that had latched and kept him inside. Weak with relief, I stumbled over and kissed Cory's small, pale face, turned a funny colour from lack of oxygen. His slitted eyes were unfocused. He was very nearly unconscious. 'Momma,' he whispered, 'I want my momma.'

But Momma was miles away, learning how to type and take shorthand. There was only a pitiless grandmother we didn't know how to reach in an emergency.

'Run quick and fill the bathtub with hot water,' said Chris, 'but not too hot. We don't want to scald him.' Then he was racing with Cory in his arms towards the stairwell.

I reached the bedroom first, then sped on towards the bath. I glanced backwards to see Chris lay Cory down on his bed. Then he bent above, held Cory's nostrils, and then Chris lowered his head until his mouth covered Cory's blue lips, which were spread apart. My heart jumped! Was he dead? Had he stopped breathing?

Carrie took one glance at what was going on – her small twin blue and not moving – and she began to scream.

In the bathroom I turned on both faucets as far as they would go; full blast they gushed. Cory was going to die! Always I was dreaming of death and dying . . . and most of the times my dreams came true! And as always, just when I thought God had turned his back on us and didn't care, I whirled to grab hold of my faith, and prayed, demanding Him not to let Cory die '. . . *please God, please God, please, please, please* . . .'

Maybe my desperate prayers did as much to help Cory back to life as the artificial resuscitation Chris performed.

'He's breathing again,' said Chris, pale-faced and trembling as he carried Cory to the tub. 'Now all we have to do is warm him up.'

In no time at all we had Cory undressed and in the tub of warm water.

'Momma,' whispered Cory as he came to, 'I want Momma.' Over and over again he kept saying it, and I could have pounded my fists through the walls it was so damned unfair! He should have his mother, and not just a pretend mother who didn't know what to do. I wanted out of this, even if I had to beg in the streets!

But I said in a calm way that made Chris lift his head and smile at me with approval, 'Why can't you pretend *I'm* Momma? I'll do everything for you that she would. I'll hold you on my lap, and rock you to sleep while I sing you a lullaby, just as soon as you eat a little lunch, and drink some milk.'

Both Chris and I were kneeling as I said this. He was massaging Cory's small feet, while I rubbed his cold hands and made them warm again. When his flesh was coloured normally again, we dried Cory off, put on his warmest pyjamas, wrapped him in a blanket, and, in the old rocker Chris had brought down from the attic, I sat down and cuddled my small brother on my lap. I covered his wan face with kisses, and whispered sweet nothings in his ear that made him giggle.

If he could laugh, he could eat, and I fed him tiny bits of sandwich, and gave him sips of lukewarm soup, and long drinks of milk. And as I did this, I grew older. Ten years I aged in ten minutes. I glanced over at Chris as he sat down to eat his lunch, and saw that he, too, had changed. Now we knew there was real danger in the attic beyond that of slow withering from lack of sunlight and fresh air. We all faced threats much worse than the mice and spiders that insisted on living, despite all we did to kill every last one.

All alone Chris stalked up the narrow, steep stairs to the attic, his face grim as he entered the closet. I rocked on and on, holding both Carrie and Cory on my lap, and singing 'Rock-a-bye, Baby'. Suddenly there was a fierce hammering coming from above, a terrible clamour the servants might hear.

'Cathy,' said Cory in a small whisper while Carrie nodded off into sleep, 'I don't like not having a momma any more.'

'You do have a momma – you have me.'

'Are you as good as a real momma?'

'Yes, I think I am. I love you very much, Cory, and that's what makes a real mother.'

Cory stared up at me with wide blue eyes, to see if I was sincere, or if I were only mocking his need. Then his small arms crept up around my neck, and he cuddled his head on my shoulder. 'I'm so sleepy, Momma, but don't stop singing.'

I was still rocking, still singing softly, when Chris came back wearing a satisfied expression. 'Never again will a trunk lock inadvertently,' he said, 'for I smashed every last lock and the wardrobes, now they won't lock, either!'

I nodded.

He sat on the nearest bed and watched the slow rhythm of the rocking-chair, listening to the childish tune I kept right on singing. A slow flush heated his face so he seemed embarrassed. 'I feel so left out, Cathy. Would it be all right if I sat in the rocker first, and then the three of you piled on?'

Daddy used to do that. He'd hold all of us on his lap, even Momma. His arms had been long enough, and strong enough, to embrace us all, and give us the nicest, warmest feeling of security and love. I wondered if Chris could do the same.

As we sat in the rocker with Chris underneath, I caught a glimpse of us in the dresser mirror across the way. An eerie feeling stole over me, making all of this seem so unreal. He and I looked like doll parents, younger editions of Momma and Daddy.

'The Bible says there is a time for everything,' whispered Chris so as not to awaken the twins, 'a time to be born, a time to plant, a time to harvest, a time to die, and so on, and this is our time to sacrifice. Later on will come our time to live and enjoy.'

I turned my head and nestled it down on his boyish shoulder, grateful he was always so optimistic, always so cheerful. It felt good to have his strong young arms about me – almost as protective and good as Daddy's arms had been.

Chris was right, too. Our happy time would come the day we left this room and went downstairs to attend a funeral.

HOLIDAYS

On the tall stalk of the amaryllis a single bud appeared – a living calendar to remind us that Thanksgiving and Christmas were drawing nigh. It was our only plant alive now, and it was, by far, our most cherished possession. We carried it down from the attic to spend warm nights with us in the bedroom. Up first every morning, Cory rushed to see the bud, wanting to know if it had survived the night. Then Carrie would shortly follow him, to stand close at his side and admire a hardy plant, valiant, victorious, where others had failed. They checked the wall calendar to see if a day was encircled with green, indicating the plant needed to be fertilized. They felt the dirt to see if it needed water. They never trusted their own judgment, but would come to me and ask, 'Should we give Amaryllis water? Do you think she's thirsty?'

We never owned anything, inanimate or alive, that we didn't name, and Amaryllis was determined to live. Neither Cory nor Carrie would trust their frail strength to carry the heavy pot up to the attic windows, where the sunshine lingered but shortly. I was allowed to carry Amaryllis up, but Chris had to bring her down at night. And each night we took turns marking off a day with a big red X. We now had crossed off one hundred days.

The cold rains came, the fierce winds blew – sometimes heavy fog shut out the morning sunlight. The dry branches of the trees scraped the house at night and woke me up, making me suck in my breath, waiting, waiting, waiting for some horror to come in and eat me up.

On a day when it was pouring rain that might later turn into snow, Momma came breathless into our bedroom, bringing with her a box of pretty party decorations to put on our Thanksgiving Day table and make it festive. She had included a bright yellow tablecloth and orange linen napkins with fringe.

'We're having guests tomorrow for a midday dinner,' she

explained, dumping her box on the bed nearest the door, and already turning to leave. 'And two turkeys are being roasted: one for us, one for the servants. But they won't be ready early enough for your grandmother to put in the picnic basket. Now don't worry, I'm not allowing my children to live through a Thanksgiving Day without the feast to fit the occasion. Somehow I'll find a way to slip up some hot food, a little bit of everything we have. I think I'll make a big to-do about wanting to serve my father myself, and while I'm preparing his tray, I can put food on another tray to bring up to you. Expect to see me about one tomorrow.'

Like the wind through the door, she blew in, blew out, leaving us with happy anticipations of a huge, hot, Thanksgiving Day meal.

Carrie asked, 'What's Thanksgiving?'

Cory answered, 'Same as saying grace before meals.'

In a way he was right, I think. And since he'd said something voluntarily, darned if I was going to squelch him by any criticism.

While Chris cuddled the twins on his lap, sitting in one of the big lounge chairs, and told them of the first Thanksgiving Day so long ago, I bustled about like any hausfrau, very happy to set a festive holiday table. Our place cards were four small turkeys with tails that fanned out to make orange and yellow honeycombed paper plumage. We had two big pumpkin candles to burn, two Pilgrim men, two Pilgrim women, and two Indian candles, but darned if I could light such pretty candles and see them melt down into puddles. I put plain candles on the table to light, and saved the costly candles for other Thanksgiving Day meals when we were out of this place. On our little turkeys, I carefully lettered our names then fanned them open and placed one of them before each plate. Our dining-table had a small shelf underneath, and that's where we kept our dishes and silverware. After each meal I washed them in the bathroom in a pink plastic basin. Chris dried, then stacked the dishes in a rubber rack under the table to await the next meal.

I laid out the silverware most carefully, forks to the left, the knives to the right, blades facing the plates, and next to the knives, the spoons. Our china was Lenox with a wide blue rim, and edged in twenty-four-carat gold – all that was written on the back. Momma had already told me this was old dinnerware that the servants wouldn't miss. Our crystal today was footed, and I couldn't help but stand back to admire my own artistry. The only thing missing was flowers. Momma should have remembered to bring flowers.

One o'clock came and went. Carrie complained loudly. 'Let's eat our lunch now, Cathy!'

'Be patient. Momma is bringing us special hot food, turkey and all the fixings – and this will be dinner, not lunch.' My house-wifely chores done for a while, I curled up happily on the bed to read more of *Lorna Doone*.

'Cathy, my stomach don't have patience,' said Cory now, bringing me back from the mid-seventeenth century. Chris was deep into some Sherlock Holmes mystery that would be solved fast on the last page. Wouldn't it be wonderful if the twins could calm their stomachs, capacity about two ounces, by reading as Chris and I did?

'Eat a couple of raisins, Cory.'

'Don't have no more.'

'The correct way to say that is: I don't have any more, or there aren't any more.'

'Don't have no more, honest.'

'Eat a peanut.'

'Peanuts are all gone – did I say that right?'

'Yes,' I sighed. 'Eat a cracker.'

'Carrie ate the last cracker.'

'Carrie, why didn't you share those crackers with your brother?'

'He didn't want none then.'

Two o'clock. Now all of us were starving. We had trained our stomachs to eat at twelve o'clock sharp. Whatever was keeping Momma? Was she going to eat first herself, and then bring us our food? She hadn't told it that way.

A little after three o'clock, Momma rushed in, bearing a huge silver tray laden with covered dishes. She wore a dress of periwinkle-blue wool jersey, and her hair was waved back from her face and caught low at the nape of her neck with a silver barrette. Boy, did she look pretty!

'I know you're starving,' she immediately began to apologize, 'but my father changed his mind and decided at the last minute to use his wheelchair and eat with the rest of us.' She threw us a harried smile. 'Your table-setting is lovely, Cathy. You did everything just right. I'm sorry I forgot the flowers. I shouldn't have forgotten. We have nine guests, all busy talking to me, and asking a thousand questions about where I was for so long, and you just don't know the trouble I had slipping into the butler's pantry when John wasn't looking – that man has eyes in back of his head. And you never saw anyone hop up and down as much as I did; the guests must have thought I was very impolite, or just plain foolish – but I did manage to fill your dishes, and hide them away, then back to the dining-table I'd dash, and smile, and eat a bite before I had to get up again to blow my nose in another room. I answered three telephone calls that I made to myself from the private lines in my bedroom. I had to disguise my voice so no one would guess, and I really did want to bring you slices of pumpkin pie, but John had it sliced and already put on the dessert plates, so what could I do? He'd have noticed four missing pieces.'

She blew us a kiss, bestowed a dazzling, but hurried smile, and disappeared out the door.

Good-golly day! We sure did complicate her life, all right!

We rushed to the table to eat.

Chris bowed his head to say a hasty grace that couldn't have impressed God very much on this day, of all days, when His ears must ring with more eloquent phrasing: 'Thank you, Lord, for this belated Thanksgiving Day meal. Amen.'

Inwardly I smiled, for it was so like Chris to get directly to the point, and that was to play host, and dish up the food on to the plates we handed him one by one. He gave 'Finicky' and 'Picky' one slice of white turkey meat apiece, and tiny portions of the vegetables, and to each a salad that had been shaped in a pretty mould. The medium-sized portions were mine, and, of course, he served himself last – huge amounts for the one who needed it most, the brain.

Chris appeared ravenous. He forked into his mouth huge gobs

of mashed potatoes that were almost cold. Everything was on the verge of being cold, the gelatin salad was beginning to soften, and the lettuce beneath it was wilted.

'We-ee don't like cold food!' Carrie wailed as she stared down at her pretty plate with such dainty portions placed neatly in a circle. One thing you could say for Chris, he was precise.

You would have thought Miss Picky was looking at snakes and worms from the way she scowled at that plate, and Mr Finicky duplicated his twin's sour expression of distaste.

Honestly, I felt kind of sorry for Momma, who had tried so hard to bring us up a really good hot meal, and messed up her own meal in the process, making herself look silly in front of the guests, too. And now those two weren't going to eat anything! After three hours of complaining, and telling us how hungry they were! Kids!

The egghead across the way closed his eyes to savour the delight of having something different: deliciously prepared food, and not the hasty picnic junk thrown together in a hurry before six o'clock in the morning. Although to be fair to the grandmother, she didn't ever forget us. She must have had to get up in the dark to beat the chef and the maids into the kitchen.

Chris then did something that really shocked me. He knew better than to stab into a huge slice of white turkey meat and shove the whole slice into his mouth! What was the matter with him?

'Don't eat like that, Chris. It sets a bad example for you-know-who.'

'They aren't watching me,' he said with a mouthful, 'and I'm starving. I've never been so hungry before in my whole life, and everything tastes so good.'

Daintily, I cut my turkey into small bits, and put some in my mouth to show the hog across the way how it was properly done. I swallowed first, then said, 'I pity the wife you'll have. She'll divorce you within a year.'

He went on eating, deaf and dumb to everything but enjoyment.

'Cathy,' said Carrie, 'don't be mean to Chris, 'cause we don't like cold food, anyway, so we don't want to eat.'

'My wife will adore me so much, she'll be charmed to pick up my dirty socks. And Carrie, you and Cory like cold cereal with raisins, so *eat*!'

'We don't like cold turkey . . . and that brown stuff in the potatoes looks funny.'

'That brown stuff is called gravy, and it tastes delicious. And Eskimos *love* cold food.'

'Cathy, do Eskimos like cold food?'

'I don't know, Carrie. I suppose they'd better like it, or starve to death.' For the life of me, I couldn't understand what Eskimos had to do with Thanksgiving. 'Chris, couldn't you have said something better? Why bring up Eskimos?'

'Eskimos are Indians. Indians are part of the Thanksgiving Day tradition.'

'Oh.'

'You know, of course, the North American continent used to be connected with Asia,' he said between mouthfuls. 'Indians trekked over from Asia, and some liked ice and snow so much, they just stayed on, while others had better sense, and moved on down.'

'Cathy, what's this lumpy and bumpy stuff that looks like Jell-O?'

'It's cranberry salad. The lumps are whole cranberries; the bumps are pecan nuts; and the white stuff is sour cream.' And, boy, was it good! It had bits of pineapple, too.

'We don't like lumpy-bumpy stuff.'

'Carrie,' said Chris, 'I get tired of what you like and don't like – *eat*!'

'Your brother is right, Carrie. Cranberries are delicious, and so are nuts. Birds love to eat berries, and you like birds, don't you?'

'Birds don't eat berries. They eat dead spiders and other bugs. We saw them, we did. They picked them out of the gutters, and ate them without chewing! We can't eat what birds eat.'

'Shut up and eat,' said Chris, with a mouthful.

Here we were with the best food (even if it was almost cold) since we'd come upstairs to live in this hateful house, and all the twins could do was stare down at their plates, and so far hadn't eaten a single bite!

And Chris – he was demolishing everything in sight like the prize-winning hog at the county fair!

The twins tasted the mashed potatoes with the mushroom gravy. The potatoes were 'grainy' and the gravy was 'funny'. They tasted the absolutely divine stuffing, and declared that 'lumpy, grainy, and funny'.

'Eat the sweet potatoes, then!' I almost yelled. 'Look at how pretty they are. They're smooth because they've been whipped, and marshmallows have been added, and you love marshmallows, and it's flavoured with orange and lemon juice.' And pray to God they didn't notice the 'lumpy' pecans.

I guess between the two of them, sitting across from one another, fussily stirring the food into mishmash, they managed to put away three or four ounces of food.

While Chris was longing for dessert, pumpkin pie, or mince-meat pie, I began to clear away the table. Then, for some reason extraordinaire, Chris began to help! I couldn't believe it. He smiled at me disarmingly, and even kissed my cheeks. And, boy, if good food could do that for a man, I was all for learning gourmet cooking. He even picked up his socks before he came to help me wash and dry the dishes, glasses, and silverware.

Ten minutes after Chris and I had everything neatly stored away under the table and covered over with the clean towel, the twins simultaneously announced, 'We're hungry! Our stomachs hurt!'

Chris read on at his desk. I got up from the bed after laying aside *Lorna Doone*, and without saying one word, I gave to each of the twins a peanut-butter-and-jelly sandwich from the picnic basket.

As they ate, taking tiny bites, I threw myself down on the bed and watched them with real puzzlement. Why did they enjoy that junk? Being a parent wasn't as easy as I used to presume, nor was it such a delight.

'Don't sit on the floor, Cory. It's colder down there than in a chair.'

'Don't like chairs,' said Cory. Then he sneezed.

*   *   *

The very next day, Cory came down with a severe cold. His small face was red and hot. He complained that he ached all over and his bones hurt. 'Cathy, where is my momma, my real momma?' Oh, how he wanted his mother. Finally, she did show up.

Immediately she became anxious as she viewed Cory's flushed face, and she rushed away to fetch a thermometer. Unhappily, she returned, trailed by the detested grandmother.

With the slim stem of glass in his mouth, Cory stared up at his mother as if at a golden angel come to save him in his time of distress. And I, his pretend mother, was forgotten.

'Sweetheart, darling baby,' she crooned. And she picked him up from the bed and carried him to the rocker, where she sat down to put kisses on his brow. 'I'm here, darling. I love you. I'll take care of you and make the pains go away. Just eat your meals, and drink your orange juice like a good little boy, and soon you'll be well.'

She put him to bed again, and hovered over him before she popped an aspirin into his mouth and gave him water to swallow it down. Her blue eyes were misted over with troubled tears, and her slim white hands worked nervously.

I narrowed my eyes as I watched her eyes close, and her lips move as if in silent prayer.

Two days later Carrie was in the bed beside Cory, sneezing and coughing, too, and her temperature raged upwards with terrifying swiftness, enough to panic me. Chris looked scared, too. Listless and pale, the two of them lay side by side in the big bed, with little fingers clutching the covers high under their rounded chins.

They seemed made of porcelain, they were so waxy white, and their blue eyes grew larger and larger as they sank deeper and deeper into their skulls. Dark shadows came under their eyes, to make them seem haunted children. When our mother wasn't there, those two sets of eyes pleaded mutely with Chris and me to do something, anything, to make the misery go away.

Momma took a week off from the secretarial school so she could be with her twins as much as possible. I hated it that the grandmother felt it so necessary to trail after her every time she showed up. Always putting her nose in where it didn't belong, and her advice, when we didn't want her advice. Already she'd told us we didn't exist, and had no right to be alive on God's earth, save for those saintly and pure – like herself. Did she come merely to distress us more, and take from us the comfort of having our mother to ourselves?

The whisper of her menacing grey dresses, the sound of her voice, the tread of her heavy feet, the sight of her huge pale hands, soft and puffy, flashing with diamond rings, and spotted brown with dying pigment . . . oh, yes, just to see her was to loathe her.

Then there was our mother, rushing to us often, doing what she could to help the twins back to health. Shadows were under her eyes, too, as she gave the twins aspirins and water, and later on orange juice, and hot chicken soup.

One morning Momma rushed in carrying a big Thermos of orange juice she had just squeezed. 'It's better than the frozen or canned kind,' she explained, 'full of vitamins C and A, and that's good for colds.' Next she listed what she wanted Chris and me to do, saying that Chris and I were to give orange juice often. We stored the Thermos on the attic steps – as good as any refrigerator in the wintertime.

One glance at the thermometer from Carrie's lips, and a frenzied panic blew away all of Mamma's cool. 'Oh, God!' she cried out in distress. 'One hundred three-point-six. I have to take them to a doctor, a hospital!'

I was before the heavy dresser holding to it lightly with one hand and exercising my legs, as I did each day, now that the attic was too cold to limber up in. I threw my grandmother a quick glance, trying to read her reactions to this.

The grandmother had no patience for those who lost control and made waves. 'Don't be ridiculous, Corrine. All children run high fevers when they are sick. Doesn't mean a thing. You should know that by now. A cold is just a cold.'

Chris jerked his head up from the book he was pursuing. He believed the twins had the flu, though how they had caught the virus he couldn't guess.

The grandmother continued: 'Doctors, what do they know about curing a cold? We know just as much. There are only three things to do: stay in bed, drink lots of liquids, and take aspirins – what else? And aren't we doing all of those things?' She flashed me a mean look. 'Stop swinging your legs, girl. You make me nervous.' Again she directed her eyes, and her words, at our mother. 'Now, *my* mother had a saying, colds take three days coming, three days staying, and three days leaving.'

'What if they have the flu?' asked Chris. The grandmother turned her back and ignored his question. She didn't like his face; he resembled our father too much. 'I hate it when people who should know better question those who are older and far wiser. Everyone knows the rule for colds: six days to start and stay, and three to leave. That's the way it is – they'll recover.'

As the grandmother predicted, the twins recovered. Not in nine days . . . in nineteen days. Only bed rest, aspirins, and fluids did the trick – no prescriptions from a doctor to help them back to health more quickly. By day the twins stayed in the same bed; by night Carrie slept with me, and Cory with his brother. I don't know why Chris and I didn't come down with the same thing.

All night long we jumped up and down, to run for water, for orange juice kept cold on the attic stairs. They cried for cookies, for Momma, for something to unstop their nostrils. They tossed and fretted, weak and uneasy, worried by bothersome things they couldn't express except by large tearful eyes that tore at my heart. They asked questions while they were sick that they didn't ask while they were well . . . and wasn't that odd?

'Why do we stay upstairs all the time?'

'Has downstairs gone away?'

'Did it go where the sun hides?'

'Don't Momma like us no more?'

'Any more,' I corrected.

'Why are the walls fuzzy?'

'Are they fuzzy?' I asked in return.

'Chris, he looks fuzzy, too.'

'Chris is tired.'

'Are you tired, Chris?'

'Kinda. I'd like for you both to go to sleep and stop asking so many questions. And Cathy is tired, too. We'd both like to go to sleep, and know the two of you are sleeping soundly, too.'

'We don't *sound* when we sleep.'

Chris sighed, picked up Cory, and carried him over to the

rocker, and soon Carrie and I were seated on his lap. There we rocked back and forth, back and forth, telling stories at three o'clock in the morning. We read stories on other nights till four in the morning. If they cried and wanted Momma, as they incessantly did, Chris and I acted as mother and father and did what we could to soothe them with soft lullabies. We rocked so much the floorboards started to creak, and surely below someone could have heard.

And all the while we heard the wind blowing through the hills. It scraped the skeleton tree branches, and squeaked the house, and whispered of death and dying, and in the cracks and crevices it howled, moaned, sobbed, and sought in all ways to make us aware we weren't safe.

We read so much aloud, sang so much, both Chris and I grew hoarse and half-sick ourselves from fatigue. We prayed every night, down on our knees, asking God to make our twins well again. 'Please, God, give them back to us the way they were.'

A day came when the coughing eased, and sleepless eyelids drooped, and eventually closed in peaceful sleep. The cold, bony hands of death had reached for our little ones, and was reluctant to let go, for so tortuously, slowly, the twins drifted back to health. When they were 'well' they were not the same robust, lively pair. Cory, who had said little before, now said even less. Carrie, who had adored the sound of her own constant chatter, now became almost as truculent as Cory. And now that I had the quiet I so often longed for, I wanted back the bird-like chitchat that rattled on incessantly to dolls, trucks, trains, boats, pillows, plants, shoes, dresses, underpants, toys, puzzles, and games.

I checked her tongue, and it seemed pale, and white. Fearfully, I straightened to gaze down on two small faces side by side on one pillow. Why had I wanted them to grow up and act their proper ages? This long illness had brought about instant age. It put dark circles under their large blue eyes, and stole their healthy colour. The high temperatures and the coughing had left them with a wise look, a sometimes sly look of the old, the tired, the ones who just lay and didn't care if the sun came up, or if it went down, and stayed down. They scared me; their haunted faces took me into dreams of death.

And all the while the wind kept blowing.

Eventually they left their beds and walked about slowly. Legs once so plump and rosy and able to hop, jump, and skip were now as weak as thin straws. Now they were inclined to only creep instead of fly, and smile instead of laugh.

Wearily, I fell face down on my bed and thought and thought and thought – what could Chris and I do to restore their babyish charm?

There was nothing either he or I could do, though we would have given our health to restore theirs.

'Vitamins!' pronounced Momma when Chris and I took pains to point out the unhealthy differences in our twins. 'Vitamins are exactly what they need, and what you two need, as well – from now on, each one of you must take a daily vitamin capsule.' Even as she said this, her slim and elegant hand rose to fluff the glory of her beautifully coiffed, shining hair.

'Does fresh air and sunshine come in capsules?' I asked, perching on a nearby bed, and glaring hard at a mother who refused to see what was wrong. 'When each of us has swallowed a vitamin capsule a day, will that give to us the radiant good health we had when we lived normal lives, and spent most of our days outside?'

Momma was wearing pink – she did look lovely in pink. It put roses in her cheeks, and her hair glowed with rosy warmth.

'Cathy,' she said, tossing me a patronizing glance while she moved to hide her hands, 'why do you incessantly persist in making everything so hard for me? I do the best I can. Really I do. And, yes, if you want the truth, in vitamins you *can* swallow the good health the outdoors bestow – that is exactly the reason so many vitamins are made.'

Her indifference put more pain in my heart. My eyes flashed over to Chris, who had bowed his head low, taking all this in, but saying nothing. 'How long is our imprisonment going to last, Momma?'

'A short while, Cathy, only a short while longer – believe that.'

'Another month?'

'Possibly.'

'Could you manage, somehow, to sneak up here and take the twins outside, say for a ride in your car? You could plan it so the servants wouldn't see. I think it would make an immense amount of difference. Chris and I don't have to go.'

She spun around and glanced at my older brother to see if he were in this plot with me, but surprise was a dead giveaway on his face. 'No! Of course not! I can't take a risk like that! Eight servants work in this house, and though their quarters are quite cut off from the main house, there is always someone looking out a window, and they would hear me start up the car. Being curious, they'd look to see which direction I took.'

My voice turned cold. 'Then would you please see if you can manage to bring up fresh fruit, especially bananas. You know how the twins love bananas, and they haven't had one since we came.'

'Tomorrow I'll bring bananas. Your grandfather doesn't like them.'

'What has *he* got to do with it?'

'It's the reason bananas are not purchased.'

'You drive back and forth to secretarial school every weekday – stop yourself and buy the bananas – and more peanuts, and raisins. And why can't they have a box of popcorn once in a while? Certainly that won't rot their teeth!'

Pleasantly she nodded, and verbally agreed. 'And what would you like for yourself?' she asked.

'Freedom! I want to be let out. I'm tired of being in a locked room. I want the twins out; I want Chris out. I want you to rent a house, buy a house, steal a house – but get us out of *this* house!'

'Cathy,' she began to plead, 'I'm doing the best I can. Don't I bring you gifts every time I come through the door? What is it you lack besides bananas? Name it!'

'You promised we'd stay up here but a short while – and it's been months.'

She spread her hands in a supplicating gesture. 'Do you expect me to kill my father?'

Numbly I shook my head.

'You leave her alone!' Chris exploded the moment the door closed behind his goddess. 'She does try to do the best she can by us! Stop picking on her! It's a wonder she comes to see us at all, what with you riding her back, with your everlasting questions, like you don't trust her. How do you know how much she suffers?

Do you believe she's happy knowing her four children are locked in one room, and left to play in an attic?'

It was hard to tell about someone like our mother, just what she was thinking, and what she was feeling. Her expression was always calm, unruffled, though she often appeared tired. If her clothes were new, and expensive, and we seldom saw her wear the same thing twice, she brought us many new and expensive clothes, too. Not that it mattered what we wore. Nobody saw us but the grandmother, and we could have worn rags, which, indeed, might have put a smile of pleasure on her face.

We didn't go up to the attic when it rained, or when it snowed. Even on clear days, there was that wind to snarl fiercely as it blew, screaming and tearing through the cracks of the old house.

One night Cory woke up and called to me, 'Make the wind go away, Cathy.'

I left my bed and Carrie, who was fast asleep on her side, crawled under the covers beside Cory, and tightly I held him in my arms. Poor little thin body, wanting to be loved so much by his real mother . . . and he had only me. He felt too small, so fragile, as if that rampaging wind could blow him away. I lowered my face into his clean, sweet-smelling curly blond hair and kissed him there, as I had when he was a baby, and I had replaced my dolls with living babies. 'I can't make the wind go away, Cory. Only God can do that.'

'Then tell God I don't like the wind,' he said sleepily. 'Tell God the wind wants to come in and get me.'

I gathered him closer, held him tightly . . . *never going to let the wind take Cory away, never!* But I knew what he meant.

'Tell me a story, Cathy, so I can forget the wind.'

There was a favourite story I had concocted to please Cory, all about a fantasy world where little children lived in a small cosy home, with a mother and father who were much, much bigger, and powerful enough to scare away frightening things. A family of six, with a garden out in back, where giant trees held swings, and where real flowers grew – the kind that knew how to die in the fall, and how to come up again in the spring. There was a pet dog named Clover, and a cat named Calico, and a yellow bird sang in a golden cage all day long, and everybody loved everybody, and nobody was ever whipped, spanked, yelled at, nor were any of the doors locked, nor the draperies closed.

'Sing me a song, Cathy. I like it when you sing me to sleep.'

I held him snugly in my arms and began to sing lyrics I had written myself to music I had heard Cory hum over and over again . . . his own mind-music. It was a song meant to take from his fear of the wind, and perhaps take from me my fears too. It was my very first attempt to rhyme.

> I hear the wind when it sweeps down from the hill,
> It speaks to me, when the night is still,
> It whispers in my ear,
> The words I never hear,
> Even when he's near.

> I feel the breeze when it blows in from the sea,
> It lifts my hair, it caresses me,
> It never takes my hand,
> To show it understands,
> It never touches me, ten-der-ly.

> Some day I know I'm gonna climb this hill,
> I'll find another day,
> Some other voice to say the words I've got to hear,
> If I'm to live, another year . . .

And my little one was asleep in my arms, breathing evenly, feeling safe. Beyond his head Chris lay with his eyes wide open, fixed upwards on the ceiling. When my song was over, he turned his head and met my eyes. His fifteenth birthday had come and gone, with a bakery cake, and ice-cream to mark the occasion as special. Gifts – they came every day, almost. Now he had a Polaroid camera, a new and better watch. Great. Wonderful. How could he be so easily pleased?

Didn't he see our mother wasn't the same any more? Didn't he notice she no longer came every day? Was he so gullible he believed everything she said, every excuse she made?

* * *

Christmas Eve. We had been five months at Foxworth Hall. Not once had we been down into the lower sections of this enormous house, much less to the outside. We kept to the rules: we said grace before every meal: we knelt and said prayers beside our beds every night; we were modest in the bathroom; we kept our thoughts clean, pure, innocent . . . and yet, it seemed to me, day by day our meals grew poorer and poorer in quality.

I convinced myself it didn't really matter if we missed out on one Christmas shopping spree. There would be other Christmases when we were rich, rich, rich, when we could go into a store and buy anything we wanted. How beautiful we'd be in our magnificent clothes, with our stylish manners, and soft, eloquent voices that told the world we were somebodies . . . somebodies who were special . . . loved, wanted, needed somebodies.

Of course Chris and I knew there wasn't a real Santa Claus. But we very much wanted the twins to believe in Santa Claus, and not miss out on all that glorious enchantment of a fat jolly man who whizzed about the world to deliver to all children exactly what they wanted – even when they didn't know what they wanted until they had it.

What would childhood be like without believing in Santa Claus? Not the kind of childhood I wanted for our twins!

Even for those locked away, Christmas was a busy time, even for one beginning to despair, and doubt, and distrust. Secretly, Chris and I had been making gifts for Momma (who really didn't need anything), and gifts for the twins – plushy stuffed animals that we tediously backstitched by hand, and then filled with cotton. I did all the embroidery work on the faces when they were still flat. I was, in private in the bathroom, knitting Chris a cap of scarlet wool – it grew and it grew and it grew; I think Momma must have forgotten to tell me something about gauge.

Then Chris came up with an absolutely idiotic and horrific suggestion. 'Let's make the grandmother a gift, too. It's really not right to leave her out. She does bring up our food and milk, and who knows, a token like this may be just the thing needed to win over her affection. And think how much more enjoyable our lives would be if she could tolerate us.'

I was dopey enough to think it might work, and for hours and hours we slaved on a gift for an old witch who hated us. In all this time she had never even once said our names.

We bonded tan linen to a stretcher frame, glued on different coloured stones, then carefully applied gold and brown cording. If we made a mistake, ever so painstakingly we'd do it over and make it right so *she* wouldn't notice. She was bound to be a perfectionist who'd see the slightest flaw and frown. And never, truly, would we give *her* anything less than our best efforts could produce.

'You see,' said Chris again, 'I really do believe we have a chance in winning her over to our side. After all, she is our grandmother, and people *do* change. No one is static. While Momma works to charm her father, we must work to charm her mother. And even if she refuses to look at me, she does look at you.'

She didn't look at me, not really, she only saw my hair – for some reason she was fascinated by my hair.

'Remember, Cathy, she did give us yellow chrysanthemums.' He was right – that alone was a strong straw to grasp.

In the late afternoon, towards dusk, Momma came to our room bearing a live Christmas tree in a small wooden tub. A balsam tree – what could smell more like Christmas? Momma's wool dress was of bright red jersey; it clung and showed off all the curves I hoped to have one day. She was laughing and gay, making us happy, too, as she stayed to help us trim the tree with the miniature ornaments and lights she'd brought along. She gave us four stockings to drape on the bedposts for Santa to find and fill.

'Next year this time we'll be living in our own house,' she said brightly, and I believed.

'Yes,' said Momma, smiling, filling all of us with cheer, 'next year this time life will be so wonderful for all of us. We'll have plenty of money to buy a grand home of our own, and everything you want will be yours. In no time at all, you'll forget this room, the attic. And all the days you have all endured so bravely will be forgotten, just like it never happened.'

She kissed us, and said she loved us. We watched her leave and didn't feel bereft, as before. She filled all our eyes, all our hopes and dreams.

* * *

Momma came in the night while we slept. In the morning I woke up to see the stockings filled to the brim. And gifts galore were stacked under the small table where the tree was, and in every empty, available space in that room were all the toys for the twins that were too large and awkward to wrap.

My eyes met with Chris's. He winked, grinned, then bounded from his bed. He grabbed for the silver bells attached to red plastic reins, and he shook them vigorously above his head. 'Merry Christmas!' he boomed. 'Wake up, everybody! Cory, Carrie, you sleepy heads – open your eyes, get up, and behold! Look and see what Santa Claus brought!'

They came so slowly out of dreams, rubbing at sticky eyes, staring in disbelief at the many toys, at the beautifully wrapped packages with name tags, at the striped stockings stuffed with cookies, nuts, candy, fruit, chewing-gum, peppermint sticks, chocolate Santas.

Real candy – at last! Hard candy, that colourful kind that churches and schools gave out at their parties, the best kind of candy for making black holes in your teeth. Oh, but it looked and tasted so Christmasy!

Cory sat on his bed, bedazzled, and again his small fists lifted to rub at his eyes, and he appeared too bewildered for speech.

But Carrie could always find words. 'How did Santa Claus find us?'

'Oh, Santa has magic eyes,' explained Chris, who lifted Carrie up and swung her to his shoulder, and then he reached to do this to Cory, too. He was doing as Daddy would have done, and tears came to my eyes.

'Santa would never overlook children deliberately,' he said, 'and besides, he knew you were here. I made sure he knew, for I sat down and wrote him one very long letter, and gave him our address, and I made out a list of things we wanted that was three feet long.'

How funny, I thought. For the list of what all four of us wanted was so short and simple. We wanted outside. We wanted our freedom.

I sat up in bed and looked around, and felt a sour-sweet lump in my throat. Momma had tried, oh, yes. She'd tried, done her best from the way it looked. She did love us. she did care. Why, it must have taken her months to buy all of this.

I was ashamed and full of contrition for everything mean and ugly I'd thought. That's what came from wanting everything, and at once, and having no patience, and no faith.

Chris turned to look at me questioningly. 'Aren't you ever gonna get up? Gonna sit there the whole day through – you don't like gifts any more?'

While Cory and Carrie tore off gift wrappings, Chris came over to me and stretched out his hand. 'Come, Cathy, enjoy the only Christmas you'll have in your thirteenth year. Make this a unique Christmas, different from any we will experience in the future.' His blue eyes pleaded.

He was wearing rumpled red pyjamas piped in white, and his gold hair fluffed out wildly. I was wearing a red nightgown made of fleece, and my long hair was far more dishevelled than his. Into his warm hand I put my own, and I laughed. Christmas was Christmas, no matter where you were, and whatever the circumstances, it was still a day to enjoy. We opened everything wrapped, and we tried on our new clothes while stuffing candy into our mouths before breakfast. And 'Santa' had left a note telling us to hide the candy from a certain 'you-know-who'. After all, candy still caused cavities. Even on Christmas Day.

I sat on the floor wearing a stunning new robe of green velvet. Chris had a new robe of red flannel to match his pyjamas. I dressed the twins in their new robes of bright blue. I don't think there could have been four happier children than we were early that morning. Chocolate bars were devilishly divine and made even sweeter because they were forbidden. It was pure heaven to hold that chocolate in my mouth and slowly, slowly let it melt while I squeezed my eyelids tight to better savour the taste. And when I looked, Chris had his eyes closed too. Funny how the twins ate their chocolate, with wide open eyes, so full of surprise. Had they forgotten about candy? It seemed so, for they appeared to be holding paradise in their mouths. When we heard the doorknob rattle, we quickly hid the candy under the nearest bed.

It was the grandmother. She came in quietly, with the picnic basket. She put the basket on the gaming table. She didn't greet us with 'Merry Christmas', nor did she say good morning, nor even smile, or show in any way that this was a special day. And we were not to speak to her unless she spoke to us first.

It was with reluctance and fear, and also with great hope, that I picked up the long package wrapped in red foil that had come from one of Momma's gifts to us. Beneath that beautiful paper was our collage painting on which all four of us had worked to create a child's version of the perfect garden. The old trunks in the attic had provided us with fine materials, such as the gossamer silk to make the pastel butterflies that hovered over bright yarn flowers. How Carrie had wanted to make purple butterflies with red spots – she loved purple combined with red! If ever a more glorious butterfly existed – it wouldn't be a live one – it would be Cory's made of yellow, with green and black splotches, and tiny little red stone eyes. Our trees were made of brown cording, combined with tiny tan pebbles to look like bark, and the branches gracefully entwined so brightly coloured birds could perch or fly between the leaves. Chris and I had taken chicken feathers from old pillows and dipped them in watercolours, and dried them, and used an old toothbrush to comb the matted hairs, and make them lovely again.

It may be conceited to say that our picture showed signs of true artistry, and a great deal of creative ingenuity. Our composition was balanced, yet it had rhythm, style . . . and a charm that had brought tears to our mother's eyes when we showed it to her. She had to turn her back so we, too, wouldn't cry. Oh, yes, by far this collage was the very best piece of artwork we had as yet turned out.

Trembling, apprehensive, I waited to time my approach so her hands would be empty. Since the grandmother never looked at Chris, and the twins were so terrified of her they shrivelled in her presence, it was up to me to give her the gift . . . and darned if I could make my feet move. Sharply, Chris nudged me with his elbow. 'Go on,' he whispered, 'she'll go out the door in a minute.'

My feet seemed nailed to the floor. I held the long red package across both my arms. From the very positioning it seemed a sacrificial offering, for it wasn't easy to give her anything, when she had given us nothing but hostility, and was waiting her chance to give us pain.

That Christmas morning, she succeeded very well in giving us pain, even without a whip or a word.

I wanted to greet her in the proper way and say, 'Merry Christmas Day, Grandmother. We wanted to give you a little something. Really, don't thank us; it was no trouble at all. Just a little something to show how much we appreciate the food you bring to us each day, and the shelter you have given us.' No, no, she would think me sarcastic if I put it that way. Much better to say something like this: 'Merry Christmas, we hope you like this gift. We all worked on it, even Cory and Carrie, and you can keep it so when we're gone, you'll know we did try, we did.'

Just to see me near with the gift held before me took her by surprise.

Slowly, with my eyes lifting to bravely meet hers, I held out our Christmas offering. I didn't want to plead with my eyes. I wanted her to take it, and like it, and say thank you, even if she said it coldly. I wanted her to go to bed this night and think about us, that maybe we weren't so bad, after all. I wanted her to digest and savour all the work we'd put into her gift, and I wanted her to question the right and wrong of how she treated us.

In the most withering way, her cold and scornful eyes lowered to the long box we'd wrapped in red. On the top was a sprig of artificial holly and a huge silver bow. A card was tied to the bow, and read: 'To Grandmother, from Chris, Cathy, Cory and Carrie.'

Her grey-stone eyes lingered on the card long enough to read it. Then she lifted her gaze to stare directly into my hopeful eyes, pleading, begging, wanting so much to be assured we weren't – as I sometimes feared – evil. Back to the box her eyes skipped, then deliberately she turned her back. Without a word she stalked out of the door, slammed it hard, then locked it from the other side. I was left in the middle of the room, holding the end product of many long hours of striving for perfection and beauty.

Fools – that's what we'd been! Damned fools!

We'd never win her over! She'd always consider us Devil's spawn! As far as she was concerned, we really *didn't* exist.

And it hurt, oh, you bet, it did hurt. Right down to my bare feet I ached, and my heart became a hollow ball shooting pains through my chest. Behind me, I could hear Chris raspily breathing in and out, and the twins began to whimper.

This was my time to be adult, and keep the poise that Momma used so well and so effectively. I patterned my movements, and my expressions, after those of my mother. I used my hands the way she used hers. I smiled as she did, slow and beguiling.

And what did I do to demonstrate my maturity?

I hurled the package to the floor! I swore, using words I'd never said aloud before! I raised my foot and stomped down on it, and heard the cardboard box crunch. I screamed! Wild with fury, I jumped with both feet on to the gift, and I wildly stomped and jumped until I heard the cracking of the beautiful old frame we'd found in the attic, and reglued, and refinished and made it look almost like new again. I hated Chris for persuading me that we could win over a woman made of stone! I hated Momma for putting us in this position! She should have known her mother better; she should have sold shoes in a department store; certainly there was something she could have done but what she did.

Beneath the assault of someone wild and frenzied, the dry frame shattered into splinters; all our labour was gone, gone.

'Stop!' cried Chris. 'We can keep it for ourselves!'

Though he ran fast to prevent total destruction, the fragile painting was ruined. For ever gone. I was in tears.

Then I was bending down, crying, and picking up the silk butterflies Cory and Carrie had made so painstakingly, with so much effort wasted to colour the wings gloriously. Pastel butterflies I was to keep all my life long.

Chris held me fast in his arms while I sobbed as he tried to comfort me with fatherly words: 'It's all right. It doesn't matter what she does. We were right, and she was wrong. We tried. She never tries.'

We sat on the floor silent now amidst our gifts. The twins were quiet, their big eyes full of doubts, wanting to play with their toys, and undecided because they were our mirrors, and they would reflect our emotions – whatever they were. Oh, the pity of seeing them so made me ache again. I was twelve. I should learn at some time in my life how to act my age, and hold on to my poise, and not be a stick of dynamite always ready to explode.

Into our room Momma came, smiling and calling out her Christmas greetings. She came bearing more gifts, including a huge doll house that once had been hers . . . and her hateful mother's. 'This gift is *not* from Santa Claus,' she said, putting down the house on the floor with great care, and now, I swear, there wasn't one inch of uncluttered space left. 'This is my present to Cory and Carrie.' She hugged them both, and kissed their cheeks, and told them now they could 'pretend house' and 'pretend parents' and 'pretend host and hostess', just as she used to do when she was a child of five.

If she noticed none of us was really excited by that grand doll house, she didn't comment. With laughter, and gay charm, she knelt on the floor and sat back on her heels, and told us of how very much she used to love this doll house.

'It is very valuable, too,' she gushed. 'On the right market, a doll house like this would bring a fabulous fortune. Just the miniature porcelain dolls with the moveable joints alone are priceless, their faces all hand-painted. The dolls are made in scale to the house, as is the furniture, the paintings – everything, in fact. The house was handcrafted by an artist who lived in England. Each chair, table, bed, lamp, chandelier – all are genuine reproductions of antiques. I understand it took the craftsman twelve years to complete this.

'Look at how the little doors open and close, perfectly hung which is more than you can say for the house you're living in,' she went on. 'And all the drawers slide in and out. There's a tiny little key to lock the desk, and look how some of the doors slide into the walls – pocket doors, they are called. I wish this house had doors like that; I don't know why they went out of fashion. And see the hand-carved mouldings near the ceiling, and the wain-scoting in the dining-room and library – and the teensy books on the shelves. Believe it or not, if you have a microscope, you can read the text!'

She demonstrated with knowing, careful fingers all the fascin-ations of a doll house only children of the extremely wealthy could ever hope to own.

Chris, of course, had to pull out a tiny book and hold it close to his squinting eyes, to see for himself print so small you needed a microscope. (There was a very special type of microscope he hoped to own some day . . . and I hoped to be the one to give it to him.)

I couldn't help but admire the skill and patience it would take to make such small furniture. There was a grand piano in the front parlour of the Elizabethan house. The piano was covered with a silken paisley shawl, with fringes of gold. Little-bitty silk flowers were centred on the dining-room table. Bitsy fruit made of wax was in a silver bowl on the buffet. Two crystal chandeliers hung down, and real candles were fitted into sockets. Servants were in the kitchen, wearing aprons while they prepared dinner. A butler wore livery white while he stood near the front door to greet the arriving guests, while in the front parlour the beautifully gowned ladies stood stiffly near poker-faced men.

Upstairs in the nursery were three children, and a baby was in the crib, arms outstretched and ready to be lifted up. A side building was attached, somewhat to the rear, and in there was such a coach! And two horses were in the stables! Golly day! Who would ever dream people could make things so small! My eyes jumped to the windows, drinking in the dainty white curtains and heavy drapes, and dishes were on the dining-table, and silverware, and pots and pans were in the kitchen cupboards – all so tiny they were no bigger than large green peas.

'Cathy,' said Momma, putting her arms around me, 'look at this little rug. It is a genuine Persian, made of pure silk. The rug in the dining-room is an Oriental.' And on and on she extolled the virtues of this remarkable plaything.

'How can it look so new, yet be so old?' I asked.

A dark cloud passed over Momma and shadowed her face. 'When it belonged to my mother, it was kept in a huge glass box. She was allowed to look at it, but she could never touch it. When it was given to me, my father took a hammer and broke the glass box and he allowed me to play with everything – on the condition that I would swear, with my hand on the Bible, not to break anything.'

'Did you swear and did you break anything?' questioned Chris.

'Yes, I swore, and yes, I did break something.' Her head bowed low so we couldn't watch her eyes. 'There was another doll, a very handsome young man, and his arm came off when I tried to take off his coat. I was whipped, not only for breaking the doll, but for wanting to see what was underneath the clothes.'

Chris and I sat silent, but Carrie perked up and showed great interest in the funny little dolls in their fancy, colourful costumes. She particularly favoured the baby in the crib. Because she was so interested, Cory moved so he, too, could investigate the many treasures of the doll house.

That was when Momma turned her attention on me. 'Cathy, why were you looking so solemn when I came in? Didn't you like your gifts?'

Because I couldn't answer, Chris answered for me. 'She's unhappy because the grandmother refused the gift we made for her.' Momma patted my shoulder but she avoided my eyes. Chris continued, 'And thank you for everything – there's nothing you didn't remind Santa Claus to bring. Thank you most of all for the doll house. I think our twins are going to have more fun with that than anything else.'

I fixed my gaze on the two tricycles for the twins to ride in the attic and strengthen their thin, weak legs while they pedalled. There were roller-skates for Chris and me to use in the attic schoolroom only. That room was insulated with plastered walls, and hardwood flooring, making it more soundproof than the rest of the attic.

Momma got up from her knees, smiling mysteriously before she left. Just outside the door she said she'd be back in a second or two, and that is when she really gave us the best gift of all – a small, portable TV set! 'My father gave this to me to use in my bedroom. And immediately I knew just who would enjoy it the most. Now you have a real window through which you can view the world.'

Just the right words to send my hopes flying high into the sky! 'Momma!' I cried out. 'Your father gave you an expensive gift? Does that mean he likes you now? Has he forgiven you for marrying Daddy? Can we go downstairs now?'

Her blue eyes went dark and troubled again, and there was no joy when she told us that yes, her father was friendlier – he had forgiven her for committing a sin against God, and society. Then she said something that jumped my heart right up against my throat.

'Next week, my father is having his lawyer write me into his will. He is going to leave me everything; even this house will be mine after my mother dies. He isn't planning on leaving her money, because she has wealth she inherited from *her* father and mother.'

Money – I didn't care anything about it. All I wanted was out! And suddenly I was very happy – so happy I flung my arms around Momma, kissed her cheek, and hugged her tight. Golly-lolly, this was the best day since we'd come to this house . . . and then I remembered, Momma hadn't said we could go downstairs yet. *But*, we were one step on our way to freedom.

Our mother sat on the bed and smiled with her lips, though not her eyes. She laughed at some silly things Chris and I said, and it was laughter brittle and hard, not at all her kind of laugh. 'Yes, Cathy, I have become the dutiful, obedient daughter your grandfather always wanted. He speaks, I obey. He orders, I jump. I have at last managed to please him.' She stopped abruptly and looked towards the double windows and the pale light beyond. 'As a matter of fact, I have pleased him so well he is giving me a party tonight to reintroduce me to my old friends, and the local society. It is to be a grand affair, for my parents do everything in a big way when they entertain. They don't imbibe themselves, but they don't mind serving liquor to those who don't fear hell. So, of course, it will be catered, and there will also be a small orchestra for dancing.'

A party! A Christmas party! With an orchestra for dancing! And catered! And Momma was being written into the new will. Was there ever such a happy wonderful day?

'Can we watch?' Chris and I cried out almost simultaneously.

'We'll be very quiet.'

'We'll hide so no one can see us.'

'Please, Momma, please, it's been so long since we saw other people, and we've never been to a Christmas Day party.'

We pleaded and pleaded until at last she could resist no longer.

She drew Chris and me aside, to a far corner where the twins couldn't overhear, and she whispered, 'There is one place where the two of you can hide and still be able to watch, but I cannot risk the twins. They're too young to be trusted and you know they can't sit still for longer than two seconds, and Carrie would probably scream out in delight, and rivet everyone's attention. So, swear on your word of honour you will not tell them.'

We promised. No, of course we wouldn't tell them, even without a vow to keep our silence. We loved our little twins, and we wouldn't hurt their feelings by letting them know they were missing out.

We sang Christmas carols after Momma had gone, and the day passed cheerfully enough, though there was nothing special in the picnic basket for us to eat: ham sandwiches, which the twins didn't like, and cold slices of turkey that were still icy, as if they had been taken from the freezer. Left-overs from Thanksgiving Day.

As evening came on so early, I sat for the longest time gazing over at the doll house, where Carrie and Cory played happily with the tiny porcelain people and the priceless miniatures.

Funny how much you can learn from inanimate objects that a little girl had once owned, and been allowed to look at, but never touch. And then another little girl came along, and the doll house was given to her, and the glass box smashed just so she COULD touch the objects inside so she could be punished – when she broke something.

A shivering thought came: I wondered just what Carrie or Cory would break, and what their punishment would be.

I shoved a bit of chocolate into my mouth, and sweetened the sourness of my roving, wicked thoughts.

THE CHRISTMAS PARTY

True to her word, not long after the twins were sound asleep, Momma slipped into our room. She looked so beautiful my heart swelled with pride and admiration, and with some envy too. Her long formal gown had a skirt of flowing green chiffon; the bodice was of a deeper green velvet, cut low to show off a lot of cleavage. Underneath the streaming panels of lighter green chiffon were shoestring straps that glittered. Diamond-and-emerald earrings dangled long and sparkling. Her scent reminded me of a musky, perfumed garden on a moonlit night somewhere in the Orient. No wonder Chris stared at her as if dazzled. Wistfully I sighed. *Oh God, please let me look like that one day . . . let me have all those swelling curves that men so admire.*

And when she moved, the panels of chiffon floated as wings, leading us out of our sequestered dim place for the first time. Down all the dark and wide halls of the northern wing we followed close at Momma's silver heels. She whispered, 'There's a place where I used to hide when I was a child, to watch the adult parties without my parents knowing. It's going to be cramped for the two of you, but it's the only place where you can hide and still see. Now promise again to be quiet, and if you get sleepy, slip unseen back to your room – remember how to get there.' She told us not to watch longer than an hour, for the twins would be frightened to wake up and find themselves alone. Then, possibly, they'd wander out into the hall, looking for us – and God alone knew what could happen if they did.

We were secreted inside a massive oblong dark table, with cabinet doors underneath. It was uncomfortable, and very stuffy, but we could see well enough through the fine, mesh-like screen on the back side.

Silently, Momma stole away.

Far below us was a mammoth room brilliantly lit with candles fitted in the five tiers of three gigantic crystal and gold chandeliers suspended from a ceiling so high above, we couldn't see it. I never saw so many candles burning all at once! The scent of them, the way flickering lights glowed and caught in the sparkling prisms, to scatter and defract beams of iridescence from all the jewellery the women wore, made it a scene from a dream – no, better, more like a movie, sharp, clear, a ballroom where Cinderella and Prince Charming might dance!

Hundreds of richly dressed people milled about, laughing, talking. And over in the corner towered a Christmas tree that was beyond belief! It must have been more than twenty feet high, and it sparkled all over with thousands of golden lights to shine on the colourful ornaments and bedazzle your eyes!

Dozens of servants in black-and-red uniforms flowed in and out of the ballroom, bearing silver trays laden with dainty party food, and they set them on long tables where a giant crystal fountain sprayed pale amber fluid into a silver receiving bowl. Many men and women came to hold stemmed goblets and catch the sparkling liquid. There were two other punchbowls of silver, with small matching cups – both bowls large enough for a child to bathe in. It was beautiful, glamorous, exciting, exhilarating, . . . and so good to know that happy living was still going on outside our locked door.

'Cathy,' whispered Chris into my ear, 'I'd sell my soul to the Devil to have just one single sip from that crystal-and-silver fountain!'

My very same thought!

Never had I felt so hungry, so thirsty, so deprived. Yet we both were charmed, enchanted, and bedazzled by all the splendour of what great wealth could buy and display. The floor where couples danced was laid out in mosaic patterns, and was waxed so it gleamed like reflecting glass. Huge gold-framed mirrors were on the walls, reflecting back the dancers so you could hardly tell the images from the reality. The frames of the many chairs and sofas lining the walls were gold-coloured, and the padded seats and backs were of red velvet, or white brocade. French chairs, of course – they just had to be Louis XIV or XV. Fancy, good-golly day!

Chris and I stared at the couples, who were the most beautiful and young. We commented on their clothing, their hairstyles, and speculated on what relationships they had going for them. But most of all we watched our mother, who was the centre of attention. Most often she danced with a tall, handsome man with dark hair and a big moustache. He was the one who brought her stemmed goblets, and a plate of food, and they sat on a velvet couch to eat canapés and hors d'oeuvres. I thought they sat too close. Quickly I took my eyes from them, to take a look at the three chefs behind the long tables, still cooking what looked like pancakes to me, and little sausages to be stuffed with fillings. The aroma of all that drifted up to us, making our salivary glands overwork.

Our meals were monotonous, boring things: sandwiches, soups, and that everlasting fried chicken and eternal potato salad. Down there was a gourmet feast of everything delicious. Food was hot down there. Ours was seldom even warm. We kept our milk on the attic stairs so it wouldn't sour – and sometimes we found ice on the top. If we kept our picnic basket of food on the attic stairs, the mice stole down to nibble on everything.

From time to time, Momma disappeared with that man. Where did they go, and what did they do? Did they kiss? Was she falling in love? Even from my high and remote place in the cabinet, I could tell that man was fascinated by Momma. He couldn't take his eyes from her face, or keep his hands from touching her. And when they danced to music that was slow, he held her so his cheek pressed to hers. When they stopped dancing, he kept his arm around her shoulders, or her waist – and once he dared to even touch her breast!

I thought that now she would slap his good-looking face – for I would! But she only turned and laughed, and pushed him away, saying something that must have been a warning not to do that in public. And he smiled and took her hand and raised it to his lips while their eyes locked long and meaningfully – or so I thought.

'Chris, do you see Momma with that man?'

'Sure I see them. He's just as tall as Daddy was.'

'Did you see what he just did?'

'They're eating and drinking, and laughing and talking, and

dancing, just like everybody else. Cathy, just think, when Momma inherits all that money, we can have parties like this on Christmas, and on our birthdays. Why, in the future, we might even have some of the very same guests we see now. Let's send invitations to our friends back in Gladstone. Boy, won't they be surprised to see what we inherit!'

Just then, Momma and that man got up from the couch and left. So we fastened our charmed eyes on the second most attractive woman in the group below and watched her, and pitied her, for how could she compete with our mother?

Then into the ballroom strode our grandmother looking neither left nor right, nor smiling at anyone. Her dress wasn't grey – and that alone was enough to astonish us. Her long formal gown was of ruby-red velvet, tight in the front and flowing in the back, and her hair was piled high on her head, and curled elaborately, and ruby and diamond jewellery sparkled on her neck, ears, arms and fingers. Who would ever think that impressive, regal-looking woman down there was the menacing grandmother who visited us each day?

Reluctantly, we had to admit in whispers back and forth: 'She does look magnificent.'

'Yes, very impressive. Like an Amazon, too big.'

'A mean Amazon.'

'Yeah, a warrior Amazon, ready to do battle with the glare of her eyes alone. She doesn't really need any other weapon.'

That's when we saw him! Our unknown grandfather!

It stole my breath away to look down and see a man so very much like our father, if he had lived long enough to become old and feeble. He sat in a shiny wheelchair, dressed in a tuxedo, and his formal shirt was white with black trim. His thinnning blond hair was almost white, and it shone silver under the lights. His skin was unlined, at least viewed from our far and high and hidden place. Appalled, as well as fascinated, neither Chris nor I could move our eyes anywhere else once we spied him.

He was fragile looking, but still unnaturally handsome for a man of his great age of sixty-seven, and a man who was near dead. Suddenly, frighteningly, he raised his head and he gazed upwards, directly at our hiding place! For one awful, terrifying moment, it seemed he knew we were there, hidden behind the wire screen! A small smile played on his lips. Oh, dear God, what did that smile mean?

Still, he didn't look nearly as heartless as the grandmother. Could he truly be the cruel and arbitrary tyrant we presumed him to be? From the gentle, kindly smiles he bestowed on all those who came up to greet him, and shake his hand, and pat his shoulder, he seemed benign enough. Just an old man in a wheelchair, who really didn't look very sick. Yet, he was the one who had ordered our mother to be stripped and whipped from her neck down to her heels, and he had watched. So, how could we ever forgive him for that?

'I didn't know he would look like Daddy,' I whispered to Chris.

'Why not? Daddy was his much younger half-brother. Grandfather was a grown man before our father was born, and married, too, with two sons of his own, before he had a half-brother.'

That was Malcolm Neal Foxworth down there, the one who had kicked out his younger step-mother and her little son.

Poor Momma. How could we blame her for falling in love with a half-uncle when he was young, and as handsome and charming as our father had been? With such parents as she'd described, she *did* have to have someone to love, and she *did* need to be loved in return . . . she did . . . he did.

Love, it came unbidden.

You couldn't help whom you fell in love with – Cupid's arrows were ill aimed. Such ran the whispered comments between Chris and me.

Then, we were suddenly hushed by the footfalls and voices of two people approaching our hiding place.

'Corrine hasn't changed at all,' said a man unseen by us, 'only to grow more beautiful, and even more mysterious. She's a very intriguing woman.'

'Hah! That's because you always did have a yen for her, Al,' responded his female companion. 'Too bad she didn't have eyes for you instead of Christopher Foxworth. Now there was a man who was really something else. But I marvel that those two narrow-minded bigots down there would allow themselves to forgive Corrine for marrying her half-uncle.'

'They have to forgive her. When you have only one child left out of three, you are forced to take that one back into the fold.'

'Isn't it peculiar how things work out?' asked the woman, her voice thick and guttural from too much liquor. 'Three children . . . and only the despised, regretted one is left to inherit all of this.'

The half-drunken man chortled. 'Corrine wasn't always so despised. Remember how the old man adored her? She could do no wrong in his eyes until she eloped with Christopher. But that harridan mother of hers never had any patience with her daughter. Jealous, maybe. But what a luscious, rich plum to fall into the hands of Bartholomew Winslow. Wish it were mine!' said the unseen Al, wistfully.

'I'll bet you do!' sarcastically scoffed the woman, who set something down on our table that sounded like a glass with ice inside. 'A beautiful, young, and rich woman is indeed a plum for any man. Much too heady for a slob like you, Albert Donne. Corrine Foxworth would never look at you, not now, not even when you were young. Besides, you're stuck with me.'

The bickering pair drifted out of earshot. Other voices came and went as the long hours passed. My brother and I were tired now of watching, and we were both very much needing the bathroom. Plus we were worried about the twins, left alone in the bedroom. What if one of the guests wandered into the forbidden room and saw the sleeping twins? Then all the world – and our grandfather – would know that our mother had four children.

A crowd gathered around our hiding place to laugh, talk, and drink. It took them for ever to move away and give us the opportunity to open the cabinet door with extreme caution. Seeing no one, we scampered out, then dashed pell-mell in the direction from which we'd come. Breathless and panting, our bladders full enough to pop, we reached our quiet, cloistered place unseen, unheard.

And just as we'd left them, our twins lay deeply asleep in separate beds. They seemed identical, weak-looking pale dolls . . . like children used to look a long time ago in the pictures in history books. They weren't today's kind of children at all – but once they'd been. And they would be again, I vowed!

Next thing, Chris and I were arguing over who got to use the bathroom first – and this was easily settled. He just pushed me down on a bed and took off, slamming the bathroom door behind him and locking it. I fumed that it seemed to take him for ever to empty his bladder. Good golly, how could he hold so much?

Nature's calls eased, bickering over, we huddled together to discuss what we'd just witnessed and overheard.

'Do you think Momma plans to marry Bartholomew Winslow?' I asked, twisting my ever-present anxieties into a knot.

'How do I know?' answered Chris in an offhand manner. 'Though it certainly seems everybody else thinks she will, and, of course, they know more about that side of her than we do.'

What an odd thing to say. Didn't we, her children, know our mother better than anyone else?

'Chris, why did you say that?'

'What?'

'What you did – about others knowing her better than we do.'

'People are multi-faceted, Cathy. To us, our mother is only our mother. To others, she is a beautiful, sexy young widow who is likely to inherit a fortune. No wonder the moths all come swarming to encircle the kind of bright flame she is.'

Wow! And he was taking all of this so casually, just as if it didn't matter to him one whit – when I knew it did. I thought I knew my brother very well. He must be suffering inside, just as I was, for I knew he didn't want our mother to marry again. I turned my most intuitive eyes upon him . . . ah, he wasn't nearly as detached as he seemed, and that pleased me.

I sighed, though, for I would so much like to be the eternal optimist, like him. Deep down I thought life was sure to always put me between Scylla and Charybdis, and give to me always Hobson's choice. I had to make myself over, make myself better, and become like Chris – eternally cheerful. When I suffered, I had to learn to hide it, as he did. I had to learn to smile and never frown, and not be the genuine clairvoyant I was.

Already we had discussed between us the possibility that our mother might marry again, and neither one of us wanted that to happen. We thought of her as still belonging to our father; we wanted her to be faithful to his memory, ever constant to his first love. And if she remarried, just where would the four of us fit in? Would that Winslow man, with his handsome face and big moustache, want four children who weren't his?

'Cathy,' mused Chris aloud. 'Do you realize this is the perfect time to explore this house? Our door is unlocked, the grandparents are downstairs. Momma is occupied – the perfect chance to find out all we can about this house.'

'No!' I cried, frightened. 'Suppose the grandmother found out? She'd whip the skin off all of us!'

'Then you stay with the twins,' he said with surprising firmness. 'If I'm caught, which I won't be, I'll suffer the whipping and take all the blame. Think of it this way, some day we may need to know how to escape this house.' An amused smile curved his lips before he went on. 'I'm going to disguise myself, anyway, just in case I'm seen.'

Disguise? How?

But I'd forgotten the treasure trove of old clothes in the attic. He was up there only a few minutes before he came down, wearing an old-fashioned dark suit that wasn't much too large. Chris was big for his age. Over his blond head he'd fitted a ratty, dark wig he'd found in a trunk. Just possibly he *might* be mistaken for a small man if the lights were dim enough – a ridiculously funny-looking man!

Jauntily, he paraded back and forth in front of me. Then he leaned forward and stalked around Groucho Marx-style, holding an invisible cigar. He stopped directly in front of me, grinning self-consciously as he bowed deeply and doffed an invisible top hat in a wide and gentlemanly gesture of respect. I had to laugh, and he laughed too, and not just with his eyes, then he straightened up to say, 'Now, tell me truthfully, who could recognize this dark and sinister small man as belonging to the giant Foxworth clan?'

No one! For who had ever seen a Foxworth such as he? An awkward, lean and gangling one, with clear-cut features, and dark birdnest hair, plus a smudgy pencil moustache? Not a photograph in the attic resembled what swaggered about, showing off.

'Okay, Chris, cut the act. Go on, find out what you can, but don't stay away too long, either, I don't like it here without you.'

He came closer to whisper in a sly and conspiratorial stage

whisper, 'I'll be back soon, my fair beauty, and when I'm back, I shall bring with me all the dark and mysterious secrets of this huge, huge, old, old house.' And suddenly, he caught me by surprise, and swooped to plant a kiss on my cheek.

Secrets? And he said *I* was given to exaggerations! What was the matter with him? Didn't he know that *we* were the secrets?

I was already bathed and shampooed and dressed for bed, and, of course, on Christmas night, I couldn't go to bed in a nightgown I'd worn before – not when I had several new ones 'Santa' had brought. It was a lovely gown I wore, white, with full long sleeves that ruffled at the wrists, and was beaded through with blue satin ribbon, and everything was lace-edged, with smocking across the front and back of the bodice, and dainty pink roses with a tracery of delicately embroidered green leaves. It was one lovely nightgown, exquisitely made, and it made me feel beautiful and exquisite just to have it on.

Chris swept his eyes from my hair down to my bare toes that just barely peeked from beneath my long gown, and his eyes told me something they'd never said quite as eloquently before. He stared at my face, at my hair that cascaded down past my waist, and I knew it gleamed from all the brushing I gave it every day. He seemed impressed and dazzled, just as he had when he'd gazed so long at Momma's swelling bosom above the green velvet bodice.

And no wonder he had kissed me voluntarily – I was so princess-like.

He stood in the doorway, hesitating, still looking at me in my new nightgown, and I guess he was very happy to be playing the knight gallant, protective of his lady fair, of small children, and everyone who relied upon his audacity.

'Take care until you see me again,' he whispered.

'Christopher,' I whispered back, 'all you need is a white horse and a shield.'

'No,' he whispered again, 'a unicorn, and a lance with a green dragon's head upon its point, and back I'll gallop in my shining white armour while the blizzard blows in the month of August and the sun is mid-sky, and when I dismount you'll be looking up at someone who stands twelve feet high, so speak respectfully when you speak to me, my lady Catherine.'

'Yes, my lord. Go forth and slay yonder dragon – but take not overlong, for I could be undone by all that menaces me and mine in this stone-cold castle, where all the drawbridges are up, and the portcullises are down.'

'Farewell,' he whispered. 'Have no fear. Soon I'll be back to care for thee and thine.'

I giggled as I climbed into bed to lie down beside Carrie. Sleep was an elusive stranger that night as I thought about my mother and that man, about Chris, about all boys, about men, about romance – and love. As I slipped softly into dreams, with music playing down below, my hand lifted to touch the small ring with the garnet heart-stone that my father had put on my finger when I was only seven years old. A ring I'd outgrown so long ago. My touchstone. My talisman, worn now on a very fine gold chain.

Merry Christmas, Daddy.

CHRISTOPHER'S EXPLORATION AND ITS REPERCUSSIONS

Suddenly rough hands seized me by the shoulders and shook me awake! Jolted, startled, I stared with frightened eyes at a woman I hardly recognized as my mother. She glared at me and demanded in an angry voice, 'Where is your brother?'

Taken aback that she could speak and look as she did, so out of control, I cringed from her attack, then rolled my head to look at the bed three feet from the one I was in. Empty. Oh, he had stayed too long.

Should I lie? Protect him, and say he was in the attic? No, this was our mother who loved us; she'd understand. 'Chris went to look over the rooms on this floor.'

Honesty was the best policy, wasn't it? And we never lied to our mother, or to each other. Only to the grandmother, and then only when necessary.

'Damn, damn, damn!' she swore, reddened by a new flood of temper that was now directed at me. Most certainly her precious older son, whom she favoured above all, would never betray her without my devilish influence. She shook me until I felt like a rag-doll, and my eyes were loose and rolling.

'Just for this, I will never, for any reason, or any special occasion, allow you and Christopher out of this room again! You both gave me your word – and you broke it! How can I trust either one of you now? And I thought I could. I thought you loved me, that you would never betray me!'

My eyes widened more. Had we betrayed her? I was shocked too that she could act the way she was – it seemed to me she was betraying *us*.

'Momma, we haven't done anything bad. We were very quiet in the chest. People came and went all around us, but nobody knew we were there. We *were* quiet. No one knows we're here. And you can't say you won't let us out again. You've got to let us out of here! You can't keep us locked up and hidden away for ever.'

She stared at me in an odd, harassed way, without answering. I thought she might slap me, but no, she released her hold on my shoulders and spun around to leave. The flaring chiffon panels of her couturier gown seemed like wild fluttering wings, wafting sweet, flowery perfume that went ill with her fierce demeanour.

Just as she was about to leave the room, apparently going to hunt up Chris herself, the door opened, and my brother stole quietly inside. He eased to the door, then turned and looked in my direction. His lips parted to speak. That's when he saw our mother and the strangest expression came over his face.

For some reason, his eyes didn't light up as they customarily did when he saw our mother.

Moving swiftly and with strong purpose, Momma reached his side. Her hand lifted and she delivered a hard, stinging slap against his cheek! Then, before he could recover from the shock of that, her left hand lifted, and the opposite cheek felt the strength of her anger!

Now Chris's pale and stunned face wore two large red splotches.

'If you ever do anything like this again, Christopher Foxworth, I will myself whip not only you, but Cathy, as well.'

What colour Chris had left in his unnaturally pale face drained away, leaving those red slap marks on his wan cheeks like smeary handprints of blood.

I felt my own blood drain down into my feet; a stinging sensation began behind my ears as my strength grew small, and I stared at that woman who seemed a stranger now, like some woman we didn't know, and one I didn't care to know. Was that our mother who usually spoke to us only with kindness and love? Was that the mother who was so understanding of our misery from such a long, long confinement? Was the house already doing 'things' to her – making her different? It came then in a rush . . . yes, all the little things totalled up . . . she *was* changing. She didn't come as often as she used to, not every day, most certainly not twice a day as she had in the beginning. And, oh, I was scared, like everything trusted and dependable was torn from beneath our feet – and only toys, games, and other gifts were left.

She must have seen something in Chris's stunned expression, something that made her hot anger disappear. She drew him into her open arms and covered his wan, splotched, moustached face with quick little kisses that sought to take away the harm she'd done. Kiss, kiss, kiss, finger his hair, stroke his cheek, draw his head against her soft, swelling breasts, and let him drown in the sensuality of being cuddled close to that creamy flesh that must excite even a youth of his tender years.

'I'm sorry, darling,' she whispered, tears in her eyes and in her voice, 'forgive me, please forgive me. Don't look so frightened. How can you be afraid of me? I didn't mean it about the whippings. I love you. You know that. I would never whip you or Cathy. Have I ever? I'm not myself, because I have everything going my way now – our way. You just can't do anything to spoil it for all of us. And that's the only reason I slapped you.'

She cupped his face between her palms and kissed him full on lips that were puckered from the tight squeeze of her hands. And those diamonds, those emeralds kept flashing, flashing . . . signal lights, meaning something. And I sat and watched, and wondered, and felt . . . felt, oh, I didn't know how I felt, except confused and bewildered, and very, very young. And the world all about us was wise, and old, so old.

Of course he forgave her, just as I did. And of course we had to know what was going her way and our way.

'Please, Momma, tell us what it is – please.'

'Another time,' she said, in a terrible hurry to get back to the party before she was missed. More kisses for the both of us. And it came to me then. I had never felt my cheek against the softness of her breast.

'Another time, perhaps tomorrow, and I'll tell you everything,' she said, hurriedly giving us more kisses, and saying more soothing words to take away our anxieties. She leaned over me to kiss Carrie, and then went over to Cory to kiss his cheek too.

'You have forgiven me, Christopher?'

'Yes, Momma. I understand, Momma. We should have stayed in this room. I should never have gone exploring.'

She smiled and said 'Merry Christmas, and I'll be seeing you soon.' And then out the door she went, closing and locking it behind her.

Our first Christmas Day upstairs was over. The clock down the hall had struck one. We had a room full of gifts, a TV set, the chess game we'd asked for, one red and one blue tricycle, new clothes that were heavy and warm, plus many sweet things to eat, and Chris and I had been to a magnificent party – in a way. Yet, something new had come into our lives, a facet of our mother's character we had never experienced before. For just a brief moment or two, Momma seemed exactly like our grandmother!

In the dark, on one bed, with Carrie on one side of me, and Chris on the other, he and I lay holding each other. He smelled different than I did. My head was on his boyish chest and he was losing weight. I could hear his heart throbbing along with the faint music still drifting to our ears. He had his hand in my hair, curling a tendril over and over around his fingers.

'Chris, being grown up is awfully complicated, isn't it?'

'Guess so.'

'I always thought when you were an adult you knew how to handle any situation. You were never in doubt as to what is wrong, and what is right. I never guessed adults floundered around, too, just like us.'

'If you're thinking of Momma, she didn't mean what she said and did. I believe, though I'm not sure, once you are an adult, and come back to the home of your parents to live, for some odd reason, you're reduced to being a child again, and dependent. Her parents tug her one way – and we pull her another way – and now she's got that man with the moustache. He must be tugging her his way, too.'

'I hope she never marries again! We need her more than that man does!'

Chris didn't say anything.

'And that TV set she brought us – she waited for her father to give her one, when she could have bought us one herself months ago, instead of buying herself so many clothes. And the jewellery! She's always wearing new rings, and new bracelets, earrings and necklaces.'

Very slowly he expressed a careful explanation of our mother's motives. 'Look at it this way, Cathy. If she had given us a TV the first day we came, we would have sat down in front of it and stared all day long. Then we wouldn't have created a garden in the attic where the twins can play happily. We wouldn't have done anything but sit and watch. And look how much we've learned during our long, long days, like how to make flowers and animals. I paint better now than when I came, and look at the books we've read to improve our minds. And you, Cathy, you've changed too.'

'How? How have I changed? Name it.'

He rolled his head from side to side on the pillow, expressing a sort of embarrassed helplessness.

'All right. You don't have to say anything nice to me. But before you leave this bed and get into your own, tell me all you found out – everything. Don't leave out a thing, not even your thoughts. I want you to make me feel I was there with you, at your side, seeing and feeling what you did.'

He turned his head so our eyes locked and he said in the weirdest voice, 'You *were* there beside me. I felt you there, holding on to my hand, whispering in my ear, and I looked all the harder, just so you could see what I did.'

This giant house, ruled by the sick ogre beneath, had intimidated him; I could tell that by his voice. 'It's an awfully big house, Cathy, like a hotel. There are rooms and rooms, all furnished with beautiful expensive things, but you can tell they are never used. I counted fourteen rooms on this floor alone, and I think I missed a few small ones.'

'Chris!' I cried out, disappointed. 'Don't tell it to me that way! Make me feel I was there beside you. Start over, and tell me how it went from the second you were out of my sight.'

'Well,' he said, sighing, like he'd rather not, 'I stole along the dark corridor of this wing, and I ran to where this hall joins that large centre rotunda where we hid in the chest near the balcony. I didn't bother looking in any of the northern-wing rooms. As soon as I was where people might see me, I had to be careful. The party was nearing its peak. The revelry down there was even louder, everybody sounded drunk. In fact, one man was singing in a foolish way something about wanting his missing two front teeth. It was so funny sounding, I stole over to the balustrade and looked down on all the people. They looked odd, foreshortened, and I thought, I'll have to remember that, so when I draw people from an above the eye-level viewpoint, they'll look natural. Perspective makes all the difference in a painting.'

It made all the difference in everything, if you asked me.

'Of course it was Momma I searched for,' he continued after I urged him on, 'and the only people I recognized down there were our grandparents. Our grandfather was beginning to look tired, and even as I watched, a nurse came and pushed him out of sight. And I watched, for it gave me the general direction to his room in back of the library.'

'Was she wearing a white uniform?'

'Of course. How else would I know she was a nurse?'

'Okay, go on. Don't leave out a thing.'

'Well, no sooner did the grandfather leave than the grandmother left, too, and then I heard voices coming up one of the stairways! You never saw anyone move quicker than I did! I couldn't hide in the chest without revealing myself, so I ducked into a corner where a suit of armour stood on a pedestal. You know that armour must have been worn by a fully grown man, and yet I'll bet you a hundred it wouldn't fit me, though I would have liked to try it on. And as for who was coming up the stairs, it was Momma, and with her she had the same dark haired man with the moustache.'

'What did they do? Why were they upstairs?'

'They didn't see me hiding in the shadows, I guess, because they were so preoccupied with each other. That man wanted to see some bed Momma has in her room.'

'Her bed – he wanted to see her bed? Why?'

'It's a special kind of bed, Cathy. He said to her, "C'mon, you've held out long enough." His voice sounded teasing. Then he added, "It's time you showed me that fabulous swan bed I've heard so much about." Apparently Momma was worried that we might still be hidden in the chest. She glanced that way, looking uneasy. But she agreed and said, "All right, Bart – however, we can linger but a moment, for you know what everyone will suspect if we stay away too long." And he chuckled and teased back, "No, I can't guess what everyone would think. Tell me what they will suspect."

To me, this sounded like a challenge to let everyone think what they would. It made me angry, him saying that.' And at this point Chris paused, and his breathing got heavier and faster.

'You're holding something back,' I said, knowing him like a book I'd read a hundred times over. 'You're protecting her! You saw something you don't want to tell me! Now that's not fair! You know we agreed the first day we came here to always be honest and fully truthful with each other – now you tell me what you saw!'

'Good gosh,' he said, squirming and turning his head and refusing to look me straight in the eyes, 'what difference does a few kisses make?'

'*A FEW kisses?*' I stormed. 'You saw him kiss Momma more than once? What kind of kisses? Hand kisses – or real mouth-to-mouth kisses?'

A blush heated up his chest, on which my cheek was resting. It burned right through his pyjamas. 'They were passionate kisses, weren't they?' I threw out, convinced even without his say-so. 'He kissed her, and she let him, and maybe he even touched her breasts, and stroked her buttocks, like I once saw Daddy do when he didn't know I was in the room and watching! Is that what you saw, Christopher?'

'What difference does it make?' he answered, a choke in his voice. 'Whatever he did, she didn't seem to mind, though it made me feel sick.'

It made me feel sick, too. Momma was only a widow of eight months then. But, sometimes eight months can feel more like eight years, and, after all, of what value was the past when the present was so thrilling, and pleasing . . . for, you bet, I could guess a lot went on that Chris wasn't ever going to tell me.

'Now, Cathy, I don't know what you're thinking, but Momma did command him to stop, and if he didn't, she wouldn't show him her bedroom.'

'Oh boy, I bet he was doing something gross!'

'Kisses,' said Chris, staring over at the Christmas tree, 'only kisses, and a few caresses, but they did make her eyes glow, and then that Bart, he was asking her if the swan bed had once belong to a French courtesan.'

'For heaven's sake, what is a French courtesan?'

Chris cleared his throat. 'It's a noun I looked up in the dictionary, and it means a woman who saves her favours for men of the aristocracy, or royalty.'

'Favours – what kind of favours?'

'The kind rich men pay for,' he said quickly, and went on, putting his hand over my mouth to shut me up. 'And, of course, Momma denied such a bed would be in this house. She said a bed with a sinful reputation, no matter how beautiful, would be burned at night, while prayers were said for its redemption, and the swan bed was her grandmother's bed, and when she was a girl, she wanted her grandmother's bedroom suite more than she wanted anything else. But her parents wouldn't let her have those rooms, fearful she'd be contaminated by the ghost of her grandmother who wasn't exactly a saint, and not exactly a courtesan either. And then Momma laughed, kind of hard and bitterly, and told Bart her parents believed she was now so corrupted that nothing could, or would, make her worse than she already was. And you know, that made me feel so bad. Momma isn't corrupted – Daddy loved her . . . they were married . . . and what married people do in private is no one else's business.'

My breath caught and held. Chris always knew everything – absolutely everything!

'Well, Momma said, "One quick look, Bart, and then back to the party." They disappeared down a wing softly lit and inviting, and of course that gave me the general directions of her room. I cautiously peered in all directions first, before I came from out of hiding, and dashed away from the suit of armour, and into the first closed door that I saw. I rushed in, thinking that since it was dark, and the door was closed, it would be unoccupied. I closed the door behind me very softly, and then stood perfectly still, just to absorb the scent and feel of the place, the way you say you do. I had my flashlight, and I could have beamed that around right away, but I wanted to learn how you can be so intuitive, and so wary and suspicious, when everything seems perfectly normal to me. And darned if you aren't right. If the lights had been on, or I'd used the flashlight, maybe I wouldn't have noticed the strangest unnatural odour that filled the room. An odour that made me feel uneasy and kind of scared. Then, by golly, I nearly dropped my skin!'

'What – what?' I said, pushing his hand that tried to hush me. 'What did you see – a monster?'

'Monster? Oh, you bet I saw *monsters*! Dozens of monsters! At least I saw their heads mounted and hung on the walls. All about me eyes were glistening – amber, green, topaz, and lemon eyes. Boy, was it scary! The light coming through the windows was coloured bluish because of the snow, and it caught on the shiny teeth, and on the fangs of the lion which had its mouth wide open and was silently roaring. It had a tawny ruff of mane that made its head seem huge – it had a mute expression of anguish, or anger. And for some reason, I felt sorry for it, decapitated, mounted, stuffed – made just a thing to decorate when it should have lived out its life stalking free on the veld.'

Oh, yes, I knew what he meant. My anguish was always like a mountain of rage.

'It was a trophy room, Cathy, a huge room with many animal heads. There was a tiger, and an elephant with its trunk uplifted. All the animals from Asia and Africa were displayed on one side of the huge room, and the big game from America was on the opposite wall: a grizzly bear, a brown-and-black bear, an antelope, a mountain lion, and so on. Not a fish or bird was represented, as if they didn't present enough of a challenge to the hunter who had killed to decorate that room. It was a creepy room, and yet I wanted so much for you to see it. You've just got to see it!'

Oh, heck – what did I care about the trophy room? I wanted to know about people – their secrets – that's what I wanted.

'There was a stone fireplace at least twenty feet long on the wall with the windows on either side, and above it hung a life-sized oil portrait of a young man who was so much like our father it made me want to cry out. But it wasn't Daddy's portrait. As I neared, I saw a man much like our father, except in the eyes. He wore a khaki hunting outfit, with a blue shirt. The hunter rested on his rifle and he had one leg up on a log that lay on the ground. I know a little about art, enough to know that painting is a masterpiece. The artist really captured the soul of the hunter. You never saw such hard, cold, cruel and pitiless blue eyes. That alone told me it couldn't be our father even before I read the small metal plate fastened to the bottom of the goldleaf frame. It was a painting of Malcolm Neal Foxworth, our grandfather. The date showed Daddy had been five years old when that portrait was painted. And as you know, when Daddy was three, he and his mother, Alicia, had been driven away from Foxworth Hall, and he and his mother were living in Richmond then.'

'Go on.'

'Well, I was very fortunate nobody saw me stealing around, for I really did poke into every room. And finally I found Momma's suite of rooms. It has double doors over two steps up, and, boy, when I took a look inside, I thought I was looking into a palace! The other rooms made me anticipate something splendid, but her rooms are just beyond belief! And they had to be our mother's rooms, for Daddy's photograph was on her nightstand, and the rooms smelled of her perfume. In the centre of the room, on a dais, was the fabulous swan bed! Oh! What a bed! You've never seen anything like it! It has a sleek ivory head, turned in profile, and appears ready to plunge its head under the ruffled underside of a lifted wing. It has one sleepy red eye. The wings curve gently to cup the head of an almost oval bed – I don't know how they fit sheets on it, unless they are custom-made. The designers arranged for the wingtip feathers to act as fingers, and they hold back the delicate, transparent draperies that are in all shades of pink and rose, and violet, and purple. It is really some bed . . . and those bed curtains . . . why, she must feel like a princess sleeping there. The pale mauve carpet is so thick you sink up to your ankles, and there's a large rug of white fur near the bed. There are lamps four feet high of cut-crystal, decorated with gold and silver, and two of them have black shades. There's an ivory chaise-longue upholstered in rose-coloured velvet – something like you'd see in a Roman orgy. And at the foot of that big swan bed – and hold your breath, for you're not going to believe this – there was an infant swan bed! Imagine that! Placed at the foot, and crossways. I just had to stand and wonder why anyone would need a big wide bed, and then a little narrow bed across the bottom. There must be a good reason, beside that of taking a nap and not mussing the larger bed. Cath, you've just got to see that bed to believe it!'

I knew he'd seen a whole lot more that he didn't mention. More that I was to see later for myself. So much I did see that I knew why he came back and made so much of the bed without telling me everything.

'Is this house prettier than our house in Gladstone?' I asked, for, to me, our ranch house – eight rooms and two and a half baths – had been the best possible.

He hesitated. It took him some time to find the right words to say, for he was not one to speak hastily. He weighed his words carefully that night, and that alone told much. 'This is not a pretty house. It's grand, it's big, it's beautiful, but I wouldn't call it pretty.'

I thought I knew what he meant. Prettiness was more akin to cosiness than grand, rich, and beautiful, plus huge.

And now there was nothing left to say but good night – and don't let the bedbugs bite. I put a kiss on his cheek and pushed him off the bed. This time he didn't complain that kisses were only for babies and sissies – and girls. Soon he was snuggled down beside Cory, only three feet away.

In the dark, the little live Christmas tree, two feet tall, sparkled with tiny coloured lights, like the tears I saw glistening in my brother's eyes.

THE LONG WINTER, AND SPRING, AND SUMMER

Never had our mother spoken truer words when she said now we had a real window to look into the lives of others. That winter, the TV set took over our lives. Like others – invalids, sick people, old people – we ate, bathed, and dressed, so we could sit down to watch other people living fake lives.

During January, February, and most of March the attic was much too cold to enter. A frigid vapour hung in the air up there, eerily misting everything over, and it was scary, you bet. And miserable; even Chris had to admit that.

All of this made us very content to stay in the warmer bedroom, cuddled close together as we stared and stared and stared. The twins adored the TV so they never wanted to turn it off; even at night while we slept they wanted it on, knowing it would then wake them up in the mornings. Even the scramble of dots after the late-late shows was better to them than nothing at all. Cory, in particular, liked to wake up and see the little people behind the desks giving the news, talking about the weather; for certainly their voices welcomed him more cheerfully into another day than did the covered, dim windows.

The TV shaped us, moulded us, taught us how to spell and pronounce difficult words. We learned how important it was to be clean, odourless, and never let wax accumulate on your kitchen floor; never let the wind muss your hair, and God forbid if you had dandruff! Then the entire world would hold you in scorn. In April I'd be thirteen, approaching the age of acne! Each day I examined my skin to see what horrors might pop up any moment. Really, we took commercials literally, believing in their value as a book of rules to see us safely through the dangers life held.

Each day that passed brought about changes in Chris and in me. Peculiar things were happening to our bodies. We grew hair where we hadn't had hair before – funny-looking, crispy, amber-coloured hair, darker than what was on our heads. I didn't like them, and I took the tweezers and plucked them out whenever they appeared, but they were like weeds; the more you plucked, the more came back. Chris found me one day with my arm upraised, seeking diligently to grasp one single, crinkly amber hair and ruthlessly yank it out.

'What the heck are you doing?' he shot out.

'I don't want to have to shave under my arms and I don't want to use that depilatory cream that Momma uses – it stinks!'

'You mean you've been pulling hairs from your body wherever they appear?'

'Sure I do. I like my body nice and neat – even if you don't.'

'You're fighting a losing battle,' he said with a wicked grin. 'That hair is supposed to grow where it does – so leave it alone and stop thinking about looking childishly neat, and begin to think of that hair as sexy.'

Sexy? Big bosoms were sexy, not crinkly, wiry hair. But I didn't say this, for little hard apples were beginning to poke out my chest, and I just hoped Chris hadn't noticed. I was very pleased I was beginning to swell out in front – when I was alone, in a private place – but I didn't want anyone else to notice. I had to abandon that forlorn hope, for I saw Chris glance quite often at my chest, and no matter how loosely my sweaters or blouses fitted, I believe those little hills betrayed my modesty.

I was coming alive, feeling things I hadn't felt before. Strange achings, longings. Wanting something, and not knowing what it was that woke me up at night, pulsating, throbbing, excited, and knowing a man was there with me, doing something I wanted him to complete, and he never did . . . he never did . . . always I woke up too soon, before I reached those climactic heights I knew he would take me to – if only I wouldn't wake up and spoil it all.

Then there was another puzzling thing. It was me who made up the beds every morning, as soon as we were up and dressed, and before the witch came in with the picnic basket. I kept seeing stains on the sheets, and they weren't large enough to be another of Cory's dreams of going to the bathroom. They were on Chris's side of the bed. 'For heaven's sakes, Chris. I sure hope *you* don't take to dreaming of being in the bathroom while you're still in bed.'

I just couldn't believe his fantastic tale of something he called 'nocturnal emissions!'

'Chris, I think you should tell Momma, so she can take you to a doctor. Whatever you have might be contagious, something Cory could catch, and he's messy enough already in the bed without adding more.'

He threw me a look of contempt while red colour heated his face. 'I don't need to see a doctor,' he said in the stiffest way. 'I've heard older boys talk in the school rest-rooms, and what is happening to me is perfectly normal.'

'It cannot be normal – it is much too messy to be normal.'

'Hah!' he scoffed, flashing his eyes with hidden laughter sparkling them. 'Your time to mess up your sheets is coming.'

'What do you mean?'

'Ask Momma. It's about time she told you. I've already noticed you're beginning to develop – and that's a sure sign.'

I hated that he always knew more about everything than I did! Where did he learn so much – from nasty, idle talk in the boys' room? I'd heard some nasty, idle talk in the girls' room too, but darned if I was gonna believe one word of it. It was all just too gross!

The twins seldom used a chair, and they couldn't loll about on the beds, for that would make them rumpled, and the grandmother insisted that we keep everything 'shipshape'. And though they liked the soaps, they still kept on playing as they occasionally glanced up to see the most spellbinding scenes. Carrie had that doll house, with all its little people and its many small fascinations, to keep her constantly chattering in a singsong, lilting way that could grate on your nerves. Many an annoyed glance I'd throw her way, hoping she'd shut up for two seconds, and let me hear and enjoy without all the chitchat – but I never said anything to her, for that would bring about howls worse than the low murmur of her back-and-forth conversations.

While Carrie moved the dolls about, and conversed for male and female, Cory would fiddle with his many boxes of Tinkertoys. He refused to use the directions that Chris tried to teach him how to follow. Cory would design whatever suited his needs most, and what he constructed was always something he could beat upon to make musical notes. With the television to make noise and give a constantly changing variety of scenes, the doll house with its many charms to please Carrie, and the Tinkertoys which happied away the hours for Cory, the twins managed to make the best of their confined lives. The young are very adaptable; I know that from watching them. Sure, they complained some, about two things the most. Why didn't Momma come as often as she used to? That hurt, really hurt, for what could I tell them? And then there was the food; they never liked the food. They wanted ice-cream cones that they saw on TV, and the hot dogs TV children were always eating. In fact, they wanted everything that was aimed at a child's appetite for sweet things, or toy things. The toys they got. The sweets they didn't.

And while the twins crawled about on the floor, or sat cross-legged making their particular kind of annoying racket, Chris and I tried to keep our minds concentrated on the complicated situations that unfolded daily before our eyes. We watched unfaithful husbands deceive loving wives, or nagging wives, or wives too concerned with their children to give the husbands the attentions they deemed so necessary. It was vice-versa, too. Wives could be just as unfaithful to husbands good, or husbands bad. We learned love was just like a soap bubble, so shining and bright one day, and the next day it popped. Then came the tears, the woebegone expressions, the anguish over endless cups of coffee while seated at the kitchen table with a best friend who had her own troubles, or his own troubles. But, no sooner was one love over and done with, than along came another love to start that shining soap bubble soaring again. Oh, how very hard those beautiful people sought to find the perfect love and lock it away, keep it safe; and they never could.

One afternoon in late March Momma came into the room with a large box tucked under her arm. We were accustomed to seeing her enter our room with many gifts, not just one, and the strangest thing was, she nodded at Chris, who seemed to understand, for he got up from where he sat to study, caught hold of the small hands of our twins, and he took them up into the attic. I didn't understand in the least. It was still cold up there. Was this some secret? Was she bringing a gift just for me?

We sat side by side on the bed Carrie and I shared and before I could have a look at the 'gift' meant especially for me, Momma said we had to have a 'woman-to-woman' talk.

Now, I'd heard about man-to-man talks from watching old Andy Hardy movies, and I knew these particular kinds of discussions had something to do with growing up and sex, so I grew thoughtful and tried not to show too much interest, which would be unladylike – though I was dying to know at last.

And did she tell me what I'd waited to hear for many a year? No! While I sat solemnly and awaited the disclosing of all the evil, unholy things boys knew from the moment they were born, according to one particular witch-grandmother, I sat stunned and disbelieving while she did the explaining of how likely any day I would start to bleed!

Not from a wound, an injury, but from God's plan of how a woman's body should function. And, to add to my amazement, not only was I going to bleed once every month from now on until I was an old woman of fifty, this bloody thing was going to last five days!

'Until I'm fifty?' I asked in a voice weak and small, afraid, oh so afraid she wasn't joking.

She gave me a sweet and tender smile. 'Sometimes it stops before you're fifty, and sometimes it goes on for a few years more – there's no set rule. But somewhere around that age bracket you can expect to go into "the change of life". And that is called menopause.'

'Is it going to hurt?' was the most important thing I needed to know at that moment.

'Your monthly periods? There may be a little crampy pain, but it's not so bad, and I can tell you this from my own experience, and that from other women I know, the more you dread it, the more it pains.'

I knew it! Never did I see blood that I didn't feel pain – unless it was the blood of someone else. And all this mess, this pain, these cramps, just so my uterus could ready itself to receive a 'fertilized egg' that would grow into a baby. Then she gave me the box which contained everything I would need for 'that time of month'.

'Hold up, Momma!' I cried, having found a way to avoid all this. 'You've forgotten I plan to be a ballerina, and dancers are never supposed to have babies. Miss Danielle was always telling us it was better never to have a child. And I don't want any, not ever. So you can take all this stuff back to the store, and get back your money, for I'm calling off this monthly period mess!'

She chuckled, then hugged me closer and put on my cheek a kiss. 'I guess I must have overlooked telling you something – for there isn't anything you can do to prevent menstruation. You have to accept all of nature's ways of changing your body from that of a child, into that of a woman. Certainly you don't want to remain a child all your life, do you?'

I floundered, wanting very much to be a grown woman, with all the curves she had, and yet I wasn't prepared for the shock of such messiness – and once each month!

'And, Cathy, please don't be ashamed, or embarrassed, or dread a little discomfort, and the trouble – having babies is very rewarding. Some day you'll fall in love and marry, and you'll want to give your husband children – if you love him enough.'

'Momma, there's something you're not telling me. If girls go through this sort of thing to become a woman, what must Chris endure to become a man?'

She giggled girlishly and pressed her cheek to mine. 'They have changes, too, though none that make them bleed. Chris will soon have to be shaving – and every day too. And there are certain other things he will have to learn to accomplish, and control, that you don't have to worry about.'

'What?' asked I, eager to have the male gender share some of the miseries of maturing. When she didn't answer, I asked, 'Chris, he sent you to me with instructions to tell me, didn't he?' She nodded and said yes, though she had meant to tell me long ago, but downstairs there was a hassle every day to keep her from doing what she should.

'Chris – what does he have to endure that's painful?'

She laughed, seemingly amused. 'Another day, Cathy. Now put your things away, and use them when you have the need. Don't panic if it starts in the night, or while you're dancing. I was twelve the day mine started, and out riding a bicycle, and you know I rode home at least six times and changed my panties before my mother finally noticed, and took the time to explain to me what it was all about. I was furious because she hadn't warned me in advance. She never told me anything. Believe it or not, you'll soon get used to it, and it won't make one bit of difference in your lifestyle.'

Despite the boxes of hateful things I wished I would never need – for I wasn't going to have a baby – that was a very good warm talk that my mother and I shared.

And yet, when she called Chris and the twins down from the attic, and she kissed Chris and ruffled his blond curls, and played with him in teasing ways, and almost ignored the twins, the closeness shared but a moment ago began to fade. Carrie and Cory seemed ill at ease in her presence now. They came running to me and climbed up on my lap, and with my arms hugging them close, they watched as Chris was fondled, kissed, and fawned over. It bothered me so much the way she treated the twins, as if she didn't like to look at them. As Chris and I moved on into puberty, and towards adulthood, the twins stagnated, went nowhere.

The long cold winter passed into spring. Gradually the attic grew warmer. We went, all four, up there to take down the paper snowflakes, and we made it bloom again with our brilliant spring flowers.

My birthday came in April, and Momma didn't fail to come with presents, and the treats of ice-cream and bakery cake. She sat down to spend the Sunday afternoon, and taught me how to do crewel embroidery, and a few needlepoint stitches. Thus, with the kits she gave me, I had another way to fill my time.

My birthday was followed by the twins' day – their sixth birthday. Again, Momma bought the cake, the ice-cream, and the many gifts, including musical instruments that made Cory's blue eyes light up. He took one long, charmed look at that toy accordion, gave it a squeeze or two while punching the keys, cocking his head to listen attentively to the sounds he made. And darned, if he wasn't soon playing a tune on that thing! None of us could believe it. Then again we were dumbfounded, for he turned to Carrie's toy piano and did the same thing. 'Happy birthday to you, happy birthday dear Carrie, happy birthday to you and me.'

'Cory has an ear for music,' said Momma, looking sad and yearning as she at last turned her gaze upon her youngest son. 'Both my brothers were musicians. The pity of it was my father had no patience for the arts, or the type of men who were artists – not only those who were musicians, but painters, poets, and so forth. He thought them weak and effeminate. He forced this older brother to work in a bank he owned, not caring if his son detested the job that didn't suit him at all. He was named after my father, but we called him Mal. He was a very good-looking young man, and on week-ends, Mal would escape the life he hated by riding up into the mountains on his motor-cycle. In his own private retreat, a log cabin he had built himself, he composed music. One day he took a curve too fast in the rain. He careened off the road and crashed down hundreds of feet into a chasm. He was twenty-two years old and dead.

'My younger brother was named Joel, and he ran away the day of his brother's funeral. He and Mal had been very close, and I guess he just couldn't bear the thought that now he would have to take Mal's place, and be the heir to his father's business dynasty. We received one single postcard from Paris, in which Joel told us he had a job with an orchestra touring Europe. Next thing we heard, perhaps three weeks later, Joel had been killed in a skiing accident in Switzerland. He was nineteen when he died. He had fallen into some deep ravine filled with snow, and to this day, they never found his body.'

Oh, golly! I was greatly disturbed, kind of numb-feeling inside. So many accidents. Two brothers dead, and Daddy, too, all from accidents. My bleak look met with Chris's. He wasn't smiling. As soon as our mother was gone we escaped to the attic and our books.

'We've read every damned thing!' said Chris in deep disgust, flashing me an annoyed look. Wasn't my fault he could read a book in a few hours!

'We could read through those Shakespeare books again,' I suggested.

'I don't like to read plays!'

Gosh-golly, I loved reading Shakespeare and Eugene O'Neill, and anything that was dramatic, fanciful, and fraught with tempestuous emotions.

'Let's teach the twins to read and write,' I suggested, I was that frantic to do something different. And in this way we could give *them* another way to entertain themselves. 'And Chris, we'll save their brains from turning into mush from looking at that tube so much, and keep them from going blind, too.'

Down the stairs we determinedly stalked, and right up to the twins who had their eyes glued to Bugs Bunny, who was signing off.

'We are going to teach the two of you to read and write,' said Chris.

With loud wails they protested. '*No!*' howled Carrie. '*We don't want to learn to read and write! We don't write letters! We want to watch* "I Love Lucy"*!*'

Chris grabbed her, and I seized hold of Cory, and quite literally we had to drag them both into the attic. It was like trying to handle slippery snakes. One of them could bellow like a mad bull charging!

Cory didn't speak, nor did he scream, nor did he beat at me with small fists to inflict some damage; he just clung fiercely to whatever came within reach of his hands, and he used his legs to wrap around things too.

Never did two amateur teachers have a more unwilling student body. But finally, through tricks and threats and fairy tales, we began to interest them. Maybe it was pity for *us* that soon had them carefully toiling over books, and tediously memorizing and reciting letters. We gave them a McGuffey's first grade primer to copy words from.

Not acquainted with other children the same age as our twins, Chris and I thought our six-year-olds did remarkably well. And though Momma didn't come every day now as she had in the beginning, or every other day, she did show up once or twice a week. How anxiously we waited to give her the short note Cory and Carrie had printed, making sure each had the same amount of words to print.

They printed in letters at least two inches high, and very crooked:

Dear Momma,

We love you,
And candy, too.

Goodbye,

Carrie and Cory

Such sweating diligence they used to concoct their own message, not coached by either Chris or me – a message which they hoped our mother would get. Which she didn't.

Tooth cavities, of course.

Then summer was upon us. And again it was hot and sweltering, so horribly stuffy, though, strangely, not as unbearable as it had been the previous summer. Chris reasoned our blood was thinner now, so we could tolerate the heat better.

Our summer was filled with books. Apparently Momma just reached in and took books from the shelves downstairs without bothering to read the titles, or wondering if they would be of interest to us, or suitable reading for young minds so easily impressed. It didn't really matter. Chris and I would read anything.

One of our favourite books that summer was a historical novel that made history better than that taught in school. We were surprised to read that in the old days women didn't go to the hospitals to have babies. They had them at home on a small, narrow cot, so the doctor could reach them more easily than on a large, wide bed. And sometimes only 'midwives' were in attendance.

'A baby swan bed, to give birth to an infant child,' mused Chris aloud, lifting his head to stare off into space.

I rolled over on my back and smiled at him wickedly. We were in the attic, both lying on the old stained mattress near the open windows that let in soft warm breezes. 'And kings and queens who held court in their bedroom – or bedchambers, as they called them – and having the nerve to sit up in bed entirely naked. Do you think everything that's written in books can be entirely true?'

'Of course not! But much of it is. After all, people didn't used to wear nightgowns, or pyjamas to bed. They only wore nightcaps to keep their skulls warm, and the heck with the rest.'

We laughed, both of us, picturing kings and queens who weren't embarrassed to be naked in front of their nobles and foreign dignitaries.

'Naked skin wasn't sinful then, was it? Way back in medieval days?'

'Guess not,' he answered.

'It's what you do when you're naked that's sinful, isn't it?'

'Guess so.'

For the second time now, I was coping with that curse nature sent to make me a woman, and it did hurt so much the first time that I stayed in bed all day, and made a big to-do about feeling crampy.

'You don't think it's disgusting, what is happening to me – do you?' I asked Chris.

His face lowered into my hair. 'Cathy, I don't think anything about the human body and the way it functions is disgusting or revolting. I guess this is the doctor in me coming out. I think like this about your particular situation . . . if it takes a few days a month to make you into a woman like our mother, then I'm all for it. And if it pains, and you don't like it, then think about dancing, for that hurts, too, you've told me so. And yet, you think the price you pay is worth the rewards.' My arms closed tighter about him when he paused. 'And I pay a price too in becoming a man. I don't have a man to talk to, as you have Momma. I'm all alone in a sticky situation, full of frustrations, and sometimes I don't know which way to turn, and how to get away from temptations, and I'm so damned scared I'll never get to be a doctor.'

'Chris,' I began, then stumbled on quicksand, I knew, 'don't you ever have any doubts about her?'

I saw his frown, and spoke again before he could fire back some angry retort. 'Doesn't it strike you as . . . as *odd*, that she keeps us locked up for so long? She's got lots of money, Chris, I know she has. Those rings and bracelets, they're not fake like she tells us. I know they're not!'

He had drawn away when first I brought up 'her'. He adored his goddess of all female perfection, but then he was embracing me again, and his cheek was on my hair, his voice tight with thick emotion, 'Sometimes I am not the eternal cockeyed optimist you call me. Sometimes I am just as doubting of what she does as you are. But I think back to the time before we came here, and I feel I have to trust her, and believe in her, and be like Daddy was. Remember how he used to say, "For everything that seems strange, there is a good reason. And everything always works out for the best." That's what I make myself believe – she has good reasons for keeping us here, and not sneaking us out to some boarding school. She knows what she's doing, and Cathy, I love her so much. I just can't help it. No matter what she does, I feel I will go right on loving her.'

He loved her more than me, I thought bitterly.

Our mother now came and went with no regularity. Once, a whole week passed with no visit. When she finally arrived she told us her father was very ill. I was overjoyed to hear the news.

'Is he getting worse?' I asked, feeling a little pang of guilt. I knew it was wrong to wish him dead, but his death meant our salvation.

'Yes,' she said solemnly, 'much worse. Any day now, Cathy, any day. You wouldn't believe his pallor, his pain; soon as he goes, you'll be free.'

Oh, good golly, to think I was so evil as to want that old man to die this very second! God forgive me. But it wasn't right for us to be shut up all the time; we needed to be outside, in the warm sunlight, and we did get so lonesome, seeing no new people.

'It could be any hour,' said Momma, and got up to leave.

'Swing low, sweet chariot, comin' for t' carry me home . . .' was the tune I hummed as I made the beds, and waited for the news to come that our grandfather was on his way to heaven if his gold counted, and to hell if the Devil couldn't be bribed.

'If you get there before I do . . .'

And Momma was at the door, tired looking as she poked only her face in. 'He's passed the crisis . . . he's going to recover – this time.' The door closed, and we were alone, with dashed hopes.

I tucked the twins into bed that night for seldom did Momma show up to do this. I was the one who kissed their cheeks and heard their prayers. And Chris did his share, too. They loved us, it was easy to read in their big, shadowed blue eyes. After they fell asleep, we went to the calendar to make an 'X' through another day. August had come again. We had now lived in this prison a full year.

PART TWO

Until the day break,
and the shadows flee away,
The Song of Solomon 2:17

GROWING UP, GROWING WISER

Another year passed, much as the first did. Mother came less and less frequently, but always with the promises that kept us hoping, kept us believing our deliverance was only a few weeks away. The last thing we did each night was to mark off that day with a big red X.

We now had three calendars with big red Xs. The first one was only half-bloodied with red, the second one X'd all the way through, and now a third over half filled with Xs. And the dying grandfather, now sixty-eight, always about to breathe his last breath, lived on, and on, and on while we waited in limbo. It seemed he'd live to be sixty-nine.

On Thursdays, the servants of Foxworth Hall went into town, and that was when Chris and I stole out on to the black roof, to lie on a steep slope, soaking up the sunlight, and airing under the moon and stars. Though it was high and dangerous, it was the real outdoors, when we could feel fresh air on our thirsting skins.

In a place where two wings met and formed a corner, we could brace our feet against a sturdy chimney and feel quite safe. Our positioning on the roof hid us from anyone who might be on the ground.

Because the grandmother's wrath had not yet materialized, Chris and I had grown careless. We were not always modest in the bedroom, nor were we always fully dressed. It was difficult to live, day in, day out, and always keep the intimate places of our bodies secret from the other sex.

And to be perfectly honest, none of us cared very much who saw what.

We should have cared.

We should have been careful.

We should have kept the memory of Momma's bloody welted back sharply before us, and never, never have forgotten. But the day she'd been whipped seemed so long, long ago. An eternity ago.

Here I was a teenager, and I'd never seen myself naked all over, for the mirror on the medicine cabinet door was placed too high for good viewing. I'd never seen a naked woman, or even a picture of one, and paintings and marble statues didn't show details. So I waited a time when I had the bedroom to myself, and before the dresser mirror I stripped off everything, and then I stared, preened, and admired. Incredible the changes hormones brought about! Certainly I was much prettier than when I came here, even my face, my hair, my legs – much less that curvy body. From side to side I twisted, keeping my eyes glued to my reflection as I performed ballet positions.

A rippling sensation on the back of my neck gave me the awareness that someone was near, and watching. I whirled about suddenly to catch Chris standing in the deep shadows of the closet. Silently he'd come from the attic. How long had he been there? Had he seen all the silly, immodest things I'd done? Oh, God, I hoped not!

He stood as one frozen. A queer look glazed his blue eyes, as if he'd never seen me before without my clothes on – and he had, many a time. Perhaps when the twins were there, sunbathing with us, he kept his thoughts brotherly and pure, and didn't really stare.

His eyes lowered from my flushed face down to my breasts, then lower, and lower, and down to my feet before they travelled upwards ever so slowly.

I stood trembling, uncertain, wondering what to do that wouldn't make me seem a foolish prude in the judgment of a brother who knew well how to mock me when he chose. He seemed a stranger, older, like someone I had never met before. He also seemed weak, dazed, perplexed, and if I moved to cover myself, I'd steal from him something he'd been starving to see.

Time seemed to stand still as he lingered in the closet, and I hesitated before the dresser which revealed to him the rear view, too, for I saw his eyes flick to the mirror to take in what that reflected.

'Chris, please go away.'

He didn't seem to hear.

He only stared.

I blushed all over and felt perspiration under my arms, and a funny pounding began in my pulse. I felt like a child caught with her hand in the cookie jar, guilty of some petty crime, and terribly afraid of being severely punished for almost nothing. But his look, his eyes, made me come alive, and my heart began a fierce, mad throbbing, full of fright. Why should I be afraid? It was only Chris.

For the first time I felt embarrassed, ashamed of what I had now, and quickly I reached to pick up the dress I'd just taken off. Behind that I would shield myself, and I'd tell him to go away.

'Don't,' he said when I had the dress in my hands.

'You shouldn't . . .' I stammered, trembling more.

'I know I shouldn't be, but you look so beautiful. It's like I never saw you before. How did you grow so lovely, when I was here all the time?'

How to answer a question like that? Except to look at him, and plead with my eyes.

Just then, behind me, a key turned in the door lock. Swiftly I tried to put the dress over my head and pull it down before she came in. Oh, God! I couldn't find the sleeves. My head was all covered by the dress, while the rest of me was bare, and *she* was there – the grandmother! I couldn't see her, but I *felt* her!

Finally I found the armholes, and quickly I yanked the dress down. But she had seen me in my naked glory, it was in those glittering grey stone eyes. She turned those eyes away from me and nailed Chris with a stabbing glare. He was still in the daze that put him nowhere.

'So!' she spat. 'I have at last caught you! I knew I would sooner or later!'

She had spoken to us first. This was just like one of my nightmares . . . without clothes in front of the grandmother and God.

Chris snapped out of the fog and stepped forward to fire back, 'You have caught us? What have you caught? Nothing!'

Nothing . . .

   Nothing . . .

      Nothing . . .

One word that reverberated. In her eyes, she had caught us doing everything!

'Sinners!' she hissed as she once again turned those cruel eyes on me. They held no mercy. 'You think you look pretty? You think those new young curves are attractive? You like that long, golden hair that you brush and brush and curl?' She smiled then – the most frightening smile I ever saw.

My knees were clicking nervously together; my hands were working too. How vulnerable I felt without underwear and with a wide-open zipper in back. I darted a glance to Chris. He advanced slowly, his eyes flickering around to search out some weapon.

'How many times have you allowed your brother to use your body?' shot out the grandmother. I just stood there, unable to speak, not comprehending what she meant.

'Use? What do you mean?'

Her eyes narrowed to mere slits that sharply turned to catch an embarrassed blush on Chris's face, clearly revealing even to me that he knew what she meant, even if I didn't.

'What I mean is,' he said, turning redder, 'we haven't really done anything bad.' He had a man's voice now, deep and strong. 'Go on, look at me with your hateful, suspicious eyes. Believe what you will, but Cathy and I have never done one single, wicked, sinful or unholy thing!'

'Your sister was naked – she has allowed you to look on her body – so, you have done wrong.' She whipped her eyes to me and flared them with hate before she pivoted around and stalked from the room. She left me quivering. Chris was furious with me.

'Cathy, why the hell did you have to undress in this room! You know she spies on us, just hoping to catch us doing something!' A wild, distraught look came upon him, making him seem older and terribly violent. 'She's going to punish us. Just because she left without doing anything, doesn't mean she won't come back.'

I knew that . . . I knew it. She was coming back – with the whip!

Sleepy and irritable, the twins drifted down from the attic. Carrie settled in front of the doll house. Cory squatted down on his heels to watch TV. He picked up his expensive, professional guitar and began to play. Chris sat on his bed and faced the door.

I hedged, ready to run when she came back. I'd run into the bathroom, lock the door . . . I'd . . .

The key turned in the door. The doorknob twisted.

I jumped to my feet, as did Chris. He said, 'Get in the bathroom, Cathy, and stay there.'

Our grandmother walked into the room, towering like a tree, and she bore not a whip, but a huge pair of scissors, the kind women use when cutting fabric to make clothes. They were chrome-coloured, shiny, long, and looked very sharp.

'Sit down, girl!' she snapped. 'I am going to cut off your hair to the scalp – and then maybe you won't feel pride when you look in the mirror.'

Scornfully, cruelly, she smiled when she saw my surprise – the first time I'd seen her smile.

My worst fear! I'd rather be whipped! My skin would heal, but it would take years and years to grow back the beautiful, long hair I'd cherished since Daddy first said it was pretty, and he liked long hair on little girls. Oh, dear God, how could she know that almost every night I dreamed she stole into this room while I slept and sheared me as one does a sheep? And sometimes I dreamed not only did I wake up in the mornings bald and ugly, but she cut off my breasts, too!

Whenever she looked at me, it was at some particular place. She didn't see me as a whole person, but in sections that seemed to arouse her anger . . . and she would destroy whatever made her angry!

I tried to dash into the bathroom, and lock the door behind me. But for some reason my dancer's legs, trained so well, refused to move. I was paralysed by the very threat of those long, shiny scissors and above them – the grandmother's chrome-coloured eyes were sparked with hate, scorn, contempt.

That's when Chris spoke up in a strong man's voice. 'You are not going to cut off one strand of Cathy's hair, Grandmother! Take just one step in her direction, and I will pound you over the head with this chair!'

He held one of the chairs we used for dining, ready to carry out his threat. His blue eyes snapped fire as hers shot hate.

She flicked him a scathing glance, as if what he threatened were of no consequence, as if his puny strength could never overcome the mountain of steel she appeared. 'All right. Have it your way. I will give you your choice, girl – the loss of your hair, or no food or milk for an entire week.'

'The twins have done nothing wrong,' I implored. 'Chris has done nothing. He didn't know I was unclothed when he came down from the attic – it was all my fault. I can go without food and milk for a week. I won't starve, and besides, Momma won't let you do this to me. She'll bring us food.'

I didn't say that with any confidence, though. Momma had been gone so long. She didn't come very often; I'd grow very hungry.

'Your hair – or no food for a week,' she repeated, untouched and unflinching.

'You are wrong to do this, old woman,' said Chris, coming closer with his lifted chair. 'I caught Cathy by surprise. We did nothing sinful. We never have. You judge us by circumstantial evidence.'

'Your hair, or *none* of you will eat for a week,' she said to me, ignoring Chris, as she always did. 'And if you lock yourself in the bathroom, or hide yourself in the attic, then not one of you will eat for two weeks! Or when you come down with a bald head!' Next, she riveted her cold and calculating eyes on Chris for a long, excruciating moment. 'I think you will be the one to shear off your sister's long, cherished hair,' she said with a secret smile. On the dresser top she laid the shiny scissors. 'When I come back, and see your sister without hair, then the four of you will eat.'

She left us, locked us in, left us in a quandary, with Chris staring at me, and me staring back at him.

Chris smiled. 'Come now, Cathy, she's all bluff! Momma will come any hour. We'll tell her . . . no problem. I'll never cut off your hair.' He came to put his arm around me. 'Isn't it fortunate we've hidden a box of crackers and a pound of cheddar cheese in the attic? And we still have today's food – the old witch forgot that.'

We seldom ate very much. We ate even less that day, just in case Momma didn't show up. We saved half our milk, and the oranges. The day ended without a visit from Momma. All night

I tossed and turned, fretting in and out of sleep. When I slept I had horrible nightmares. I dreamed Chris and I were in a deep dark woods, running lost, looking for Carrie and Cory. We called their names in the silent voices of dreams. The twins never answered. We panicked and ran in utter blackness.

Then suddenly, out of the dark loomed up a cottage made of gingerbread! Made of cheese, too, with a roof of Oreo cookies, and hard Christmas candy made a colourful winding path to the Hershey bar door. The picket fence was of peppermint sticks, the shrubbery of ice-cream cones, seven flavours. I flashed a thought over to Chris. *No!* This is a trick! We can't go in!

He messaged back: We have to go in! We have to save the twins!

Quietly we stole inside and saw the hot-roll cushions, dripping with golden butter, and the sofa was of freshly baked bread, buttered, too.

In the kitchen was the witch to end all witches! Beak-nosed, jutting jaw, sunken, toothless mouth, and her head was a mop of strings coloured grey and pointing wildly in all directions.

She held up our twins by their long golden hair. They were about to be thrust into her hot ovens! Already they were frosted pink and blue, and their flesh, without cooking, was beginning to turn into gingerbread, and their blue eyes into black raisins!

I screamed! Over and over again I screamed!

The witch whirled to glare at me with her grey flintstone eyes, and her sunken mouth, thin as a red knife slash, opened wide to laugh! Hysterically, she laughed on and on as Chris and I cringed in shock. She threw back her head, her wide open mouth exposing fang-like tonsils – and startlingly, frighteningly, she began to change from the grandmother. From a caterpillar into a butterfly she emerged as we stood frozen, and could only watch . . . and there from the horror came our mother!

Momma! Her blonde hair flowed as silken, streaming ribbons, writhing forward on the floor to snare us both like snakes! Slithering coils of her hair twined up and around our legs, to creep nearer our throats . . . trying to strangle us into silence . . . no threat to her inheritance then!

I love you, I love you, I love you, she whispered without words.

I woke up, but Chris slept on and on, just as the twins did.

I grew desperate as sleep wanted to come and take me again. I tried to fight it off, the terrible drowsiness of drowning, drowning, and then again I was sunken deep in dreams, in nightmarish dreams. I ran wild into the dark, and into a pool of blood I fell. Blood sticky as tar, smelling of tar, and diamond-spangled fish with swan heads and red eyes came and nibbled on my arms and legs so they went numb and unfeeling, and the fish with the swan heads laughed, laughed, laughed, glad to see me done in, and made bloody all over. See! See! They shouted in whiny voices that echoed and re-echoed. *You can't get away!*

The morning came pale behind the heavy drawn draperies that shut out the yellow light of hope.

Carrie turned over in her sleep and cuddled up closer to me, 'Momma,' she murmured, 'I don't like this house.' Her silky hair on my arm felt like goose-down, as slowly, slowly, feeling began to return to my hands and arms, feet and legs.

I lay still on the bed as Carrie squirmed restlessly, wanting my arms about her, and I felt so drugged I couldn't move my arms. What was wrong with me? My head so heavy, as if it were stuffed full of rocks so my skull was pressured from the inside and the pain was so great my skull was likely to split wide open! My toes and fingers still tingled. My body was leaden. The walls advanced, then retreated, and nothing had straight vertical lines.

I tried to see my reflection in the shimmering mirror across the way, yet when I tried to turn my swollen head, it refused to budge. And always before I went to sleep, I spread my hair on my pillow so I could turn my head, and nestle my cheek in the sweet-smelling silkiness of very pampered, well-cared-for, healthy, strong hair. It was one of the sensual things I enjoyed, the feel of my hair against my cheek to take me into sweet dreams of love.

And yet, today, there was no hair on my pillow. Where was my hair?

The scissors, they still lay on the dresser top. I could vaguely see them. Swallowing repeatedly to clear the way, I forced out a small cry, uttering Chris's name, not Momma's. I prayed to God to make Him let my brother hear. 'Chris,' I finally managed to whisper in the strangest, gritty voice, 'something is the matter with me.'

My whispered, weak words roused Chris, though I don't know how he heard. He sat up and sleepily rubbed his eyes. 'What yuh want, Cathy?' he asked.

I mumbled something that took him from his bed, and in his rumpled blue pyjamas, his hair a golden mop, he ambled over to my bed. He jerked up short. He drew in his breath and made small gasping sounds of horror and shock.

'Cathy, oh my God!'

His cry sent shivers of fear down my spine.

'Cathy . . . oh, Cathy,' he moaned.

As he stared, and as I wondered what he was seeing that made his eyes bulge, I tried to lift my leaden arms and feel my swollen, heavy head. Somehow I managed to get my hands up there – and that's when I found a loud voice to scream! Really scream! Over and over again I howled like someone demented until Chris ran to gather me in his arms.

'Stop, please stop,' he sobbed. 'Remember the twins . . . don't scare them more . . . please don't scream again, Cathy. They've been through so much, and I know you don't want to scar them permanently, and you will, if you don't calm down. It's all right, I'll get rid of it. I swear on my life, that today, somehow, I'll get the tar from your hair.'

He found a small red prick on my arm where the grandmother had plunged in a hypodermic needle to keep me asleep with some drug. And while I slept, she had poured hot tar on my hair. She must have gathered it all into a neat bunch before she used the tar, for not a strand was left free of the gook.

Chris tried to keep me from looking into the mirror, but I shoved him away, and had to stare with my mouth agape at the horrible black blob that was my head now. Like a huge wad of black bubble gum, chewed and left in an unsightly mess, it even ran down my face and streaked my cheeks with black tears!

I looked, and I knew that he'd never get the tar out. Never!

Cory woke up first, ready to run to the windows and draw aside the closed draperies and peek outside to see the sun that kept hiding from him. He was out of bed and ready to dash to the windows when he saw me.

His eyes widened. His lips parted. His small fluttering hands reached upwards to rub at his eyes with fists, and then he was staring at me again with so much disbelief. 'Cathy,' he managed finally, 'is that you?'

'I guess it is.'

'Why is your hair black?'

Before I could reply to that question, Carrie was awake. '*Oooh!*' she howled. 'Cathy – your head looks funny!' Big tears came to glisten her eyes and slide down her cheeks. 'I don't like your head now!' she wailed, then began to sob as if the tar were on *her* hair.

'Calm down, Carrie,' said Chris, in the most ordinary, everyday tone of voice. 'It's only tar on Cathy's hair – and when she takes a bath, and shampoos her hair, it will be the same as yesterday. While she does that, I want the two of you to eat the oranges for breakfast, and look at TV. Later on we'll all eat a real breakfast, when Cathy's hair is clean.' He didn't mention our grandmother for fear of instilling in them even more terror of our situation. So they sat on the floor close as book-ends, supporting only each other, and peeled and ate orange sections, losing themselves in the sweet nothingness of cartoons and other Saturday morning violence and foolishness.

Chris ordered me into a tub full of hot water. In that almost scalding water I dunked my head over and over again while Chris used shampoo to soften the tar. The tar did soften, but it didn't come out and leave my hair clean. His fingers moved in a sodden mass of sticky goo. I heard myself making small whimpering sounds. He did try, oh, he did try to take out the tar without taking out all my hair. And all I could think of was the scissors – the shiny scissors the grandmother had laid on the dresser top.

On his knees by the tub, Chris finally managed to work his fingers through the mass, but when he withdrew them, they were clogged with sticky black hair. 'You'll have to use the scissors!' I cried out, tired of the whole thing after two hours. But no, the scissors were the last resort. He reasoned there must be some chemical solution that would dissolve the tar, without dissolving my hair. He had a very professional chemistry set Momma had given him. On the lid was a stern warning: 'This is not a toy. This box contains dangerous chemicals and is for professional use only.'

'Cathy,' he said, sitting back on his bare heels, 'I'm going up to the attic schoolroom and mix some compound to take the tar from your hair.' He grinned at me shyly then. The light from the ceiling caught on the soft downy fuzz that covered his upper lip, and I knew he had stronger, darker hair on the lower part of his body, the same as I did. 'I've got to use the john, Cathy. I've never done that in front of you, and I'm kind of embarrassed. You can turn your back, and put your fingers in your ears, and maybe if you go in the water too, the ammonia might unglue your hair.'

I couldn't help but stare at him in amazement. The day had taken on nightmarish proportions. To sit in boiling water and use it for a toilet and then wash my hair in that? Could it be real that I would do this as Chris streamed urine into the commode behind my back? I said to myself, no, this wasn't real, just a dream. Carrie and Cory wouldn't use the bathroom, too, while I was in the tub, dunking my hair in foul water.

It was real enough. Hand in hand, Cory and Carrie came to the tub and stared at me, wanting to know why I was taking so long.

'Cathy, what is that stuff on your head?'

'Tar.'

'Why did you put tar in your hair?'

'I must have done it in my sleep.'

'Where did you find the tar?'

'In the attic.'

'Why did you want to put tar in your hair?'

I hated lying! I wanted to tell her who put the tar in my hair, but I couldn't let her know. Already she and Cory were scared enough of that old woman. 'Go back and look at TV, Carrie,' I ordered, testy and irritable from all the questions she asked, and hating to look at her thin, hollowed-out cheeks, her sunken eyes.

'Cathy, don't you like me no more?'

'Any more . . .'

'Don't you?'

'Of course I like you, Cory. I love you both, but I put the tar on my hair by mistake, and now I'm mad at myself.'

Carrie wandered off to sit once more near Cory. They whispered back and forth in that strange language that only they could understand. Sometimes, I think they were far wiser than Chris and I suspected.

For hours I was in the tub, while Chris concocted a dozen different compounds to test on a bit of my hair. He tried everything, making me change the water often, always making it hotter. I shrivelled into a puckered prune as bit by bit he cleared the gooey mess from my hair. The tar came out, eventually, along with a great loss of hair. But I had a lot, and could afford to lose much without making a noticeable difference. And when it was over, the day was gone, and neither Chris nor I had eaten a bite. He had given cheese and crackers to the twins, but he himself hadn't wasted time to eat. Wrapped in a towel, I sat on the bed and dried my much thinned hair. What was left was fragile. It broke easily, and the colour was almost platinum.

'You might as well have saved yourself the effort,' I said to Chris, who was hungrily eating two crackers with cheese. 'She hasn't brought up any food – and she won't bring any up until you cut it all off.'

He came to me, bearing a plate with cheese and crackers, and holding a glass of water. 'Eat and drink. We will out-smart her. If by tomorrow she doesn't bring up some food, or if Momma doesn't show up, I'll cut off just your front hair, over your forehead. Then you can wrap your head with a scarf, like you're ashamed to be seen bald-headed, and soon enough that hair will grow back in.'

Sparingly, I ate the cheese and crackers, not answering. I washed down my one meal of the day with water from the bathroom tap. Then Chris brushed that pale, pale weak hair that had endured so much. Peculiar how fate works things out: my hair had never gleamed more, or felt so much like gossamer silk, and I was grateful to have any left at all. I lay back on the bed, worn out, enervated by emotion torn asunder, and watched Chris sitting on the bed just looking at me. When I fell asleep, he was still there, watching me, and in his hand he held a long coil of my spider-web, silken hair.

That night I fretted in and out of sleep, restless, tormented. I felt helpless, angry, frustrated.

And then I saw Chris.

He was still in the clothes he'd worn all day. He'd moved the heaviest chair in the room so that it was against the door, and in that chair he sat and dozed, while in his hand he held the pair of long and sharp scissors. He had barred the way, so the grandmother couldn't sneak in again and use the scissors. He was, even in his sleep, guarding me from her.

As I stared over at him, his eyes opened, jolted, as if he hadn't meant to doze off and leave me unprotected. In the dimness of that locked room, always rosy at night, he caught my gaze, and our eyes locked, and ever so slowly he smiled. 'Hi.'

'Chris,' I sobbed, 'go to bed. You can't keep her out for ever.'

'I can while you sleep.'

'Then let me be the sentry. We'll take turns.'

'Who's the man here, you or me? Besides, I eat more than you do.'

'What's that got to do with it?'

'You're too thin now, and staying awake all night would make you thinner, whereas I can afford to lose weight.'

He was underweight, too. We all were, and his slight weight wouldn't keep that grandmother out if she really wanted to shove the door open. I got up and went to sit with him in the chair, though he gallantly protested.

'Ssh,' I whispered. 'The two of us together can keep her out better, and we can both sleep.' Embraced in each other's arms, we fell asleep.

And the morning came . . . without the grandmother . . . without food.

The hungry days passed by endlessly, miserably.

Only too soon the cheese and crackers were gone, though we ate most sparingly of what we had. And that was when we really began to suffer. Chris and I drank only water, and saved what milk there was for the twins.

Chris came to me with the shears in his hand, and reluctantly, with tears, he cut off the front top hair close to my scalp. I wouldn't look in a mirror when it was done. The long part that was left, I wrapped about my head, and over that I formed a scarf into a turban.

Then came the irony, the bitter irony of the grandmother not coming to check!

She didn't bring us food, or milk, or clean linens, or towels, or even the soap and toothpaste we had run out of. Not even toilet paper. Now I regretted throwing out all the tissue our expensive clothes came in. There was nothing left to do but tear pages from the oldest books in the attic and use that.

Then the toilet bowl stopped up, and overflowed, and Cory began to scream as filth flooded over and filled the bathroom. We didn't have a plunger. Frantically, Chris and I wondered what to do. As he ran for a coat hanger made of wire to straighten out and push down whatever clogged the drain, I ran to the attic to get old clothes to mop up the flooding mess.

Somehow Chris managed to use the wire coat hanger, and the commode worked normally again. Then, without a word, he got down on his knees beside me, and we both mopped up the floor with the old clothes from the attic trunks.

Now we had filthy, smelly rags to fill up a trunk, and add to the secrets of the attic.

We escaped the full horror of our situation by not talking about it much. We just got up in the mornings, splashed water on our faces, cleaned our teeth with plain water, drank a little water, moved about a little, then lay down to watch TV, or to read, and the devil to pay if she came in and caught us rumpling a bedspread. What did we care now?

To hear the twins cry for food put scars on my soul that I would bear for the rest of my life. And I hated, oh, how I hated that old woman – and Momma – for doing this to us!

And when mealtimes rolled by with no food, we slept. For hours on end we slept. Asleep you don't feel pain or hunger, or loneliness, or bitterness. In sleep you can drown in false euphoria, and when you awaken, you just don't care about anything.

There was one hazy, unreal day when we lay listless, all four of us, with the only life going on confined to the small box over in the corner. Dazed and tired, I turned my head for no reason at all just to look at Chris and Cory, and I lay without much feeling at all as I watched Chris take his pocket-knife and slash his wrist. He put his bleeding arm to Cory's mouth, and made him drink his blood, though Cory protested. Then it was Carrie's turn. The two of them, who wouldn't eat anything lumpy, bumpy, grainy, too stringy, or just plain 'funny looking', drank of their older brother's blood and stared up at him with dull, wide, accepting eyes.

I turned my head away, sickened by what he had to do, and full of admiration that he *could* do it. He could always solve a difficult problem.

Chris came to my side of the bed and perched on the edge, and looked at me for the longest moment, then his eyes lowered to the cut on his wrist that wasn't bleeding as freely now. He lifted his pocket-knife and prepared to make a second slash so I too could be nourished by his blood. I stopped him, and seized hold of his jack-knife and hurled it away. He ran fast to get it, and again he cleaned it with alcohol, despite my vow never to taste his blood, and drain from him more of his strength.

'What will we do, Chris, if she never comes back?' I asked dully. 'She will let us starve to death.' Meaning the grandmother, of course, whom we hadn't seen in two weeks. And Chris had exaggerated when he said we had a full pound of cheddar cheese stashed away. We baited our mousetrap with cheese, and had been forced to take back the bits of cheese to eat ourselves, when everything else was gone. Now we'd been without one bit of food in our stomachs for three whole days and four days with only a little cheese and crackers. And the milk we saved for the twins to drink – gone ten days ago, too.

'She won't let us starve to death,' said Chris as he lay down beside me and took me into his weak embrace. 'We'd be idiots, and spineless, to allow her to do that to us. Tomorrow, if she doesn't show up with food, and our mother doesn't show up, we'll use our sheet-ladder to reach the ground.'

My head was on his chest and I could hear his heart thumping. 'How do you know what she'd do? She hates us. She wants us dead – hasn't she told us that time and time again we should never have been born?'

'Cathy, the old witch is not dumb. She'll bring food soon, before Momma comes back from wherever she's been.'

I moved to bandage his slashed wrist. Two weeks ago Chris

and I should have tried to escape, when both of us had the strength to make the perilous descent. Now, if we tried to make it, surely we'd fall to our deaths, what with the twins tied to our backs to make it even more difficult.

But when morning came, and there was still no food brought up to us, Chris forced us into the attic. He and I carried the twins who were too weak to walk. It was a torrid zone up there. Sleepily, the twins sagged in the corner of the schoolroom where we put them down. Chris set about fashioning slings so we could attach the twins securely to our backs. Neither of us mentioned the possibility that we could be committing suicide, and murder, too, if we fell.

'We'll do it another way,' said Chris, reconsidering. 'I'll go first. When I reach the ground, you'll put Cory into a sling, tie him in fast so he can't kick free, and then you'll lower him down to me. Next, you can do that for Carrie. And you can come down last. And for God's sake, put forth your very best efforts! Call upon God to give you the strength – don't be apathetic! Feel anger, wrath, think of revenge! I've heard great anger gives you super-human strength in an emergency!'

'Let me go first. You're stronger,' I said weakly.

'No! I want to be down there to catch in case anyone comes down too fast, and your arms don't have the strength mine do. I'll brace the rope about a chimney so all the weight won't be on you – and Cathy, this is really an emergency!'

God, I couldn't believe what he expected me to do next!

With horror I stared at the four dead mice in our traps. 'We've got to eat these mice to gain some strength,' he said to me grimly, 'and what we have to do, we *can* do!'

Raw meat? Raw mice? 'No,' I whispered, revolted by the sight of those tiny stiff and dead things.

He grew forceful, angry, telling me I could do anything that was necessary to keep the twins alive, and myself alive. 'Look, Cathy, I'll eat my two first, after I've run downstairs for salt and pepper. And I need that coat hanger to tighten up the knots – leverage, you know. My hands, they're not working too good now.'

Of course they weren't. We were all so weak we could barely move.

He shot me a quick appraising glance. 'Really, with salt and pepper, I think the mice might be tasty.'

Tasty.

He sliced off the heads, then skinned and gutted them next. I watched him slice open the small bellies and withdraw long, slimy intestines, little bitty hearts, and other miniature 'innards'.

I could have vomited if there had been anything in my stomach.

And he didn't run for the salt and pepper, or the coat hanger. He only walked, and slowly at that – telling me in this way he wasn't too eager to partake of raw mice, either.

While he was gone, my eyes stayed glued to the skinned mice that were to be our next meal. I closed my eyes and tried to will myself into taking the first bite. I was hungry but not hungry enough to enjoy the prospect.

I thought then of the twins, who sagged in the corner with their eyes closed, holding each other, their foreheads pressed togethér, and I thought they must have embraced like that when they were inside Momma's womb, waiting to be born, so they could be put away behind a locked door, and starved. Our poor little buttercups who once had known a father and mother who loved them well.

Yet, there was the hope the mice would give Chris and me enough strength and we could take them safely to the ground, and some kind neighbour who was at home would give them food, give all of us food – if we lived through the next hour.

I heard the slow returning steps of Chris. He hesitated in the door-frame, half-smiling, his blue eyes meeting with mine . . . and shining. In both of his hands he carried the huge picnic basket we knew so well. It was so filled with food the wooden lids that folded backwards couldn't lie flat.

He lifted out two Thermos jugs: one with vegetable soup, the other with cold milk, and I felt so numb, confused, hopeful. Had Momma come back and sent this up to us? Then why hadn't she called for us to come down? Or why didn't she come looking for us?

Chris took Carrie and I took Cory on our laps, and we spooned soup into their mouths. They accepted the soup as they had accepted his blood – as just another event in their extraordinary lives. We fed them bits of sandwich. We ate most sparingly, as Chris cautioned, lest we threw it up.

I wanted to stuff the food into Cory's mouth, so I could get around to ramming food into my own ravenous stomach. He ate so darned slow! A thousand questions ran through my brain: Why today? Why bring food today and not yesterday, or the day before? What was her reasoning? When finally I could eat, I was too apathetic to be overjoyed, and too suspicious to be relieved.

Chris, after slowly eating some soup, and half a sandwich, unwrapped a foil package. Four powdered-sugar doughnuts were disclosed. We, who were never given sweets, were given a dessert – from the grandmother – for the first time. Was this her way of asking our forgiveness? We took it that way, whatever her purpose.

During our week of near starvation, something peculiar had happened between Chris and me. Perhaps it became enhanced that day when I sat in the hot tub of concealing bubble bath, and he toiled so valiantly to rid my hair of the tar. Before that horrible day, we'd been only brother and sister, play-acting the roles of parents to the twins. Now our relationship had changed. We weren't play-acting any more. We were the genuine parents of Carrie and Cory. They were our responsibility, our obligation, and we committed ourselves to them totally, and to each other.

It was obviously drawn now. Our mother didn't care any more what happened to us.

Chris didn't need to speak and say how he felt to recognize her indifference. His bleak eyes told me. His listless movements said more. He'd kept her picture near his bed, and now he put that away. He'd always believed in her more than I, so naturally he was hurt the most. And if he ached more than I was aching, then he was in agony.

Tenderly he took my hand, indicating that now we could go back to the bedroom. Down the stairs we drifted as pale sleepy ghosts, in sub-normal states of shock, all of us feeling sick and weak, especially the twins. I doubted they weighed thirty pounds each. I could see how they looked, and how Chris looked, but I couldn't see myself. I glanced towards the tall, wide mirror over the dresser, expecting to see a circus freak, short-cropped hair on top, long, lank pale hair in back. And lo, when I looked, there was no mirror there!

Quickly I ran to the bathroom to find the medicine cabinet mirror smashed! Back I raced to the bedroom, to lift the lid of the dressing-table that Chris often used as a desk . . . and that mirror, too, was broken!

We could gaze in shattered glass and see distorted reflections of ourselves. Yes, we could view our faces in faceted broken pieces as a fly would, one side of the nose riding up higher than the other. It wasn't pleasant viewing. Turning away from the dressing-table, I put the basket of food down on the floor where it was coldest, then went to lie down. I didn't question the reason for the broken mirrors, and the one taken away. I knew why she'd done what she did. Pride was sinful. And in her eyes Chris and I were sinners of the worst kind. To punish us, the twins would suffer, as well, but why she brought us food again, I couldn't guess.

Other mornings came, with baskets of food carried up to us. The grandmother refused to look our way. She kept her eyes averted and swiftly retreated out the door. I wore a turban made of a pink towel around my head which revealed the front portion over my brow, but if she noticed, she didn't comment. We watched her come and go, not asking where Momma was, or when she was coming back. Those so easily punished learn their lesson well, and don't speak unless spoken to first. Both Chris and I stared at her, filling our eyes with hostility, with anger and hate, hoping she'd turn and see how we felt. But she didn't meet a pair of our eyes. And then I would cry out and make her see, and make her look at the twins, and see for herself how thin they were, how shadowed their large eyes were. But she wouldn't see.

Lying on the bed beside Carrie, I looked deep into myself and realized how I was making all of this worse than it ought to be. Now Chris, once the cheerful optimist, was turning into a gloomy imitation of me. I wanted him back the way he used to be – smiling and bright, making the best out of the worst.

He sat at the dressing-table with the lid down, with open medical books before him, his shoulders sagging. He wasn't reading, or making notes. Just sitting there.

'Chris,' I said, sitting up to brush my hair, 'in your opinion, what percentage of teen-aged girls in the world have gone to bed with clean, shining hair and awakened a tar baby?'

Swivelling around, he shot me a glance full of surprise that I would mention that horrible day. 'Well,' he drawled, 'in my opinion, I suspect you might well be the one and only . . . unique.'

'Oh, I don't know about that. Remember when they were putting down asphalt on our street? Mary Lou Baker and I turned over a huge tub of that stuff, and we made little tar babies, and put black beds in black houses, and the man in charge of the street-repair gang came along and bawled us out.'

'Yeah,' he said, 'I remember you came home looking filthy-dirty, and you had a wad of tar in your mouth, chewing to make your teeth whiter. Gosh, Cathy, all you did was pull out a filling.'

'One good thing about this room, we don't have to visit dentists twice a year.' He gave me a funny look. 'And another nice thing is to have so much time! We'll complete our Monopoly tournament. The champion player has to wash everyone's underwear in the bathtub.'

Boy, he was all for that. He hated bending over the tub, kneeling on the hard tile, doing his wash and Cory's.

We set up the game, and counted out the money, and looked around for the twins. Both had disappeared! Where was there to go but up in the attic? They'd never go there without us, and the bathroom was empty. Then we heard some small twittering noises behind the TV set.

There they were, crouched in the corner in back of the set, sitting and waiting for the tiny people inside to come out. 'We thought maybe Momma was in there,' explained Carrie.

'I think I'll go up in the attic and dance,' I said, getting up from the bed and moving towards the closet.

'Cathy! What about our tournament Monopoly game?'

Pausing, I half-turned. 'Oh, you'd only win. Forget the tournament.'

'Coward!' he taunted now, the same as he used to. 'Come on, let's play.' He looked long and hard at the twins, who always acted as our bankers. 'And no cheating this time,' he warned sternly, 'if I catch one of you slipping Cathy money when you think I'm not looking – then I'll eat every one of those four doughnuts myself!'

I'll be darned if he would! The doughnuts were the best part of our meals, and saved for night-time dessert. I threw myself down on the floor, crossed my legs, and busied my brain with clever ways in which I would get to buy the best property first, and the railroads, and the utilities, and I'd get my red houses up first, then the hotels. He'd see who was good at doing something better than him.

For hours and hours we played, stopping only to eat meals or go to the bathroom. When the twins grew tired of playing bankers, we counted out the money ourselves, closely watching each other to see if any cheating was going on. And Chris kept landing up in jail, and had to miss out on passing Go and collecting two hundred dollars, and the Community Chest made him give, and he had to pay inheritance tax . . . and *still* he won!

Late in August Chris came to me one night and whispered in my ear, 'The twins are sound asleep. And it's so hot in here. Wouldn't it be just great if we could go for a swim?'

'Go away – leave me alone – you know we can't go swimming.' I was, of course, still sulky from always losing at Monopoly.

Swimming, what an idiotic idea. Even if we could, I didn't want to do anything in which he excelled, like swimming. 'And just where are we going to swim? In the bathtub?'

'In the lake Momma told us about. It's not far from here,' he whispered. 'We ought to practice reaching the ground with that rope we made, anyway, just in case there's a fire. We're stronger now. We can reach the ground easily, and we won't be gone long.' On and on he pleaded, as if his very existence depended on escaping this house just once – just to prove that we could.

'The twins might wake up and find us gone.'

'We'll leave a note on the bathroom door, telling them we're up in the attic. And besides, they never wake up until morning, not even to go to the bathroom.'

He argued, and pleaded until I was won over. Up into the attic we went, and out on to the roof where he fastened the sheet-ladder securely to the chimney closest to the back side of the house. There were eight chimneys on the roof.

Testing the knots one by one, Chris gave me instructions: 'Use the large knots as a ladder rung. Keep your hands just above the higher knot. Go down slowly, feeling with your feet for the next knot – and be sure to keep the rope twisted between your legs, so you can't slip and fall.'

Smiling with confidence, he held to the rope and inched his way to the very edge of the roof. We were going down to the ground for the first time in more than two years.

A TASTE OF HEAVEN

Slowly, carefully, hand under hand, and foot under foot, Chris descended to the ground while I lay flat on my stomach near the roof's edge watching his descent. The moon was out and shining brightly as he lifted his hand and waved: his signal to send me on my way. I had watched the way he handled himself, so I could duplicate his method. I told myself it was no different from swinging on the ropes tied to the attic rafters. The knots were big and strong, and we had judiciously made them about four and a half feet apart. He had told me not to look down once I left the roof, just to concentrate on notching one foot securely on a lower knot before I reached with my other foot to find an even lower knot. In less than ten minutes, I was standing on the ground next to Chris.

'Wow!' he whispered, hugging me close. 'You did that better than me!'

We were in the back gardens of Foxworth Hall, where all the rooms were dark, though in the servants' quarters over the huge garage every window was brightly yellow. 'Lead on, MacDuff, to the swimming hole,' I said in a low voice, 'if you know the way.'

Sure, he knew the way. Momma had told us how she and her brothers used to steal away and go swimming with their friends.

He caught my hand as we tiptoed away from the huge house. It felt so strange to be outside, on the ground, on a warm summer night. Leaving our small brother and sister alone in a locked room. When we crossed over a small footbridge, and knew we were now outside the realm of Foxworth property, we felt happy, almost free. Still we had to be cautious and not let anyone see us. We ran towards the woods, and the lake Momma had told us about.

It was ten o'clock when we went out on the roof; it was ten-thirty when we found the small body of water surrounded by trees. We were fearful others would be there to spoil it for us, and send us back unsatisfied, but the lake water was smooth, unruffled by winds, or bathers, or sailboats.

In the moonlight, under a bright and starry sky, I looked on that lake and thought I'd never beheld such beautiful water, or felt a night that filled me with such rapture.

'Are we going to skinny-dip?' asked Chris, looking at me in a peculiar way.

'No. We are going to swim in our underwear.'

The trouble was, I didn't own a single bra. But now that we were here, silly prudery wasn't going to stop me from enjoying that moonlit water. 'Last one in is a rotten egg!' I called. And I took off, on the run towards a short dock. But when I reached the end of the dock, I somehow sensed the water might be icy cold, and most gingerly I cautiously stuck a toe in first – and it was ice cold! I glanced back at Chris, who had taken off his watch and flung it aside, and now he was coming at me fast. So darned fast, before I could brave myself to dive into the water, he was behind me, and shoved me! Splash – flat down in the water I was, soaked from head to toe, and not inch by inch, as I would have had it!

I shivered as I came to the surface and paddled around, looking for Chris. Then I spied him crawling up a pile of rocks, and for a moment he was silhouetted. He lifted his arms and gracefully made a swan dive into the middle of the lake. I gasped! What if the water wasn't deep enough? What if he hit the bottom and broke his neck or back?

And then, and then . . . he didn't surface! Oh God . . . he was dead . . . drowned!

'Chris,' I called, sobbing, and began to swim towards the spot where he had disappeared beneath the cold water.

Suddenly I was seized by the legs! I screamed and went under, pulled down by Chris, who kicked his legs strongly and took us both up to the surface, where we laughed, and I splashed water into his face for playing such a dirty trick.

'Isn't this better than being shut up in that damned hot room?' he asked, frolicking around like someone demented, delirious, wild, and crazy! It was as if this bit of freedom had gone to his head like strong wine, and he was drunk! He swam in circles around me, and tried again to catch my legs and drag me under. But I was wise to him now. He kicked to the surface and back-stroked, he also did the breaststroke, the crawl, side-stroked, and named what he did as he performed. 'This is the back crawl,' he said as he demonstrated, showing off techniques I'd never seen before.

He surfaced from a dive under, and treaded water as he began to sing, 'Dance, ballerina, dance,' – and in my face he threw water, as I splashed it back at him – 'and do your pirouette in rhythm with your aching heart . . .' And then he had me in his embrace, and laughing and screaming, we fought, gone crazy just to be children again. Oh, he was wonderful in the water, like a dancer. Suddenly I was tired, extremely tired, so tired I felt weak as a wet dishcloth. Chris put his arm about me and assisted me up on to shore.

Both of us fell on a grassy bank to lie back and talk.

'One more swim, and then back to the twins,' he said, lying supine on the gentle slope beside me. Both of us stared up at a sky full of glittering, twinkling stars, and there was a quarter-moon out, coloured silvery-gold, and it ducked and hid, and played hide-and-seek with the strung-out long, dark clouds.

'Suppose we can't make it back up to the roof?'

'We'll make it, because we have to make it.'

That was my Christopher Doll, the eternal optimist, sprawled beside me, all wet and glistening, with his fair hair pasted to his forehead. His nose was the same as Daddy's as it aimed at the heavens, his full lips so beautifully shaped he didn't need to pout to make them sensual, his chin square, strong, clefted, and his chest was beginning to broaden . . . and there was that hillock of his growing maleness before his strong thighs, beginning to swell. There was something about a man's strong, well-shaped thighs that excited me. I turned away my head, unable to feast my eyes on his beauty without feeling guilty and ashamed.

Birds were nested overhead in the tree branches. They made sleepy little twittery noises that for some reason made me think of the twins, and that made me sad and put tears in my eyes.

Fireflies bobbed up every so often and flashed their lemon-coloured tail-lights off and on, signalling male to female, or vice-versa. 'Chris, is it the male firefly that lights up, or the female?'

'I'm really not sure,' he said as if he didn't care. 'I think they both light up, but the female stays on the ground signalling, while the male flies around looking for her.'

'You mean you aren't positive about everything – you, the all-knowing?'

'Cathy, let's not quibble. I don't know everything – a long way from it.' He turned his head and met my eyes; our gazes locked and neither of us seemed capable of looking elsewhere.

Soft southern breezes came and played in my hair and dried the wisps about my face. I felt them tickling like small kisses, and again I wanted to cry, for no reason at all, except the night was so sweet, so lovely, and I was at the age for high romantic yearning. And the breeze whispered loving words in my ears . . . words I was so afraid no one was ever going to say. Still, the night was so lovely under the trees, near the shimmering moonlit water, and I sighed. I felt that I'd been here before, on this grass near the lake. Oh, the strange thoughts I had as the night-fliers hummed and whirred, and the mosquitoes buzzed and somewhere far off an owl hooted, taking me quickly back to the night when first we came to live as fugitives, hidden from a world that didn't want us.

'Chris, you're almost seventeen, the same age Daddy was when he first met Momma.'

'And you're fourteen, the same age she was,' he said in a hoarse voice.

'Do you believe in love at first sight?'

He hesitated, mulling that over . . . his way, not mine. 'I'm not an authority on that subject. I know when I was in school, I'd see a pretty girl and right away feel in love with her. Then when we'd talk, and she was kind of stupid, then I didn't feel anything at all about her. But if her beauty had been matched by other assets, I think I could fall in love at first sight, though I've read that kind of love is only physical attraction.'

'Do you think I'm stupid?'

He grinned and reached out to touch my hair. 'Gosh, no. And I hope you don't think you are, because you're not. Your trouble is, Cathy, you have too many talents; you want to be everything, and that's not possible.'

'How do you know I'd like to be a singer and an actress, too?'

He laughed soft and low. 'Silly girl, you're acting ninety per cent of the time, and singing to yourself when you feel contented; unfortunately, that's not very often.'

'Are *you* contented often?'

'No.'

So we lay, silent, from time to time staring at something that drew our attention, like the fireflies that met on the grass and mated, and the whispering leaves, and the floating clouds, and the play of the moonlight on the water. The night seemed enchanted and set me to thinking again of nature, and all its strange ways. Though I didn't understand fully many of its ways, why I dreamed as I did at night now, why I woke up throbbing and yearning for some fulfilment that I could never reach.

I was glad Chris had persuaded me into coming. It was wonderful to be lying on grass again, feeling cool and refreshed, and most of all, feeling fully alive again.

'Chris,' I began tentatively, afraid to spoil the soft beauty of this star-filled moonlit night, 'where do you think our mother is?'

He kept right on staring at Polaris, the north star.

'I have no idea where she is,' he answered finally.

'Don't you have any suspicions?'

'Sure. Of course I do.'

'What are they?'

'She could be sick.'

'She's not sick; Momma's never sick.'

'She could be away on a business trip for her father.'

'Then why didn't she come and tell us she was going, and when to expect her back?'

'I don't know!' he said irritably, like I was spoiling the evening for him, and of course he couldn't know, any more than I could.

'Chris, do you love and trust her as much as you used to?'

'Don't ask me questions like that! She's my mother. She's all we've got, and if you expect me to lie here and say mean things about her, I'm not going to do it! Wherever she is tonight, she's thinking of us, and she's coming back. She'll have a perfectly good reason for going away and staying so long, you can count on that.'

I couldn't say to him what I was really thinking, that she could have found time to come in and tell us of her plans – for he knew that as well as I did.

There was a husky tone to his voice that came about only when he was feeling pain – and not the physical kind. I wanted to take away the hurt I'd inflicted with my questions. 'Chris, on TV, girls my age, and boys your age – they start to date. Would you know how to act on a date?'

'Sure, I've watched a lot on TV.'

'But watching isn't the same as doing.'

'Still it gives you the general idea of what to do, and what to say. And besides, you're still too young to date guys.'

'Now let me tell you something, Mr Big Brain, a girl of my age is actually one year older than a boy of your age.'

'You're crazy!'

'Crazy? I read that fact in a magazine article, written by an authority on the subject – a doctor of psychology,' I said, thinking he was sure to be impressed. 'He said girls mature emotionally much quicker than boys do.'

'The author of that article was judging all mankind by *his own* immaturity.'

'Chris, you think you know everything – and nobody knows everything!'

He turned his head and met my eyes and scowled, like he used to do so often. 'You're right,' he agreed pleasantly. 'I know only what I read, and what I'm feeling inside has me as mystified as any first-grader. I'm mad as hell at Momma because of what she's done, and I'm feeling so many different things, and I don't have a man to talk them over with.' He rose on an elbow to stare down in my face. 'I wish it wasn't taking your hair so long to grow back. I wish now I hadn't used the scissors . . . didn't do any good, anyway.'

It was better when he didn't say anything to make me think of Foxworth Hall. I just wanted to look up at the sky and feel the fresh night air on my wet skin. My pyjamas were of thin white batiste, scattered all over with rosebuds, and edged with lace. They clung to me like a second skin, just as Chris's white jockey shorts clung to him.

'Let's go now, Chris.'

Reluctantly, he got up and stretched out a hand. 'Another swim?'

'No. Let's go back.'

Silently, we headed away from the lake, walking slowly through the woods, drinking in the sensation of being outside, on the ground.

We headed back to our responsibilities. For the longest time we stood by the rope we'd made, fastened to a chimney far above. I wasn't thinking of how we'd make the ascent, only wondering what we'd gained by this brief little escape from a prison we had to enter again.

'Chris, do you feel different?'

'Yes. We didn't do very much but walk and run on the ground, and swim for a short while, but I feel more alive and more hopeful.'

'We could get away if we wanted to – tonight – and not wait for Momma to come back. We could go up, make slings to carry the twins, and while they sleep we could carry them down. We could run away! We'd be *free*!'

He didn't answer, but began the ascent to the roof, hand over hand, with the sheet-ladder caught fast between his legs as he worked his way up. As soon as he was on the roof, I began, for we didn't trust the rope to hold the weight of two people. It was much harder going up than coming down. My legs seemed so much stronger than my arms. I reached above for the next knot, and lifted my right leg. Suddenly my left foot slipped from where I'd notched it and I was swinging free – held only by weak hands!

A short scream tore from my lips! I was more than twenty feet from the ground!

'Hold on!' called Chris from above. 'The rope is directly between both your legs. All you have to do is squeeze them together quick!'

I couldn't see what I was doing. All I could do was follow his directions. I grasped the rope between my thighs, quivering all over. Fear made me weaker. The longer I stayed in one place, the more fearful I became. I began to gasp, to tremble. And then came the tears . . . stupid girlish tears!

'You are almost within reach of my hands,' called Chris. 'Just a few more feet up, and I can reach you. Cathy, don't panic. Think of how much the twins need you! Try . . . try hard!'

I had to talk myself into letting go with one hand, to reach higher for another knot. I said over and over again to myself, I *can* do it. I can. My feet were slippery from the grass – but then, Chris's feet had been slippery, too, and he managed. And if he could do it, then I could too.

Bit by terrifying bit I climbed up that rope to where Chris could reach down and grasp my wrists. Once his strong hands had me, a surge of relief tingled my blood down to my fingertips and to my toes. In a few seconds he hauled me up, and I was seized in a tight embrace while we both laughed and then almost cried. Then we crawled up the steep slope, keeping fast hold of the rope until we reached the chimney. That's when we fell down in our accustomed place and shivered all over.

Oh, the irony of it – that we would be glad to be back!

Chris lay on his bed and stared over at me. 'Cathy, for just a second or two, when we were lying on the bank of the lake, it seemed a bit like heaven. Then when you faltered on the rope, I thought I might die too, if you did. We can't do that again. You don't have the strength in your arms that I do. I'm sorry I forgot about that.'

The night lamp was burning with a rosy glow over in the corner. Our eyes met in the dimness. 'I'm not sorry we went. I'm glad. It's been so long since I felt real.'

'Did you feel like that?' he asked. 'So did I . . . just like we had left a bad dream that was lasting too long.'

I dared again, had to. 'Chris, where *do* you think Momma is? She's drifting away from us gradually, and she never really looks at the twins, like they scare her now. But she's never stayed away this long before. She's been gone over a month.'

I heard his heavy, sad sigh. 'Honestly, Cathy, I just don't know. She hasn't told me any more than she's told you – but you can bet she's got a good reason.'

'But what kind of reason could she have to leave without an explanation? Isn't that the least she could do?'

'I don't know what to say.'

'If I had children, I would never leave them the way she does. I'd never stick my four children away in a locked room and then forget them.'

'You're not going to have any children, remember?'

'Chris, some day I'm going to dance in the arms of a husband who loves me, and if he really wants a baby, then I might agree to have one.'

'Sure, I knew all along you'd change your mind once you grew up.'

'You really think I'm pretty enough for a man to love?'

'You're *more* than pretty enough.' He sounded embarrassed.

'Chris, remember when Momma told us that it was money that made the world go around and not love? Well, I think she's wrong.'

'Yeah? Give that a bit more thought. Why can't you have both?'

I gave it thought. Plenty of thought. I lay and stared up at the ceiling that was my dancing floor, and I mulled life and love over and over. And from every book I'd ever read, I took one wise bead of philosophy and strung them all into a rosary to believe in for the rest of my life.

Love, when it came and knocked on my door, was going to be enough.

And that unknown author who'd written that if you had fame, it was not enough, and if you had wealth as well, it was still not enough, and if you had fame, wealth, and also love . . . still it was not enough – boy, did I feel sorry for him.

ONE RAINY AFTERNOON

Chris was at the windows, both hands holding open the heavy tapestry draperies. The sky was leaden, the rain came down in a solid sheet. Every lamp in our room was lit, and the TV was on, as usual. Chris was waiting to see the train that would pass by around four. You could hear its mournful whistle before dawn, around four, and then later if you were awake. You could just barely catch a glimpse of the train that appeared to be a toy, it was so far away.

He was in his world, I was in mine. Sitting cross-legged on the bed Carrie and I shared, I cut pictures from decorating magazines Momma had brought up for my entertainment before she went away to stay so long. I cut each photograph out carefully and pasted them into a large scrapbook. I was planning my dream house, where I would live happily ever after, with a tall, strong, dark-haired husband who loved only me and not a thousand others on the side.

I had my life mapped out: my career first, a husband and children when I was ready to retire and give someone else a chance. And when I had my dream home, I'd have an emerald-glass tub situated on a dais where I could soak in beauty oil all day long if I wanted to – and nobody would be outside the door, banging and telling me to hurry up! (I never had the chance to sit in the tub long enough.) From that emerald tub I'd step, smelling sweet of flowered perfume, and my skin soft as satin, and my pores would be for ever cleansed of the rotten stench of dry old wood and attic dust permeated with all the miseries of antiquity . . . so that we, who were young, smelled as old as this house.

'Chris,' I said, turning to stare at his back, 'why should we stay on and on, and wait for Momma to come back, much less wait for that old man to die? Now that we are strong, why don't we find a way to escape?'

He didn't say a word. But I saw his hands clutch the fabric of the draperies harder.

'Chris . . .'

'I don't want to talk about it!' he flared.

'Why are you standing there waiting for the train to pass, if you aren't thinking about getting away?'

'I'm not waiting for the train! I'm just looking out, that's all!'

His forehead was pressed against the glass, daring a close neighbour to look out and see him.

'Chris, come away from the window. Someone might see you.'

'I don't give a damn who sees me!'

My first impulse was to run to him, to put my arms around him, and lavish a million kisses on his face to make up for those he was missing from Momma. I'd draw his head down against my breast and cuddle it there as she used to do, and he'd go back to being the cheerful, sunny optimist who never had a sullen angry day like I used to. Even if I did all that Momma did once, I was wise enough to know it wouldn't be the same. It was *her* he wanted. He had all his hopes, dreams, and faith wrapped up in one single woman – Momma.

She'd been gone more than two months! Didn't she realize one day up here was longer than a month of normal living? Didn't she worry about us, and wonder how we were faring? Did she believe that Chris would always be her staunchest supporter when she left us without an excuse, a reason, an explanation? Did she really believe that love, once gained, couldn't be torn asunder by doubts and fears, and could never, never be put back together again?

'Cathy,' said Chris suddenly, 'where would you go if you had your choice of anywhere?'

'South,' I said, 'down to some warm, sunny beach, where the waves wash in gentle and low . . . don't want high surf with white caps . . . don't want the grey sea chafing against big rocks . . . I want to go where the wind never blows, I just want soft warm breezes to whisper in my hair and on my cheeks, while I lie on pure white sand, and drink up the sunlight.'

'Yeah,' he agreed, sounding wistful, 'sounds nice the way you say it. Only I wouldn't mind a strong surf; I'd like to ride the crest of a wave on one of those surfboards. It would sort of be like skiing.'

I put my scissors down, my magazines, my pot of rubber cement, and laid aside the magazines and scrapbook to fully concentrate on Chris. He was missing out on so many sports he loved, shut up here in one room, made old and sad beyond his years. Ah, how I wanted to comfort him, and I didn't know how.

'Come away from the windows, Chris, please.'

'Leave me alone! I get so damned sick and tired of this place! Don't do this, don't do that! Don't speak until spoken to – eat those damned meals every day, none of it hot enough, or seasoned right – I think *she* does it deliberately, just so we'll never have anything to enjoy, even food. Then I think about all that money – half of it should be Momma's, and ours. And I tell myself, no matter what, it is worth it! That old man can't live for ever!'

'All the money in the world isn't worth the days of living we've lost!' I flared back.

He spun around, his face red. 'The hell it isn't! Maybe you can get by with your talent, but I've got years and years of education ahead of me! You know Daddy expected me to be a doctor, so come hell or high water, I'm getting my MD! And if we run away, I'll never be a doctor – you know that! Name what I can do to earn a living for us – quick, list the jobs I can get other than a dish-washer, a fruit-picker a short-order cook – will any of those put me through college, and then through med. school? And I'll have you and the twins to support, as well as myself – a ready-made family at age sixteen!'

Fiery anger filled me. He didn't give me credit for being able to contribute anything! 'I can work, too!' I snapped back. 'Between us we can manage. Chris, when we were starving, you brought me four dead mice, and you said God gives people extra strength and abilities in the time of great stress. Well, I believe He does. When we leave here and are on our own, somehow or other we will make our way, and you will be a doctor! I'll do anything to see that you get that damned MD behind your name!'

'What can *you* do?' he asked in a hateful, sneering way. Before I could reply, the door behind us opened and the grandmother was there! She paused without stepping into the room and fixed her glare on Chris. And he, stubborn and unwilling to co-operate as before, refused to be intimidated. He didn't move from the window, but he turned to stare out at the rain again.

'Boy!' she lashed out. *'Move away from that window – this instant!'*

'My name is not "boy". My name is Christopher. You can address me by my given name, or don't address me at all – but never call me "*boy*" again!'

She spat at his back: 'I hate that particular name! It was your father's; out of the kindness of my heart, I pleaded his cause when his mother died, and he didn't have a home. My husband didn't want him here, but I felt pity for a young boy without parents, or means, and robbed of so much. So I kept nagging my husband to let his younger half-brother live under our roof. So your father came . . . brilliant, handsome, and he took advantage of our generosity. Deceived us! We sent him to the best of schools, bought him the best of everything, and he stole our daughter, his own half-niece! She was all we had left then . . . the only one left . . . and they eloped in the night, and came back two weeks later, smiling, happy, asking us to forgive them for falling in love. That night, my husband had his first heart attack. Has your mother told you that – that she and that man were the cause of her father's heart disease? He ordered her out – told her never to come back – and then he fell down on the floor.'

She stopped, gasping for breath, putting a large strong hand flashing with diamonds to her throat. Chris turned away from the window and stared at her, as did I. This was more than she had said to us since we came up the stairs to live, an eternity ago.

'We are not to blame for what our parents did,' Chris said flatly.

'You are to blame for what you and your sister have done!'

'What have we done so sinful?' he asked. 'Do you think we can live in one room, year after year, and not see each other? You helped put us here. You have locked this wing so the servants cannot enter. You *want* to catch us doing something you consider evil. You want Cathy and me to prove your judgment of our mother's marriage is right! Look at you, standing there in your iron-grey dress, feeling pious and self-righteous while you starve small children!'

'Stop!' I cried, terrified by what I saw on the grandmother's face. 'Chris, don't say anything else!'

But he had already said too much. She slammed out of the room as my heart came up in my throat. 'We'll go up in the attic,' said Chris calmly. 'The coward is afraid of the stairwell. We'll be safe enough, and if she starves us, we'll use the sheet-ladder and reach the ground.'

Again the door opened. The grandmother came, striding forward with a green willow switch in her hand, and grim determination in her eyes. She must have stashed the switch somewhere nearby, to have fetched it so quickly. 'Run into the attic and hide,' she lashed out, reaching to seize Chris by his upper arm, 'and none of you will eat for another week! And not only will I whip you, but your sister, as well, if you resist, and the twins.'

It was October. In November, Chris would be seventeen. He was still only a boy compared to her huge size. He was considering resistance, but glanced at me, then at the twins, who whimpered and clung to each other, and he allowed that old woman to drag him into the bathroom. She closed and locked the door. She ordered him to strip, and to lean over the bathtub.

The twins came running to me, burying their faces in my lap. 'Make her stop!' pleaded Carrie. 'Don't let her whip Chris!'

He didn't make a sound as that whip slashed down on his bare skin. I heard the sickening thuds of green willow biting into flesh. And I felt every painful blow! Chris and I had become as one in the past year; he was like the other side of me, the way I'd like to be, strong and forceful, and able to stand that whip without crying out. I hated her. I sat on that bed, and gathered the twins in my arms, and felt hate so large looming up inside of me that I didn't know how to release it except by screaming. He felt the whip, and I let loose his cries of pain. I hoped God heard! I hoped the servants heard! I hoped that dying grandfather heard!

Out of the bathroom she came, with her whip in her hand. Behind her, Chris trailed, a towel swathed around his hips. He was dead-white. I couldn't stop screaming.

'Shut up!' she ordered, snapping the whip before my eyes. 'Silence this second, unless you want more of the same!'

I couldn't stop screaming, not even when she dragged me off to the bed and threw the twins aside when they tried to protect me. Cory went for her leg with his teeth. She sent him reeling with one blow. I went then, my hysteria quelled, into the bathroom, where I, too, was ordered to strip. I stood there looking at her diamond brooch, the one she always wore, counting the stones, seventeen tiny ones. Her grey taffeta was patterned with fine red lines, and the white collar was hand-crocheted. She fixed her eyes on the short stubble of hair the scarf about my head revealed with an expression of gloating satisfaction.

'Undress, or I will rip off your clothes.'

I began to undress, slowly working on the buttons of my blouse. I didn't wear a bra then, though I needed one. I saw her eyeing my breasts, my flat stomach, before she turned her eyes away, apparently offended. 'I'm going to get even one day, old woman,' I said. 'There's going to come a day when you are going to be the helpless one, and I'm going to hold the whip in my hands. And there's going to be food in the kitchen that you are never going to eat, for, as you incessantly say, God sees everything, and he has his way of working justice, an eye for an eye is his way, Grandmother!'

'Never speak to me again!' she snapped. She smiled then, confident there would never come that day when I was in control of her fate. Foolishly, I had spoken, using the worst possible timing, and she let me have it. While the whip bit down on my tender flesh, in the bedroom the twins screamed, 'Chris, make her stop! Don't let Cathy be hurt!'

I fell down on my knees near the tub, crouching in a tight ball to protect my face, my breasts, my most vulnerable areas. Like a wild woman out of control, she lashed at me until the willow switch broke. The pain was like fire. When the switch broke, I thought it was over, but she picked up a long-handled brush and with that she beat me about the head and shoulders. Try as I would to keep from screaming, like the brave silence Chris had kept, I had to let it out. I yelled, 'You're not a woman! You're a monster! Something unhuman and inhumane!' My reward for this was a belting whack against the right side of my skull. Everything went black.

I drifted into reality, hurting all over, my head splitting with pain. Up in the attic a record was playing the 'Rose Adiago' from the ballet *The Sleeping Beauty*. If I live to be a hundred I will never forget that music, and the way I felt when I opened my eyes to see Chris bending over me, applying antiseptic, taping on adhesive plasters, tears in his eyes dropping down on me. He'd ordered the twins up into the attic to play, to study, to colour, to do anything to keep their minds off of what was going on down here. When he had done for me all that he could with his inadequate medical supplies, I took care of his welted, bloody back. Neither of us wore clothes. Clothes would adhere to our oozing cuts. I had the most bruises from the brush she'd wielded so cruelly. On my head was a dark lump that Chris feared might be a concussion.

Doctoring over, we turned on our sides, facing one another under the sheet. Our eyes locked and melded as one set. He touched my cheek, the softest, most loving caress. 'Don't we have fun, my brother . . . don't we have fun?' I sang in a parody of that song about Bill Bailey. 'We'll hurt the livelong da-ay . . . you'll do the doctoring and I'll pay the rent . . .'

'Stop!' he cried out, looking hurt and defenceless. 'I know it was my fault! I stood at the window. She didn't have to hurt you, too!'

'It doesn't matter, sooner or later she would do it. From the very first day, she planned to punish us for some trifling reason. I just marvel that she held back for so long in using that whip.'

'When she was lashing me, I heard you screaming – and I didn't have to. You did it for me, Cathy, and it helped; I didn't feel any pain but yours.'

We held each other carefully. Our bare bodies pressed together; my breasts flattened out against his chest. Then he was murmuring my name, and tugging off the wrapping from my head, letting loose my spill of long hair before he cupped my head in his hands to gently ease it closer to his lips. It felt odd to be kissed while lying naked in his arms . . . and not right. 'Stop,' I whispered fearfully, feeling that male part of him grow hard against me. 'This is just what she thought we did.'

Bitterly, he laughed before he drew away, telling me I didn't know anything. There was more to making love than just kissing, and we hadn't done more than kiss, ever.

'And never will,' I said, but weakly.

That night I went to sleep after thinking of his kiss, and not the whipping or the blows from the brush. Swelling up in both of us was a turmoil of whirling emotions. Something sleeping deep inside of me had awakened, quickened, just as Aurora slept until the Prince came to put on her quiet lips a long lover's kiss.

That was the way of all fairy tales – ending with the kiss, and the happy-ever-after. There had to be some other prince for me to bring about a happy ending.

TO FIND A FRIEND

Somebody was screaming on the attic stairs! I bolted awake and looked around to see who was missing. Cory!

Oh, God – what had happened now?

I bounded from bed and raced towards the closet, and I heard Carrie wake up and add her yowls to Cory's, not even knowing what he was yelling about. Chris cried out, 'What the hell is going on now?'

I sped through the closet, raced up six steps, and then stopped dead and just stared. There was Cory in his white pyjamas, yelling his head off – and darned if I could see why.

'Do something! Do something!' he screamed at me, and finally he pointed to the object of his distress.

Ohhh . . . on the step was a mousetrap, the same place we left one every night, set with cheese. But this time the mouse wasn't dead. It had tried to be clever, and steal the cheese with a forepaw instead of his teeth, and it was a tiny foot caught beneath the strong wire spring. Savagely that little grey mouse was chewing on that trapped foot to free itself, despite the pain it must have felt.

'Cathy, do something quick!' cried Cory, throwing himself into my arms. 'Save his life! Don't let him bite off his foot! I want him alive! I want a friend! I've never had a pet; you know I always wanted a pet. Why do you and Chris always have to kill all the mice?'

Carrie came up behind me to beat on my back with her tiny fists. 'You're *mean*, Cathy! *Mean! Mean! You won't let Cory have nothin'!*'

As far as I knew, Cory had just about everything money could buy except a pet, his freedom and the great outdoors. And truly, Carrie might have slaughtered me on the stairs if Chris hadn't rushed to my defence and unhinged the jaws clenched on my leg, which was fortunately well covered over with a very full night-gown that reached my ankles.

'Stop all this racket!' he ordered firmly. And he bent over to use the wash cloth he must have gone for just to pick up a savage mouse, and save his hand from being bitten.

'Make him well, Chris,' pleaded Cory. 'Please don't let him die!'

'Since you seem to want this mouse so badly, Cory, I'll do what I can to save his foot and leg, though it's pretty mangled.'

Oh, what a hustle and bustle to save the life of one mouse, when we had killed hundreds. First Chris had to carefully lift the wire spring, and when he did, that uncomprehending wild thing almost hissed as Cory turned his back and sobbed, and Carrie screamed. Then the mouse seemed to half-faint, from relief, I suppose.

We raced down to the bathroom, where Chris and I scrubbed up and Cory held his near-dead mouse well wrapped in the pale blue washcloth, as Chris warned not to squeeze too tight.

On the countertop I spread all the medication we had on a clean towel.

'He's dead!' yelled Carrie, and she struck Chris. 'You killed Cory's only pet!'

'This mouse is not dead,' said Chris calmly. 'Now please, all of you, be quiet, and don't move. Cathy, hold him still. I've got to do what I can to repair the torn flesh, and then I'll have to splint up that leg.'

First he used antiseptic to clean the wound, while the mouse lay as if dead, only its eyes were open and staring up at me in a pitiful way. Next he used gauze that had to be split lengthwise to fit such a tiny foot and leg, and then over that he wrapped cotton and for a splint he used a toothpick, broke it in half and taped that in place with adhesive.

'I'm going to call him Mickey,' said Cory – a thousand candles behind his eyes because one small mouse would live to become his pet.

'It may be a girl,' said Chris, who flicked his eyes to check.

'No! Don't want no girl mouse – want a Mickey mouse!'

'It's a boy all right,' said Chris. 'Mickey will live and survive to eat all of our cheese,' said the doctor, having completed his first surgery, and made his first cast, and looking, I must admit, rather proud of himself.

He washed the blood from his hands, and Cory and Carrie were lit up like something marvellous had finally come into their lives.

'Let me hold Mickey now!' cried Cory.

'No, Cory, let Cathy hold him for a while longer. You see, he's in shock and her hands are larger and will give Mickey more warmth than yours. And you might, just accidentally, squeeze too much.'

I sat in the bedroom rocker and nursed a grey mouse that seemed on the verge of having a heart attack – its heart beat so fiercely. It gasped and fluttered its eyelids. As I held it, I felt its small, warm body struggling to live on, I wanted it to live and be Cory's pet.

The door opened and the grandmother came in.

None of us was fully clothed; in fact, we still wore only our nightclothes, without robes to conceal what might be revealed. Our feet were bare, our hair was tousled, and our faces weren't washed.

One rule broken.

Cory cringed close at my side as the grandmother swept her discerning gaze ever the disorganized (well, truthfully, really messy) room. The beds weren't made, our clothes were draped on chairs, and socks were everywhere.

Two rules broken.

And Chris was in the bathroom washing Carrie's face, and helping her put on her clothes, and fasten the buttons of her pink coveralls.

Three rules broken. The two of them came out, with Carrie's hair up in a neat pony tail, tied with a pink ribbon.

Immediately, when she saw the grandmother, Carrie froze. Her blue eyes went wide and scared. She turned and clung to Chris for protection. He picked her up and carried her over to me and put her down in my lap. Then he went on to where the picnic basket was on the table and began to take out what she had brought up.

As Chris neared, the grandmother backed away. He ignored her, as he swiftly emptied the basket.

'Cory,' he said, heading towards the closet, 'I'll go up and find a suitable bird-cage and while I'm gone, see if you can't put on all of your clothes, without Cathy's help, and wash your face and hands.'

The grandmother remained silent. I sat in the rocker and nursed the ailing mouse, as my little children crowded in the seat with me, and all three of us fixed our eyes on her, until Carrie could bear it no longer and turned to hide her face against my shoulder. Her small body quivered all over.

It troubled me that she didn't reprimand us and speak of the unmade beds, the cluttered, messy room that I tried to keep neat and tidy – and why hadn't she scolded Chris for dressing Carrie? Why was she looking, and seeing, but saying nothing?

Chris came down from the attic with a bird-cage and some wire screening he said would make the cage more secure.

Those were words to snap the grandmother's head in his direction. Then her stone eyes fixed on me, and the pale blue wash-cloth I held. 'What do you hold in your hands, girl?' she fired in a glacial tone.

'An injured mouse,' I answered, my voice as icy as hers.

'Do you intend to keep that mouse as a pet, and put it in that cage?'

'Yes, we do.' I stared at her defiantly and dared her to do something about it. 'Cory has never owned a pet, and it is time that he did.'

She pursed her thin lips and her stone-cold eyes swept to Cory, who trembled on the verge of tears. 'Go on,' she said, 'keep the mouse. A pet like that suits you.' With that she slammed out the door.

Chris began to fiddle with the bird-cage, and the screening, and spoke as he worked. 'The wires are much too far apart to keep Mickey inside, Cory, so we'll have to wrap the cage with this screen, and then your little pet can't escape.'

Cory smiled. He peeked to see if Mickey still lived. 'It's hungry. I can tell, its nose is twitching.'

The winning over of Mickey the attic mouse was quite a feat. First of all, he didn't trust us, though we'd set his foot free from the trap. He hated the confinement of the cage. He wobbled about in circles on the awkward thing we'd put on his foot and leg, seeking a way out. Cory dropped cheese and bread crumbs through the bars to entice him into eating and gaining strength. He ignored the cheese, the bread, and in the end, walked as far away as he could get, his tiny bead-black eyes wary with fear, his body a-tremble as Cory opened the rusty cage door, to put in a miniature soup tureen filled with water.

Then he put his hand in the cage and pushed a bit of cheese closer. 'Good cheese,' he said invitingly. He moved a bit of bread nearer to the trembling mouse whose whiskers twitched. 'Good bread. It will make you strong and well.'

It took two weeks before Cory had a mouse that adored him and would come when he whistled. Cory hid tidbits in his shirt pockets to tempt Mickey into them. When Cory wore a shirt with two breast pockets, and the right one held a bit of cheese, and the left a bit of peanut-butter-and-grape-jelly sandwich, Mickey would hesitate indecisively on Cory's shoulders, his nose twitching, his whiskers jerking. And only too plainly could you see we had not a gourmet mouse, but a gourmand who wanted what was in both pockets at the same time.

Then, when finally he could make up his mind as to which he would go for first, down he'd scamper into the peanut-butter pocket, and eat upside down, and in a squiggle he'd race back up to Cory's shoulder, around his neck, and down into the pocket with the cheese. It was laughable the way he never went directly over Cory's chest to the other pocket, but always up and around his neck, and then down, tickling every funnybone Cory had.

The little leg and foot healed, but the mouse never walked perfectly, nor could he run very fast. I think the mouse was clever enough to save the cheese for last, for that he could pick up and hold as he daintily nibbled, whereas the bit of sandwich was a messy meal.

And believe me, never was there a mouse better at smelling out food, no matter where it was hidden. Willingly, Mickey abandoned his mice friends to take up with humans who fed him so well, and petted him, and rocked him to sleep, though oddly enough, Carrie had no patience with Mickey at all. It could be just because that mouse was as charmed by her doll house as she was. The little stairways and halls fitted his size perfectly, and once on the loose, he headed directly for the doll house. In through a window he clambered, and tumbled down on the floor; and porcelain people, so delicately balanced, fell right and left, and the dining-room table turned over when he wanted a taste.

Carrie screamed at Cory, 'Your Mickey is eating all the party food! Take him away! Take him out of my living-room!'

Cory captured his lame mouse, which couldn't move too quickly, and he cuddled Mickey against his chest. 'You must learn to behave, Mickey. Bad things happen in big houses. The lady who owns that house over there, she hits you for anything.'

He made me giggle, for it was the first time I'd ever heard him make even the slightest disparaging remark about his twin sister.

It was a good thing Cory had a little, sweet grey mouse to delve deep into his pockets for the goodies his master hid there. It was a good thing all of us had something to do to occupy our time, and our minds, while we waited and waited for our mother to show up, when it was beginning to seem like she never would come to us again.

AT LAST, MOMMA

Chris and I never discussed what had happened between us on the bed the day of the whippings. Often I caught him staring at me, but just as soon as my eyes turned to meet his, his would shift away. When he turned suddenly to catch me watching him, mine were the eyes to flee.

We were growing more day by day, he and I. My breasts filled out fuller, my hips widened, my waist diminished, and the short hair above my forehead grew out longer and curled becomingly. Why hadn't I known before that it would curl without so much weight to pull the curls into waves only? As for Chris, his shoulders broadened, his chest became more manly, and his arms too. I caught him once in the attic staring down at that part of him he seemed so taken with – and measuring it too! 'Why?' I asked, quite astonished to learn that the length mattered. He turned away before he told me once he'd seen Daddy naked, and what he had seemed so inadequate in size. Even the back of his neck was red as he explained this. Oh, golly – just like I wondered what size bra Momma wore! 'Don't do it again,' I whispered. Cory had such a small male organ, and what if he had seen and felt as Chris did, that *his* was inadequate?

Suddenly I stopped polishing the school desks, and stood very still, thinking of Cory. I turned to stare at him and Carrie. Oh, God, how too much closeness dims your perspective! Two years, and four months we had been locked away – and the twins were very much as they had been the night they came! Certainly their heads were larger and that should have diminished the size of their eyes. Yet their eyes appeared extraordinarily large. They sat listless on that stained and smelly old mattress we'd pulled close to the windows. Butterflies danced nervously in my stomach to view them objectively. Their bodies seemed frail flower stems too weak to support the blossoms of their heads.

I waited until they fell asleep in the weak sunlight, then said in an undertone to Chris, 'Look at the buttercups, they don't grow. Only their heads are larger.'

He sighed heavily, narrowed his eyes, and neared the twins, hovering above them, and bending to touch their transparent skins. 'If only they would go outside on the roof with us to benefit from the sun and fresh air like we do. Cathy, no matter how much they fight and scream, we've got to force them outside!'

Foolishly, we thought if we carried them out on the roof while they were asleep, they would awaken in the sunlight, held safe in our arms, and they'd feel secure enough. Cautiously, Chris lifted up Cory, while I leaned to heft Carrie's slight weight. Stealthily, we approached an open attic window. It was Thursday, our day to enjoy outdoors on the roof, while the servants spent their day off in town. It was safe enough to use the back part of the roof.

Barely had Chris cleared the window ledge with Cory when the warm Indian summer air brought Cory suddenly out of sleep. He took one look around, seeing me with Carrie in my arms, obviously planning to take her out on the roof too, when he let out a howl! Carrie bolted out of sleep. She saw Chris with Cory on the steep roof, she saw me and where I was taking her, and she let out a scream that must have been heard a mile away!

Chris called to me through the racket, 'Come on! For their own good, we have to do this!'

Not only did they scream, they kicked and beat at us with small fists! Carrie clamped her teeth down on my arm, so I screamed, too. Little as they were, they had the strength of those in extreme danger. Carrie was battering her fists into my face so I could hardly see, plus screaming in my ear! Hastily, I turned around and headed back towards the schoolroom window. Trembling and weak, I stood Carrie on her feet beside the teacher's desk. I leaned against that desk, gasping and panting, and thanking God for letting me get her safely back inside. Chris returned Cory to his sister. It was no use. To force them out on the roof endangered the lives of all four of us.

Now they were angry. Resentfully they struggled when we pulled them towards the markings on the wall, where we'd measured their height the first day in the schoolroom. Chris held them both in place, while I backed up to read the inches they'd grown.

I stared and I stared, shocked and disbelieving it was possible. In all this time to grow only two inches? Two inches, when Chris and I had gained many, many inches between the ages of five and seven, though they had been exceptionally small at birth, Cory weighing only five pounds and Carrie five pounds and one ounce.

Oh, I had to put my hands up to cover my face so they couldn't see my stunned and horrified expression. Then that wasn't enough. I spun around so they saw only my back as I choked on the sobs stuck in my throat.

'You can let them go now,' I finally managed. I turned to catch a glimpse of them scurrying away like two small flaxen-haired mice, racing for the stairwell, heading towards the beloved television and the escape it offered, and the little mouse which was real and waiting for them to come and pleasure *his* imprisoned life.

Directly behind me Chris stood and waited. 'Well,' he asked when I just wilted, speechless, 'how much have they grown?'

Quickly I brushed away the tears before I turned, so I could see his eyes when I told him. 'Two inches,' I said in a flat way, but the pain was in my eyes, and that was what he saw.

He stepped closer and put his arms about me, then held my head so it was against his chest, and I cried, really bawled. I hated Momma for doing this! Really hated her! She knew children were like plants – they had to have sunshine if they were to grow. I trembled in the embrace of my brother, trying to convince myself that as soon as we were freed, they'd be beautiful again. They would, of course they would; they'd catch up, make up the lost years, and as soon as the sunshine was upon them again, they'd shoot up like weeds – they would, yes, they would! It was only all the long days hidden indoors that made their cheeks so hollow, and their eyes so sunken. And all of that could be undone, couldn't it?

'Well,' I began in my hoarse, choked voice, while clinging to the only one who seemed to care any more, 'does money make the world go round, or is it love? Enough love bestowed on the twins, and I would have read six or seven or maybe eight inches gain in height, not only two.'

*   *   *

Chris and I headed for our dim sequestered prison to eat lunch, and as always I sent the twins into the bathroom to wash their hands, for they certainly didn't need mouse germs to imperil their health more.

As we sat quietly at the dining-table, eating our sandwiches, and sipping our lukewarm soup and milk, and watching TV lovers meet and kiss and make plans to run away and leave their respective spouses, the door to our room opened. I hated to look away, and miss what would happen next, yet I did.

Gaily into our room strode our mother. She wore a beautiful, lightweight suit, with soft grey fur at the cuffs and around the neck of the jacket.

'Darlings!' she cried in enthusiastic greeting, then hesitated uncertainly when not one of us jumped up to welcome her back. 'Here I am! Aren't you glad to see me? Oh, you just don't know how very glad I am to see all of you. I've missed you so much, and thought about you, and dreamed of you, and I've brought you all so many beautiful presents that I chose with such care. Just wait until you see them! And I had to be so sneaky – for how could I explain buying things for children? I wanted to make up for being away for so long. I did want to tell you why I was leaving, really I did, but it was so complicated. And I didn't know exactly how long I'd be gone, and though you missed me, you were cared for, weren't you? You didn't suffer, did you?'

Had we suffered? Had we only missed her? Who was she, anyway? Idiot thoughts while I stared at her and listened to how difficult four hidden children made the lives of others. And though I wanted to deny her, keep her from ever really being close again, I faltered, filling with hope, wanting so much to love her again, and trust her again.

Chris got up and spoke first, in a voice that had finally resolved from one that was high and squeaky at times into reliable, deep and masculine tones. 'Momma, of course we're glad you're back! And yes, we missed you! But you were wrong to go away, and stay away for so long, no matter what complicated reasons you had.'

'Christopher,' she said, her eyes widening in surprise, 'you don't sound like yourself.' Her eyes flicked from him to me, then to

241

the twins. Her vivaciousness simmered down. 'Christopher, did anything go wrong?'

'Wrong?' he repeated. 'Momma, what can be right about living in one room? You said I don't sound like myself – look me over good. Am I a little boy now? Look at Cathy – is she still a child? Look longest at the twins; notice in particular how tall they've grown. Then turn your eyes back on me, and tell me that Cathy and I are still children to be treated with condescension, and are incapable of understanding adult subjects. We haven't remained idle, twiddling our thumbs while you were off having a good time. Through books Cathy and I have lived a zillion lives . . . our vicarious way to feel alive.'

Momma wanted to interrupt, but Chris overrode her small voice which faltered. He threw her many gifts a scornful glance. 'So, you have come back bearing peace offerings, like you always do when you know you have done wrong. Why do you keep thinking your stupid gifts can make up for what we've lost, and what we are constantly losing? Sure, once we were delighted with the games and toys and clothes you brought up to our prison room, but we're older now, and gifts are just not enough!'

'Christopher, please,' she begged, and looked uneasily at the twins again, and so quickly she averted her eyes. 'Please don't speak as if you've stopped loving me. I couldn't bear that.'

'I love you,' was his reply. 'I *make* myself keep on loving you, despite what you do. I've *got* to love you. We all have to love you, and believe in you, and think you are looking out for our best interests. But look at us, Momma, and really see us. Cathy feels, and I feel, that you close your eyes to what you are doing to us. You come to us smiling, and dangle before our eyes and our ears bright hopes for the future, but nothing ever materializes. Long ago, when you first told us about this house and your parents, you said we'd only be shut up in this room for *one* night, and then you changed it to a *few* days. And then it was another few weeks, and then another few months . . . and over two years have passed while we wait for an old man to die, who may never die from the skilled way his doctors keep pulling him back from the grave. This room is not improving *our* health. Can't you see that?' he almost shouted, his boyish face suffused with red as his limit of self-control was reached at last. I thought I would never live to see the day when he would attack our mother – *his* beloved mother.

The sound of his loud voice must have startled him, for he lowered his tone and spoke more calmly, and yet his words had the impact of bullets: 'Momma, whether or not you inherit your father's immense fortune, we want out of this room! Not next week, or tomorrow – but today! Now! This minute! You turn that key over to me, and we'll go away, far away. And you can send us money, if you care to, or send nothing, if that's what you want, and you need never see us again, if that is your choice, and that will solve all your problems, we'll be gone from your life, and your father need never know we existed, and you can have what he leaves you, all to yourself.'

Momma went pale from shock.

I sat in my chair, with my lunch half-eaten. I felt sorry for her, and I felt betrayed by my own compassion. I closed the door, slammed it hard, just by thinking of those two weeks when we were starved . . . four days of eating nothing else but crackers and cheese, and three days without any food at all, and nothing but water to drink. And then the whippings, the tar in my hair, and, most of all, the way Chris had to slash his wrist to feed the twins his nourishing blood.

And Chris, what he was saying to her, and the hard determined way he said it, was mostly my doing.

I think she guessed this, for she shot me a stabbing glance, full of resentment.

'Say no more to me, Christopher – it's clear to see you are not yourself.'

Jumping to my feet, I stepped over to his side. 'Look at us, Momma! Observe our radiant, healthy complexions, just like yours. Look especially long on your two youngest. They don't look frail, do they? Their full cheeks don't look gaunt, do they? Their hair isn't dull, is it? Their eyes – they're not dark and hollowed out, are they? When you look, and register, do you see how much they've grown, how healthily they thrive? If you can't have pity for Christopher and me, have pity for them.'

'Stop!' she yelled, jumping up from the bed where she'd sat to have us crowd cosily around, in our former way. She spun on her heel so she wouldn't have to see us. Choking sobs were in her voice that cried, 'You have no right to talk to your mother in this manner. But for me you would all be starving in the streets.' Her voice broke. She turned sideways, throwing Chris an appealing, woebegone look. 'Haven't I done the best I could by you? Where did I go wrong? What do you lack? You knew how it would be until your grandfather died. You agreed to stay here until he did. And I've kept my word. You live in a warm, safe room. I bring to you the best of everything – books, toys, games, the best clothes that money can buy. You have good food to eat, a TV set.' Fully she faced us now, spreading wide her hands in a supplicating gesture, appearing ready to fall down on her knees, pleading with her eyes at me now. 'Listen to this – your grandfather is so ill now he is confined to bed all day long. He isn't even allowed to sit in the wheelchair. His doctors say he can't last long, a few days or the maximum of a few weeks. The day he dies, I'll come up and unlock your door and lead you down the stairs. I'll have money enough then to send all four of you to college, and Chris to medical school, and you, Cathy, can continue on with your ballet lessons. I'll find for Cory the best of musical teachers, and for Carrie, I'll do anything she wants. Are you going to throw away all the years you've suffered and endured without waiting for rewards – just when you're on the verge of reaching your goal! Remember how you used to laugh and talk of what you'd do when you were blessed with more money than you knew how to spend? Recall all the plans we made . . . our house where we could all live together again. Don't throw everything away by becoming impatient just when we're due to win! Tell me I've had pleasure while you've suffered, and I'll agree that I have. But I'll make up for that by tenfold!'

Oh, I admit I was touched, and wanted so much to step away from disbelief. I hovered near, trusting her again, and quivered with the suspicious fear that she was lying. Hadn't she told us from the very beginning that our grandfather was taking his last breath . . . years and years of his breathing his last breath? Should I yell out, *Momma, we just don't believe you any more?* I wanted to wound her, make her bleed as we had bled with our tears, isolation, and loneliness – to say nothing of the punishments.

But Chris looked at me forbiddingly, making me ashamed. Could I be as chivalrous as he was? Would that I could open my mouth, ignore him, and shout all the grandmother had done to punish us for nothing. For some strange reason I stayed quiet. Maybe I was protecting the twins from knowing too much. Maybe I was waiting for Chris to tell her first.

He stood and gazed at her with soft compassion, forgetting the tar in my hair, and the weeks without food, and the dead mice he would make tasty with salt and pepper – and then the whippings. He was beside me, his arm brushing mine. He trembled with indecision, and in his eyes were tormented visions of hopes and despair as he watched our mother begin to cry.

The twins crept closer to cling to my skirt as Momma crumpled down on the nearest bed to sob and beat her fists into the pillow, just like a child.

'Oh, but you are heartless and ungrateful children,' she wailed pitifully, 'that you should do this to me, your own mother, the only person in this world who loves you! The only one who cares about you! I came so joyfully to you, so happy to be with you again, wanting to tell you my good news so you could rejoice with me. And what do you do? You attack me viciously, unjustly! Making me feel so guilty, and so ashamed, when all along I have done the best I could, and yet you won't believe!'

She was on our level now, crying, face down on the bed in the same way I would have done years ago, and Carrie would do this day.

Immediately, spontaneously, Chris and I were stricken contrite and sorry. Everything she said was only too true. She *was* the only person who loved us, who cared, and in her only lay our salvation, our lives, our futures, and our dreams. We ran to her, Chris and I, and threw our arms around her as best we could, pleading for forgiveness. The twins said nothing, only watched.

'Momma, please stop crying! We didn't mean to hurt your feelings. We're sorry, we really are. We'll stay. We believe you. The grandfather *is* almost dead – he has to die sometime, doesn't he?'

On and on she wept, inconsolable.

'Talk to us, Momma, please! Tell us your good news. We want

245

to know, we want to be glad and rejoice with you. We said those things only because we were hurt when you left us and didn't tell us why. Momma, please, please, Momma.'

Our pleas, our tears, our anguish finally reached her. She somehow managed to sit up, and she dabbed at her eyes with a white linen handkerchief with five inches of fine lace all around, and monogrammed with a big white C.

She shoved Chris and me aside, then brushed off our hands as if they burned, and she got to her feet. Now she refused to meet our eyes which begged, pleaded, cajoled.

'Open your gifts that I selected with such care,' she said in a cold voice filled with choked sobs, 'and then tell me whether or not you are thought about and loved. Tell me then that I didn't think of your needs, and think of your best interests, and try to cater to your every whim. Tell me then I am selfish and that I don't care.'

Dark mascara streaked her cheeks. Her bright red lipstick was smeared. Her hair, customarily worn on her head like a perfect hat, was mussed and displaced. She had strolled into our room a vision of perfection and now she appeared a broken mannequin.

And why did I have to go and think she was like an actress, playing her part for all she was worth?

She looked at Chris, and ignored me. And the twins – they could have been in Timbuktu for all the concern she showed for their welfare, and their sensitivities.

'I have ordered a new set of encyclopaedias for your upcoming birthday, Christopher,' she choked out, still dabbing at her face and trying to take off the mascara smudges. 'The very set you always wanted – the best that is published, bound in genuine red leather, tooled in twenty-four-carat gold around all four sides, and hubbed-spined a full half-inch outwards. I went directly to the publishing house, to order them for you especially. They'll bear your name, and the date, but they won't be mailed directly here, lest someone should see them.' She swallowed heavily and put away her fancy handkerchief. 'I thought and thought about a gift to please you the most, just like I have always given you the very best to educate yourself.'

Chris appeared dumbfounded. The play of mixed emotions

upon his face made his eyes look confused, bewildered, dazed, and sort of helpless. God, how he must have loved her, even after all she'd done.

My emotions were straightforward, with no indecision. I smouldered with rage. Now she was bringing up genuine, leather-bound, hubbed-spined, twenty-four-carat gold-tooled encyclopaedias! Books like that must cost more than a thousand dollars – maybe two or three thousand! Why wasn't she putting that money into our escape fund? I wanted to yell out like Carrie and protest, but something broken in Chris's blue eyes kept my mouth shut. He'd always wanted a set of genuine red-leather-bound encyclopaedias, and she'd already ordered them, and money was nothing to her now, and maybe, just maybe, the grandfather really would die today or tomorrow, and she wouldn't *need* to rent an apartment, or buy a house.

She sensed my doubts.

Momma raised her head regally high and turned towards the door. We had not opened our gifts, and she wasn't staying to watch our reactions. Why was I crying inside when I hated her? I didn't love her now . . . I didn't.

She said when she reached the door and had it open, 'When you have thought about the pain you have given me today, and when you can treat me with love and respect again, then I will come back. Not before.'

So she came.

So she went.

So she had come and gone and left Carrie and Cory untouched, unkissed, unspoken to, and hardly glanced at. And I knew why. She couldn't bear to look and see what gaining a fortune was costing the twins.

They jumped up from the table and came running to me, to cling to my skirts, and stare up into my face. Their small faces were fraught with anxieties, with fears, studying my expression to see if I were happy, so they, too, could feel happy. I knelt to lavish them with all the kisses and caresses she had overlooked – or just couldn't give to those she'd harmed so.

'Do we look funny?' asked Carrie worriedly, her small hands plucking at mine.

'No, of course not. You and Cory just look pale, because you stay inside too much.'

'Did we grow much?'

'Yes, yes, of course you have.' And I smiled, even as I lied. And with a pretence of joy, and keeping that false smile like a mask to wear, I sat down on the floor with the twins and Chris, and we all four began to open our gifts like it was Christmas Day. They were all beautifully wrapped in expensive paper, or gold or silver foil, and sporting huge satin bows of assorted colours.

Tear off the paper, toss away the ribbons, the bows, rip off the lids of boxes, pull out the inside tissue . . . see all the pretty clothes for each of us. Glance at the new books, hooray! See the new toys, the games, the puzzles, hurrah! My, oh, my, what a big, big box of maple sugar candy shaped like identical leaves!

Here before us was the display of her concern. She knew us well, I admit, our tastes, our hobbies – all but our sizes. With gifts she paid us for all those long empty months when we were left in the care of the witch-grandmother who would quite willingly see us dead and buried.

And she knew what kind of mother she had – she knew!

With games and toys and puzzles, she sought to buy us off, and beg our forgiveness for doing what she knew in her heart was wrong.

With sweet maple sugar candy she hoped to take the sour gall of loneliness from our mouths, hearts, and minds. To her way of thinking, it was very obvious, we WERE still only children, though Chris needed to shave, and I needed to wear a bra . . . still children . . . and children she would keep us for ever as the titles of the books she bought plainly indicated. *Little Men.* I'd read that years ago. Fairy tales by the brothers Grimm and Hans Christian Andersen – we knew them by heart. And *Wuthering Heights* and *Jane Eyre again*? Didn't she keep a list of what we'd already read? What we had?

I managed to smile though as I pulled over Carrie's head a new red dress, and in her hair I tied a purple ribbon. Now she was dressed as she'd always wanted to be, in her favourite colours. I put purple socks on her feet and new white sneakers. 'You look beautiful, Carrie.' And in a way she did, she was so happy to own bright, grown-up, royally coloured clothes.

Next I helped Cory on with his bright red short pants, and a white shirt monogrammed on the pocket in red, and his tie had to be knotted by Chris, the way Daddy had shown him how a long time ago.

'Shall I dress you now, Christopher?' I asked sarcastically.

'If that is your heart's desire,' he said wickedly, 'you can dress me from skin out.'

'Don't be vulgar!'

Cory had another new instrument to play – a shining banjo! Oh, golly day, he'd always wanted a banjo! She'd remembered. His eyes lit up. *Oh, Susannah, don't you cry for me, for I'm going to Louisiana with a banjo on my knee . . .*

He played the tune, and Carrie sang the lyrics. It was one of his favourite happy songs, and one he could play on the guitar, though it never sounded right. On the banjo it sounded right, as it should. God blessed Cory with magic fingers.

God blessed me with mean thoughts to take the joy from everything. What good were pretty clothes when no one ever saw them? I wanted things that didn't come wrapped in fancy paper, and tied around with satin ribbons, and put in a box from an expensive store. I wanted all the things money couldn't buy. Had she noticed my hair cut so short on top? Had she seen how thin we were? Did she think we looked healthy with our pale, thin skins?

Bitter, ugly thoughts as I pushed a maple sugar leaf into Carrie's eager mouth, and then a leaf into Cory's, and next one into my own mouth. I glared at the beautiful clothes meant for me. A blue velvet dress, such as should be worn to a party. A pink and blue nightgown and peignoir set, with slippers to match. I sat there with the candy melting on my tongue, and it had the acrid taste of the iron lump in my throat. Encyclopaedias! Were we going to be here for ever?

Yet candy made from maple sugar was my topmost favourite, always had been. She brought this box of candy for me, *for me*, and I could only swallow one piece, and that with great difficulty.

They sat on the floor with the candy box centred between them, Cory, Carrie, and Chris. They stuffed the candy in, piece after piece, laughing and pleased. 'You should make that candy last,' I told them with sour hatefulness. 'That may well be the last box of candy you see for a long, long time.'

Chris threw me a look, his blue eyes happy and shining. Easy enough to see all *his* faith and trust was restored by just one short visit from Momma. Why couldn't he see that gifts were just a way of hiding the fact that she no longer cared about us? Why didn't he know, as I did, that we weren't as real to her now as once we'd been? We were another of those unpleasant subjects that people don't like to talk about, like mice in the attic.

'Sit there and act dumb,' said Chris, sparkling his happiness on me. 'Deny yourself the candy, while we three satisfy our sweet tooth all at once before the mice come down and eat it for us. Cory, Carrie, and I will scrub our teeth clean, while you sit and cry, and feel sorry for yourself, and pretend by self-sacrifice you can change our circumstances. Go on, Cathy! Cry! Play the martyr. Suffer! Pound your head on the wall! Scream! And we'll still be here until the grandfather dies, and all the candy will be gone, gone, gone.'

I hated him for making fun of me! I jumped to my feet, ran to the far side of the room, turned my back, and tried on my new clothes. Three beautiful dresses I yanked down over my head one by one. Easily they zipped up to the waist, and fitted there loosely. But try as I would, the zipper wouldn't close in back when it reached my bust. I tore off the last dress, looking for the darts in the bodice. None there! She was buying me little-girl dresses – silly, sweet little-girl garments that screamed out she *didn't* see! I threw those three dresses down on the floor and stomped on them, crushing the blue velvet so it could never be returned to the store.

And there sat Chris on the floor with the twins, looking devilish, and laughing with a raffishly wicked and boyish charm that would win me over to laughter, too – if I would let it. 'Make out a shopping list,' he joked. 'It's time you started wearing bras and stopped bobbing up and down. And while you're at it, write down a girdle, too.'

I could have slapped his grinning face! My abdomen was a hollowed-out cave. And if my buttocks were rounded and firm, it was from exercise – not from fat! 'Shut up!' I yelled. 'Why should I have to write out a list and tell Momma anything? She'd know what clothes I have, and what I should be wearing, if she really looked at me! How do I know what size bra to order? And I don't need a girdle! What you need is a jock strap – and some sense in your head that doesn't come from a book!' I glared at him, happy to see his stunned expression.

'Christopher,' I screamed, unable to control myself. 'Sometimes I hate Momma! And not only that, sometimes I hate you, too! Sometimes I hate everybody – most of all myself! Sometimes I wish I were dead, because I think we would all be better off dead than buried alive up here! Just like rotting, walking, talking vegetables!'

My secret thoughts had been thrown out, spewed forth like garbage to make both my brothers wince and go paler. And my small sister shrank even smaller as she began to tremble. Immediately after the cruel words were out of my mouth, I wanted them back in. I was drowning in shame but unable to apologize and take it all back. I whirled about and ran for the closet, running for the tall, slender door that would take me up the stairs and into the attic. When I hurt, and I hurt often, I raced for the music, the costumes, the ballet shoes on which I could spin and twirl and dance away my troubles. And somewhere in that crimson-coloured never-never land where I pirouetted madly, in a wild and crazy effort to exhaust myself into insensibility, I saw that man, shadowy and distant, half-hidden behind towering white columns that rose clear up to a purple sky. In a passionate *pas de deux* he danced with me, for ever apart, no matter how hard I sought to draw nearer and leap into his arms, where I could feel them protective about me, supporting me . . . and with him I'd find, at last, a safe place to live and love.

Then, suddenly, the music was over. I was back in the dry and dusty attic, on the floor, with my right leg twisted beneath me. I had fallen! When I struggled to my feet, I could barely walk. My knee hurt so much, tears of another kind came to my eyes. I limped through the attic and on into the schoolroom, not caring if I ruined my knee for ever. I opened up a window wider and stepped out on to the black roof. Painfully I eased my way down the steep incline, stopping only when I was at the very edge with the leaf-clogged gutters. Far below was the ground. With tears of self-pity and pain streaking my face and blurring my vision, I closed my eyes and let myself sway off balance. In a minute it would all be over. I'd be sprawled down there on top of the thorny rose bushes.

The grandmother and Momma could claim it was some idiot strange girl who climbed up on their roof and fell off accidentally, and Momma would cry when she saw me dead and broken and lying in a coffin, dressed in blue leotards and tulle tutu. Then she'd realize what she'd done, she'd want me back, she'd unlock the door to free Chris and the twins, and let them live real lives again.

And that was the golden side of my suicide coin.

But I had to turn it over, and see the tarnish. What if I didn't die? Suppose I just fell, and the rose bushes cushioned my fall, and I only ended up crippled and scarred for the rest of my life?

Then, again, suppose I really did die, and Momma didn't cry, or feel sorry, or any regret, and was only glad to be rid of a pest like me? Just how would Chris and the twins survive without me to take care of them? Who would mother the twins, and lavish them with the affection that was sometimes embarrassing for Chris to give as easily as I did? As for Chris – maybe he thought he didn't really need me, that books and red-leather, gold-tooled, hubbed-spined new encyclopaedias were enough to take my place. When he got that MD behind his name, that would be enough to satisfy him all his life through. But when he was a doctor, I knew it still wouldn't be enough, never enough, if I wasn't there, too. And I was saved from death by my own ability to see both sides of the coin.

I stumbled away from the edge of the roof, feeling silly, childish, but still crying. My knee hurt so badly I ascended the roof by crawling to the special place near the back chimney, where two roofs met and made a safe corner. I lay on my back and stared up at that unseeing, uncaring sky. I doubted God lived up there; I doubted heaven was up there, too.

God and heaven were down there on the ground, in the gardens, in the forests, in the parks, on the seashores, on the lakes, and riding the highways, going somewhere!

Hell was right here, where I was, shadowing me persistently, trying to do me in, and make me into what the grandmother thought I was – the Devil's issue.

I lay on that hard, cold slate roof until darkness came on and the moon came out, and the stars flashed angrily at me, as if knowing me for what I was. I wore only a ballet costume, leotards, and one of those silly frilly tutus.

Goosebumps came and chicken-skinned my arms, and still I stayed to plan all my revenge, my vengeance against those who had turned me from good to evil, and made of me what I was going to be from this day forward. I convinced myself there would come a day when both my mother and my grandmother would be under my thumb . . . and I'd snap the whip, and handle the tar, and control the food supply.

I tried to think of exactly what I would do to them. What was the right punishment? Should I lock them both up and throw away the key? Starve them, as we had been starved?

A soft noise interrupted the dark and twisted flow of my thoughts. In the gloom of early evening Chris spoke my name hesitatingly. No more, just my name. I didn't answer, I didn't need him – I didn't need anybody. He had let me down by not understanding, and I didn't need him, not now.

Nevertheless, he came and lay close by my side. He'd brought a warm woollen jacket with him that he spread over me without saying a word. He stared as I did up at the cold and forbidding sky. The longest, most fearful silence grew between us. There was nothing I really hated about Chris, or even disliked, and I wanted so much to turn on my side and say this to him, and thank him for bringing me the warm jacket, but I couldn't say a word. I wanted to let him know I was sorry that I struck out at him, and the twins, when God knows none of us needed another enemy. My arms, shivering under the warmth of the jacket, longed to slide around him, and comfort him as he so often comforted me when I woke up from another nightmare. But all I could do was lie there, and hope he understood that I was all tied up in knots.

Always he could raise the white flag first, and for that I'm for ever grateful. In a stranger's husky, strained voice that seemed to span across a great distance, he told me he and the twins had already eaten dinner, but my share had been saved.

'And we only pretended to eat all of the candy, Cathy. There's plenty left for you.'

Candy. He spoke of candy. Was he still in the child's world where candy stood for something sweet enough to hold back tears? I had grown older, and had lost enthusiasm for childish delights. I wanted what every teenager wants – freedom to develop into a woman, freedom to have full control over my life! Though I tried to tell him this, my voice had dried up along with my tears.

'Cathy . . . what you said . . . don't ever say ugly, hopeless things like that again.'

'Why not?' I choked out. 'Every word I said is true. I only expressed what I feel inside – I let out what *you* keep hidden deep. Well, keep on hiding from yourself, and you'll find all those truths turn into acid to eat up your insides!'

'Not once have I ever wished myself dead!' he cried out in the hoarse voice of one with an everlasting cold. 'Don't you ever say such a thing again – or think about death! Sure I've got doubts and suspicions hidden away in me, but I smile and I laugh, and make myself believe because I want to survive. If you died by your own hand, you would take me down with you, and soon the twins would follow, for who would be their mother then?'

It made me laugh. Hard, brittle, ugly laughter – duplicating my mother's way of laughing when *she* felt bitter. 'Why, Christopher Doll, remember we have a dear, sweet, loving mother who thinks first of our needs, and she will be left to care for the twins.'

Chris turned towards me then, reaching out to seize my shoulders. 'I hate it when you talk that way, like she talks sometimes. Do you think I don't know that you are more a mother to Cory and Carrie than *she* is? Do you think I failed to see the twins only stared at their mother, like she was a stranger? Cathy, I'm not blind or stupid. I know Momma takes care of herself first, and us next.' That old moon was out to sparkle the tears frozen in his eyes. His voice in my ear had been gritty, hushed and deep.

All of this he said without bitterness, only regret – just the flat, emotionless way a doctor tells his patient he has a terminal illness.

That's when it came over me in a cataclysmic flood – I loved Chris – and he was my brother. He made me whole, he gave me what I lacked, a stability when I would run off wild and frantic – and what a perfect way to strike back at Momma and the grandparents. God wouldn't see. He'd closed his eyes to everything the day Jesus was put on the cross. But Daddy was up there, looking down, and I cringed in shame.

'Look at me, Cathy, please look at me.'

'I didn't mean any of it, Chris, really I didn't. You know how melodramatic I am – I want to live as much as anyone does, but I'm so afraid something terrible is going to happen to us, shut up all the time. So I say awful things just to shake you up, make you see. Oh, Chris, I just ache to be with lots of people. I want to see new faces, new rooms. I'm scared to death for the twins. I want to go shopping, and ride horses, and do all the things we can't do in here.'

In the dark, on the roof, in the cold, we reached for each other intuitively. We clung as one, our hearts throbbing loud against each other. Not crying, not laughing. Hadn't we already cried an ocean of tears? And they hadn't helped. Hadn't we already said a zillion prayers and waited for deliverance that never came? And if tears didn't work, and prayers weren't heard, how were we to reach God and make him do something?

'Chris, I've said it before, and I'm saying it again. We've got to take the initiative. Didn't Daddy always say God helps those who help themselves?'

His cheek was tight against mine while he reflected for so darned long. 'I'll give it some thought, though, as Momma said, we could come any day into that fortune.'

OUR MOTHER'S SURPRISE

Each day of the ten that passed before Momma visited us again, Chris and I speculated for hours on end just why she had gone away and stayed away so long, and most of all – what was the big news she had to tell us?

We thought of those ten days as just another form of punishment. For punishment was what it was, and it hurt to know she was in this same house, and yet she could ignore us and shut us out, as if we *were* only mice in the attic.

So, when she showed up, at long last, we were thoroughly chastised, and most fearful she would never come back if Chris and I showed more hostility or repeated our demands to be let out. We were quiet, timid and accepting of our fate. For what would we do if she never returned? We couldn't escape by using the ladder made of torn-up sheets – not when the twins went hysterical just to be on the roof.

So we smiled at Momma, and uttered not one word of complaint. We didn't ask why she had punished us again by staying away ten days, when already she'd been gone for months. We accepted what she was willing to give us. We were, as she had told us she had learned to be with her father, her dutiful, obedient, and passive children. And, what's more, she liked us this way. We were again her sweet, her loving, her private 'darlings'.

Since we were so good, so sweet, so approving of her now, and so very respectful, and apparently trusting, this was the time she chose to drop her bombshell.

'Darlings, rejoice for me! I am so happy!' She laughed and spun around in a circle, hugging her arms over her chest, loving her own body, or so it seemed to me. 'Guess what happened – go on, guess!'

Chris and I glanced at each other. 'Our grandfather has died,' he said cautiously, while my heart was doing pirouettes, preparing to really leap and bound if she gave us the glad tidings.

'No!' she said sharply, as if her happiness had dimmed some.

'He's been taken to the hospital,' said I, guessing second best.

'No. I really don't hate him now, so I wouldn't come to you and say I was rejoicing over his death.'

'Why don't you just tell us your good news, then,' I said dully. 'We'll never be able to guess; we don't know much about your life any more.'

She ignored what I implied and rhapsodized on: 'The reason I was gone for so long, and what I found so difficult to explain – I've married a wonderful man, an attorney named Bart Winslow. You're going to like him. He's going to love all of you. He's dark-haired and so handsome, and tall and athletic. And he loves to ski, like you do, Christopher, and he plays tennis, and he's brilliant, like you are, darling,' and she was looking at Chris, of course. 'He's charming and everybody likes him, even my father. And we went to Europe on our honeymoon, and the gifts I brought to you all come from England, France, Spain or Italy.' And on and on she raved about her new husband, while Chris and I sat silent.

Since the night of the Christmas party, Chris and I had voiced our suspicions many times. For as young as we had been back then, we were wise enough to know that a beautiful young woman who was as needing of a man as our mother, was not likely to remain a widow for long. But still, almost two years passed without a wedding, and that had given us reason enough to believe that the handsome, dark-haired man with the big moustache was of no real importance to Momma – just a passing fancy – one suitor amongst many. And deep down in our foolish hearts, we had convinced ourselves that she was going to be ever-faithful, ever-devoted to our dead father – our blond and blue-eyed Grecian-god father whom she had to love beyond reason to have done what she did – marry a man so closely related.

I closed my eyes to try and shut out her hateful voice, telling us of another man who was taking our father's place. Now she was another man's wife, a totally different kind of man, and he'd been in her bed and sleeping with her now, and we'd see even less of her than we had. Oh, dear God, how long, how long?

Her news and her voice gave birth to a little grey bird of panic that fluttered wild in the cage of my ribs . . . wanting out, out, out!

'Please,' Momma begged, her smiles and laughter, joy and happiness all struggling to survive in the bleak, sterile air of our reception to her news. 'Try and understand, and be happy for me. I loved your father, you know that, but he's gone, and been gone for so long, and I need someone else to love, and someone to love me.'

I saw Chris open his mouth to say he loved her, that we all loved her, but then he tightened his lips, realizing, as I did, that love from her children wasn't the kind of love she was speaking about. And *I* didn't love her any more. I wasn't even sure I liked her now, but I could smile and pretend, and say the words just so the twins would not be frightened by my expression. 'Yes, Momma, I'm glad for you. It's nice you found someone to love you again.'

'He's been in love with me for a long time, Cathy,' she rushed on, encouraged and smiling with confidence again, 'though he did have his mind set on being a bachelor. It wasn't easy to convince him he needed a wife. And your grandfather never wanted me to marry a second time, just as another punishment for the evil I did when I married your father. But he likes Bart, and when I kept on begging and begging, he finally relented, and said yes, that I could marry Bart and still inherit.' She paused to chew on her lower lip. Then she swallowed nervously. Her beringed fingers fluttered to her throat, to nervously work the string of genuine pearls she wore, and thus betrayed all the ways of a woman in distress, who could smile, even so. 'Of course, I don't love Bart as much as I did your father.'

Hah! How weakly she said this. Her glowing eyes and radiant complexion betrayed a love that loomed larger than any she'd known before. And I sighed. Poor Daddy.

'The gifts you brought us, Momma . . . they weren't all from Europe, or the British Isles. That box of maple sugar candy came from Vermont – did you go to Vermont, too? Is that where he's from?'

Her laughter came with lilting joy, uninhibited and even a little sensual, as if Vermont had given her much. 'No, he isn't from

258

Vermont, Cathy. But he has a sister living there and we visited her for a week-end after we came from Europe, and that's where I bought the box of candy, for I know how much you love maple sugar candy. He has two other sisters living down South. He's from some little town in South Carolina – Greenglena, Grenglenna, or something like that. But he stayed so long in New England, where he graduated from Harvard Law School, that he sounds more like a Yankee than a Southerner. And oh, it is so beautiful in Vermont in the autumn; it absolutely took my breath away. Of course, when you're on your honeymoon, you don't want to be with other people, so we visited his sister and her family only a short while, and then spent some time on the seashore.' She flicked her eyes uneasily at the twins, and again her pearls were twisted so likely they'd break any second. Apparently, genuine pearls are more strongly strung than the simulated kind.

'Did you like the little boats I brought you, Cory?'

'Yes, ma'am,' he answered, very politely, staring at her with his large, shadowed eyes, just as if she were a stranger.

'Carrie, sweetheart . . . the little dolls, I picked those up for you in England, to add to your collection. I hoped to find you another cradle, but they don't seem even to make doll house cradles any more.'

'It's all right, Momma,' answered Carrie, her eyes on the floor. 'Chris and Cathy made me a cradle out of cardboard, and I like it fine.'

Oh, God, didn't she see?

They didn't know her now. They felt uncomfortable with her now.

'Does your new husband know about us?' I asked, dead serious. Chris glowered at me for asking, telling me mutely that of course our mother wouldn't be deceitful and not tell the man she'd married that she had four hidden children – that some considered the Devil's issue.

Shadows came to darken and pain Momma's happiness. Again I had asked a wrong question. 'Not yet, Cathy, but just as soon as Daddy dies, I'll tell him about you four. I'll explain in minute detail. He'll understand; he's kind and gentle. You're going to like him.'

She had already said that more than once. And here was another thing that had to wait until an old man died.

'Cathy, stop looking at me like that! I couldn't tell Bart before our marriage! He's your grandfather's attorney. I couldn't let him know about my children, not yet, not until the will is read, and I have the money in my name.'

Words were on the tip of my tongue to say a man should know when his wife had four children by her first husband. Oh, how I wanted to say this! But Chris was glaring meanly at me, and the twins were huddled over, crouching small, with their large eyes fixed on the TV set. And I didn't know if I should speak, or stay silent. At least when you were silent, you didn't make any new enemies. Maybe she was right, too. *God, let her be right. Let my faith be renewed. Let me believe in her again. Let me believe that she is not just beautiful on the surface, but all the way through.*

God didn't reach down and lay a warm, reassuring hand on my shoulder. I sat there, realizing my suspicions were stretching the cord between her and me, very, very fine.

Love. How often that word came up in books. Over and over again. If you had wealth and health, and beauty and talent . . . you had nothing if you didn't have love. Love changed all that was ordinary into something giddy, powerful, drunken, enchanted.

Thus ran the course of my thoughts on a day early in winter, when rain pelted on the roof, and the twins sat on the floor in the bedroom, before the TV. Chris and I were in the attic, lying side by side on the old mattress, near the window in the school-room, reading together one of the antique books Momma had brought up from the big library downstairs. Soon the attic would again turn arctic winter, so we spent as much time up there as possible now, while we still could. Chris liked to scan a page, and then quickly leap to another. I liked to dawdle over the beautiful lines, going back to read through them twice, sometimes three times. We argued incessantly about this. 'Read faster, Cathy! You try to absorb the words.'

Today he was patient. He turned his back and stared up at the ceiling while I took my time, pursuing each beautifully written line, and soaking up the feel of Victorian times, when people wore such fancy clothes, and spoke in such elegant ways, and felt so deeply about love. From paragraph one, the story had captivated both of us with its mystical, romantic charm. Each slow page spinning out an involved tale of star-crossed lovers named Lily and Raymond, who had to overcome monumental obstacles to find and stand upon the magic place of purple grass, where all dreams are fulfilled. God, how I wanted them to find that place! Then I discovered the tragedy of their lives. All along they had stood on the purple grass . . . can you imagine? On that special grass all the time, and they never looked down even once to see it. I hated unhappy endings! I slammed that hateful book shut and hurled it against the nearest wall. 'If that isn't the most stupid, silly, ridiculous story!' I raged at Chris, as if he had written the book. 'No matter whom I love, I'll learn to forgive and forget!' I continued to rail along with the storm outside, the weather and me beating out the same crescendo. 'Now why couldn't it have been written differently? How is it possible for two intelligent people to float along with their heads in the clouds, not realizing happenstance can always bring about bad luck? Never, never am I going to be like Lily, or Raymond, either! Idealistic fools who don't know enough to look down at the ground on occasion!'

My brother seemed amused that I took a story so seriously, but then he reconsidered, and stared thoughtfully at the driving rain. 'Perhaps lovers aren't supposed to look down at the ground. That kind of story is told in symbols – and earth represents reality, and reality represents frustrations, chance illnesses, death, murder, and all kinds of other tragedies. Lovers are meant to look up at the sky, for up there no beautiful illusions can be trampled upon.'

Frowning, sulky, I gazed moodily at him. 'And when I fall in love,' I began, 'I will build a mountain to touch the sky. Then, my lover and I will have the best of both worlds, reality firmly under our feet, while we have our heads in the clouds with all our illusions still intact. And the purple grass will grow all around, high enough to reach our eyes.'

He laughed, he hugged me, he kissed me lightly, tenderly, and his eyes were so gentle and soft in the murky, cold gloom of the attic. 'Oh, yes, my Cathy could do that. Keep all her fanciful illusions, dancing eye-high in purple grass, wearing clouds for gossamer clothes. She'd leap, she'd bound and pirouette until her clumsy-footed, awkward lover was dancing, too, just as gracefully.'

Put on quicksand, I quickly jumped to where I was sure-footed. 'It was a beautiful story though in its own peculiar way. I feel so sorry that Lily and Raymond had to take their own lives, when it should have worked out differently. When Lily told Raymond the full truth, how she was virtually raped by that awful man, Raymond shouldn't have accused her of seducing him! Nobody in their right mind would want to seduce a man with eight children.'

'Oh, Cathy, sometimes, really, you are just too much.'

His voice sounded deeper than usual when he said that. His soft look travelled slowly over my face, lingering on my lips, then down to my bosom, to my legs, sheathed in white leotards. Over the leotards I wore a short wool skirt and a wool cardigan sweater. Then his eyes moved upwards again, coming to lock with my surprised look. He flushed as I kept on staring at him, and turned aside his face for the second time today. I was close enough to hear his heart drumming fast, faster, racing, and all of a sudden my own heart caught the rhythm of his, in the only tempo hearts can have – thumpity-bump, thumpity-bump. He shot me a quick glance. Our eyes melded and held. He laughed nervously, trying to hide and pretend none of this could possibly be serious.

'You were right the first time, Cathy. It was a stupid, silly story. Ridiculous! Only insane people would die for the sake of love. I'll bet you a hundred to one a woman wrote that junky romantic trash!'

Just a minute ago I'd despised that author for bringing about such a miserable ending, then there I went, rushing to the defence. 'T. M. Ellis could very well have been a man! Though I doubt any woman writer in the nineteenth century had much chance of being published, unless she used her initials, or a man's name. And why is it all men think everything a woman writes is trivial or trashy – or just plain silly drivel? Don't men have romantic notions? Don't men dream of finding the perfect love? And it seems to me, that Raymond was far more mushy-minded than Lily!'

'Don't ask me what men are like!' he stormed with such bitterness he didn't seem himself at all. He raged on: 'Up here, living as we do, how am I ever going to know how it feels to be a man? Up here, I'm not allowed to have any romantic notions. It's don't do this, and don't do that, and keep your eyes averted, and don't see what's before your very eyes gliding about, showing off, pretending I'm just a brother, without feelings, without any emotions but childish ones. It seems some stupid girls think a gonna-be doctor is without sexuality!'

My eyes widened. Such a vehement outburst from one seldom upset took me completely by surprise. In all our lives he'd never spoken so fervently to me, and with such anger. No, I was the sour lemon, the bad apple in the barrel of good. I'd contaminated him. He was acting now like he had when Momma went away and stayed so long. Oh, it was wicked of me to make him the troublesome thing *I* was. He should stay always what *he* was, the happy-go-lucky cheerful optimist. Had I robbed him of his greatest asset, besides his good looks and charm?

I put out my hand to touch his forearm. 'Chris,' I whispered, near tears. 'I think I know exactly what you need to feel manly.'

'Yeah,' he bit out. 'What can *you* do?'

Now he wouldn't even look at me. Instead, he fixed his gaze on the ceiling above. I ached for him. I knew what had him down; he was letting go of his dream, for my benefit, so he could be like me, and not care whether or not we inherited a fortune. And to be like me, he had to be sour, bitter, hating everyone, and suspicious of their hidden motives.

Tentatively, I reached out to touch his hair. 'A haircut, that's what you need. Your hair is much too long and pretty. To feel a man, you must have shorter hair. Right now, your hair looks like mine.'

'And who has ever said your hair is pretty?' he asked in the tightest of voices. 'Maybe once you had pretty hair, before the tarring.'

Really? It seemed I could recall many times his eyes had told me my hair was more than just pretty. And I could recall the way he looked when he picked up the shiny shears to cut off that front hair, so delicate and brittle. He snipped with such reluctance it seemed he was cutting off fingers and not just hair that didn't feel pain. Then one day I caught him sitting in the attic sunshine, holding the long lengths of cut-off hair in his hands. He'd sniffed it, then put it to his cheek, and then to his lips, and then he hid it away in a box to keep under his pillow.

Not easily could I force laughter to deceive him and not let him know I'd seen. 'Oh, Christopher Doll, you have the most expressive blue eyes. When we are free of this place, and out in the world, I pity all the girls who are going to fall for you. Most especially I'll feel sorry for your wife, with such a handsome husband to charm all his beautiful patients into wanting affairs. And if I were your wife I'd kill you if you even had one extramarital affair! I'd love you so much, I'd be so jealous . . . I might even make you retire from medicine at age thirty-five.'

'I never told you even once your hair was pretty,' he said sharply, ignoring everything I'd said.

Ever so lightly I stroked his cheek, feeling the whiskers that needed shaving off.

'Sit right where you are. I'll run for the scissors. You know, I haven't given you a haircut for the longest time.' Why should I bother cutting his hair and Cory's when the way our hair looked didn't seem important to our lifestyle? Not since we came had Carrie and I had our hair trimmed. Only the top of mine had been snipped off to signify our submission to a mean old woman made of steel.

And while I raced for the scissors, I thought how odd it was that none of our green plants would grow, yet each of us grew lots of hair. It seemed in all the fairy tales I'd read, the damsels in distress always had long, long blonde hair. Had any brunette ever been locked away in a turret – if an attic could be considered a turret?

Chris sat on the floor, I knelt behind him, and though his hair hung below his shoulders, he didn't want much taken off. 'Now go easy with those shears,' he ordered nervously. 'Don't cut off too much all at once. Feeling manly too suddenly, on a rainy afternoon in the attic, just might be dangerous,' he teased, and grinned, and then he was laughing with a brilliant show of even, white teeth. I had charmed him back to how he should be.

Oh, I did love him as I crawled around and earnestly snipped and trimmed. Constantly I had to move backwards for perspective, to check and see if his hair hung evenly, for most certainly, I wouldn't want to make his head lopsided.

I held his hair with a comb, as I'd seen barbers do, and I carefully snipped beneath that comb, not daring to take off more than a quarter of an inch a clip. I had a mental vision of how I wanted him to look – like someone I admired very much.

And when I'd finished, I brushed the bright hair snippings from his shoulders, and leaned back to see that I hadn't done a bad job at all.

'There!' I said in triumph, pleased with my unexpected mastery of what seemed to be a difficult art. 'Not only do you look exceptionally handsome, but extremely manly as well! Though, of course, you have been manly all along, it's a pity you didn't know it.'

I thrust the silver-backed mirror with my initials into his hands. This mirror represented one-third of the sterling-silver set Momma had given me on my last birthday. Brush, comb, mirror: all three to be hidden away so the grandmother wouldn't know I had expensive items of vanity and pride.

Chris stared and stared into that mirror, and my heart faltered as he looked, for a moment, displeased and undecided. Then, slowly, a wide grin lit up his face.

'My God! You've made me look like a blond Prince Valiant! At first I didn't like it, but now I see you changed his style just a bit, so it isn't squared off. You've curved it, and layered it to flatter my face like a loving cup. Thank you, Catherine Doll. I had no idea you were so skilled at cutting hair.'

'I have many skills you don't know about.'

'I am beginning to suspect that.'

'And Prince Valiant should be so lucky as to look like my handsome, manly, blond brother,' I teased, and couldn't help but admire my own artistry. Oh, golly-gee, what a heartbreaker he'd be one day.

He still had the mirror, and casually he laid it aside, and before I knew what he was about, like a cat he pounced! He wrestled with me, bearing me back to the floor, and reached for the scissors at the same time! He yanked them from my hand, and then grabbed a handful of my hair!

'Now, my lovely, let's see if I can't do the same thing for you!' Terrified, I yelped!

I thrust him away so he fell backwards, and I jumped to my feet. No one was going to shear off one-eighth of an inch of my hair! Maybe it was too fine and too thin now, and maybe it wasn't as sensational as it used to be, but it was all the hair I had, and prettier even now than what most girls had. I took off on the run from the schoolroom. I raced through the doorway and into the immense attic, dodging behind posts, circling old trunks. leaping over low tables, and bounding over sheet-shrouded sofas and chairs. The paper flowers fanned frantically as I ran, and he chased. The flames of the low fat candles that we kept burning during the day just to cheer up and warm up a dreary, vast and cold place, bent low in our wakes, and almost guttered.

And no matter how swiftly I ran, or how cleverly I dodged, I couldn't shake off my pursuer! I threw a glance over my shoulder, and I couldn't even recognize his face – and that scared me even more. Lunging forward, he made an effort to seize hold of my long hair which bannered out behind me, and seemed so very intent on cutting it off!

Did he hate me now? Why had he spent one entire day so devotedly trying to save my hair, only to cut off my crowning glory for the sheer fun of it?

I fled back towards the schoolroom, planning on reaching there first. Then I'd slam the door, and lock it, and he'd come to his senses and realize the absurdity of it all.

Perhaps he sensed my purpose, and put some extra speed into his longer legs – he bounded forward, and caught hold of my long, streaming locks, causing me to scream as I tripped and fell forward!

Not only did I fall, but he fell too – straight on top of me! A sharp pain pierced my side! I screamed again – not in terror this time, but in shock.

He was over me, supported by his hands on the floor, staring down into my face, his face deadly white and frightened. 'Are you hurt? Oh, God, Cathy, are you all right?'

Was I all right, was I? Lifting my head, I stared down at the heavy flow of blood quickly staining my sweater. Chris saw it, too. His blue eyes went stark, bleak, wild, distraught. With trembling fingers he began to unbutton my sweater, so he could spread it open and take a look at my wound.

'Oh, Lord . . .' he breathed, then expelled a low whistle of relief. 'Wow! Thank God. I was so scared it would be a puncture. A deep puncture would be serious, but it's only a long cut, Cathy. Nasty, and you're losing a lot of blood. Now don't move a muscle! Stay right where you are, and I'll dash down to the bath and fetch medicine and bandages.'

He kissed me first on the cheek, then was up and in a terrible hurry, racing madly towards the stairwell, whereas I thought I could have gone with him and saved time. Yet the twins were down there, and they'd see the blood. And all they had to do was see blood and they'd go to pieces and scream.

In a few minutes Chris came speeding back with our medical emergency kit. He fell down on his knees beside me, his hands still glistening with water from a fast scrub-up. He was in too much of a hurry to dry them well.

I was fascinated to see he knew so precisely what to do. First he folded a heavy towel, and used that to press down hard on the long cut. Looking very serious and intent, he bore down on the pad, checking every few seconds to see if the bleeding had stopped. When it did, he busied himself with antiseptic that stung like fire, and hurt worse than the injury itself.

'I know it stings, Cathy . . . can't help that . . . have to put it on to avoid infection. Wish I had sutures, but maybe it won't make a permanent scar; and I pray it doesn't. It would be so nice if people could go through all of their life without ever cutting into the perfect envelope they're born with. And here I am, the first one to really scar your skin. If you had died because of me – and you could have if the shears had been slanted differently – then I would want to die too.'

He had finished playing doctor, and was now winding the remaining gauze up in a neat roll before replacing it in the blue wrapping-paper, and into a box. He stashed away the adhesive, closed the kit.

Leaning above me, his face hovered over mine, his serious eyes so delving, worried, and intense. His blue eyes were like the eyes we all had. Yet on this rainy day they were catching colours from the paper flowers, making them limpid dark pools of iridescence. A lump came in my throat as I wondered where the boy was I used to know. Where was that brother – and who was this young man with the blond whiskers, staring so long into my eyes? Just that look of his held me in thrall. And greater than any pain, or ache, or hurt I ever felt before, or since, was the pain caused me by the suffering I saw in the shifting kaleidoscopic, rainbowed colours of his tortured eyes.

'Chris,' I murmured, feeling unreal, 'don't look like that. It wasn't your fault.' I cupped his face in my palms first, then drew his head down to my breast as I'd seen Momma do in the past. 'It's only a scratch, doesn't hurt a bit [though it hurt dreadfully], and I know you didn't do it deliberately.'

Hoarsely he choked, 'Why did you run? Because you ran, I had to chase. And I was only teasing. I wouldn't cut one strand from your head; it was just something to do, to have fun. And you were wrong when you said I thought your hair was pretty. It's more than just pretty. I think you may grow on your head the most glorious hair in the world.'

A little knife twisted in my heart as he lifted his head long enough to spread my hair fanlike and cover my bare breast. I could hear him breathing deeply my scent. We lay there quietly listening to the winter rain drumming on the slate roof not so far above. Deep silence all around. Always silence. Nature's voices were the only ones to reach us in the attic, and so seldom did nature speak in friendly, soft tones.

The rain on the roof pitter-pattered down into only drops, and the sun came out and shone down on us to shimmer his hair and mine like long glimmering strands of silken diamonds. 'Look,' I said to Chris, 'one of the slats from a western window shutter has fallen out.'

'Nice,' he said, sounding sleepy and content. 'Now we'll have sun where once there was none. See, I've made a rhyme.' And then in a sleepy whisper, he said, 'I'm thinking of Raymond and Lily and their quest for the purple grass where all dreams are fulfilled.'

'Were you? In a way, I was kinda thinking the same things,' I answered, whispery, too. Over and over again I twirled a strand of his hair around my thumb, pretending not to notice one of his hands was ever so cautiously stroking my breast, the one his face didn't cover. Because I didn't object, he dared to kiss the nipple. I jumped, startled, wondering why that should feel so strange, and so extraordinarily thrilling. What was a nipple but a tannish-pink little peak? 'I can picture Raymond kissing Lily, just when you kissed,' I went on breathlessly, wanting him to stop, and wanting him to go on, 'but I can't imagine them doing what comes next.'

Words to make his head pop up. Just the right words to make him look at me intensely again, with strange lights flickering in his eyes which wouldn't stay only one colour. 'Cathy, do you know what comes next?'

A blush heated my face. 'Yes, I know, sort of. Do *you* know?'

He laughed, one of those dry chuckles you read about in novels. 'Sure I know. My very first day in school, I was told in the boys' rest-room; that's all the older boys could talk about. They had four-letter words on the walls that I didn't understand. But they were soon explained, in detail. Girls, baseball, girls, football, girls, girls, girls were all they could talk about, and all the ways they were different from us. It's a fascinating subject for most boys, and, I suppose, men.'

'But not fascinating for you?'

'Me? I don't think about girls, or sex, though I wish to God you weren't so damned pretty! And it would help if you weren't always so near, and so available.'

'Then you do think about me? You do think I'm pretty?'

A smothered groan escaped his lips – more like a moan. He bolted up to sit straight, staring down at what my open sweater revealed, for the fan of my hair was displaced. If I hadn't cut off the top of my leotards, he wouldn't be seeing so much. But I had had to cut off the too-small bodice.

With trembling, clumsy fingers he fastened the buttons of my sweater, keeping his eyes averted from mine. 'Get this straight in your head, Cathy. Of course you are pretty, but brothers don't think about sisters as girls – nor do they feel any sort of emotion for them other than tolerance and brotherly affection – and some-times, hate.'

'I hope God strikes me dead this second if you hate me, Christopher.'

His hands lifted to cover his face, hiding, and when he came out from behind the shield, he was smiling, cheerful, clearing his throat. 'Come on, it's time we went down to the twins before they burn their eyes into black holes from staring at the boob-tube for so long.'

It hurt to rise, though he assisted me up. In his arms I was held close while my cheek was pressed against his heart. And though he would put me from him quickly, I clung tighter. 'Chris – what we did just now – was it sinful?'

Again, he cleared his throat. 'If you think it so, then it was.'

What kind of an answer was that? If thoughts of sin stayed out of it, those moments lying on the floor when he touched me so tenderly with magical tingling fingers and lips were the sweetest moments since we'd come to live in this abominable house. I looked up to see what he was thinking and saw that strange look in his eyes. Paradoxically he seemed happier, sadder, older, younger, wiser . . . or was it he was feeling a man now? And if he was, then I was glad, sinful or not.

We walked hand in hand down the steps to the twins, where Cory was plucking a tune on the banjo, while keeping his eyes glued to the TV. He picked up the guitar and began his own composition, as Carrie chanted simple lyrics he'd composed. The banjo was for happy tunes to move your feet. This melody was like rain on the roof, long, dreary, monotonous.

> Gonna find my home,
> Gonna see the sun,
> Gonna find my home,
> Gonna feel the wind,
> See the sun ag'in.

I sat on the floor near Cory, and took the guitar from his hands, for I could play a bit, too. He had taught me how – taught us all how. And I sang to him that special, wistful song that belonged to Dorothy in the movie *The Wizard of Oz*, – a movie that the twins adored every time they saw it. And when I had finished singing of bluebirds that flew over the rainbow, Cory asked, 'Don't you like my song, Cathy?'

'You bet I like your song – but it's so sad. How about writing a few happy lyrics, with a little hope?'

The little mouse was in his pocket, just his tail poking out as he fingered down there for bread crumbs. Mickey made a twisting movement, and then his head was out of the shirt pocket, and in his forefeet he held a bit of bread and daintily began to nibble. The look on Cory's face as he stared down at his first pet touched me so deeply I had to turn away to keep from crying.

'Cathy, you know Momma, she never said nothing about my pet.'

'She hasn't noticed him, Cory.'

'Why don't she notice?'

I sighed, not really knowing who and what my mother was any more, except a stranger we used to love. Death wasn't the only thing that took away someone you loved and needed; I knew that now.

'Momma's got a new husband,' said Chris brightly, 'and when you're in love, you don't see anyone's happiness but your own. Soon enough she'll notice you've got a friend.'

Carrie was staring at my sweater. 'Cathy, what's that stuff on your sweater?'

'Paint,' said I without the slightest hesitation. 'Chris was trying to teach me how to paint, and he got mad when my picture was better than anything he's ever done, so he picked up the little pan with red, and he threw it at me.'

My older brother sat there with the darnedest look on his face.

'Chris, can Cathy paint better than you can?'

'If she says she can, then she must.'

'Where is her painting?'

'In the attic.'

'I want to see it.'

'Then you go up and get it. I'm tired. I want to look at TV while Cathy prepares dinner.' He shot me a swift look. 'My dear sister, would you mind, for the sake of propriety, putting on a clean sweater before we sit down to eat dinner? There's something about that red paint that makes me feel guilty.'

'It looks like blood,' said Cory. 'It's stiff like blood when you don't wash it off.'

'Poster colours,' said Chris, as I left to go into the bathroom to change into a sweater many sizes too large. 'Poster colours stiffen up.'

Satisfied, Cory began to tell Chris of how he'd missed seeing dinosaurs. 'Chris, they were bigger than this house! They came up out of the water, and swallowed the boat, and two men! I knew you'd be sorry to miss seeing that!'

'Yeah,' said Chris dreamily, 'I sure would have liked to have seen that.'

That night I felt strangely ill at ease, and restless, and my thoughts kept returning to the way Chris had looked at me in the attic.

I knew then what the secret was I'd been searching so long to find – that secret button that switched on love . . . physical, sexual desire. It wasn't just the viewing of naked bodies, for many a time I'd bathed Cory, and seen Chris naked, and I'd never felt any particular arousal because what he and Cory had was different from what Carrie and I had. It wasn't being naked at all.

It was the eyes. The secret of love was in the eyes, the way one person looked at another, the way eyes communicated and spoke when the lips never moved. Chris's eyes had said more than ten thousand words.

And it wasn't just the way he touched me, caressingly, tenderly; it was the way he touched, when he looked as he did, and that's why the grandmother made it a rule that we shouldn't look at the other sex. Oh, to think that old witch knew the secret of love. She couldn't have ever loved, no, not her, the iron-hearted, the steel-spined . . . never could other eyes have been soft.

And then, as I delved deeper into the subject, it was more than the eyes – it was what was behind the eyes, in the brain, wanting to please you, make you happy, give you joy, and take away the loneliness of never having anyone understand as you want to be understood.

Sin had nothing at all to do with love, real love. I turned my head and saw that Chris was awake, too, curled up on his side, staring over at me. He smiled the sweetest smile, and I could have cried for him, for me.

Our mother didn't visit us that day, nor had she visited us the day before, but we'd found a way to cheer ourselves by playing Cory's instruments and singing along. Despite the absence of a mother grown very negligent, we all went to bed more hopefully that night. Singing happy songs for several hours had convinced us all that sun, love, home and happiness were just around the bend, and our long days of travelling through a deep dark forest were almost over.

Into my bright dreams crept something dark and terrifying. Everyday forms took on monstrous proportions. With my eyes closed, I saw the grandmother steal into my bedroom, and thinking me asleep, she shaved off all my hair! I screamed but she didn't hear me – nobody heard me. She took a long and shiny knife and sliced off my breasts and fed them into Chris's mouth. And there was more. I tossed, writhed, and made small whimpering sounds that awakened Chris as the twins slept on as children dead and buried. Sleepily, Chris stumbled over to sit on my bed, and asked as he fumbled to find my hand, 'another nightmare?'

Nooo! This was no ordinary nightmare! This was precognition, and psychic in nature. I felt it in my bone marrow, something dreadful was about to happen. Weak and trembling I told Chris what the grandmother had done. 'And that wasn't all. It was Momma who came in and cut out my heart, and she was sparkled all over with diamonds!'

'Cathy, dreams don't mean anything.'

'Yes, they do!'

Other dreams and other nightmares I'd willingly told my brother and he'd listened, and smiled, and expressed his belief that it must be wonderful to have nights like being in a movie theatre, but it wasn't that way at all. In a movie, you sit and watch a big screen, and you know you are only watching a story that someone wrote. I participated in my dreams. I was in the dreams,

273

feeling, hurting, suffering, and I'm sorry to say, very seldom did I really enjoy them.

Since he was so accustomed to me and my strange ways, why did Chris sit as still as a marble statue, as if this dream affected him more than any other? Had he been dreaming, too?

'Cathy, on my word of honour, we are going to escape this house! All four of us will run away! You've convinced me. Your dreams must mean something, or else you wouldn't keep having them. Women are more intuitive than men; it's been proven. The subconscious is at work at night. We won't wait any longer for Momma to inherit the fortune from a grandfather who lives on and on and never dies. Together, you and I, we'll find a way. From this second on, I vow on my life, we depend only on ourselves . . . and your dreams.'

From the intense way he said this, I knew he wasn't joking, making fun – he meant what he said! I could have shouted, I felt so relieved. We were going to get away. This house wasn't going to do us in after all!

In the gloom and chill of that big shadowed and cluttered room, he stared down into my eyes. Maybe he was seeing me, as I saw him, looking larger than life, and softer than dreams. Slowly his head inclined towards mine, and he kissed me full on the lips as a way to seal his promise in a strong and meaningful way. Such a peculiar long kiss, to give me the sensation that I was falling down, down, down, when I was already lying down.

What we needed most was a key to our bedroom door. We knew it was the master key to every room in this house. We couldn't use the sheet-ladder because of the twins, and we didn't antici-pate, either Chris or I, that our grandmother would be so thought-lessly careless as to lay aside the key negligently. That just wasn't her way. Her way was to open the door, and immediately stash the key in her pocket. Always her hateful grey dresses had pockets.

Our mother's way was to be careless, forgetful, indifferent. And she didn't like pockets in her clothes to add extra bulk to her svelte figure. We counted on her.

And what did she have to fear from us – the passive, the meek, the quiet? Her private little captive 'darlings', who were never going to grow up and be a threat. She was happy, in love; it lit up her eyes and made her laugh often. She was so damned unobservant you wanted to scream and make her see – make her see the twins so quiet and sick looking! She never mentioned the mouse – why wasn't she seeing the mouse? He was on Cory's shoulder, nibbling on Cory's ear, and she never said a word, not even when tears streamed down Cory's face because she wouldn't congratulate him on winning the affections of a very stubborn mouse that would have gone his way, if allowed.

She came a generous two or three times a month, and each time she bore with her the gifts that gave *her* solace if they gave us none. She came in gracefully to sit a while, wearing her beautiful, expensive clothes trimmed with furs, and decorated with jewels.

On her throne she sat as a queen and doled out the painting sets to Chris, the ballet slippers to me, and to each of us she brought sensational-looking clothes, well suited for attic wearing, for up here it didn't matter if they seldom fit, being too large, or too small, and our sneakers were sometimes comfortable, sometimes not, and I was still waiting for the bra she kept promising but always forgot.

'I'll bring you a dozen or so,' she said with a benevolent cheerful smile, 'all sizes, all colours, and you can try them on and see which you like best, and fit best, and I can give the ones you don't want to the maids.' And on and on she chatted vivaciously, always true to her false façade, pretending we still mattered in her life.

I sat, I fixed my eyes on her, and I waited for her to ask me how the twins were. Had she forgotten that Cory had hay fever which kept his nose running all the time, and sometimes his nostrils stuffed up so he couldn't breathe except through his mouth? She knew he was supposed to be receiving allergy shots once a month, and years had passed since the last one. Didn't it hurt her to see Cory and Carrie clinging to me as if I were the one who had given them birth? Did one single thing reach out and tell her something was wrong?

If it did, in no way did she indicate that she saw us as less than perfectly normal, though I took pains to name our small illnesses: the way we threw up so often now, and how our heads ached from time to time, and we had stomach cramps, and sometimes very little energy.

'Keep your food in the attic, where it's cold,' she said without flinching.

She had the nerve to speak to us of parties, of concerts, of the theatre, of movies, and going to balls and on trips with her 'Bart'. 'Bart and I are going on a shopping spree in New York,' she said. 'Tell me what you want me to bring you. Make out a list.'

'Momma, after you Christmas-shop in New York, where will you go then?' I asked, careful not to turn my eyes on that key she had so casually tossed on the dresser top. She laughed, liking my question, and clasped her slender white hands together, and began to list her plans for the long dull days after the holidays. 'A trip south, perhaps a cruise, or a month or so in Florida. And your grandmother will be here to take good care of you.'

While she chatted on and on, Chris stole stealthily near to slip the key into his pants pocket. On into the bathroom he sauntered, excusing himself. He needn't have bothered; she didn't notice he was gone. She was doing her duty, visiting her children – and thank God she had chosen the right chair to sit in. In the bathroom I knew Chris was pressing the key into a bar of soap we kept ready for just this way to make a clear impression. Just one of the many things watching endless hours of television had taught us.

Once our mother had gone, Chris pulled out the piece of wood he had and began immediately to carve a rough wooden key. Though we had metal from the old trunk locks, we had nothing strong enough to cut and shape it. For hours and hours Chris slaved meticulously, carving that key, fitting and refitting it into the hardened soap impression. Purposefully, he had chosen very hard wood, fearing soft wood might break in the lock and give away our escape plan. It took three days of work before he had a key that worked.

Jubilance was ours! We threw our arms about each other and danced around the room, laughing, kissing, almost crying. The twins watched us, amazed we were so happy with a little key.

We had a key. We could open our prison door. Yet, strangely, we hadn't planned our future beyond the opening of the door.

'Money. We must have money,' reasoned Chris, stopping in

the middle of our wild dance of triumph. 'With lots of money, all doors are open, and all roads are ours to travel.'

'But where can we get money?' I asked, frowning and unhappy now. He had found another reason for stalling.

'There is no way but to steal it from Momma, her husband, and the grandmother.'

He said this so pronounced, exactly as if thieving were an old and honoured profession. And in dire need, perhaps it was, and still is.

'If we're caught, it will mean the whip for all of us, even the twins,' I said, casting my eyes on their fearful expressions. 'And when Momma goes on a trip with her husband, *she* could starve us again, and God alone knows what else *she* would do to us.'

Chris fell down on the small chair before the dressing-table. He propped his chin in his hand, thoughtful and considering for minutes. 'One thing for sure, I don't want to see you or the twins punished. So I will be the one to steal out of here, and I alone will stand guilty if caught. But I'm not going to be caught; it *is* too risky to take from that old woman – she's too observant. No doubt she knows to a penny exactly the amount of money in her purse. Momma never counts money. Remember how Daddy used to complain about that?' He grinned at me reassuringly. 'I will be just like Robin Hood, stealing from the rich to give to the needy poor – us! And only on the nights Momma and her husband tell us they are going out.'

'You mean *when* she tells us,' I corrected. 'And we can always watch from the window, on those days she doesn't come.' When we dared, we had a fine view of the curved drive to watch the comings and goings.

Soon enough Momma told us she was going to a party. 'Bart doesn't care much for the social life; he'd rather stay home. But I hate this house. He asks then why we don't move into our own home, and what can I say?'

What could she say? *Darling, I have a secret to tell you: upstairs, hidden away in the far northern wing, I have four children.*

It was easy enough for Chris to find money in his mother's grand, splendid bedroom. She was careless about money. Even he was shocked at how casually she left tens and twenties scattered over the dresser. It made him frown and put suspicions in his head. Wasn't she supposed to be saving up for that day when she could take us all out of our prison . . . even if she did have a husband now? More bills were in her many pocketbooks. Chris found change in her husband's trousers pockets. No, he was not as careless with *his* money. However, when Chris searched under the chair cushions, a dozen or more coins were there. He felt like a thief, an unwanted intruder in his mother's room. He saw her beautiful clothes, her satin mules, her negligées trimmed with fur, or marabou feathers, making his trust shrink even smaller.

Time after time that winter, he visited that bedroom, growing ever more careless since it was all so easy to steal. He came back to me, looking jubilant, looking sad. Day by day our hidden cache was increasing – why did he look sad? 'Come with me next time,' he said in way of reply. 'See for yourself.'

I could go with a clear conscience now, knowing the twins wouldn't awaken and find us gone. They slept so soundly, so deeply, that even in the mornings they woke up blurry-eyed, slow, reluctantly coming into reality. It scared me sometimes to look at them asleep. Two small dolls, never growing, so sunken into oblivion it seemed more a small death than normal night-time rest.

Go away, run away, spring was approaching, we had to leave soon, before it was too late. A voice inside, intuitive, kept drumming out this tune. Chris laughed when I told him. 'Cathy, you and your notions! We need money. At least five hundred. What is the terrible hurry? We have food now, and we aren't being whipped; even when *she* catches us half-undressed, she doesn't say a word.'

Why didn't the grandmother punish us now? We had not told Momma of her other punishments, her sins against us, for to me, they were sins, and not justified in any way. Yet, that old woman stayed her hand. Daily she brought up the picnic basket, filled to the brim with sandwiches, with lukewarm soups in Thermos bottles, with milk, and always four powdered-sugar doughnuts. Why couldn't she vary our menus and bring brownies, cookies, slices of pie or cake?

'C'mon,' urged Chris, dragging me along the corridors so dark and sinister. 'Lingering in one place is dangerous. We'll take a quick look in the trophy room, then rush on into Momma's bedroom suite.'

All I needed was one glance in that trophy room. I hated – actually detested that oil portrait over the stone fireplace – so much like our father – and yet so very different. A man as cruel and heartless as Malcolm Foxworth had no right to be handsome, even when he was young. Those cold blue eyes should have corrupted the rest of him with sores, boils. I saw all those heads of dead animals, and the tiger and bear skins on the floor, and I thought, how like him to want a room like this.

If Chris would let me, I would look into every room. But he insisted we pass by the closed doors, allowing me to peek in only a few. 'Nosy!' he whispered. 'There's nothing of interest in any of them.' He was right. Right in so many things. I learned that night what Chris meant when he said this house was only grand and beautiful, not pretty or cosy. Nevertheless, I couldn't help being impressed. Our home in Gladstone shrank in the comparison.

When we had quietly traversed many a long and stingily lit dim hall, we came at last upon our mother's grand suite of rooms. Sure, Chris had told me in detail of the swan bed, and the infant bed at the foot – but hearing wasn't seeing! My breath pulled in. My dreams took off on wings of fancy! Oh, glory be to heaven! This wasn't a room, but a chamber fit for a queen or a princess! I couldn't believe the posh splendour, the opulence! Overwhelmed, I flitted from here to there, awed to touch the walls, covered with silk damask, coloured a delicious strawberry pink, richer than the pale mauve of the two-inch-thick carpet. I fingered the soft, furry coverlet and I threw myself upon it and rolled about. I touched the filmy bed curtains, and heavier drapes of purple velvet. I jumped up from the bed, to stand at the foot, and gazed in admiration at that marvellous swan that kept his observant, but sleepy red eye riveted on me.

Then I backed off, not liking a bed where Momma slept with a man not our father. I walked into her huge walk-in closet, drifting about in a dream of riches that could never be mine, *except* in dreams. She had more clothes than a department store. Plus shoes, hats, handbags. Four full-length fur coats, three fur stoles, a white mink cape, and a dark sable one, plus fur hats of a dozen different styles and made of different animal pelts, plus a leopard coat with green wool in between the fur trim. Then there were negligées, nightgowns, peignoir sets, flounced, beruffled, beribboned, feathered, furred, made of velvet, satin, chiffon, combinations – good glory be! She'd have to live a thousand years to wear all she owned just once!

What caught my eye most, I took from the closet and carried into the golden dressing-room Chris showed me. I glanced in her bath, with the mirrors all around, live green plants, real flowers growing, two commodes – one didn't have a lid. (I know now one was a bidet.) A separate shower stall, too. 'All this is new,' explained Chris. 'When I first came, you know, the night of the Christmas party, it wasn't so . . . well, so opulent as it is now.'

I spun about to glare at him, guessing it had been all along, but he hadn't told me. He had been deliberately shielding her, not wanting me to know about all those clothes, the furs, plus the fabulous amount of jewellery she kept hidden in a secret compartment of her long dressing-table. No, he hadn't lied – just omitted. It showed in his betraying, shifting eyes, his flushed face, and the quick way he hurried to escape more of my embarrassing questions – no wonder she didn't want to sleep in *our* room!

I was in the dressing-room trying on the clothes from Momma's big closet. For the first time in my life I slipped on nylon hose, and, oh, did my legs look heavenly – divine! No wonder women liked these things! Next, I put on a bra for the first time, one that was much too large, to my dismay. I stuffed the cups full of tissues until they bulged way out. Next came the silver slippers, again, too large. And then I topped off the splendour of me with a black dress cut very low in front to show off what I didn't have much of.

Now came the fun part – what I used to do when I was little whenever I had the chance. I sat down at Momma's dressing-table and began to apply her make-up with a lavish hand. She had ten carloads. On my face I slathered the whole works: foundation, rouge, powder, mascara, eyeshadow, lipstick. And then I swept my hair up in a way I considered sexy and stylish, stuck in hairpins and began to put on jewellery. And, last of all, perfume – lots of it.

Tottering awkwardly on the high heels, I teetered over to Chris. 'How do I look?' I asked, flirtatiously smiling, and fluttering my sooty lashes. Truly, I was prepared for compliments. Hadn't the mirrors already told me I looked sensational?

He was carefully going through a drawer, putting everything back exactly as he had found it, but he turned to take a glance. Astonishment widened his eyes, and then he heavily scowled, while I rocked back and forth and sideways, seeking my balance on four-inch heels, and kept on batting my eyelids – maybe I didn't know how to put on false eyelashes right. I felt I was looking through spider legs.

'How do you look?' he began in a sarcastic way. 'Let me tell you precisely. You look like a street-walker – that's how!' He turned away in disgust, as if unable to bear the sight of me. 'An adolescent whore – that's what! Now go wash your face, and put back all that stuff where you found it, and clean up the dressing-table!'

I tottered over to the nearest full-length mirror. It had right and left wings so she could adjust them, and see herself from every angle, and in those three very revealing mirrors I took a fresh perspective – and what a fascinating mirror; it closed like a three-page-book, and then there was a beautiful French pastoral scene to view.

Twisting and turning, I checked over my appearance. This wasn't the way my mother looked in the same dress – what had I done wrong? True, she didn't ladder so many bracelets up her arms. And she didn't wear three necklaces at once, while long, dangling diamond earrings brushed her shoulders, plus a tiara; nor did she ever wear two or three rings on each finger – including her thumbs.

Oh, but I did dazzle the eyes all right. And my jutting bosom was absolutely magnificent! Truthfully, I had to admit I'd over-done it.

I took off seventeen bracelets, twenty-six rings, the necklaces, the tiara, and the black chiffon formal gown that didn't look as elegant on me as when Momma wore it to a dinner party with only pearls at the throat. Oh, but the furs – nobody could help but feel beautiful in furs!

'Hurry up, Cathy. Leave that stuff alone and come help me search.'

'Chris, I'd love to take a bath in her black marble tub.'

'God Almighty! We don't have time for you to do that!'

I took off her clothes, her black lace bra, the nylon hose, and the silver slippers, and put on my own things. But on second thoughts, I sneaked a plain white bra from her drawer of many, and tucked it down inside my blouse. Chris didn't need my help. He'd been here so often, he could find money without my assistance. I wanted to see what was in every drawer, but I'd have to move fast. I pulled open a small drawer of her nightstand, expecting to find cold cream, tissues, but nothing of value for servants to steal. And there was night cream in the drawer, and tissues, plus two paperback books to read when sleep was evasive. (Were there nights when she tossed and turned and thought uneasily about us?) Underneath those paperbacks was a very large and thick book with a colourful dustjacket. *How to Create Your Own Needlework Designs*. Now, that was a title to really intrigue me. Momma had taught me to do some needlepoint stitches, and also crewelwork on my first birthday in that locked room. And how to create your own designs would indeed be inspiring.

Casually I lifted out the book and flipped through the pages at random. Behind me Chris was making soft noises as he opened and closed drawers, and moved on sneakered feet from here to there. I had expected to see flower designs – anything but what I actually saw. Silent, wide-eyed, full of stunned fascination, I stared down at the photographs in full colour. Unbelievable pictures of naked men and women doing . . . did people really do such things as that? Was this love-making?

Chris wasn't the only one who'd heard whispered tales accompanied by much snickering from older children clustered in groups in the bathroom at school. Why, I had believed it was a sacred, reverent thing to do in complete privacy, behind locked doors. This book depicted many couples all in one room, all naked, and all into each other in one way or another. Against my will, or so

I wanted to think, my hand stole out to slowly turn each page, growing ever more incredulous! So many ways to do it! So many positions! My God, was *this* what lovesick Raymond and Lily had in mind from page one of that Victorian novel? I lifted my head and stared blankly into space. From the beginning of life, were we all headed towards this?

Chris spoke my name, informing me he had found enough money. Couldn't steal too much all at once, or it might be noticed. He was taking only a few fives, and many ones, and all the change under chair cushions. 'Cathy, what's the matter, are you deaf? Come on.'

I couldn't move, couldn't leave, couldn't close that book without pursuing it from cover to cover. Because I stood so enthralled, unable to respond, he came up behind me to look over my shoulder at what held me so mesmerized. I heard his breath pull in sharply. After an eternal time, he exhaled a low whistle. He didn't say a single word until I reached the end and closed the book. Then he took over and began at the beginning, looking at each page he had missed as I stood beside him and looked again, too. There was small printed text opposite the full-page pictures. But the photographs didn't need explanations – not to my mind.

Chris closed the book. I glanced at his face quickly. He appeared stunned. I returned the book to the drawer, placing the paperbacks on top, just as I had found it. He took my hand and pulled me towards the door. Down all the long and dark halls we went silently back to the northern wing. Now I knew only too well why the witch-grandmother had wanted Chris and me put in separate beds, when that compelling call to human flesh was so strong, so demanding, and so thrilling it could make people act more like demons than saints. I leaned above Carrie, staring down in her sleeping face, which, in her sleep, regained the innocence and child-ishness that evaded her during her waking hours. She seemed a small cherub lying there on her side, curled up tight, her face rosy and flushed, her hair damp and curling on the nape of her neck and on her rounded forehead. I kissed her, and her cheek felt hot, and then I went over to Cory to touch his soft curls and kissed his flushed cheek. Children like the twins were made from a little of what I had just viewed in that erotic picture book, so it couldn't all be totally wicked, or else God wouldn't have made men and women the way He did. And yet I was so troubled, and so uncertain, and deep down really stunned and shocked, and still . . .

I closed my eyes and silently prayed: *God, keep the twins safe and healthy until we're out of here . . . let them live until we reach a bright and sunny place where doors are never locked . . . please.*

'You can use the bath first,' said Chris, sitting on his side of the bed with his back towards me. His head was bowed down, and this was his night to take his bath first.

Under a kind of spell I drifted into the bath and did what I had to, then came out wearing my thickest, warmest, and most concealing granny-gown. My face was scrubbed clean of all make-up. My hair was shampooed and still a little damp as I sat down on the side of my bed to brush it into shining waves.

Chris rose silently and entered the bath without looking my way, and when he came out much later, and I was still sitting and brushing my hair, he didn't meet my eyes. Nor did I want him to look at me.

It was one of the grandmother's rules that we were to kneel down by our beds each night and say prayers. Yet, that night, neither of us knelt to say prayers. Often, I was on my knees by the bed, with my palms together under my chin, and I didn't know what to pray, since already I'd prayed so much, and none of it helped. I'd just kneel there, empty-minded, bleak-hearted, but my body and its nerve endings felt everything and screamed out what I couldn't bring myself to think, much less say.

I stretched out beside Carrie on my back, feeling soiled and changed by that big book that I wished to see again and wished, if I could, to read every word of the text. Maybe it would have been the ladylike thing to just put the book back when I'd found out its subject – and most certainly I should have slammed it shut when Chris came to look over my shoulder. Already I knew I wasn't a saint, or an angel, or a puritan prude, and I felt in my bones that some day in the near future I was going to need to know all there was to know about how bodies were used in ways of love.

Slowly, slowly, I turned my head to peer through the rosy dimness and see what Chris was doing.

He was on his side, under the covers, gazing over at me. His eyes glimmered in some faint meandering light that filtered through the heavy draperies, for what light was in his eyes wasn't rose-coloured.

'Are you all right?' he asked.

'Yes, I'm surviving.' And then I said good night in a voice that didn't even sound like me.

'Good night, Cathy,' he said, using someone else's voice, too.

MY STEPFATHER

That spring, Chris got sick. He looked greenish around his mouth and threw up every few minutes, staggering back from the bathroom to fall weakly on the bed. He wanted to study *Gray's Anatomy*, but threw it aside, irritated with himself. 'Must have been something I ate,' he grouched.

'Chris, I don't want to leave you alone,' I said at the door, preparing to fit the wooden key into the lock.

'Look here, Cathy!' he yelled. 'It's time you learned to stand on your own two feet! You don't need me at your side every live-long minute of the day! That was Momma's trouble. She thought she'd always have a man to lean on. Lean on yourself, Cathy, always.'

Terror jumped into my heart, flooded up in my eyes. He saw, and he spoke more gently. 'I'm all right, really. I can take care of myself. We need the money, Cathy, so go on alone. We might not have another chance.'

I ran back to his bed, falling down on my knees, and pressing my face down on his pyjamaed chest. Tenderly he caressed my hair. 'Really, Cathy, I'll survive. It's not so bad you have to cry about it. But you've got to understand, no matter what happens to either one of us, the one left has to get the twins out.'

'Don't say things like that!' I cried out. Just to think of him dying made me sick inside. And as I knelt there, staring at him, it fleetingly crossed my mind, how often one or the other of us was sick.

'Cathy, I want you to leave now. Stand up. Force yourself. And when you get there, take only ones and fives. Nothing larger. But take all the coins our stepfather lets fall from his pockets. And in the back of his closet, he keeps a big tin box full of change. Take a handful of the quarters.'

He looked pale and weak, thinner, too. Quickly I kissed his cheek, loath to leave when he felt so unwell. Glancing at the sleeping twins, I backed off towards the door, clutching the wooden key in my hand. 'I love you, Christopher Doll,' I said in a joking way before opening the door.

'I love you too, Catherine Doll,' he said. 'Good hunting.'

I threw him a kiss, then closed and locked the door behind me. It was safe enough to go stealing in Momma's room. Only this afternoon she had told us she and her husband were attending another party, at a friend's who lived down the road. And I thought to myself, as I stole quietly along the corridors clinging to the walls, keeping to the shadows, I *was* going to take at least one twenty, and one ten. I was going to risk somebody noticing. Maybe I'd even steal a few pieces of Momma's jewellery. Jewellery could be pawned, just as good as money, maybe better.

All business, all determination, I didn't waste time looking in the trophy room. Straight on to Momma's bedroom I crept, not expecting to see the grandmother, who retired very early, at nine. And the hour was ten.

With all brave determined confidence, I stole through the double doors to her rooms, and silently closed them behind me. One dim light was burning. Often she left lights burning in her rooms – sometimes every last one, according to Chris. For what was money to our mother now?

Hesitating uncertainly, I stood just inside the doors and looked around. Then I froze in terror.

There, in a chair, with his long legs stretched before him and crossed at the ankles, sprawled Momma's new husband! I was directly in front of him, wearing a transparent blue nightie that was very short, though little matching panties were underneath. My heart beat out a mad tune of panic as I waited for him to bellow out and demand to know who I was, and what the hell was I doing coming uninvited into his bedroom?

But he didn't speak.

He wore a black tuxedo, and his formal shirt was pink with black-edged ruffles down the front. He didn't bellow, he didn't question, because he was dozing. I almost turned about and left, I was so terrified he'd awaken and see me.

However, curiosity overcame my trepidations. On my toes I stole closer to peer down at him. I dared to go so close, up to his chair, that I could reach out and touch him, if I chose. Close enough to put my hand in his pocket and rob him if I chose, which I didn't.

Robbery was the last thing I had in mind as I gazed down into his handsome sleeping face. I was amazed to see what was revealed now that I was so very close to my mother's dearly beloved Bart. I had viewed him from a distance a number of times: first, the night of the Christmas party, and another time when he was down there near the stairs, holding a coat for Momma to slip her arms in. He'd kissed the back of her neck, and behind her ear, and whispered something that made her smile, and so tenderly he'd drawn her against his chest before they both went out the door.

Yes, yes, I had seen him, and heard much about him, and knew where his sisters lived, and where he was born, and where he'd gone to school, but nothing had prepared me for what was so clearly revealed now.

Momma – how could you? You should be ashamed! This man is younger than you – years younger! She hadn't told us that.

A secret. How well she could keep such an important secret! And no wonder she adored him, worshipped him – he was the kind of man any woman would want. Just to look at him so casually, elegantly sprawled, I guessed he was both tender and passionate when he made love to her.

I wanted to hate that man dozing in the chair, but somehow I just couldn't. Even asleep, he appealed to me, and made my heart beat faster.

Bartholomew Winslow, smiling in his sleep, innocently, unknowingly responding to my admiration. A lawyer, one of those men who knew everything – like doctors – like Chris. Certainly he must be seeing and experiencing something exceptionally pleasing. What was going on behind his eyeballs? I wondered, too, if his eyes were blue or brown. His head was long and lean, his body slim, and hard and muscular. A deep cleft was near his lips, looking like a stretched vertical dimple to play games of hide and seek as it came and went with his vague sleepy smiles.

He wore a wide sculptured gold wedding band, and of course I recognized it as the twin to the slimmer one my mother wore. On the index finger of his right hand he wore a large square-cut diamond ring that sparkled even without much light. On a small finger he wore a fraternity ring. His long fingers had square nails buffed so they shone as much as mine. I remembered when Momma used to buff Daddy's nails, while they played teasing games with their eyes.

He was tall . . . I already knew that. And of everything he had that pleased me well, it was his full and sensual lips beneath the moustache that intrigued me most. Such a beautifully shaped mouth – sensual lips that must kiss my mother . . . everywhere. That book of sexual pleasures had educated me well along that line of how adults gave and took when they were bare.

It came over me all of a sudden – the impulse to kiss him – just to see if the dark moustache tickled. Just to know also, what a kiss was like from a stranger who was no blood relation at all.

Not forbidden, this one. Not sinful to tentatively reach out and very lightly stroke his closely shaven cheek, so softly challenging him to wake up.

But he slept on.

I leaned above him and pressed my lips down on his ever so lightly, then drew away fast, my heart pounding in a paralysing kind of fear. I was almost wishing that he would waken, but I was still fearful and afraid. I was too young and unsure of what I had to believe he would come rushing to my defence, when he had a woman like my mother madly in love with him. Would he, if I took his arm and shook him awake, sit and listen calmly to my story about four children sequestered in a lonely, isolated room year after year, waiting impatiently for their grandfather to die? Would he understand and sympathize with us, and would he force Momma to set us free, and give up hopes of inheriting that immense fortune?

My hands fluttered nervously to my throat, the way Momma's did when she was caught in a dilemma, not knowing which way to turn. My instinct was shouting loud: *Wake him up!* My suspicions whispered slyly, keep quiet, don't let him know; he won't want you, not four children he didn't father. He'll hate you for preventing his wife from inheriting all the riches and pleasures that money can buy. Look at him, so young, so handsome. And though our mother was exceptionally beautiful, and on the way to being one of the wealthiest women in the world, he could have had somebody younger. A fresh virgin who'd never loved anyone else, nor slept with another man.

And then my indecision was over. The answer was so simple. What were four unwanted children when compared to unbelievable riches?

They were nothing. Already Momma had taught me that. And a virgin would bore him.

Oh, it was unfair! Foul! Our mother had everything! Freedom to come and go as she wished; freedom to spend lavishly and buy out the world's best stores, if she chose. She even had the money to buy a much younger man to love, and sleep with – and what did Chris and I have but broken dreams, shattered promises, and unending frustrations?

And what did the twins have, but a doll house and a mouse and ever-declining health?

Back to that forlorn, locked room I went with tears in my eyes and a helpless, hopeless feeling heavy as stone in my chest. I found Chris sleeping with *Gray's Anatomy* lying face down and open on his chest. Carefully I marked his place, closed the book, and put it aside.

Then I lay beside him, and clung to him, and silent tears came to streak my cheeks and wet his pyjama jacket.

'Cathy,' he said, waking up, and coming sleepily into focus. 'What's the matter? Why are you crying? Did someone see you?'

I couldn't meet his concerned look squarely, and for some inexplicable reason, I couldn't tell him what happened. I couldn't speak the words to say I'd found mother's new husband dozing in her room. Much less could I tell him I'd been so childishly romantic as to kiss him while he slept.

'And you didn't even find a single cent?' he asked with so much disbelief.

'Not even a cent,' I whispered in return, and I tried to hide my face from his. But he cupped my chin and forced me to turn my head so he could delve deep into my eyes. Oh, why did we have to know each other so well? He stared at me, while I tried to keep my eyes blank, but it was no use. All I could do was close my eyes and snuggle closer in his arms. He bowed his face into my hair while his hands soothingly stroked my back. 'It's all right. Don't cry. You don't know where to look like I do.'

I had to get away, run away, and when I ran away, I would take all of this with me, no matter where I went, or who I ended up with.

'You can get in your own bed now,' said Chris in his hoarse voice. 'The grandmother could open the door and catch us, you know.'

'Chris, you didn't throw up again after I left, did you?'

'No. I'm better. Just go away, Cathy. Go away.'

'You really feel better now? You're not just saying that?'

'Didn't I just say I was better?'

'Good night, Christopher Doll,' I said, then put a kiss on his cheek before I left his bed and climbed into my own bed to snuggle up with Carrie.

'Good night, Catherine. You make a pretty good sister, and mother to the twins . . . but you're one helluva liar, and one damned no-good thief!'

Each of Chris's forays into Momma's room enriched our hidden cache. It was taking so long to reach our goal of five hundred dollars. And now summer was upon us again. Now I was fifteen, the twins recently turned eight. Soon August would mark the third year of our imprisonment. Before another winter set in, we had to escape. I looked at Cory, who was listlessly picking at black-eyed peas because they were 'good luck' peas. First time on New Year's Day, he wouldn't eat them: didn't want any little brown eyes looking at his insides. Now he'd eat them because each pea gave him one full day of happiness – so we'd told him. Chris and I had to make up tales like this or else he'd eat nothing but the doughnuts. As soon as that meal was over, he crouched down on the floor, picked up his banjo, and fixed his eyes on a silly cartoon. Carrie glued in beside him, as close as possible, watching her twin's face and not the TV. 'Cathy,' she said to me in her bird twitter. 'Cory, he don't feel so good.'

'How do you know?'

'Jus' know.'

'Has he told you he feels sick?'

'He don' have to.'

'And how do *you* feel?'

'Like always.'

'And how is that?'

'Don't know.'

Oh yes! We had to get out, and fast!

Later on I tucked the twins in one bed. When they were both asleep, I'd lift out Carrie, and put her in our bed, but for now, it was comforting for Cory to go to sleep with his sister by his side. 'Don't like this pink sheet,' complained Carrie, scowling at me. 'We all like white sheets. Where are our white sheets?'

Oh, rue the day when Chris and I had made white the safest colour of all! White chalk daisies drawn on the attic floor kept away evil demons, and monsters, and all the other things the twins feared would get them if white wasn't somewhere near to hide inside, or under, or behind. Lavender, blue or pink, or flower-strewn sheets and pillowcases were not to be tolerated . . . little coloured places gave small imps a hole through which to drive a forked tail, or glare a mean eye, or stab with a wicked, tiny spear! Rituals, fetishes, habits, rules – Lord – we had them by the millions! Just to keep us safe.

'Cathy, why does Momma like black dresses so much?' asked Carrie, waiting as I took off the pink sheets and replaced them with plain white ones.

'Momma is blonde and very fair, and black makes her look even more fair, and exceptionally beautiful.'

'She's not scared of black?'

'No.'

'How old do you get before black doesn't bite you with long teeth?'

'Old enough to know such a question as that is absolutely silly.'

'But all the black shadows in the attic have shiny, sharp teeth,' said Cory, scooting backwards so the pink sheets wouldn't touch his skin.

'Now look,' I said, seeing Chris's laughing eyes watching as he anticipated some gem I would certainly deliver. 'Black shadows don't have shiny sharp teeth unless your skin is emerald green, and your eyes are purple, and your hair is red, and you have three ears instead of two. Only then is black a threat.'

Comforted, the twins scurried under the white sheet and white blankets, and were soon fast asleep. Then I had time to bathe, and shampoo my hair, and put on wispy baby-doll pyjamas. I ran up into the attic to open a window wide, hopeful of catching a cool breeze to freshen the attic so I'd feel like dancing and not wilting. Why was it the wind could find its way inside only during a wintry blast? Why not now, when we needed it most?

Chris and I shared all our thoughts, our aspirations, our doubts, and our fears. If I had small problems, he was my doctor. Fortunately, my problems were never of much consequence, only those monthly cramps, and that womanly time never showed up on schedule, which he, my amateur doctor, said was only to be expected. Since I was of a quixotic nature, all my internal machinery would follow suit.

So I can write now of Chris and what happened one September night when I was in the attic, and he had gone stealing, just as if I were there, for later, when the shock of something totally unexpected had died down a bit, he told me in great detail of this particular trip to Momma's grand suite of luxurious rooms.

He told me it was that book in the nightstand drawer that drew him always; it lured him, beckoned to him, was to shipwreck him later, and me too. As soon as he found his quota of money – enough, but not too much – he drifted over to the bed and that table as if magnetized.

And I thought to myself, even as he told me: Why did he have to keep on looking, when each of those photographs was for ever engraved on my brain?

'And there I was, reading the text, a few pages at a time,' he said, 'and thinking about right and wrong, and wondering about nature and all its strange exhilarating calls, and thinking about the circumstances of our lives. I thought about you and me, that these should be blossoming years for us, and I had to feel guilty and ashamed to be growing up, and wanting what other boys my age could take from girls who were willing.

'And, as I stood there, leafing through those pages, burning inside with so many frustrations, and wishing in a way you hadn't ever found that damned book that never drew my attention with its dull title, I heard voices approaching in the hall. You know who it was – it was our mother, and her husband, returning. Quickly I shoved the book back into the drawer and tossed in the two paperbacks which no one was ever going to finish reading, for the bookmarks were always in the same place. Next I dashed into Momma's closet – that big one, you know, the one nearest her bed – and way back near the shoe shelves I crouched down on the floor beneath her long formal gowns. I thought if she came in, she wouldn't see me and I doubt she would have. But no sooner did I feel this security, than I realized I'd forgotten to close the door.

'That's when I heard our mother's voice. "Really, Bart," she said as she came into the room and switched on a lamp, "it's just plain carelessness for you to forget your wallet so often."

'He answered, "I can't help but forget it when it's never in the same place I put it down." I heard him moving things about, opening and closing drawers and so forth. Then he explained, "I'm certain I left it in this pair of trousers . . . and damned if I'm going anywhere without my driver's licence."

'"The way you drive, I can't say I blame you," said our mother, "but this is going to make us late again. No matter how fast you drive, we'll still miss the first act."

'"Hey!" exclaimed her husband, and I heard surprise in his voice, and inwardly groaned, remembering what I'd done. "Here's my wallet, on the dresser. Darned if I recall leaving it there. I could swear I put it in these trousers."

'He really had hidden it in his chest of drawers,' Chris explained, 'under his shirts, and when I found it, I took out a few small bills, I just laid it down and went on to look at that book. And Momma, she said, "Really, Bart!" as if she was out of patience with him.

'And then he said, "Corrine, let's move out of this place. I believe those maids are stealing from us. You keep missing money, and so do I. For instance, I know I had four fives, and now I have only three."

'I groaned again. I thought he had so much he never counted.

And the fact that Momma knew what cash she carried in her purse really came as a shock.

'"Just what difference does a five make?" questioned our mother, and that sounded like her, to be indifferent about money, just as she had been with Daddy. And then she went on to say the servants were under-paid, and she didn't blame them for taking what they could when it was left so opportunely before them, "actually inviting them to steal".

'And he answered, "My dear wife, money may come easily to you, but I've always had to work hard to earn a buck, and don't want ten cents stolen from me. Besides, I can't say my day starts out right when I have your mother's grim face across the table from me every morning." You know, I'd never given that any thought, how he felt about that old witch ironface.

'Apparently he feels just as we do, and Momma, she grew kind of irritated, and said, "Let's not go through all that again." And her voice had a hard edge to it; she didn't even sound like herself, Cathy. It never occurred to me before that she talked one way to us, and another way to other people. And then she said, "You know I can't leave this house, not yet, so if we're going, come on, let's go – we're late already."

'And that's when our stepfather said he didn't want to go if they'd already missed the first act, for that spoiled the whole show for him, and besides, he thought they could find something more entertaining to do than sit in an audience. And, of course, I guessed he meant they could go to bed and do a little love-making, and if you don't think that didn't make me feel sick, then you don't know me very well – darned if I wanted to be there when that was going on.

'However, our mother can be very strong-willed, and that surprised me. She's changed, Cathy, from the way she was with Daddy. It's like she is the boss now, and no man is going to tell her what to do. And she said to him then, "Like last time? Now, that was really embarrassing, Bart! You came back to get your wallet, swearing to me you'd only be gone a few minutes and what did you do but fall asleep – and there I was at that party without an escort!"

'Now our stepfather sounded somewhat irritated, both by her

words, and her tone, if I judged him correctly, and there's a lot you can read into voices even when you don't see facial expressions. "Oh, how you must have suffered!" he replied, sounding sarcastic. But that didn't last long, for he must be basically a jovial fellow. "As for me, I had the sweetest dream, and I'd come back every time if I knew that for certain, a lovely young girl with the long, golden hair would steal into the room and kiss me while I dozed. Oh, she was pretty, and she looked at me so longingly, yet, when I opened my eyes she was gone, and I thought she must have been a dream."

'What he said made me gasp, Cathy — it was you, wasn't it? How could you be so bold, so indiscreet? I got so damned mad with you I felt ready to explode if just one more little thing happened to set me off. You think you're the only one wound up, right? You think you're the only one with frustrations, with doubts, suspicions, and fears. Well, take comfort from knowing I have them too — you've seen to that. And, boy, was I mad at you, madder than I've ever been before.

'And then Momma said sharply to her husband, "God, I am sick of hearing about the girl and her kiss — why, to hear you tell it, you've never been kissed before!" And I thought that then and there they might have an argument. But Momma changed her voice, and sounded sweet and loving, like she used to sound with Daddy. But it proved she was more determined to leave this house than a would-be lover who would use the swan bed then and there, for Momma said, "Come along, Bart, we'll stay overnight in a hotel, and then you won't have to see my mother's face in the morning." And that solved my concern about how I was going to escape that room before they used that swan bed — for damned if I would stay and listen, or spy.'

This was all happening while I was up in the attic, sitting on a windowsill, waiting for Chris to reappear. I was thinking of the silver music box Daddy had given me, and wishing I had it back. I didn't know then that the episode in Momma's room was to have its repercussions.

Something creaked behind me! A soft step on rotting wood! I jumped, startled, scared, and turned, expecting to see — God knows what! Then I sighed, for it was only Chris standing in the gloom, silently staring at me. Why? Did I look prettier than usual? Was it the moonlight, shining through my airy clothes?

All random doubts were cleared when he said in a voice gritty and low, 'You look beautiful sitting there like that.' He cleared the frog in his throat. 'The moonlight is etching you with silver-blue, and I can see the shape of your body through your clothes.'

Then, bewilderingly, he seized me by the shoulders, digging in his fingers, hard! They hurt. 'Damn you, Cathy! You kissed that man! He could have awakened and seen you, and demanded to know who you were! And not thought you only a part of his dream!'

Scary the way he acted, the fright I felt for no reason at all. 'How do you know what I did? You weren't there; you were sick that night.'

He shook me, glaring his eyes, and again I thought he seemed a stranger. 'He saw you, Cathy – he wasn't soundly asleep!'

'He saw me?' I cried, disbelieving. It wasn't possible . . . wasn't!

'Yes!' he yelled. This was Chris, who was usually in such control of his emotions. 'He thought you a part of his dream! But don't you know that Momma can guess who it was, just by putting two and two together – just as I have? Damn you and your romantic notions! Now they're on to us! They won't leave money casually about as they did before. He's counting, she's counting, and we don't have enough – not yet!'

He yanked me down from the windowsill! He appeared wild and furious enough to slap my face – and not once in all our lives had he ever struck me, though I'd given him reason to when I was younger. But he shook me until my eyes rolled, until I was dizzy and crying out: 'Stop! Momma knows we can't pass through a locked door!'

This wasn't Chris . . . this was someone I'd never seen before . . . primitive, savage.

He yelled out something like, 'You're mine, Cathy! Mine! You'll always be mine! No matter who comes into your future, you'll always belong to me! I'll make you mine . . . tonight . . . now!'

I didn't believe it, not Chris!

And I did not fully understand what he had in mind, nor, if I am to give him credit, do I think he really meant what he said, but passion has a way of taking over.

297

We fell to the floor, both of us. I tried to fight him off. We wrestled, turning over and over, writhing, silent, a frantic struggle of his strength against mine.

It wasn't much of a battle.

I had the strong dancer's legs; he had the biceps, the greater weight and height . . . and he had much more determination than I to use something hot, swollen and demanding, so much it stole reasoning and sanity from him.

And I loved him. I wanted what he wanted – if he wanted it *that* much, right or wrong.

Somehow we ended up on that old mattress – that filthy, smelly, stained mattress that must have known lovers long before this night. And that is where he took me, and forced in that swollen, rigid male sex part of him that had to be satisfied. It drove into my tight and resisting flesh which tore and bled.

Now we had done what we both swore we'd never do.

Now we were doomed through all eternity, damned to roast for ever, hung upside down and naked over the everlasting fires of hell. Sinners, just as the grandmother had forecast so long ago.

Now I had all the answers.

Now there might be a baby. A baby to make us pay in life and not wait for hell, and everlasting fires reserved for such as us.

We drew apart and stared at each other, our faces numb and pale from shock, and barely could we speak as we drew on our clothes.

He didn't have to say he was sorry . . . it was all over him . . . the way he quivered, the way his hands trembled and were so clumsy with his buttons.

Later, we went out on the roof.

Long strings of clouds blew across the face of the full moon, so it would duck and hide, then peek out again. And on the roof, on a night that was made for lovers, we cried in each other's arms. He hadn't meant to do it. And I had meant never to let him. The fear of the baby that might be the result of one single kiss on moustached lips rose high in my throat, and hesitated on my tongue. It was my worst fear. More than hell, or God's wrath, I feared giving birth to a monstrous baby, deformed, a freak, an idiot. But how could I speak of this? Already he was suffering enough. However, his thoughts were more knowledgable than mine.

'The odds are all against a baby,' he said fervently. 'Just one time – there won't be a conception, I swear there won't be another time – no matter what! I'll castrate myself before I'll let it happen again!' Then he had pulled me tightly against him so I was crushed so hard it hurt my ribs. 'Don't hate me, Cathy, please don't hate me. I didn't mean to rape you, I swear to God. There's been many a time when I've been tempted, and I was able to turn it off. I'd leave the room, go into the bathroom, or into the attic. I'd bury my nose in a book until I felt normal again.'

Tight as I could, I wrapped my arms around him. 'I don't hate you, Chris,' I whispered, pressing my head tightly against his chest. 'You didn't rape me. I could have stopped you if I'd really wanted to. All I had to do was bring my knee up hard, where you told me to. It was my fault, too.' Oh yes, my fault too. I should have known better than to kiss Momma's handsome young husband. I shouldn't have worn skimpy little see-through garments around a brother who had all a man's strong physical needs, and a brother who was always so frustrated by everything, and everyone. I had played upon his needs, testing my femininity, having my own burning yearnings for fulfilment.

It was a peculiar kind of night, as if fate had planned this night, long ago, and this night was our destiny, right or wrong. It was darkness lit up by the moon so full and bright, and the stars seemed to flash Morse code beams to one another . . . fate accomplished . . .

The wind in the leaves rustled and made an eerie, melancholy music that was tuneless, yet music just the same. How could anything as human and loving be ugly on such a beautiful night as this one?

Perhaps we stayed too long on the roof.

The slate was cold, hard, rough. It was early September. Already the leaves were beginning to fall, so soon to be touched by the winter's frosty hand. Hot as hell in the attic. On the roof, it was beginning to turn very, very cold.

Closer Chris and I huddled, clinging to each other for safety and warmth. Youthful, sinful lovers of the worst kind. We had dropped ten miles in our own esteem, done in by yearnings stretched too thin by constant closeness. Just once too often we'd tempted fate, and our own sensuous natures . . . and I hadn't even known at the time that I was sensuous, much less that he was. I'd thought it was only beautiful music that made my heart ache and my loins crave; I hadn't known it was something far more tangible.

Like one heart shared between us, we drummed out a terrible tune of self-punishment for what we'd done.

A colder breeze lifted a dead leaf to the roof and sent it scuttling merrily on its way to catch in my hair. It crackled dry and brittle when Chris plucked it out and held it, just staring down at a dead maple leaf as if his very life depended on reading its secret for knowing how to blow in the wind. No arms, no legs, no wings . . . but it could fly when dead.

'Cathy,' he began in a crackling, dry voice, 'we now have exactly three hundred and ninety-six dollars and forty-four cents. Won't be long before the snow starts to fall. And we don't own winter coats or boots that fit, and the twins are already so weakened that they will catch cold easily, and might pass from colds into pneumonia. I wake up in the night, worrying about them, and I've seen you lying on your bed staring at Carrie, so you must be worrying, too. I doubt very much we'll be finding money lying about in Momma's suite of rooms now. They suspect a maid is stealing from them – or they did. Maybe now Momma suspects that it could be you . . . I don't know . . . I hope not.

'Regardless of what either of them thinks, the next time I play thief, I'm forced to steal her jewellery. I'll make a grand sweep, take it all – and then we'll run. We'll take the twins to a doctor as soon as we're far enough away, and we'll have enough money to pay their bills.'

Take the jewellery – what I'd begged him to do all along! Finally he would do it, agree to steal the hard-won prizes Momma had struggled so to gain, and in the process, she was going to lose us. But would she care – would she?

That old owl that might be the same one that greeted us at the train depot on the first night we came, hooted in the far distance, sounding ghostly. While we watched, thin, slow, grey mists began to rise up from the damp ground, chilled by the night's sudden cold. The thick and billowing fog swelling up to the roof . . . undulating curling waves, rolling as a misty sea to shroud over us.

And all we could see in the murky-grey and cold, damp clouds was that single great eye of God – shining up there in the moon.

I awakened before dawn. I stared over to where Cory and Chris slept. Even as my sleepy eyes opened, and my head turned, I sensed that Chris was awake, too, and had been for some time. He was already looking at me, and shiny, glistening tears sparkled the blue of his eyes and smeared the whites. The tears that rolled to fall on his pillow, I named as they fell: shame, guilt, blame.

'I love you, Christopher Doll. You don't have to cry. For I can forget, if you can forget, and there's nothing to forgive.'

He nodded and said nothing. But I knew him well, right down to his bone marrow. I knew his thoughts, his feelings, and all the ways to wound his ego fatally. I knew that through me he had struck back at the one woman who had betrayed him in trust, faith and love. All I had to do was look in my hand mirror with the big C. L. F. on the back, and I could see my own mother's face as she must have looked at my age.

And so it had come to pass, just as the grandmother predicted. Devil's issue. Created by evil seed sown in the wrong soil, shooting up new plants to repeat the sins of the fathers.

And the mothers.

COLOUR ALL DAYS BLUE, BUT SAVE ONE FOR BLACK

We were leaving. Any day. As soon as Momma gave the word that she'd be out for the evening, she'd also be out of all her valuable, transportable possessions. We would not go back to Gladstone. There the winter came and lasted until May. We would go to Sarasota, where the circus people lived. They were known for having and showing kindness to those from strange backgrounds. Since Chris and I'd grown accustomed to high places, the roof, the many ropes attached to the rafter beams, I blithely said to Chris, 'We'll be trapeze performers.' He grinned, thinking it a ridiculous idea – at first – next calling it inspired.

'Golly, Cathy, you'll look great in spangled pink lights.' He began to sing: 'She flies through the air with the greatest of ease, the daring young beauty on the flying trapeze . . .'

Cory jerked up his blond head. Blue eyes wide with fear. *'No!'*

Said Carrie, his more proficient voice, 'We don't like your plans. We don't want you to fall.'

'We'll never fall,' said Chris, 'because Cathy and I are an unbeatable team.' I stared over at him, recalling the night in the schoolroom, and on the roof afterwards when he'd whispered, 'I'm never going to love anyone but you, Cathy. I know it . . . I've got that kind of feeling . . . just us, always.'

Casually I'd laughed. 'Don't be silly, you know you don't really love me in *that* way. And you don't have to feel guilty, or ashamed. It was my fault, too. And we can pretend it never happened, and make sure it never happens again.'

'But Cathy . . .'

'If there were others for you and me, never, never would we feel this way for each other.'

'But I *want* to feel this way about you, and it's too late for me to love or trust anyone else.'

How old I felt, looking at Chris, at the twins, making plans for all of us, speaking so confidently of how we would make our way. A consolation token for the twins, to give them peace, when I knew we would be forced to do anything, and everything to earn a living.

September had passed on into October. Soon the snow would fly.

'Tonight,' said Chris after Momma took off, saying a hasty goodbye, not pausing in the doorway to look back at us. Now she could hardly bear to look at us. We put one pillowcase inside another, to make it strong. In that sack Chris would dump all Momma's precious jewellery. Already I had our two bags packed and hidden in the attic, where Momma never went now.

As the day wore on towards evening, Cory began to vomit, over and over again. In the medicine cabinet we had non-prescription drugs for abdominal upsets.

Nothing we used would stop the terrible retching that left him pale, trembling, crying. Then his arms encircled my neck and he whispered, 'Momma, I don't feel so good.'

'What can I do to make you feel better, Cory?' I asked, feeling so young and inexperienced.

'Mickey,' he whispered weakly. 'I want Mickey to sleep with me.'

'But you might roll over on him and then he'd be dead. You wouldn't want him to die, would you?'

'No,' he said, looking stricken at the thought, and then that terrible gagging began again, and in my arms he grew so cold. His hair was pasted to his sweaty brow. His blue eyes stared vacantly into my face as over and over again he called for his mother, 'Momma, Momma, my bones hurt.'

'It's all right,' I soothed, picking him up and carrying him back to his bed, where I could change his soiled pyjamas. How could he throw up again when there couldn't be anything left? 'Chris is going to help you, don't worry.' I lay beside him and held his weak and quivering body in my arms.

Chris was at his desk poring over medical reference books, using Cory's symptoms to name the mysterious illness that struck each one of us from time to time. He was almost eighteen now, but far from being a doctor.

'Don't go and leave me and Carrie behind,' Cory pleaded. He cried out later, and louder, 'Chris, don't go! Stay here!'

What did he mean? Didn't he want us to run away? Or did he mean never sneak into Momma's suite of rooms again to steal? Why was it Chris and I believed the twins seldom paid attention to what we did? Surely he and Carrie knew we'd never go away and leave them behind – we'd die before we did that.

A little shadowy thing wearing all white drifted over to the bed, and stood with big watery blue eyes staring and staring at her twin brother. She was barely three feet high. She was old, and she was young, she was a tender little plant brought up in a dark hothouse, stunted and withered.

'May I' – she began very properly (as we had tried to teach her, and she had consistently refused to use the grammar we tried to teach, but on this night of nights, she did the best she could) – 'sleep with Cory? We won't do anything bad, or evil, or unholy. I just want to be close to him.'

Let the grandmother come and do her worst! We put Carrie to bed with Cory, and then Chris and I perched on opposite sides of the big bed and watched, full of anxiety, as Cory tossed about restlessly, and gasped for breath, and cried out in his delirium. He wanted the mouse, he wanted his mother, his father, he wanted Chris, and he wanted me. Tears were pooling down on the collar of my nightgown, and I looked to see Chris with tears on his cheeks. 'Carrie, Carrie . . . where is Carrie?' he asked repeatedly, long after she'd gone to sleep. Their wan faces were only inches apart, and he was looking directly at her, and still he didn't see her. When I took the time to look from him to Carrie, she seemed but a bit better off.

Punishment, I thought. God was punishing us, Chris and me, for what we'd done. The grandmother had warned us . . . every day she'd warned us up until the day we were whipped.

All though the night Chris read one medical book after another while I got up from the twins' bed and paced the room.

Finally Chris raised his red-rimmed, bloodshot eyes. 'Food poisoning – the milk. It must have been sour.'

'It didn't taste sour, or smell sour,' I answered in a mumble. I was always careful to sniff and taste everything first before I'd

304

give it to the twins or Chris. For some reason, I thought my taste-buds keener than Chris's, who liked everything, and would eat anything, even rancid butter.

'The hamburger, then. I thought it had a funny taste.'

'It tasted all right to me.' And it must have tasted fine to him, as well, for he'd eaten half of Carrie's hamburger on a bun, and all of Cory's. Cory hadn't wanted anything to eat all day.

'Cathy, I noticed you hardly ate anything yourself all day. You're almost as thin as the twins. She does bring us enough food, such as it is. You don't have to stint on yourself.'

Whenever I was nervous, or frustrated, or worried – and I was all three now – I'd begin the ballet exercises, and holding lightly to the dresser that acted as a barre, I began to warm up by doing pliés.

'Do you have to do that, Cathy? You're already skin and bones. And why didn't you eat today – are you sick, too?'

'But Cory so loves the doughnuts, and that's all I want to eat too. And he needs them more than I do.'

The night wore on. Chris returned to reading the medical books. I gave Cory water to drink – and right away he threw it up. I washed his face with cold water a dozen times, and changed his pyjamas three times, and Carrie slept on and on and on.

Dawn.

The sun came up and we were still trying to figure out what made Cory ill, when the grandmother came in, bearing the picnic basket of food for today. Without a word she closed the door, locked it, put the key in her dress pocket, and advanced to the gaming-table. From the basket she lifted the huge Thermos of milk, the smaller Thermos of soup, then the packets wrapped in foil, containing sandwiches, fried chicken, of bowls of potato salad or coleslaw – and, last of all, the packet of four powdered-sugar doughnuts. She turned to leave.

'Grandmother,' I said tentatively. She had not looked Cory's way. Hadn't seen.

'I have not spoken to you,' she said coldly. 'Wait until I do.'

'I can't wait,' said I, growing angry, rising up from my place on the side of Cory's bed, and advancing. 'Cory's sick! He's been throwing up all night, and all day yesterday. He needs a doctor, and his mother.'

She didn't look at me, or at Cory. Out of the door she stalked, then clicked the lock behind her. No word of comfort. No word to say she'd tell our mother.

'I'll unlock the door and go and find Momma,' said Chris, still wearing the clothes he put on yesterday, and hadn't taken off to go to bed.

'Then they'll know we have a key.'

'Then they'll know.'

Just then the door opened and Momma came in, with the grandmother trailing behind her. Together they hovered over Cory, touching his clammy, cold face, their eyes meeting. In a corner they drifted to whisper and connive, glancing from time to time at Cory who lay quiet as one approaching death. Only his chest heaved in spasms. From his throat came gasping, choking noises. I went and wiped the beads of moisture from his brow. Funny how he could feel cool, and still sweat.

Cory rasped in, out, in, out.

And there was Momma – doing nothing. Unable to make a decision! Fearful still of letting someone know there was a child, when there shouldn't be any!

'Why are you standing there whispering?' I shouted out. 'What choice do you have but to take Cory to a hospital, and get him the best doctor available?'

They glared at me – both of them. Grim-faced, pale, trembling, Momma fixed her blue eyes on me, then anxiously they sidled over to Cory. What she saw on the bed made her lips tremble, made her hands shake and the muscles near her lips twitch. She blinked repeatedly, as if holding back tears.

Narrowly I watched each betraying sign of her calculating thoughts. She was weighing the risks of Cory being discovered, and causing her to lose that inheritance . . . for that old man downstairs just had to die one day, didn't he? He couldn't hold on for ever!

I screamed out, 'What's the matter with you, Momma? Are you just going to stand there and think about yourself, and that money while your youngest son lies there and dies? You *have* to help him! Don't you care what happens to him? Have you forgotten you are his mother? If you haven't, then, damn it, act like his mother! Stop hesitating! He needs attention now, not tomorrow!'

Sanguine colour flooded her face. She snapped her eyes back to me. 'You!' she spat. 'Always it's you!' And with that she raised her heavily ringed hand, and she slapped my face, hard! Then again she slapped me.

The very first time in my life I'd been slapped by her – and for such a reason! Outraged, without thinking, I slapped back – just as hard!

The grandmother stood back and watched. Smug satisfaction twisted her ugly, thin mouth into a crooked line.

Chris hurried to seize hold of my arms when I would strike Momma again. 'Cathy, you're not helping Cory by acting like this. Calm down. Momma will do the right thing.'

It was a good thing he held my arms, for I wanted to slap her again, and make her see what she was doing!

My father's face flashed before my eyes. He was frowning, silently telling me I must always have respect for the woman who gave me birth. I knew that's how he would feel. He wouldn't want me to hit her.

'Damn you to hell, Corrine Foxworth,' I shouted at the top of my lungs, 'if you don't take your son to a hospital! You think you can do anything you want with us, and no one will find out! Well, you can throw away that security blanket, for I'll find a way for revenge, if it takes me the rest of my life, I'll see that you pay, and dearly pay, if you don't do something right now to save Cory's life. Go on, glare your eyes at me, and cry and plead, and talk to me about money and what it can buy. But it can't buy back a child once he's dead! And if that happens, don't think I won't find a way to get to your husband and tell him you have four children you have kept hidden in a locked room with their only playground an attic . . . and you've kept them there for years and years! See if he loves you then! Watch his face and wait to see how much respect and admiration he has for you then!' She winced, but her eyes shot deadly looks at me. 'And what's more, I'll go to the grandfather and tell him, too!' I yelled even louder. 'And you won't inherit one damned red penny – and I'll be glad, glad, glad!'

From the look on her face she could kill me, but oddly enough, it was that despicable old woman who spoke in a quiet way: 'The girl is right, Corrine. The child must go to a hospital.'

They came back that night. The two of them. After the servants retired to their quarters over the huge garage. Both of them were bundled up in heavy coats, for it had turned suddenly frigid-cold. The evening sky had gone grey, chilled with early winter that threatened snow. The two of them pulled Cory from my arms and wrapped him in a green blanket, and it was Momma who lifted him up. Carrie let out a scream of anguish. 'Don't take Cory away!' she howled. 'Don't take him, don't . . .' She threw herself into my arms wailing at me to stop them from taking away a twin from whom she'd never been separated.

I stared down in her small pale face, streaked with tears. 'It's all right for Cory to go,' I said as I met my mother's glare, 'for I am going, too. I'll stay with Cory while he's in the hospital. Then he won't be afraid. When the nurses are too busy to wait on him, I'll be there. That will make him get well quicker, and Carrie will feel good knowing I'm with him.' I spoke the truth. I knew Cory would recover quicker if I was there with him. *I* was his mother now – not her. He didn't love her now, it was me he needed and me he wanted. Children are very wise intuitively; they know who loves them most, and who only pretends.

'Cathy's right, Momma,' Chris spoke up and he looked at her directly in the eye without warmth. 'Cory depends on Cathy. Please let her go, for as she says, her presence there will help him get well sooner, and she can describe to his doctor all his symptoms better than you can.'

Momma's glassy, blank stare turned his way, as if struggling to grasp his meaning. I admit she looked distraught, and her eyes jumped from me to Chris, and then to her mother, and then to Carrie, and back to Cory.

'Momma,' said Chris more firmly, 'let Cathy go with you. I can do for Carrie, if that's what you're worried about.'

Of course they didn't let me go.

Our mother carried Cory out into the hall. His head was thrown back, his cowlick bobbing up and down as she strode away with her child wrapped in a green blanket, the very colour of spring grass.

The grandmother gave me a cruel smile of derisive victory, then closed and locked the door.

They left Carrie bereft, screaming, tears flowing. Her small weak fists beat against me, as if I were to blame. 'Cathy, I wanna go, too! Make them let me go! Cory don't wanna go nowhere I don't go . . . and he forgot his guitar.'

Then all her anger dissipated, and she fell into my arms and sobbed, 'Why, Cathy, why?'

Why?

That was the biggest question in our lives.

By far it was the worst and longest day of our lives. We had sinned, and how quickly God set about punishing us. He *did* keep his sharpest eye turned on us, as if *He* knew all along sooner or later we would prove ourselves unworthy, just as the grandmother had known.

It was like it had been in the beginning, before the TV set came to take over the better part of our days. All through the day we sat quietly without turning on the television, just waiting to hear how Cory was.

Chris sat in the rocker and held out his arms to Carrie and me. We both sat on his lap as he rocked slowly back and forth, back and forth, creaking the floorboards.

I don't know why Chris's legs didn't grow numb; we sat on him for so long. Then I got up to take care of Mickey's cage, and gave him food to eat and water to drink, and I held him, and petted him, and told him soon his master would be coming back. I believe that mouse knew something was wrong. He didn't play cheerfully in his cage, and even though I left the door open, he didn't come out to scamper all over the room, and head for Carrie's doll house that enchanted him the most.

I prepared the pre-cooked meals, which we hardly touched. When the last meal of the day was over, and the dishes were put away, and we were bathed and ready for bed, we all three knelt in a row beside Cory's bed, and said our prayers to God. 'Please, please let Cory get well, and come back to us.' If we prayed for anything else, I don't recall what it was.

We slept, or tried to, all three in the same bed, with Carrie between Chris and me. Nothing gross was ever going to happen between us again . . . never, never again.

God, please don't punish Cory as a way to strike back at Chris and me and make us hurt, for already we hurt, and we didn't mean to do it, we didn't. It just happened, and only once . . . and it wasn't any pleasure, God, not really, not any.

A new day dawned, grim, grey, forbidding. Behind the drawn draperies life started up for those who lived on the outside, those unseen by us. We dragged ourselves into focus, and poked about, trying to fill our time, and trying to eat, and make Mickey happy when he seemed so sad without the little boy who laid down trails of bread crumbs for him to follow.

I changed the mattress covers, with the assistance of Chris, for that was a very hard thing to do, to slip a full-sized mattress in and out of one of those heavy quilted things, and yet we had to do it often because of Cory's lack of control. Chris and I made the beds up with clean linens, and smoothed on the spreads, and tidied up the room, while Carrie sat alone in the rocker and stared off into space.

Around ten, there was nothing left to do but sit on the bed nearest the door to the hall, with our eyes riveted upon the knob, willing it to turn and admit Momma, who would bring us news.

Shortly thereafter, Momma came in with her eyes rimmed red from crying. Behind her was the steel-eyed grandmother, tall, stern, no tears.

Our mother faltered near the door as if her legs would give way and spill her to the floor. Chris and I jumped to our feet, but Carrie only stared at Momma's empty eyes.

'I drove Cory to a hospital miles away, the nearest one, really,' explained our mother in a tight and hoarse voice that choked from time to time, 'and I registered him under a false name, saying he was my nephew, my ward.'

Lies! Always lies! 'Momma – how is he?' I asked impatiently.

Her glazed blue eyes turned our way; void eyes, staring vacantly; lost eyes, seeking something gone for ever – I guessed it was her humanity. 'Cory had pneumonia,' she intoned. 'The doctors did all they could . . . but it was . . . too . . . too late.'

Had pneumonia?

All they could?

Too late?

All past tenses!

Cory was dead! We were never going to see him again!

Chris said later the news hit him hard in the groin, like a kick, and I did see him stumble backwards and spin around to hide his face as his shoulders sagged and he sobbed.

At first I didn't believe her. I stood and I stared, and I doubted. But the look on her face convinced me, and something big and hollow swelled up inside my chest. I sank down on the bed, numb, almost paralysed, and didn't even know I was crying until my clothes were wet.

And even as I sat and cried, I still didn't want to believe Cory was gone from our lives. And Carrie, poor Carrie, she lifted up her head, threw it back, and opened up her mouth and screamed! She screamed and screamed until her voice went, and she could scream no more. She drifted to the corner where Cory kept his guitar and his banjo, and neatly she lined up all his pairs of small worn tennis shoes. And that's where she chose to sit, with the shoes, with the musical instruments, and Mickey's cage nearby, and from that moment on, not a word escaped her lips.

'Will we go to his funeral?' Chris asked in a choked way with his back still turned.

'He's already been buried,' said Momma. 'I had a false name put on the tombstone.' And then, very quickly, she escaped the room and our questions, and the grandmother followed, her lips set in a grim, thin line.

Right before our horrified eyes, Carrie shrivelled more each day. I felt God might as well have taken Carrie, too, and buried her alongside Cory in that faraway grave with the wrong name that didn't even have the comfort of a father buried nearby.

None of us could eat much. We became listless and tired, always tired. Nothing held our interest. Tears – Chris and I cried five oceans of tears. We assumed all the blame. A long time ago we should have escaped. We should have used that wooden key and gone for help. We had *let* Cory die! He'd been our responsibility, our dear quiet little boy of many talents, and we had let him die. Now we had a small sister huddled in a corner, growing weaker each passing day.

Chris said in a low voice so Carrie wouldn't overhear, just in case she was listening, though I doubted she was (she was blind, deaf, mute . . . our babbling brook, dammed), 'We've got to run, Cathy, and quick. Or we are all going to die like Cory. Something is wrong with all of us. We've been locked up too long. We've lived abnormal lives, like being in a vacuum without germs, without the infections children usually come in contact with. We are without resistance to infections.'

'I don't understand,' I said.

'What I mean is,' he whispered as we huddled in the same chair, 'like the creatures from Mars in that book *The War of the Worlds* we could all die from a single cold germ.'

Horrified, I could only stare at him. He knew so much more than I did. I turned my gaze on Carrie in the corner. Her sweet baby face, with eyes too large and shadowed underneath, stared blankly forward at nothing. I knew she had her vision fixed on eternity, where Cory was. All the love I'd given Cory, I put into Carrie now . . . so afraid for her. Such a tiny skeleton body, and her neck was so weak, too small for her head. Was this the way all the Dresden dolls were going to end?

'Chris, if we have to die, it's not going to be like mice in a trap. If germs can kill us, then let it be germs – so when you steal tonight, take everything of value you can find and we can carry! I'll pack a lunch to take along. With Cory's clothes taken from the suitcases, we'll have more room. Before the morning comes, we'll be gone.'

'No,' he said quietly. 'Only if we know Momma and her husband have gone out – only then can I take all the money and leave, and all the jewellery in one fell swoop. Take only what we absolutely need – no toys, no games. And Cathy, Momma may not go out tonight. Certainly she can't attend parties in her time of mourning.'

How could she mourn when she had to keep her husband always

312

in the dark? And no one came but the grandmother to tell us what was going on. She refused to speak to us, or look at us. In my mind we were already on our way, and I looked at her as if she were already part of the past. Now that our time to depart was so near, I felt frightened. It was big out there. We'd be on our own. What would the world think of us now?

We weren't beautiful like we used to be, only pale and sickly attic mice with long flaxen hair, wearing expensive but ill-fitting clothes, and sneakers on our feet.

Chris and I had educated ourselves from reading so many books, and television had taught us much about violence, about greed, about imagination, but it had taught us hardly anything that was practical and useful in preparing us to face reality.

Survival. That's what TV should teach innocent children. How to live in a world that really doesn't give a damn about anyone but their own – and sometimes, not even their own.

Money. If there was one thing we'd learned during the years of our imprisonment, it was that money came first, and everything else came after. How well Momma had said it long ago: 'It's not love that makes the world go 'round – it's money.'

I took Cory's small clothes from the suitcase, his second-best sneakers, two pair of pyjamas, and all the time tears fell and my nose ran. In one of the side pockets of the suitcase, I found sheet music he must have packed himself. Oh, it did hurt to pick up those sheets, and see the lines he had drawn by using a ruler, and his little black notes, and half-notes so crookedly done. And beneath the musical score (he had taught himself to write down the music from an encyclopaedia Chris had found for him) Cory had written words to a half-completed song:

> 'I wish the night would end,
> I wish the day'd begin,
> I wish it would rain or snow,
> Or the wind would blow,
> Or the grass would grow,
> I wish I had yesterday,
> I wish there were games to play . . .'

Oh, God! Was there ever such a sad, melancholy song? So these were the lyrics to a tune I'd heard him play over and over. Wishing, always wishing for something he couldn't have. Something all other little boys accepted as a normal, unremarkable part of their lives.

I could have screamed the anguish I felt.

I went to sleep with Cory on my mind. And, like always, when I was most troubled, I fell into dreams. But this time I was only me. I found myself on a winding, dirt path with wide, flat pastures that grew wild flowers of crimson and pink on the left, and on the right, yellow and white blossoms swayed gently in the soft, warm kind breezes of eternal spring. A small child clung to my hand. I looked down, expecting to see Carrie – but it was Cory!

He was laughing and happy, and he skipped along beside me, his short legs trying to keep pace with mine, and in his hand he held a bouquet of the wild flowers. He smiled up at me and was about to speak when we heard the twitterings of many brightly coloured birds in the parasol trees ahead.

A tall, slim man with golden hair, his skin deeply tanned, wearing white tennis clothes, came striding forwards from a glorious garden of abundant trees and radiant flowers, including roses of all colours. He paused a dozen yards away and held his arms out to Cory.

My heart, even in my dream, pounded in excitement and joy! It was Daddy! Daddy had come to meet Cory so he wouldn't have to travel alone the rest of the way. And though I knew I should release Cory's small hot hand, I would hold him for ever with me.

Daddy looked at me, not with pity, not with reprimand, but only with pride and admiration. And I let go of Cory's hand and stood to watch him joyfully run into Daddy's arms. He was swept up by powerful arms that once used to hold me and make me feel all the world was a wonderful thing. And I would step down the path, too, and feel those arms about me once again, and allow Daddy to take me where he would.

'Cathy, wake up!' said Chris, sitting on my bed and shaking me. 'You're talking in your sleep, and laughing and crying, and saying hello, and then goodbye. Why is it you dream so much?'

My dream spilled from me so fast my words were garbled. Chris just sat there and stared at me, as did Carrie, who had awakened to hear as well. It had been so long since I last saw my father, his face had faded in my memory, but as I looked at Chris, I grew very confused. He was so very much like Daddy, only younger.

That dream was to haunt me many a day, pleasantly. It gave me peace. It gave me knowledge I hadn't had before. People never really died. They only went on to a better place, to wait a while for their loved ones to join them. And then once more they went back to the world, in the same way they had arrived the first time around.

ESCAPE

November tenth. This was to be our last day in prison. God would not deliver us, we would deliver ourselves.

As soon as the hour passed ten, tonight, Chris would commit his final robbery. Our mother had visited to stay but a few minutes, ill at ease with us now, very obviously so. 'Bart and I are going out tonight. I don't want to, but he insists. You see, he doesn't understand why I look so sad.'

I bet he didn't understand. Chris slung over his shoulder the dual pillowcases in which to carry back heavy jewels. He stood in the open doorway and gave Carrie and me one long long look before he closed the door and used his wooden key to lock us in, for he couldn't leave the door open, and in this way alert the grandmother, if she came to check. We couldn't hear Chris steal along the long dark northern corridor, for the walls were too thick, and the hall carpet too plush and sound-proofing.

Side by side Carrie and I lay, my arms protectively around her. If that dream hadn't come to tell me Cory was well taken care of, I would have cried not to feel him close still. I couldn't help but ache for a little boy who had called me Momma whenever he was sure his older brother wouldn't overhear. Always he'd been so afraid Chris would consider him a sissy if he knew how much he missed and needed his mother, so much so, he had to make do with me. And though I'd told him Chris would never laugh, or jeer, for he had been very needing of a mother too, once upon a time, still Cory would keep it a secret just between him and me – and Carrie. He had to pretend to be manly, and convince himself it didn't matter if he had neither a mother, nor a father, when all along it did matter, a great deal.

I held Carrie tight, tight against me, vowing that if ever I had a child, or children, they'd never feel a need for me that I didn't sense and respond to. I'd be the best mother alive.

Hours dragged by like years, and still Chris didn't return from his last foray into our mother's grand suite of rooms. Why was it taking so long this time? Wide awake and miserable, I was filled with fears, and envisioned all the calamities that could stay him.

Bart Winslow . . . the suspicious husband . . . he'd catch Chris! Call the police! Have Chris thrown in jail! Momma would stand calmly by and mildly express shock and faint surprise that someone would dare steal from her. Oh, no, of course she didn't have a son. Everybody knew she was childless, for heaven's sake. Had they ever seen her with a child? She didn't know that blond boy with blue eyes so very much like her own. After all, she did have many cousins scattered about – and a thief was a thief, even if he were blood kin, some fifth or sixth distant relative.

And that grandmother! If she caught him – the worst possible punishment!

Dawn came up quickly, faint, shrilled by a cock's crow.

The sun lingered reluctantly on the horizon. Soon it would be too late to go. The morning train would pass on by the depot, and we needed several hours' head start before the grandmother opened the bedroom door and found us gone. Would she send out a search party? Notify the police? Or would she, more likely, just let us go, glad, at last, to be rid of us?

Despairing, I ascended the stairs to the attic to stare outside. Foggy, cold day. Last week's snow lay in patches here and there. A dull, mysterious day that seemed incapable of bringing us joy or freedom. I heard that rooster cockle-doodle-doo again; it sounded muffled and far away as I silently prayed that, whatever Chris was doing, and wherever he was, he heard it too, and would put some speed in his feet.

I remember, oh, how I remember that chilly early morning when Chris stole back into our room. Lying beside Carrie, I was tentatively on the edge of fretful sleep, so it was easy for me to bolt widely awake when the locked door to our room opened. I'd lain there, fully dressed, ready to go, waiting, even in the fitful dreams that came and went, for Chris to come back and save us all.

Just inside the door, Chris hesitated, his glazed eyes staring over at me. Then he drifted in my direction, in no great hurry, as he should be. All the while I could only stare at the pillowcases one inside the other – so flat! So empty looking! 'Where are the jewels?' I cried. 'Why did you stay so long? Look out the windows, the sun is rising! We'll never make it to the train depot on time!' My voice turned hard accusing, angry. 'You turned chivalrous again, didn't you? That's why you've come back without Momma's precious jewellery!'

He had reached the bed by this time, and he just stood there with the flat, empty pillowcases hanging from his hand.

'Gone,' he said dully. 'All the jewellery was gone.'

'Gone?' I asked sharply, sure he was lying, covering up, still unwilling to take what his mother so cherished. Then I looked at his eyes. 'Gone? Chris, the jewellery is always there. And what's the matter with you, anyway – why do you look so queer?'

He sagged down on his knees beside the bed, gone boneless and limp as his head drooped forward, and his face nestled down on my breast. Then he began to sob! Dear God! What had gone wrong? Why was he crying? It's terrible to hear a man cry, and I thought of him as a man now, not a boy.

My arms held him, my hands caressed and stroked his hair, his cheek, his arms, his back, and then I kissed him, all in an effort to soothe whatever awful thing had happened. I did what I had seen our mother do for him in times of distress, and intuitively I had no fears that his passions would be aroused into wanting more than just what I was willing to give.

Actually, I had to force him to talk, to explain.

He choked off his sobs, and swallowed them. He wiped away the tears and dried his face with the edge of the sheet. Then he turned his head so he could stare at those horrible paintings depicting hell and all its torment. His phrases came broken, disjointed, stopped often by sobs he had to hold back.

This was the way he told it, while on his knees beside my bed, while I held his shaky hands, and his body trembled, and his blue eyes were dark and bleak, warning me I was about to be shocked. Forewarned as I was, I still wasn't prepared for what I heard.

'Well,' he began, breathing hard, 'I realized that something was different the second I stepped into her suite of rooms. I beamed my flashlight around without turning on a lamp, and I just couldn't believe it! The irony of it . . . the hateful, despicable bitterness of making our move too late! God, Cathy – Momma and her husband have gone! Not just to some neighbour's party, but really gone! They had taken with them all those little mementoes that made their rooms personal: the trinkets gone from the dresser, the geegaws from that dressing-table, the creams, lotions, powders, and perfumes – everything that once was there, gone. Nothing was on her dressing-table.

'It made me so mad, I ran about like someone demented, dashing from here to there, pulling open drawers and ransacking them, hoping to find something of value that we could pawn . . . and I didn't find anything! Oh, they did a very good job – not even a little porcelain pillbox was left, or one of those heavy Venetian-glass paperweights that cost a fortune. I ran into the dressing-room and yanked open all the drawers. Sure, she had left *some* things – junk of no value to us, or anyone: lipsticks, cold creams, and stuff like that. Then I pulled open that special bottom drawer – you know the one she told us about a long time ago, never thinking we'd be the ones to steal from her. I pulled that drawer all the way out, like you have to, and set it aside on the floor. Then I felt in back for the tiny little button you have to push in a certain combination of numbers – her birthday numbers, or else she would herself forget the combination. Remember how she laughed when she told us that? The secret compartment sprang open, and there were the velvet trays where dozens of rings should have been fitted into small slots, and there wasn't a ring there – not one! And the bracelets, necklaces, and earrings gone, every last thing was gone, Cathy, even that tiara you tried on. Oh, golly, you don't know how I felt! So many times you pleaded with me to take just one little ring, and I wouldn't because I believed in her.'

'Don't cry again, Chris,' I begged when he choked up, and he put his face down on my chest again. 'You didn't know she'd go, not so soon after Cory's death.'

'Yeah, she grieves a lot, doesn't she?' he asked bitterly, and my fingers twined in his hair.

'Really, Cathy,' he went on, 'I lost all control. I ran from closet to closet, and threw out the winter clothes, and soon found all the summer clothes were gone, along with two sets of their fine luggage. I emptied shoe boxes, and rifled the closet drawers, and looked for the tin of coins he kept, but he'd taken that, too, or hidden it away in a better place. I searched everything, and everywhere, feeling frantic. I even considered taking one of the huge lamps, but I hefted one and it weighed a ton. She'd left her mink coats, and I thought about stealing one of those, but you'd tried them on, and all were too large – and someone on the outside would be suspicious if an adolescent girl was wearing a too-large coat of mink. The fur stoles were gone. And if I took one of the full-length fur coats, it would fill all of one suitcase, and then we wouldn't have room for our own things, and the paintings I might be able to sell – and we need what clothes we have, Really, I almost tore out my hair, I was that desperate to find something of value, for how would we ever manage without enough money? You know, at that minute, when I stood in the middle of her room and thought about our situation, and Carrie's poor health, it didn't matter a damn to me then whether or not I became a doctor. All I wanted was to get out of here!

'Then, just when it seemed I wasn't going to find anything to steal, I looked in the lower drawer of the nightstand. I'd never checked that drawer before. And in it, Cathy, was a silver-framed photograph of Daddy, and their marriage licence, and a small velvet box of green. Cathy, inside that little green velvet box, inside was Momma's wedding band, and her engagement diamond – the ones our father gave her. It hurt to think she would take everything, and leave his photograph as valueless, and the two rings he'd given her. And then the strangest thought fleeted through my mind. Maybe she knew who was stealing the money from her room, and she left those things there deliberately.'

'No!' I scoffed, tossing that gracious consideration away. 'She just doesn't care about him any more – she has her *Bart*.'

'Regardless, I was grateful to find something. So the sack isn't as empty as it may appear. We've got Daddy's photograph, and her rings – but it's gonna take an awful, unbearable crisis to make me pawn either of those rings.'

I heard the warning in his voice, and it didn't sound the least sincere, like it should have. It was as if he was putting on an act of being the same old trusting Christopher Doll, who saw good in everyone. 'Go on. What happened next?' For he'd stayed away so long, what he'd just told me wouldn't have taken all the night.

'I figured if I couldn't rob our mother, then I would go on to the grandmother's room and rob her.'

Oh, my God, I thought. He didn't . . . he couldn't have. And yet, what perfect revenge!

'You know she has jewels, lots of rings on her fingers, and that damned diamond brooch she wears every day of her life as part of her uniform, plus she has those diamonds and rubies we saw her wear at the Christmas party. And, of course, I figured she had more loot to be taken, as well. So, I stole down all the long dark halls, and I tiptoed right up to the grandmother's closed door.'

Oh, the nerve to do that. I would never . . .

'A thin line of yellow light showed underneath, to warn me she was still awake. That made me bitter for she should have been asleep. And under less driven circumstances, that light would have made me stay my hand, and act less foolhardy than I did – or maybe you could call it "audacious" now that you're planning on being a woman of words one day, after you've been a woman of action.'

'Chris! Don't meander from the subject! Go on! Tell me what crazy thing you did! If I had been you, I would have turned around and come straight back here!'

'Well, I am not you, Catherine Doll, I am *me* . . . I used some caution, and very carefully eased open her door just a slot, though I feared every second it would creak or squeak and give me away. But someone keeps the hinges well-oiled, and I put an eye to the crack without fear of her being alerted, and I peered inside.'

'You saw her naked!' I interrupted.

'No!' he answered impatiently, annoyed, 'I didn't see her naked, and I'm glad I didn't. She was in the bed, under the covers, sitting up and wearing a long-sleeved nightgown of some heavy material, and it had a collar and was buttoned down the front to her waist. But I did catch her naked in a small way. You know that steel-blue hair we hate so much. It *wasn't* on her head! It was perched crookedly on a dummy head on her nightstand, as if she wanted the reassurance of having it near in case of an emergency during the night.'

'She wears a wig?' I asked in total astonishment, though I should have known. Anybody who persistently took their hair and skinned it back from their face so tightly would sooner or later go bald.

'Yeah, you bet, she wears a wig, and that hair she had on during the Christmas party, that must have been a wig, too. What hair she's got left on her head is sparse and yellow-white, and there are wide pink places on her scalp with no hair at all, but short baby fuzz. She had rimless grasses perched on the end of that long nose, and you know we've never seen her with glasses on. Her thin lips were pursed up in a disapproving line as she moved her eyes slowly from line to line of the large black book she was holding – the Bible, of course. There she sat, reading of harlots and other wicked deeds, enough to put a terrible frown on her face. And as I watched, knowing I couldn't steal from her now, she laid aside the Bible and marked the place with a postcard, then put the Bible on the nightstand, then left the bed and knelt beside it. She bowed her head, templed her fingers under her chin, just the way we do, and she said silent prayers that lasted and lasted. Then she spoke aloud: "Forgive me, Lord, for all my sins. I have always done what I thought best, and if I made mistakes, please believe I thought I was doing right. May I for ever find grace in thine eyes. Amen." She crawled back into bed, and then she reached to turn out the lamp. I stood in the hall and wondered what to do. I just couldn't come back to you empty-handed, for I hope we never have to pawn the rings our father gave our mother.'

He continued, and now his hands were in my hair, cupping my head. 'I went to that main rotunda, where the chest is near the staircase, and found our grandfather's room. I didn't know if I would have the nerve to open *his* door, and face up to that man who lies perpetually dying, year after year.

'But, this was my only chance, and I would make the most of it. Come what may, I raced down the stairs noiselessly like a real thief, carrying my pillowcase sack. I saw the big rich rooms, so grand and fine, and I wondered, just as you have wondered how it would be to grow up in a house like this one. I wondered how it felt to be waited on by many servants, and catered to hand and foot. Oh, Cathy, it is one beautiful house, and the furniture must have been imported from palaces. It looks too fragile to sit on, and too lovely to feel comfortable with, and there are original oil paintings, I know them when I see them, and sculptures and busts, mostly on top of pedestals, and rich Persian rugs and Oriental rugs. And, of course, I knew the way to the library, since you had asked so darned many questions of Momma. And you know what, Cathy? I was darned glad you had asked so many questions or else I may well have gotten lost; there's so many halls that shoot off right and left from the centre stem.

'But it was easy enough to get to the library: a long, dark, really immense room, and it was quiet as a graveyard. The ceiling must have been twenty feet high. The shelves went all the way up, and there was a little stairway of iron that curved to a second level, and a balcony where you could reach books on that level. And on the lower level were two wooden ladders that slid along railings put there for that very purpose. Never have I seen so many books in a private home. No wonder the books Momma brought us had never been missed – though when I looked carefully, I could see the gaping spaces, like teeth, missing in the long rows of leather-bound, gold-tooled, hubbed-spined expensive books. A desk was there, dark and massive, must have weighed a ton, and a tall leather swivel chair was behind it, and I could just picture our grandfather sitting there, issuing orders right and left, and using the phones on his desk – there were six telephones, Cathy – six! Though when I checked, thinking I might have use for them, they were all disconnected. To the left of the desk was a row of tall narrow windows that looked out on a private garden – a really spectacular view, even at night. There was a dark mahogany filing system made to look like fine furniture. Two very long, soft, tan-coloured sofas were set out from the walls about three feet, giving you plenty of room to move behind them. Chairs were placed near the fireplace, and, of course, there was a batch of tables and chairs and things to stumble against, and an awful lot of bric-a-brac.'

I sighed, for he was telling me so much of what I'd longed to hear, and yet, I kept waiting for that terrible thing that kept me on edge, waiting for the knife to plunge.

'I thought that money could be hidden in that desk. I used my flashlight and set about pulling open each drawer. They were all unlocked. And it was no wonder, because they were all empty – completely empty! This sort of threw me – for why have a desk if you don't keep it full of junk? Important papers you lock away in a bank vault, or your own private vault; you don't leave them in locked desk drawers that a clever thief could force open. All those empty drawers without rubber bands, paper clips, pencils, pens, notepads, and other sorts of odds and ends – why have a desk if not for this? You just don't know the suspicions that jumped into my thoughts. And that's when I made up my mind. I could look across the long library and see the door to our grandfather's room. Slowly, I headed that way. I was going to see him at last . . . face to face with the detested grandfather, who was also our half-uncle.

'I pictured our encounter. He'd be on the bed, sick, but hard and still mean and cold as ice. I'd kick open the door, switch on the light, and he'd see me. He'd gasp! He'd recognize me . . . he'd have to know who I was, just one look and he'd know. And I'd say, "Here I am, Grandfather – the grandson you never wanted to be born. Upstairs in a locked bedroom of the northern wing, I have two sisters. And once I had a younger brother, but he's dead now – and you helped kill him!" All that was in my mind, though I doubt I would really have said any of it. Although you no doubt would have screamed it out – just as Carrie would have if she had the words to express herself – which you do. Still maybe I would have said them, just for the joy of watching him wince, or maybe he would have shown sorrow, or grief, or pity . . . or more likely, fierce indignation that we were living at all! I know this, I couldn't stand another minute of being kept a prisoner, and having Carrie pass away like Cory did.'

I held my breath. Oh, the nerve of him, to face up to the detested grandfather, even if he was still lying on his deathbed, and that solid copper coffin was still waiting for him to fill it. I was waiting breathlessly for what came next.

'I turned the knob very cautiously, planning on taking him by surprise, and then I felt ashamed to be so timid, and I thought I would act boldly – and I lifted my foot and kicked open that door!

It was so dark in there I couldn't see a damned thing. And I didn't want to use the flashlight. I reached inside the door and felt around for a wall switch, but I couldn't find one. I beamed the flashlight straight ahead and saw a hospital bed painted white. I stared and stared, for I was seeing something *I* hadn't expected to see – the blue-and-white-striped ticking of the mattress that was doubled over on itself. Empty bed, empty room. No dying grandfather there, gasping out his last breaths, and connected up to all kinds of machines to keep him alive – it was like a punch in the stomach, Cathy, not to see him there, when I'd prepared myself to meet him.

'In a corner not too far from the bed, was a walking cane, and not so far from the cane was that shiny wheelchair we'd seen him in. It still looked new – he must not have used it often. There was only one piece of furniture besides two chairs, and that was a single dresser . . . and not one item was on the top. No brush, comb, nothing. The room was as neat as the suite of rooms Momma had left, only this was a simple, plain room with panelled walls. And the grandfather's sickroom had the feel of not being used for a long, long time. The air was stale, musty. Dust was on the dresser top. I ran about, looking for something of value we could hock later on. Nothing – again nothing! I was so full of angry frustration that I dashed back into the library and sought out that special landscape painting Momma told us covered a wall safe.

'Now you know how many times we've watched thieves on TV open wall safes, and it seemed to me perfectly simple when you knew how. All you had to do was put your ear to the combination lock, and turn it slowly, slowly, and listen carefully for the betraying clicks . . . and count them . . . *I* thought. Then you would know the numbers, and dial them correctly – and next, voilà! The safe would open.'

I interrupted: 'The grandfather – why wasn't he on the bed?'

He went on as if I hadn't spoken: 'There I was, listening, hearing the clicks. I thought, if I lucked out, and the steel safe did open – it too would be empty. And you know what happened, Cathy? I heard the betraying clicks that told me the combination – hah-hah! I couldn't count fast enough! Nevertheless, I took the chance of turning the top wheel of the lock, thinking I just might by happenstance come up with the right choice of numbers, in the right sequence. The safe door didn't open. I heard the clicks, and I didn't understand. Encyclopaedias don't give you good lessons on how to become a thief – that must come naturally. Then I looked about for something slim and strong to insert into the lock, hoping maybe I could trip a spring that would open the door. Cathy, that was when I heard footsteps!'

'Oh, hell and damnation!' I swore, frustrated for him.

'Right! I quickly ducked behind one of the sofas and fell flat on my stomach – and that's when I remembered I'd left my flash-light in the grandfather's small room.'

'Oh, dear God!'

'Right! My goose was cooked, so I thought, but I lay perfectly still and quiet, and into the library strolled a man and a woman. She spoke first and had a sweet-girlish voice.

'"John," she said, "I swear I'm not just hearin' things! I did hear noises comin' from this room."

'"You're always hearin' somethin'," complained a heavy, guttural voice. It was John, the butler with the bald head.

'And the bickering pair made a half-hearted search of the library, then the small bedroom beyond, and I held my breath, waiting for them to discover my flashlight, but for some reason they didn't. I suspect it was because John didn't want to look at anything but that woman. Just as I was about to get up and make my move to leave the library, they came back, and so help me God, they fell down on the very sofa I was hiding behind! I put my head down on my folded arms and prepared for a nap, guessing you'd be on edge up here, wondering why I didn't come back. But since you were locked in, I didn't fear you'd come looking for me. It's a good thing I didn't go to sleep.'

'Why?'

'Let me tell it in my own way, Cathy, please. "See," said John, as they came back to the library and sat on the sofa, "didn't I tell yuh nobody'd be in there or in here?" He sounded smug, pleased with himself. "Really, Livvy," he went on, "you're so damned nervous all the time, it takes the pleasure out of this."

'"But, John," she said, "I *did* hear something."

"'Like I said before," John answered, "yuh hear too much of what ain't there. Hell's bells, jus' this mornin' you were speakin' of mice in the attic again, and how noisy they are." John chuckled then, a soft and low chuckle, and he must have done something to that pretty girl to send her into peals of silly giggles, and if she was protesting, she didn't do a good job of it.

'Then that John, he murmured, "That old bitch is killin' all the little mice in the attic. She carries up to them food in a picnic basket . . . enough food to kill a whole German army of mice."'

You know, I heard Chris say that, and I didn't think anything unusual, that's how dumb I was, how innocent and still trusting.

Chris cleared his throat before he continued. 'I got a qu·er feeling in my stomach, and my heart began to make so much noise, I thought that couple on the sofa would surely hear.

"'Yeah," said Livvy, "she's a mean, hard old woman, and t' tell you the truth, I always took to the old man better – at least he knew how to smile. But her – she don't know how. Time and time ag'n, I come in this room to clean up, and I find her in *his* room . . . she's just standing there staring at his empty bed, and she's got this queer, little tight smile that I take for gloating because he's dead, and she's outlived him, and now she's free, and don't have nobody ridin' her back and tellin' her not to do this, and don't do that, and jump when I speak. God, sometimes I wonder how she stood him, and he stood her. But now that he's dead, she's got his money."

"'Yeah, sure, she's got some," said John. "She's got her own money that her family left her. But her daughter, she got all the millions old Malcolm Neal Foxworth left."

"'Well," said Livvy, "that old witch, she don't need no more. Don't blame the old man for leavin' his entire estate to his daughter. She put up with a lot of mess from him, makin' her wait on him hand and foot when he had nurses to hand him things. Still he treated her like some slave. But now she's free, too, and married to that handsome young husband, and she's still young and beautiful, and with loads of money. Wonder what it would feel like to be her? Some people, they get all the luck. Me . . . I never had any."

"'What about me, Livvy, honey? You got me – at least until the next pretty face comes along."

'And there I was, behind the sofa, hearing all of this, and feeling numb with shock. I felt ready to throw up, but I lay very quiet and listened to that couple on the sofa talk on and on. I wanted to get up and run fast to you and Carrie, and take you out of this place before it was too late.

'But there I was, caught. If I moved they'd see me. And that John, he's related to our grandmother . . . third cousin, so Momma said . . . not that I think a third cousin matters one way or another, but apparently that John has our grandmother's confidence, or else she wouldn't allow him so much freedom to use her cars. You've seen him, Cathy, the bald-headed man who wears livery.'

Sure, I knew who he meant, but I could only lie there, feeling my own sort of numb shock that made me speechless.

'So,' Chris went on in that deadly monotone that didn't show that he was concerned, frightened, surprised, 'while I hid behind the sofa, and put my head down on my arms and closed my eyes and tried to make my heart stop beating so damned loud, John and the maid began to get really serious with each other. I heard their little movements as he began to take off her clothes, and she began to work on his clothes.'

'They undressed each other?' I asked. 'She actually helped him off with his clothes?'

'It sounded to me that way,' he said flatly.

'She didn't scream or protest?'

'Heck, no. She was all for it! And by golly, it took them so everlastingly long! Oh, the noises they made, Cathy – you wouldn't believe it. She moaned and screamed and gasped and panted, and he grunted like a stuck pig, but I guess he must have been pretty good at it, for she shrieked at the end like someone gone crazy. Then, when it was over, they had to lie and smoke cigarettes and gossip about what goes on in this house – and believe me, there's little they don't know. And then they made love a second time.'

'Twice in the same night?'

'It's possible to do.'

'Chris, why do you sound so funny?'

He hesitated, pulled away a bit, and studied my face. 'Cathy, weren't you listening? I went to a great deal of pains to tell you everything just as it happened. Didn't you hear?'

Hear? Sure, I'd heard, everything.

He'd waited too long to rob Momma of her hoard of hard-won jewellery. He should have been taking a little all along, like I'd begged him to do.

So, Momma and her husband were off on another vacation. What kind of news was that? They were always coming and going. They'd do anything to escape this house, and I can't say I blamed them. Weren't we prepared to do the same thing?

I screwed up my brows and gave Chris a long questioning look. Obviously he knew something he wasn't telling me. He was still protecting her; he still loved her.

'Cathy,' he began, his voice jagged and torn.

'It's all right, Chris. I'm not blaming you. So our dear, sweet, kind, loving mother and her handsome young husband have gone off on another vacation and taken all the jewellery with them. We'll still get by.' Say goodbye to security in the outside world. But we were still going! We'd work, we'd find a way to support ourselves, and pay doctors to make Carrie well again. Never mind about jewellery; never mind about the callousness of our mother's act, to leave us without explaining where she was going, and when she was coming back. By now we were accustomed to ugly, harsh, thoughtless indifference. *Why so many tears, Chris – why so many?*

'Cathy!' he raged, turning his tear-streaked face to lock his eyes with mine. 'Why aren't you listening and reacting? Where are your ears? Did you hear what I said? Our grandfather is dead! He's been dead for almost a year!'

Maybe I hadn't been truly listening, not carefully enough. Maybe his distress had kept me from hearing everything. Now it hit me fully for the first time. If the grandfather was truly dead – this was stunning good news! Now Momma would inherit! We'd be rich! She'd unlock the door, she'd set us free. Now we didn't have to run away.

Other thoughts came flooding, a torrent of devastating questions – Momma hadn't told us when her father died. When she knew how long these years had been for us, why had she kept us in the dark, waiting always? Why? Bewildered, confused, I didn't know which emotion to feel: happy, glad, sorry. A strange paralysing fear settled the indecision.

'Cathy,' whispered Chris, though why he bothered to whisper I don't know. Carrie wouldn't hear. Her world was set apart from ours. Carrie was suspended between life and death, leaning more towards Cory every moment she starved herself and abandoned the will to live on without her other half. 'Our mother deceived us deliberately, Cathy. Her father died, and months later his will was read, and all the while she kept quiet and left us here to wait and rot. Nine months ago we would all have been nine months healthier! Cory would be alive today if Momma had let us out the day her father died, or even the day after the will was read.'

Overwhelmed, I fell into the deep well of betrayal Momma had dug to drown us in. I began to cry.

'Save your tears for later,' said Chris, who had just cried himself. 'You haven't heard everything. There's more . . . much more, and worse.'

'More?' What more could he tell me? Our mother was proven a liar and a cheat, a thief who'd stolen our youth, and killed Cory in the process of acquiring a fortune she didn't want to share with children she no longer wanted, or loved. Oh, how well she explained to us what to expect that night when she gave us our little litany to say when we were unhappy. Did she know, or guess, way back then, that she would become the *thing* the grandfather would make of her? I toppled over into Chris's arms, and lay against his chest. 'Don't tell me any more! I've heard enough . . . don't make me hate her more!'

'Hate . . . you haven't begun to know what hate is yet. But before I tell you the rest, keep in mind we are leaving this place, no matter what. We will go on to Florida, just like we planned. We'll live in the sunshine and make our lives the very best we can. Not for one moment are we going to feel ashamed of what we are, or what we've done, for what we've shared between us is so small compared to what our mother has done. Even if you die before I do, I'll remember our lives up here and in the attic. I'll see us dancing beneath the paper flowers, with you so graceful, and me so clumsy. I'll smell the dust and the rotting wood, and

I'll remember it as perfume sweet as roses, because without you it would have been so bleak, and so empty. You've given me my first taste of what love can be.

'We're going to change. We're going to throw out what's worse in us and keep what's best. But come hell or high water, we three will stick together, all for one, one for all. We're going to grow, Cathy, physically, mentally, and emotionally. Not only that, we're going to reach the goals we've set for ourselves. I'll be the best damned doctor the world's ever known and you will make Pavlova seem like an awkward country girl.'

I grew weary of hearing talk of love, and what the future held, possibly, when we were still behind a locked door, and death was lying beside me curled up in foetal position, with small hands praying even in sleep.

'All right, Chris, you've given me a breather. I'm prepared for anything. And thank you for saying all of that, and for loving me, for you haven't gone unloved, or unadmired, yourself.' I kissed him quickly on the lips, and told him to go on, to hit me with his knock-out blow.

'Really, Chris, I know you must have something perfectly awful to tell me – so out with it. Keep holding me as you tell me, and I can stand anything you have to say.'

How young I was. How unimaginative – and how confidently presuming.

ENDINGS, BEGINNINGS

'Guess what she told them,' Chris continued on. 'Name the reason she gave for not wanting this room cleaned on the last Friday of the month.'

How could I guess? I'd need a mind like hers. I shook my head. So long ago the servants had stopped coming to this room, I had forgotten those first horrible weeks.

'Mice, Cathy,' Chris said, his blue eyes cold, hard. '*Mice!* Hundreds of mice in the attic, our grandmother invented . . . clever little mice that used the stairs to steal down to the second floor. Devilish little mice that forced her to lock this door, leaving in the room – food covered over with arsenic.'

I listened and thought that an ingenious, marvellous story for keeping the servants away. The attic *was* full of mice. They *did* use the stairs.

'Arsenic is white, Cathy, *white*. When mixed with powdered sugar, you cannot taste its bitterness.'

My brain went spinning! Powdered sugar on the four daily doughnuts! One for each of us. Now only three in the basket!

'But, Chris, your story doesn't make any sense. Why would the grandmother poison us bit by bit? Why not give us a sufficient amount to kill us immediately and have done with it?'

His long fingers went through my hair to cup my head between his palms. He spoke in a low voice: 'Think back to a certain old movie we saw on TV. Remember that pretty woman who would keep house for older gentlemen – rich gentlemen, of course – and when she'd won their trust, and affection, and they had written her into their wills, each day she fed them just a little arsenic? When you digest just a fraction of arsenic each day, it is slowly absorbed by your entire system, and each day the victim feels a little worse, but not too much so. The small headaches, stomach upsets that can easily be explained away, so that when the victim dies, say in a hospital, he already is thin, anaemic, and has a long history of illness, hay fever, colds, and so forth. And doctors don't suspect poisoning – not when the victim has all the manifestations of pneumonia, or just plain old age, as was the case in that movie.'

'Cory!' I gasped. 'Cory died of arsenic poisoning? Momma said it was pneumonia that killed him!'

'Can't she tell us anything she wants? How do we know when she's telling the truth? Maybe she didn't even take him to a hospital. And if she did, obviously the doctors didn't suspect any unnatural cause of death, or else she'd be in jail by now.'

'But, Chris,' I objected, 'Momma wouldn't allow the grand-mother to feed us poison! I know she wants that money, and I know she doesn't love us now as she did once – but still she would never kill us!'

Chris turned aside his head. 'Okay. We've got to make a test. We're going to feed Cory's pet mouse a bit of powdered-sugar doughnut.'

No! Not Mickey, who trusted and loved us – we couldn't do that. Cory had adored the little grey mouse. 'Chris, let's catch another mouse – a wild one that doesn't trust us.'

'C'mon, Cathy, Mickey is an old mouse, and lame, too. It's hard to catch a mouse alive, you know that. How many have lived after the cheese was nibbled on? And when we leave, Mickey won't survive when we set him free – he's a pet now, dependent on us.'

But I was planning on taking him with us.

'Look at it this way, Cathy – Cory's dead, and he hadn't even begun to live. If the doughnuts aren't poisonous, Mickey will live, and we can take him with us, if you insist. One thing for certain – we have to know. For Carrie's sake, we've got to be positive. Look at her. Can't you see she's dying, too? Day by day, she's losing ground – and so are we.'

On three well legs, he came staggering to us, dragging the lame leg, our sweet little grey mouse that nibbled trustingly on Chris's finger before he bit into the doughnut. He took a small piece and ate it, trustingly, believing in us, his gods, his parents, his friends. It hurt to watch.

He didn't die, not right away. He grew slow, listless, apathetic. Later on he had small fits of pain that made him whimper. In several hours he was on his back, stiff, cold. Pink toes curled up into claws. Small black bead eyes, sunken and dull. So now we knew . . . for sure. God hadn't taken Cory.

'We could put the mouse in a paper sack along with two of the doughnuts and take it to the police,' said Chris tentatively, keeping his eyes averted from mine . . .

'They'd put the grandmother in jail.'

'Yeah,' he said, and then turned his back.

'Chris, you're holding something back – what is it?'

'Later . . . after we've gone. Right now I've said all I can say without throwing up. We'll leave early tomorrow morning,' he said when I didn't speak. He caught both my hands in his and squeezed them tightly. 'As soon as possible, we'll get Carrie to a doctor – and ourselves too.'

Such a long day to live through. We had everything ready and nothing to do but stare at the TV for the last time. With Carrie in the corner, and the two of us on separate beds, we watched our favourite soap opera. When it was over I said, 'Chris, soap people are like us – they seldom go outdoors. And when they do, we only hear about it, never see it. They loll about in living-rooms, bedrooms, sit in the kitchens and sip coffee or stand up and drink Martinis – but never, never go outside before our eyes. And whenever something good happens, whenever they think they're finally going to be happy, some catastrophe comes along to dash their hopes.'

Somehow I sensed someone else in the room. My breath pulled in! There stood the grandmother. Something in her stance, in her cruel, hard grey-stone eyes showed her mocking scornful contempt, and informed me she'd been there for some time.

She spoke, her voice cold: 'How sophisticated the two of you have grown while locked away from the world. You think you jokingly exaggerated the way life is – but you didn't exaggerate. You forecast it correctly. Nothing ever works out the way you think it will. In the end, you are always disappointed.'

Chris and I stared at her, both chilled. The hidden sun took a nose-dive into night. She'd had her say, so she left, locking the door behind her. We sat on our separate beds, with Carrie slouched over near the corner.

'Cathy, don't look so defeated. She was only trying to put us down again. Maybe nothing did work out right for her, but that doesn't mean *we* are doomed. Let's go forth tomorrow with no great expectations of finding perfection. Then, expecting only a small share of happiness, we won't be disappointed.'

If a little hill of happiness would satisfy Chris, good for him. But after all these years of striving, hoping, dreaming, longing – I wanted a mountain high! A hill wasn't enough. From this day forward, I vowed to myself, I was in control of my life. Not fate, not God, not even Chris was ever again going to tell me what to do, or dominate me in any way. From this day forward, I was my own person, to take what I would, when I would, and I would answer only to myself. I'd been kept prisoner, held captive by greed. I'd been betrayed, deceived, lied to, used, poisoned . . . but all that was over now.

I had been barely twelve years old when Momma led us through the dense piney woods on a starry, moonlit night, . . . just on the verge of becoming a woman, and in these three years and almost five months, I'd reached maturity. I was older than the mountains outside. The wisdom of the attic was in my bones, etched on my brain, part of my flesh.

The Bible said, as Chris quoted one memorable day, there was a time for everything. I figured my time for happiness was just ahead, waiting for me.

Where was that fragile, golden-fair Dresden doll I used to be? Gone. Gone like porcelain turned into steel – made into someone who would always get what she wanted, no matter who or what stood in her way. I turned my resolved gaze on Carrie, who slumped in the corner, her head so low her long hair covered her face. Only eight and a half years old, but she was so weak she shuffled like someone old; she didn't eat or speak. She didn't play with the sweet little baby who lived in the doll house. When I asked if she wanted to take along a few of those dolls, she kept on hanging her head.

Not even Carrie, with her stubborn, defiant ways would defeat me now. There was no one anywhere, much less an eight-year-old, who could resist the strength of my will now.

I strode over and picked her up, and though she fought weakly, her efforts to free herself were fruitless. I sat down at the table and forced food into her mouth, and made her swallow when she would spit it out. I held a glass of milk to her lips, and though she clamped those lips together, I pried them apart and forced her to swallow the milk too. She cried out that I was mean. I carried her into the bathroom, and used tissue when she refused even to do that.

In the tub I shampooed her hair. Then I dressed her in several layers of warm clothing, just as I dressed myself. And when her hair was dry, I brushed it until it shone and looked somewhat like it used to look, only far thinner, and less glorious.

All through the long hours of waiting, I held Carrie in my arms, whispering to her of the plans Chris and I had for our future – the happy lives we'd live in the golden, liquid sunshine of Florida.

Chris was in the rocker, fully clothed, and was strumming idly on Cory's guitar. 'Dance, ballerina, dance,' he softly chanted, and his singing voice wasn't bad at all. Maybe we could work as musicians – a trio – if Carrie ever recovered enough to want a voice again.

On my wrist was a fourteen-carat-gold watch, made in Switzerland, that must have cost Momma several hundred dollars, and Chris had his watch, too, we weren't penniless. We had the guitar, the banjo, Chris's Polaroid camera and his many watercolours to sell – and the rings our father had given our mother.

Tomorrow morning held escape for us – but why did I keep thinking I was overlooking something very important?

Then suddenly I realized something! Something both Chris and I had ignored. If the grandmother could open our locked door, and stand quietly for so long before we noticed her . . . had she done this on other occasions? If she had, she might now know of our plans! She might have made her own plans to prevent our escape!

I looked over at Chris, wondering if I should bring this up. He couldn't hesitate *this* time and find a reason to stay . . . so I voiced my suspicion. He kept picking on the guitar, apparently not disturbed in the least. 'The minute I saw her there, that thought flashed into my mind,' he said. 'I know she puts a great deal of trust in that butler, John, and she might very well have him waiting at the bottom of the stairs to prevent us from leaving. Let him try – nothing and no one is going to stop us from leaving early tomorrow morning!'

But the thoughts of the grandmother and her butler waiting at the bottom of the steps wouldn't go away and leave me peace. Leaving Carrie on the bed asleep, leaving Chris in the rocker and strumming the guitar, I wandered up to the attic to say goodbye.

Directly under the dangling lightbulb, I stood and looked around. My thoughts went flashing back to the first day we came up here . . . I saw us, all four, holding hands, staring around, overwhelmed by the gargantuan attic and its ghostly furniture and clutter of dusty junk. I saw Chris up high, risking his life to hang two swings for Carrie and Cory to use. I ambled into the schoolroom, looking at the old desks where the twins had sat to learn to read and write. I didn't glance at the stained, smelly mattress to picture us sunbathing there. That mattress put other memories in my head. I stared at the flowers with sparkling centres – and the lopsided snail, the menacing purple worm, the signs Chris and I had lettered and through all the maze of our gardens and jungle, I saw myself dancing alone, always alone, except when Chris stood in the shadows watching, making his ache my ache. For when I waltzed with Chris, I'd made him someone else.

He called up the stairs. 'It's time to go, Cathy.'

Quickly I raced back to the schoolroom. On the blackboard I wrote very large, using white chalk:

> We lived in the attic,
> Christopher, Cory, Carrie, and me,
> Now there are only three.

I signed my name, and wrote down the date. In my heart I knew that the ghosts of the four of us would override all other ghosts of children shut away in an attic schoolroom. I left an enigma for someone in the future to unwind.

* * *

With Mickey in a paper sack along with two poisoned doughnuts stored in Chris's pocket, he used that wooden key and opened our prison door for the last time. We'd fight to the death if the grandmother and the butler were below. Chris carried the two suitcases filled with our clothes and other possessions, and over his shoulder he slung both Cory's beloved guitar and his banjo. He led the way down all the dim halls, to the back stairs. Carrie was in my arms, partially asleep. She weighed but a bit more than she had the night we'd taken her up these same stairs more than three years ago. Those two suitcases my brother carried were the very same ones Momma had been burdened with on that terrible night so long ago, when we were young, so loving and trusting.

Pinned inside our clothes were two small bags holding bills stolen from Momma's room, divided equally just in case something unforseen separated Chris from me – then neither of us would be left penniless. And Carrie was sure to be with one of us, and taken care of. In the two suitcases were the heavy coins, also put into two bags, to weigh them evenly.

Both Chris and I were very much aware of what lay waiting for us on the outside. We hadn't looked at so much TV without learning the worldly and heartless lie in wait for the naïve and innocent. We were young and vulnerable, weak, half-sick, but no longer naïve, or innocent.

My heart stood still as I waited for Chris to unlock the back door, fearful every second someone would stop us. He stepped out, smiling back at me.

It was cold outside. Patches of snow lay melting on the ground. Soon enough the snow would fly again. The grey sky above foreboded that. Still, it was no colder than in the attic. The earth felt mushy beneath our feet. Strange feeling after walking so many years on hard, level wooden floors. I was not yet feeling safe, for John could follow . . . take us back, or try to.

I raised my head to sniff the clean, sharp mountain air. It was like sparkling wine to make one drunk. For a short way I kept Carrie in my arms. Then I set her on her feet. She wobbled uncertainly, stared around, disoriented and bedazed looking. She sniffled, swiped at her reddened nose so small and finely shaped. Ohhh . . . was she going to catch cold so soon?

'Cathy,' called back Chris, 'you two have to hurry. We don't have much time, and it's a long, long way. Pick up Carrie when she tires.'

I caught her small hand and pulled her along. 'Take deep, long breaths, Carrie. Before you know it, the fresh air, good food, and sunshine will have you feeling strong and well again.'

Her small pale face tilted upwards to mine – was that hope sparking her eyes at last? 'Are we going to meet Cory?'

The first question she'd asked since that tragic day when we learned Cory had died. I gazed down at her, knowing her deepest yearning was for Cory. I couldn't say no. I just couldn't put out that flicker of hope. 'Cory is in a far-far place from here. Didn't you listen when I said I saw Daddy in a beautiful garden? Didn't you hear when I said Daddy took Cory up into his arms, and now Daddy is taking care of him? They're waiting for us, and some day we'll see them again, but not for a long, long time.'

'But, Cathy,' she complained, puckering her faint brows, 'Cory won't like that garden if I'm not there, and if he comes back looking for us, he won't know where we are.'

Earnestness like that put tears in my eyes. I picked her up and tried to hold her, but she struggled free to drag her feet and hang back, twisting halfway around so she could stare back at the huge house we were leaving.

'Come, Carrie, walk faster! Cory's watching us – he wants us to escape! He's down on his knees, praying we'll get away before the grandmother sends someone to take us back and lock us up again!'

Down all the winding trails we tagged along behind Chris, who set a very fast pace. And just as I knew he would, he led us unerringly to the same little train depot that was only a tin roof supported by four wood posts, with a rickety green bench.

The rim of the dawning sun peeked over a mountaintop, chasing away the low morning mists. The sky turned lavender-rose as we drew nearer the depot.

'Hurry, Cathy!' called Chris. 'If we miss this train, we'll have to wait until four o'clock!'

Oh. God, we couldn't miss this train! If we did, the grandmother might for sure have time to catch us again!

We saw a mail truck, with a tall, broomstraw man standing near three mailbags on the ground. He took off his cap, displaying a Brillo pad of reddish hair. Genially, he smiled in our direction. 'You folks are sure up early,' he called to us cheerfully. 'On your way to Charlottesville?'

'Yep! On our way to Charlottesville,' answered Chris, as, with relief, he put the two suitcases down.

'Pretty little girl you got there,' said the tall mailman, sweeping his pitying gaze over Carrie, who clung fearfully to my skirt. 'But if you don't mind my sayin' so, she seems kinda peaked.'

'She's been sick,' Chris confirmed. 'But soon she'll be better.'

The mailman nodded, seemingly believing this prognosis. 'Got tickets?'

'Got money.' Then Chris added sagaciously, practising for less reliable strangers, 'But just enough to pay for the tickets.'

'Well, get it out, son, 'cause here comes the five-forty-five.'

As we rode on that morning train, headed towards Charlottesville, we saw the Foxworth mansion sitting high on the hillside. Chris and I couldn't take our eyes from it, couldn't help but stare at our prison from the outside. Especially we fixed our gazes on the attic windows with the closed black shutters.

Then my attention was drawn to the northern wing, riveted on that end room on the second floor. I nudged Chris as the heavy draperies parted, and the shadowy, distant form of a large old woman appeared there, staring out, looking for us . . . then vanished.

Of course she could see the train, but we knew she couldn't see us, just as we'd never been able to see the passengers. Nevertheless, Chris and I slipped down lower on our seat. 'Wonder what she's doing up there so early?' I whispered to Chris. 'Usually she doesn't carry up our food until six-thirty.'

He laughed, sounding bitter. 'Oh, just another of her efforts to catch us doing something sinful and forbidden.'

Maybe so, but I wanted to know her thoughts, her feelings when she entered that room and found it empty, and the clothes gone from the closet and the drawers. And no voices, or steps overhead to come running – if she called.

* * *

In Charlottesville we bought bus tickets to Sarasota, and were told we had two hours to wait for the next Greyhound heading south. Two hours in which John could jump into a black limousine and overtake that slow train!

'Don't think about it,' said Chris. 'You don't know that he knows about us. She'd be a fool to tell him, though he's probably snoop enough to find out.'

We thought the best way to keep him from finding us, if he was sent to follow, would be to keep on the move. We stored our two suitcases and the guitar and banjo in a rented locker. Hand in hand, Carrie in the middle, we strolled the main streets of that city, where we knew the servants of Foxworth Hall came to visit relatives on their day off, and to shop, go to the movies, or pleasure themselves in other ways. And if this were Thursday, we'd have really been fearful. But it was Sunday.

We must have looked like visitors from another planet in our ill-fitting bulky clothes, our sneakers, our clumsily cut hair, and our pale faces. But no one really stared as I feared they would. We were accepted as just a part of the human race, and no odder than most. It felt good to be back in crowds of people, each face different.

'Wonder where everyone's going in such a hurry?' asked Chris, just when I was speculating on the same thing.

We stopped on a corner, undecided. Cory was supposed to be buried not far from here. Oh, so much I wanted to go and find his grave and put flowers there. On another day we'd come back with yellow roses, and we'd kneel and say prayers, whether or not it did any good. For now, we had to get far, far away and not endanger Carrie more . . . out of Virginia before we took her to a doctor.

It was then that Chris took the paper sack with the dead mouse and the powdered-sugar doughnuts from his jacket pocket. His solemn eyes met mine. Loosely he held that bag in front of me, studying my expression, asking with his eyes: An eye for an eye?

That paper sack represented so much. All our lost years, the lost education, the playmates and friends, and the days we could have known laughter instead of tears. In that bag were all our frustrations, humiliations, tons of loneliness, plus the punishments and disappointments – and, most of all, that bag represented the loss of Cory.

'We can go to the police and tell our story,' said Christopher, while he kept his eyes averted, 'and the city will provide for you and Carrie, and you won't have to run. You two might be put in foster homes, or an orphanage. As for me, I don't know . . .'

Chris never talked to me while he kept his eyes elsewhere unless he was hiding something – that special something that had to wait until we were outside of Foxworth Hall. 'Okay, Chris. We've escaped, so out with it. What is it you keep holding back?'

His head bowed down as Carrie moved closer and clung to my skirt, though her eyes were wide with fascination as she watched the heavy flow of traffic, and the many people hurrying by, some who smiled at her.

'It's Momma,' Chris said in a low voice. 'Recall when she said she'd do anything to win back her father's approval so she could inherit? I don't know what he made her promise, but I did over-hear the servants talking. Cathy, a few days before our grand-father died, he had a codicil added to his will. It states that if our mother is ever proven to have given birth to children by her first husband, she will have to forfeit everything she inherits – and return everything she's bought with the money, including her clothes, jewels, investments – everything. And that's not all; he even had it written in, that if she has children by her *second* marriage, she will lose everything too. And Momma thought he had forgiven her. He didn't forgive, or forget. He would keep on punishing her from his grave.'

My eyes widened with shock as I added up the pieces. 'You mean Momma . . . ? It was Momma, and not the grandmother?'

He shrugged, as if indifferent, when I knew he couldn't be. 'I heard that old woman praying by her bed. She's evil, but I doubt she would put poison on the doughnuts herself. She would carry them up to us, and know we ate the sweets, when all along she warned us not to eat them.'

'But, Chris, it couldn't have been Momma. She was on her honeymoon when the doughnuts started coming daily.'

His smile came bitter, wry. 'Yeah. But nine months ago the will was read; nine months ago Momma was back. Only Momma

342

benefits from the grandfather's will – not our grandmother – she has her own money. She only brought up the baskets each day.'

So many questions I had to ask – but there was Carrie, clinging to me, staring up at me. I didn't want her to know Cory had died from any but natural reasons. It was then Chris put the bag with the evidence in my hands. 'It's up to you to decide. You and your intuition were right all along – if I'd have listened, Cory would be alive today.'

There is no hate such as that born out of love betrayed – and my brain screamed out for revenge. Yes, I wanted to see Momma and the grandmother locked up in jail, put behind bars, convicted of premeditated murder – four counts, if intentions were counted, too. They'd be only grey mice in cages, shut up like us, only they'd have the benefit of being in the company of drug addicts, prostitutes, and other killers like themselves. Their clothes would be of grey prison cotton. No trips twice a week to the beauty salon for Momma, no make-up, no professional manicures – and a shower once a week. She'd even lose the privacy of her most personal body places. Oh, she'd suffer without furs to wear, and jewellery, and warm cruises in southern waters when the winter rolled around. There wouldn't be a handsome, adoring young husband to romp with in a grand swan bed.

I stared up at the sky where God was supposed to be – could I let Him in His own ways, balance the scales and take the burden of justice from me?

I thought it cruel, unfair, that Chris should put all the burden of decision on my shoulders. Why?

Was it because he would forgive her for anything – even the death of Cory, and her efforts to kill all of us? Would he reason that such parents as hers could pressure her into doing anything – even murder? Was there enough money in the whole world to make *me* kill my four children?

Pictures flashed in my mind, taking me back to the days before my father died. I saw us all in the back garden, laughing and happy. I saw us at the beach, sailing, swimming, or in the mountains skiing. And I saw Momma in the kitchen doing her best to cook meals to please us all.

Yeah, surely her parents would know all the ways to kill her love for us – they'd know. Or was Chris thinking, as I was, that if we went to the police and told our story, our faces would be splashed on the front pages of every newspaper in the country? Would the glare of publicity make up for what we'd lose? Our privacy – our need to stay together? Could we lose each other just to get even?

I glanced up at the sky again.

God, He didn't write the scripts for the puny little players down here. We wrote them ourselves – with each day we lived, each word we spoke, each thought we etched on our brains. And Momma had written her script, too. And a sorry one it was.

Once she'd had four children she considered perfect in every way. Now she had none. Once she had four children who loved her, and considered her perfect in every way – now she had none who saw her as perfect. Nor would she ever want to have others. Love for what money could buy would keep her for ever faithful to that cruel codicil in her father's will.

Momma would grow old; her husband was years younger. She'd have time to feel lonely and wish she'd done it all differently. If her arms never ached to hold me again, they'd ache for Chris, and maybe Carrie . . . and, most certainly, she'd want those babies that would be ours one day.

From this city we'd flee southwards on a bus to make of ourselves *somebodies*. When we saw Momma again – and to be certain fate would arrange it that way – we'd look her straight in the eyes, and turn our backs.

Into the nearest green trashcan I dropped the bag, saying goodbye to Mickey, and asking him to please forgive us for what we did.

'C'mon, Cathy,' called Chris, stretching forth his hand. 'What's done is done. Say goodbye to the past, and hello to the future. And we're wasting time, when already we've wasted enough. We've got everything ahead, waiting for us.'

Just the right words to make me feel real, *alive, free*! Free enough to forget thoughts of revenge. I laughed and spun about to run back to where I could put my hand in his, stretched ready and waiting. With his free arm, Chris swooped down to pick up Carrie, and he hugged her close and kissed her wan cheek. 'Did you hear all of that, Carrie? We are on our way to where the flowers bloom all through the winter – in fact, flowers bloom all year long down there. Does that make you want to smile?'

A tiny smile came and went on pale lips that seemed to have forgotten how to smile. But that was enough – for now.

EPILOGUE

It is with relief that I end the telling of our foundation years, on which we were to base the rest of our lives.

After we escaped Foxworth Hall, we made our way, and managed, somehow, to always keep striving towards our goals.

Our lives were always to be tempestuous, but it taught both Chris and me that we were survivors. For Carrie, it was far different. She had to be persuaded to want a life without Cory, even when she was surrounded by roses.

But how we managed to survive – that's another story.